Sign up for our newsletter to hear about
new releases, read interviews with authors, enter
giveaways, and more.

www.ylva-publishing.com

Other Books by this Author

See Right Through Me
Puppy Love
Hearts and Flowers Border

Still Life

L.T. Smith

Ylva

Acknowledgements

Firstly, a huge thanks to Astrid Ohletz for wanting to breathe life into *Still Life*. When I first wrote this story, I'd never contemplated that one day it would be primped and polished and ready to be released into the world as both an e-book and a paperback, but I am so happy that it has been given the Ylva treatment. I couldn't wish for better publishers, and I'm so happy they have the faith in me to want to keep printing my work.

To me, this story was just one I had to tell. When I was writing it, I just kept on thinking of all the emotions we go through in life and how the actions of others affect us in so many ways. A cruel word, a fear of exposing our vulnerable selves to someone we long to trust and love being two. Then I also contemplated how by taking a leap of faith, we could actually achieve our heart's desire if we believed in ourselves and not just in the actions and words of others. What a fantastic feeling of achievement that could be.

Moving on from my rambling, I would also like to thank Day Petersen for crafting, guiding, and suggesting changes in such a way that I didn't feel the sting of editing as so many others writers say. You are a wonderful woman, and I love working with you.

And what is a book without the cover? I know we shouldn't judge the work by the casing, but in this instance, I hope everyone does. Thank you, Amanda Chron, for designing such a work of art. And also thank you for including my drawing on the front—although I honestly believe you could have done a better job of the eye. Can't wait to see what you do with my next book.

Finally. Thank you, reader. With your kind words and support, I have wanted to continue to write. Considering I have to grab the time when I can to sit down and slam against the keys with fingers that refuse to type coherently, you have made the journey from opening sentence to the last one worth the frustration, the backspacing, and the consistent swearing.

Dedicated to the creative side found in all of us.

However we create, whether it is through art, writing, drama, our children, science, etc., we all have a gift to make things beautiful—a gift to make our lives, and the lives of those around us, perfect. Let's not waste it.

LT Smith

"There is only one way to avoid criticism: do nothing, say nothing, and be nothing."

Aristotle

Chapter 1

September 2010

I was bored. Bored, bored, bored. Nothing moved me from my apathy about everything. Work was living up to its name, and it seemed as if all I ever did was get up, go to the office, fart about on computers all day whilst talking to potential clients on the phone, come home and do bugger all for the rest of the evening until it was time to go to bed. The next day would appear with the crowing of an impatient alarm clock, and that day was the same as the previous. I was living through my personal Groundhog Day. Deep down, I knew I would probably do the same thing over and over again until I keeled over, hand gripping my chest, my expression a contortion of agony, splatting my face on the flat screen of my computer monitor as the final act of a woman whose life was shite.

It was a Wednesday. Actually, it was Wednesday, 8th September. Or 08/09/10 for those who think it is cool to see the chronological progression of dates through numbers—and yes, I am a sad bastard. Pity I couldn't say it was 11:12

and 13 seconds when I had the epiphany about how crap my life was, but I didn't notice the time. Sorry for getting your hopes up.

I remember it being a Wednesday, because on Wednesdays the canteen served curry for lunch. I hated curry, even the smell of it, and I hated the fact that everyone in the office knew I hated it, so on Wednesdays they would make a beeline for sitting with me whilst grinning idiotically and offering me forkfuls of the stuff. I was back in front of my computer before our allotted hour for lunch was over.

A good time to write some personal emails, don't you think?

A grin slipped across my face as I opened Hotmail and typed in my user name and password. Many junk mails had slipped through the filter, and I was silently hoping that the IT department had missed the ones asking if I needed a penis extension, when I spotted the mail from my friend Sophie.

Sophie and me went way back. Her grinning face, sans one front tooth, was the clearest memory I had from Primary School. To say she adopted me would be the easiest way to sum up our relationship, even though she was only three and a half weeks older than I was. I say "was" but in fact it should be "is," as both of us are very much alive. Carrying on... It was Sophie's personal goal to make sure I was fully integrated into school politics: where to hang out, who not to make eye contact with, which dinner lady gave the biggest portions, what teacher to suck up to, which one to play up, and the blinding one—don't touch the curry. It was made from all the things they should throw away but were too tight fisted to bin.

Leaving Primary, we advanced to High School together.

Moved on to makeup, bad fashion sense, acne, and boys. Well, Sophie moved through the boys like lightning, while I was only too happy to be her alibi when she stayed out all night. It wasn't until we both went to college that I came to some kind of self-understanding. Boys just didn't tickle my proverbial fancy, although it still took me a while to understand why. No. Actually I didn't even work it out for myself. Once again it was Sophie who led me, this time to the realisation that girls were more my bag. And here was an email from her.

Oi! Lezza! What're you doing later? Fancy meeting up at The Dog for a snifter? Text me and let me know. I've a cunning plan!!!!
SophX

I loved seeing Sophie. Loved her infectious laugh, her twinkling brown eyes, her zest for life. However, if I did go to The Dog, that would mean I would have to break the monotony of my existence. Could I, or should I say "Dare I" break away from eating a meal for one, having a soak in the tub, and then tumbling into a solitary bed at 9:30?

I slipped my phone from my bag and saw that I had a message, the very same message Sophie had sent via email. My, she was eager. Three times I wrote the reply, changing my mind each time. No. Yes. No. And then a fourth and final time:

C u l8r say 7? Btr b gud. Jess x

What has happened to the English language, eh? Sometimes it would be far easier to write with the correct spelling and grammar instead of wondering how on earth you can write "See you later, about 7? Better be good. Jess x", without blowing apart a handful of neurons. Weirdly enough, most of us still sign the bloody thing when it is obvious who sent it, as our names appear on the other person's phone.

Yes. I know. Waffling.

Seven o'clock saw me walking into The Dog—sounds strange, but I mean the pub and not our canine friend—and easily spotting Sophie chatting to the barman. Her laughter tinkled over to where I was standing, and it seemed almost instinctive on her part for her to stop her flirting, turn, and bless me with a huge grin before waving her hands wildly as if I hadn't already seen her.

As I stepped up to the bar, a vodka and lime was placed in front of me. I hadn't planned on having a drink, as just being out of the house after dark was more than my Puritan lifestyle could easily handle, but one wouldn't hurt, would it? Or two? Maybe three, just to shake off the shackles of a working day and the smell of fucking curry.

By the fourth, I was feeling relaxed. Actually, more like on the verge of passing out. I had worked my way through the giggly stage and was approaching "Homing Mode" when Sophie landed me with it.

"How's about you and me going back to school?"

And do what? Burn it down? Graffiti "Ms Edwards is a twat" over the windows in the Maths block?

"Night school, I mean."

My face took on the "I don't understand" look that I always thought made me look semi intelligent, although in reality it probably screamed, "Idiot here!"

Sophie shifted closer to me, looking over her shoulder in a conspiratorial way as if the KGB were tuning in on our conversation. "Art Class."

"What the fu—"

"Art. Class. As in Life Drawing. As in..." another look over her shoulder, "naked men."

Of course, I wasn't interested. What kind of lesbian would I be if I went to night school to see men flashing their percies? Men who likely couldn't get anyone else to look at it, even if they exposed themselves to women in the subway. I opened my mouth to tell her as much, but she spoke over me.

"And naked women."

My mouth was still on the verge of rejecting her suggestion, but I didn't. I slowly closed my mouth. Was this the only way I was ever going to see another woman naked again for the rest of my life? I can't believe I hesitated about turning her down, can't believe I didn't look affronted and say as much, but I didn't.

"Look. I was joking, Jess. I thought you might want to do something together instead of you sitting at home every night all on your own." A small smile crept over her face. "I know breaking up with Sam was hard, but holing yourself up won't make you feel better."

Sam? Why on earth had she brought Samantha James into the conversation? I had broken up with her, mainly because she felt the need to cop off with anything that barely resembled a woman. Even some that at a second glance a person could be misguided into thinking was a bloke with tits.

"Sam?"

"I know, honey. But you have to learn to let go."

"What on—"

"Night class. That will do it."

"But I wasn't—"

"No. You weren't the one to blame. She was a slut."

Fuck this for a game of soldiers. The alcohol was making me too slow to carry on what was apparently a monologue rather than a conversation. Sophie had never liked Sam, never trusted her. Funnily enough, neither had I. We had only dated for five months, and in that time, I think she aged me. As you may gather, I am not, and never was, a party animal. I am perfectly happy with a good book and an early night swaddled in my flannelette pyjamas.

"You want another?" Sophie nodded at my half full glass, and I shook my head. "Just me then." And off she toddled to chat up the barman.

I lifted my drink, then paused with the cool, sticky glass touching my bottom lip. I had always enjoyed drawing when I was at school and, if I say so myself, I was pretty good at it. On the other hand, Sophie's art gave the distinct impression she was drawing with her eyes closed. So why on earth would she want to go to night school to study art?

Looking over my shoulder, I saw my friend chatting happily to the same barman. No. Going to an art class couldn't be because she wanted to see men's winkies—with her looks and personality, she could see as many as she wanted to. As the thought trickled through my head, Sophie turned and flashed me one of her radiant smiles before turning back to the bar to pick up her drink.

For me. That's why she wanted to take an art class. She was looking out for me again.

"So, are you game, Ms Taylor?" Sophie leaned over me, her face so close it surprised me for a moment. "Come on, Jess. Let's do it. It'll be fun." Her smile was gentle, beckoning, and so typically my best friend.

"Okay. When do we start?"

Everyone in the pub turned at Sophie's triumphant whoop, but soon returned to their pub conversations which usually consisted of football, wrestling, who was shagging whom, and the price of petrol. The hug she gave me was fierce, and she mumbled a "thank you" into my ear before she ripped herself away and plonked herself on her chair.

"I think that deserves a celebratory drink, don't you?"

Aw shit.

Chapter 2

One week later, I was standing outside Stockport College of Technology waiting for my art partner to arrive whilst tutting at the drizzle that was fucking up my hair. Granted, I was thirty minutes early, and I could've waited inside the foyer, but I was too nervous. I don't know why, as it was just a night school class on still life. That was probably it. Still Life. And by the brochure I had picked up the previous Thursday when Sophie and I had enrolled, it wasn't just oranges and nuts—although I did believe there was going to be a different selection of nuts on offer, not forgetting the bananas.

What if the person came out and I knew him? Or her? What if it was Sam? Nah. She was the type to get her kit off at any given opportunity, but not in the "Jack, I want you to draw me like one of your French girls. Wearing this... and only this" kind of way. What if it was someone from work? Neil from Accounting? Bile rose in my throat at the thought of the sweaty letch who always tried to cop a feel of all the young girls. What if it was Clive from Human Resources? Or Terrence from the mail room. God. What if it was James Jackson, my boss!

Stop right there. Why on earth would my boss strip off and let complete strangers draw him buck naked? But then again, why would complete strangers want to draw him in the first place? Shit. I was taking myself on a one way trip to Complete Mental Breakdown City. Yes, Jess. Stop. Go with the flow. Go with the...flow... Deep breaths...deep... breaths.

"Evening, Dali."

I knew it was Sophie, so why did I jump? More to the point...why did I scream and hit her with my art pad?

"Jesus, Jess, I'm not going to molest you."

The red mark on the side of her face was glowing against the greyness of the evening behind her, and I did feel bad. Pity I couldn't show it instead of gripping my chest and swooning like a 1920s silent film star.

"Apology accepted," preceded a muttered, "if one was given."

I was still gripping the lapels of my raincoat.

"Shall we?"

"What?"

A sigh, one of the ones reserved for complete imbeciles, came through Sophie's pursed lips. "Go inside." When I didn't move, she said, "What the fuck is wrong with you? Anyone would think I was sending you to your death." She leaned forward. "You been on the sugar, Taylor?" I shook my head. Sophie laughed and grabbed my arm. "You definitely need to get out more."

If she wanted me to get out more, why was she taking me in? Rhetorical *and* stupid, I know.

It was packed inside. Well, there were about twenty people waiting to begin, but I hadn't thought there would be even that much call for coming out in the evening to draw pictures. Shows how much I knew, didn't it? The male/female ratio was pretty equal, especially after Sophie and I turned up.

The room was pretty much what one would expect an art room to look like—tables, chairs, pictures of people in agony on the walls...the usual. Maybe I could put my face up there on the wall next to the three legged man and the screaming banshee. Something to consider if any of my previous thoughts about knowing the nude model came to fruition.

Selecting vacant chairs beside each other, Sophie and I placed our bags on the desks, claiming ownership. To my relief, there was a table with pots, pans, and other miscellaneous kitchen stuff placed in the centre of the room. Even though the items were naked, I felt as if I had received some kind of reprieve. No naked men...better still, no naked men that I knew.

In the final few minutes before class was to start, people started getting their stuff out and slapping it onto the tables in front of them. Obviously, being a lemming, I followed suit. Placing my art materials on said desk, I finally admitted to myself that I was looking forward to getting in tune with my more artistic side, probably because I had spent a small fortune on gearing myself up for the occasion.

"You got a pencil I could use?"

For fuck's sake. Considering it was her idea in the first place, I couldn't believe Sophie hadn't brought a pencil. Opening up my pencil case, I selected one of the new ones—friends are friends, after all.

"And some paper?"

Turning to tell Sophie that she was a waste of time and space, I was cut short. A voice— not a loud voice, but a distinctly female and alluring voice—pulled me around to face the front. It was a pity that my open mouth didn't catch up as quickly, and close itself.

Standing before the class was a woman I can only describe as artistic. Long, tousled hair and a crisscross middle parting framed the thick glasses she wore. Her eyes seemed huge, and images of Emma Thompson playing Professor Trelawney in the Harry Potter films sprang to mind. Scooting my eyes downwards, I was not disappointed by the flowing, multi-coloured cardigan and brown ankle length skirt that made a not so fashionable combination. One more thing: sandals. With socks. But this woman couldn't have been the same woman who had spoken, could it? That voice was sexy. Finally, why was my mouth still open and in fly catching mode?

"If you would all like to take your places?"

No. No. I didn't mean "no I don't want to take my place," as I was already in it. I meant, no, the voice didn't belong to Barbara Hepworth on a bad day. It came from off to the side of her. I shifted my gaze slightly and...and...

"You okay, Jess?"

It may have been because my mouth had been open too long that my tongue felt like sandpaper, or it may have been that all the moisture in my body had scooted to other, needier places.

"Ug."

Ug? Where had my ability to speak gone? Why hadn't I turned to my friend and said, "Yes, Sophie. I am perfectly fine, thank you for asking. And by the way—get your own fucking pencil and paper." But no. "Ug" it was, and that's where it was staying.

"Good evening, all." There was the music again. "I'm Diana Sullivan, and I will be leading this course for the next twelve weeks."

Diana Sullivan. Di-an-a Sul-li-van. What a wonderful name. What a beautifully wonderful na—

"Oi. Dolly dreamboat. You okay?"

All I could do was move my head slowly up and down in affirmation.

"Well, close your mouth then. The flies are getting antsy."

I heard the snap of my lips as they seemed to clang together.

"And where's my paper and pencil?"

That seemed to snap me out of the daze that had fallen over me, and I finally tore my eyes away from the woman who was now standing in the place the "artistic woman" had been and rummaged through my new art pad.

"Here you go." My voice was a whisper, almost reverent. We were in class after all. It wasn't just because I believed if I spoke any louder, I would probably be told off or sent into the corner. I didn't want to disturb the flow of the woman who was still talking. Before you say it, it was not because she was the most perfect woman I had ever seen either.

"So... We'll all start with a brief introduction then. Is that okay?"

Fuck. And fuck. And triple fuck. That would mean I would have to look at her and speak at the same time. I know women are known for having the ability to multitask, but I didn't think I was capable at that moment.

What the hell was happening? I had been in the room less than twenty minutes, and I was going through a mid-life crisis at thirty-one years of age. Was it the smell of paint? Had a rebellious pencil escaped the confines of a spanking new pencil case and lodged its tip in the part of my brain that made me a quivering wreck? Art class was supposed to be the place where I could do something other than work and sleep; a place where I could spend time with my oldest and dearest—although badly organised—friend; the place where I could dip into the more artistic part of my psyche. The class was not supposed to be where I turned into a love-struck, mute teenager.

In my mental meanderings, I had missed the first three people who had kicked off the introductions, and only tuned in when it was two people away from where I sat.

"Hi. I'm Dave."

Sophie mumbled, "Well, hello there, Dave," which she followed with girlish giggling.

At Sophie's comment, I looked up to where the teacher was standing and wondered what she would think about someone flirting with another class member. And then a surge of jealousy raced through me. Diana was looking at this Dave with such affection that I wanted to get up and slap him around the head. Now, I could have understood if it was just a feeling of disappointment, but jealousy? Since I had been focused on her, she had not even looked in my direction, never mind professed her undying love.

"I'm Diana's brother."

I leaned forward and looked at his face. He was half man, half beetroot by this stage, as all eyes in the room were on him. Just like his sister, he was handsome. Well, his sister wasn't handsome, as such, she... I stopped myself from going into ramble mode there. They both had dark brown hair—although hers was long—chiselled facial features, and stunning blue eyes, but he had a moustache and goatee where she didn't. I think the last was obvious without my having to write that, but some women do have a 'tache, although they don't usually trim them and have a chic, styled strip of hair on the tip of their chins. Do they?

Turning back to the instructor, I witnessed something I would describe as one of the most amazing things I had ever seen—Diana's smile. It may have been my overactive imagination, but I was definite I witnessed rays of light sparking from her mouth. Or should I classify that as corny? Whatever it called itself, I would bet my left butt cheek I saw rays of light. It gave her face the appearance of something that came straight from a pre-Raphaelite painting—so womanly, so captivating, so goddamn gorgeous. I felt myself smiling in response to the smile that wasn't even aimed at me, and even though I was having difficulty breathing, I felt wonderful. I also felt like I could just sit and stare at her all day, whilst wishing I didn't have to blink.

A voice was coming from near me, a voice I recognised, but couldn't quite place. It seemed as if I was underwater and listening to the muffled sounds of the world above. Then came a sensation...a knocking sensation...a tapping, insistent sensation on my thigh, then on my arm, and then...

WHACK!

"Jess!"

And that was the wakeup call I really didn't need. The impression of water vanished, and I was back in the classroom with about twenty pairs of eyes staring at me, one of which belonged to an attentive teacher and another set to a friend that was trying to glare me out.

"Everyone is waiting for you, you dick head!"

The lovely epithet was squeezed through clenched teeth, and Sophie turned and flashed the fakest smile I had ever seen her use.

"Erm... I..." I was finding it difficult to breathe again, but not in the delectable way I had before when I was floating underwater in an almost Millais' *Ophelia* way. I felt more like Lichtenstein's *Drowning Girl*, wishing I had the ability to splutter, "I don't care! I'd rather sink than call Brad for help!" or even Sophie, for that matter. "I...erm..." Jesus. This was going from bad to worse to downright intolerable.

Diana came over to where I was seated and leaned over the table. I could smell her perfume—light and engaging, and exquisitely addictive. When I lifted my face, I was met by perfect blueness. Not light blue, but a deep, rich blue, the blue you see when you picture perfection. Her eyes looked as if they were made of liquid, vibrant liquid that constantly changed in reflection of the events around them. Like water. Probably the same kind of water I felt I was drowning in.

"Hey, you. Don't worry. We can skip this part."

I doubt anyone else in the room heard her say it, but her voice seemed to seep into my skin, every word leaving an imprint as it wound its way inside me.

Diana turned back to the waiting group and opened those perfect lips to speak.

"Jess Taylor. Serial dick head, and paper and pencil loan shark," I blurted.

The teacher's eyes met mine in a flash, blue meeting green and making a sea of aqua turned turquoise.

Amidst the hoots of laughter, I grinned at her and she smiled back. A slight tilt of her head, and the grin turned into something I can only describe as a clicking sensation. Her brow furrowed slightly, and a fleeting look of confusion scattered over her flawless face. Maybe she could hear the rapid beating of my heart, or see it trying to thump its way through my ribcage.

A slight shake of her head, dark hair fluttering with the movement—a definite move to clear her thoughts—and the grin was back. "Well, hello there, Jess Taylor." Diana pushed herself back from the table and straightened to her full height, her eyes never leaving mine. "But I think I will reserve judgement on the 'serial dick head' tag until after you've witnessed my attempt to claim the title of 'Serial Dick Head' when I start teaching you all."

More sniggers from around the room.

Diana turned and looked at Sophie. "And you must be the cadger."

For the first time in a long time, Sophie blushed. I knew it wasn't because the beautiful art teacher held her fancy, far from it. Sophie was straighter than a laser. It was because she knew that the delectable goatee-toting Dave was looking in her direction. Even I could taste the testosterone in the air—something I avidly avoided, so God knows how Soph was feeling.

"Not a cadger, per se."

Aw fuck, no. Sophie was going to try and sound like she had English degrees falling out of her arse. The last time she had done something like that, it was like listening to *The Bluffer's Guide to Being a Twat*. Everyone in the museum at that time knew she knew bugger all about the exhibition—well, everyone but her.

"It appears that after reaching this facility, I have come to realise that the receptacle I had purchased for the storage of my equipment is in absentia."

What the... She was going for gold here.

"Furthermore, I—"

"So you need to cadge paper and a pencil, is that right?" Diana's voice was light, amused. Her right eyebrow rose to accompany her question, and she looked drop dead gorgeous. And yes. I was beginning to drool again.

Sophie went a shade darker, her mouth opened, and all she managed to squeak out was a high pitched "Yes" followed by a cough, then a gulp, then, "Sophie Harrison."

Brown eyes darted over to where an amused Dave was sitting, and for the life of me, I thought Sophie was going to add, "Single." Thankfully, the person next to her began speaking, as if she had waited long enough for her ten seconds of embarrassment, most certainly not aware of what had preceded her except that when it should've been her turn, it was delayed by a beetroot and a dick on a stick.

"Serves you right," I whispered to my glowing friend before I slapped the paper and pencil down in from of her and turned smugly back to my overflowing pencil case and huge pad. I was definite I heard the word "anal" muttered under her breath, but I just kept fiddling for the sharpest pencil I had.

"You can sit there and look as smug as you want, git, but you've already given me paper and a pencil."

I ignored her and carried on in my serenity.

It wasn't long before the introductions were finished and Diana was bringing the class' focus back to the front, although, to be truthful, mine had not really moved from that vicinity. However, I do pride myself on being subtle. Subtlety is my forte.

"As if she needed to tell you to give her your attention," Sophie whispered, and followed it with a snort, then a yelp, as I nipped her thigh—hard.

Diana looked over quizzically, and thankfully Sophie muttered something about a cramp whilst rubbing her leg in an overly dramatic way as I looked appropriately concerned.

A hesitation, a gathering of thoughts, and then Diana was on a roll. She explained the nature of the class, and how we were there to learn how to study form. I didn't turn to my friend at that point, because I knew I would be greeted by immature nodding and grinning.

"However, we will not be drawing nudes for a few weeks. We have to come to grips with the basics first."

At that I lifted my chin higher and smiled a serene smile at the teacher before tilting my head to the right and nodding once in smugness at Sophie.

Diana continued to explain our lesson objective, and how to create form, we had to dabble with perspective. "Therefore, at timed intervals, we will be moving around and drawing the various items I have assembled on the table here." She pointed at the pots, pans, and other miscellaneous kitchen stuff I had noted upon entering the room. "Picasso used a similar technique. The trick is to draw quickly, get a feel for it, then when you change perspective, move back to an item you can relate to." She paused, her eyes sweeping the class for understanding. "It will seem odd at first, and challenging, but the effect is impressive."

Each drawing stage was no longer than five minutes, then Diana would tell us to get up and move one seat to the right.

I was so engrossed in the activity that I was startled when I heard a voice in my ear. No. That's wrong. It wasn't her voice that alerted me, or startled me, for that matter. It was the sensation rippling down my spine that told me she was there. It was that clicking again, the way I held my breath in anticipation as she drew nearer. Then her voice. Or was it? Could it have been the scent of her? The warmth of her? The sheer presence of the woman behind me that made all the small hairs on my body stand to attention? Or was it the sensation of being watched? I don't know the answer; it wasn't something I noted consciously. One thing that did stick in my mind was how much I craved her closeness.

"Well done, Jess. That's excellent work." Then she was gone, and I was left feeling the chill of empty air.

A snigger spurted from next to me. "Well done, Jess." Jesus. Sophie sounded like she did when she tormented me at Primary School. "Who's the teacher's pet?"

I leaned over and looked at the splattered objects on her paper, if they could even be described as that, then turned to look into my friend's grinning face. "Well, it's obviously not you. She said to draw it, not kill it."

Sophie's retort died on her lips as Diana brought everyone's attention back to the front of the room. "Break time."

Thoughts of running around the playground chasing each other rushed through my head.

"The canteen is open on the ground floor."

Maybe not. Although I wouldn't have minded a bit of tumbling around in the long grass with a certain blue-eyed teacher.

I should have known. Sophie wanting to come to night school to spend "quality time" with me should have made bells go off inside my head like an oncoming fire engine. But no. I once again proved that being naïve was a way of life for me and not a just phase.

And the reason I came to that conclusion? There we were, lining up for a lukewarm coffee, and who walked up to us and started a conversation? Dave. As in, Dave with goatee and chic 'tache. I thought he wanted to push in line, and was beginning to close the gap between me and Babs Hepworth. Shit coffee or not, I was a stickler for the British "We must queue" way of thinking.

"Sophie, is it?"

Huh? He remembered her? Well, she was pretty hard to forget after her blushing furiously and stammering out excuses.

"You work at Pickard's, don't you?"

Huh? Again.

But before Sophie could shove me out of the way to get closer to him, he was talking again. "So do I. Accounts."

I was beginning to feel like the piggy in the middle, as he was now in front of me and Sophie was behind me. I know I'm not the tallest of people in the world, but it still didn't give them license to talk over my head. I tried to move to the side, but I couldn't shift out of the way because all the other people were thinking exactly what I had thought when Dave came up. As if I would ever be a queue jumper!

"Now that you mention it, I think I have seen you about before."

I knew by the tone of her voice that she was lying. Spending twenty-five plus years with someone gives you the edge on details like that. Because I was so near to him, all I could see was the bottom of his chin and part way up his nose. He must've been about six three, if not taller. How had I got this close? I had been able to see all details of him when he first arrived, so why was he appearing like something from a magic eye puzzle? Then I realised that we were, in fact, moving. Slowly, granted, but moving all the same. Dave, however, seemed to be nailed to the spot.

At this rate, I would soon be inside his stylish jacket and living under his wing for the rest of my life.

"David!" A voice came from a ways behind him, and as he turned, his chest smacked me in the face.

Instead of feeling sorry for myself, I sneaked around him and got myself out of the increasingly claustrophobic situation. Sophie stayed where she was, and I wished that I had too, as the voice that had called to her love interest turned out to be Diana's.

"Shit." The reason I said shit right about there is because of what happened next. You guessed it. Dave introduced my friend to his sister, and I was left looking at stale muffins and ordering a latte from a teenager who looked as if she would rather be scooping up dog mess with her bare hands than serving a bunch of luvvies on a night out. If I had just stood my ground, or even reacted to the thump in my face, I, too, could have been in deep conversation with the gorgeous Ms Sullivan.

Taking my coffee, I made my way over to an empty table and thumped the cup down with enough va va voom to make it spill into the saucer. Not exactly the action of a woman who was out to create destruction, but just enough to piss me off a little bit more.

As I was cleaning the mess, I heard another cup placed delicately on the table. Part of me was hoping that I would hear the resounding thud of more cups, as that would mean Sophie had brought her new best friends back with her, but, alas, it was just the one.

I was upset. Who wouldn't be? I had assumed that Sophie wanted to spend time with me, wanted me to have more out of life than I had been getting, cared enough about me to drag me out to do something other than read in bed before falling asleep. But it wasn't like that at all. It had been me helping her get something, or someone, she fancied, without the embarrassment of coming to class on her own.

"I know what you're thinking, and you're wrong. I didn't come to meet Dave."

I flicked a glance in her direction and continued to wipe at the already clean saucer.

"I know you don't believe me, but it's true."

Another flick-cum-glare.

"Okay." Sophie's deep sigh resonated through the space between us. "I overheard him telling someone about it at work...about his sister holding the class."

I didn't answer. I just settled myself into my seat and looked at her expectantly.

"My first thought was of you. You loved art when we were at school. I always thought you would be a designer or something."

She waited for me to say something, but I wasn't in the mood.

"I was always so proud of you."

I wanted to stay mad at her, I really did, but her expression told me that she was, in fact, telling me the truth as she knew it. Because she had praised me, even stroked my ego a little, a small smile crept over my face.

"So, are you going to go out with him?" It wasn't an accusation, just interest, and also a step in the right direction.

For the second time that evening, Sophie was blushing.

I leaned closer, enjoying that the usually confident woman seated in front of me was looking uncomfortable. "Are you?"

"No."

Huh? "Huh? No? You must be losing your touch."

"I said no. He asked, and I turned him down."

Fuck me. That was a first. I had never known Sophie to turn down a night out with a hunky guy. Don't get me wrong. Sophie wasn't a loose woman, or, to use even more clichéd expressions, a bike or a slut/slag/manizer, if there is such a word, since men can be called womanizers. She just liked to go out with good looking men, have a laugh. You know, enjoy herself.

"You turned him down?"

"We've got to get back to class."

"Why?"

"Because its ti—"

"Not about class. Why did you turn him down?"

She didn't answer, just got up, finished off her coffee, which was probably still hot, and made her way back to the counter to drop off her cup. "Are you coming or what?"

With that, she was gone, and I was left with half a cup of coffee and a thousand questions. I couldn't work her out. Actually, I couldn't work myself out. Initially I had been mad at her for making me come to a class so she could cop off with a dishy bloke from her office, and then I was confused when she had turned him down. All I could muster was a shrug of the shoulders to dispel the fogging of my brain.

I lifted the cup and saucer and followed in Sophie's footsteps. Five minutes later, I was back in the class, my best friend seated next to me, diligently working over her mishmash of blotches and distorted lines.

It was weird. Yep. Weird. After class finished at nine and we went to the pub, Sophie didn't even mention Dave or the class. We had one drink, and then she feigned a yawn and said all the excitement had tuckered her out. She seemed reserved in an "I feel so embarrassed yet I don't know why" kind of way, so I just went along with it, but I knew then and there in the car park that this wasn't over. I would let her sleep on it. Only one night, mind you. And in the famous words of Scarlett O'Hara, "After all, tomorrow is another day."

Chapter 3

Pffft. What a wonderful word, if it can described as such. Pffffft…nearly as good as brrrrr and grrrrrr. You may be wondering why I am using such silly expressions here. Simple. Sophie. Could I get hold of her? Not a chance in hell. It was Saturday morning that I eventually came to grips with the slippery one herself, and that was by pure luck. I had left her countless messages, both on her voicemail and through texting. I had even emailed her about ten times. Nothing. I was just giving up the will to live when I bumped into her. Literally. I bumped into her in Tesco, in the feminine hygiene aisle of all places. To say I smelled a rat would actually seem out of place here. Not because of her expression when I whacked into her with my shopping trolley as I was turning into the aisle, no. Mainly because talking about smells when it is linked to a setting that involves lady bits seemed a tad coarse. I was in the process of texting her again when the collision happened, and if I'd been paying attention, I could have saved myself the price of a sms, could've just told her. But no. The velocity with which I cracked into her trolley inadvertently made me press send.

"Hey, stranger!"

Sophie seemed surprised in more ways than one.

"I've been trying to get hold of you." I wasn't the one saying this. "Where've you been?"

"Bumchickawowow!"

Once again, that wasn't me. Well, it was, but not. It was the sound of Sophie's phone notifying her that she had received a message. Part of me was glad she had got rid of the chickens repeatedly clucking that signalled the arrival of a message, whilst the other half of me was totally fucked off big time that here she stood, as bold as brass, I might add, and had tried to pass it over on me for her—yes *her*—lack of communication.

"Me? Me not contacting you?" Seemed a little obvious, me saying that, but what else could I say?

"I've been trying to contact you since Thursday. Wanted to know your plans for tonight," Sophie said.

I looked into Sophie's trolley and saw three bottles of wine and the ingredients for an evening of entertaining. I raised my eyes to meet hers. "Looks like you've already got plans." Yes. I admit it. It did sound bitter. "And, for your information, I've been trying to get hold of you for the last three days."

Sophie looked confused, I'll give her that. Instead of taking art classes, she would have excelled at drama. "But…I've sent you about fifteen messages."

Yeah right. Where were they? Cyber Land, just past I Don't Give a Fuck? "Look, Soph. I don't know what's going on and to be honest, I don't give a flying fu—"

"Ohhh, ohhhh—your text is on fi-re!"

And then again and again and again, until my phone was going crazy.

"I think you have a message."

I glared at her and pulled my phone back out of my pocket. Another text. Another. And then another. All from Sophie, and all from different times and days. Scrolling through her messages, it was apparent she had been answering mine and was wondering why I was getting increasingly pissed off. But why hadn't she called my landline? Or answered my emails? And why couldn't I ever be satisfied?

"I've been away—conference in Leeds. Don't you remember? I told you on Wednesday."

Nope. Not a spark.

"I don't have your landline number on my mobile, or I would've called you."

I squinted in disbelief.

"I haven't. Look."

She thrust her phone my way, and I pushed it back to her. "But you could've called my mobile." Simple, don't you think?

"I was on a course, Jess. We didn't finish until late, that's why I sent the texts."

Why was I being such a twat with her? Why was I being so insecure? I had known Sophie most of my life and she had never done anything to hurt me, so what was going on? Was I going through a "poor me" phase? To quote Scarlett O'Hara again, "I can't think about that right now. If I do, I'll go crazy. I'll think about that tomorrow." Jesus. I was paralleling my life with a Margaret Mitchell character.

"So, what are your plans, oh gorgeous one?" Sophie was waiting for me to return to the present and out of the pages of the American Southern saga. "You up for coming for dinner at my place? I have a surprise."

I began to speak, but she knew me too well.

"I'm not telling you. Just be at my place at seven, and dress smart but casual."

Again I opened my mouth.

"Can't stop. Can't tell. Just be there or else, okay?"

With that, she was gone, and I was left looking at panty liners and feminine wash.

⋘⊙⊙⊙⋙

I was tempted to stay home, tempted to wait for her to call at 7:01pm and demand to know why I hadn't turned up. But then I wondered, why smart / casual? Usually when I ate at Sophie's, it meant pizza from Dominos or Chinese takeaway. So, why dress up? And what was the surprise? I wouldn't have to wash up after? There was only one way to find out, and that was to get my butt in gear and go 'round to her house. Early. That would give me time to pump her for information.

⋘⊙⊙⊙⋙

I had been there for less than five minutes before the sound of the bell interrupted my interrogation. "What? Who?" That's all I got out before Sophie almost skipped off to answer the door, bringing back memories of her on the playground just before she caused trouble. My gut was giddy, and it wasn't with excitement. Anticipation? No. More like dread.

Voices filtered through the doorway of the kitchen where I was standing like a spare prick at a wedding. I straightened my back. I knew that voice. Not well, but I knew it. And then another, a female voice. A man and a woman. Jeez. I should give up my life working in an office and join CSI.

"Jess!" Sophie's high pitched voice broke through my reverie, and the only thought I knew for definite was that Sophie was shitting a brick. And I hoped it came out sideways. "Come and say hello."

It was when my legs were moving me towards the doorway and into the hallway that it came to me: It was Dave. Dave and Diana. A number of emotions vied for supremacy—anger being the initial one. Sophie had told me she had not made arrangements to meet Dave again. I also knew she would try to get out of it by saying, "I didn't go out with him. He came around to my house." What a load of bollocks. Then second emotion? Curiosity. Why had he brought his sister? Was he too scared to be alone with the man eater? Did he need a chaperone?

FUCK! His sister was here! And I was being a doddering dickhead in the cusp of the kitchen and hallway whilst there was a gorgeous woman waiting for my handshake less than five feet away. Panic shot through me. Did I look okay? Had I actually given a shit about what I looked like when I got ready to come to my supposed best friend's house tonight? I knew I should have worn the top that accentuated my cleavage instead of the fucking crew-necked jumper I was wearing. What about my ass?

"Jess! Are you coming?"

No. I'm having a fashion crisis and imagining the fashion police about to hammer down the door and arrest me for mixing cotton with wool.

Before I had a chance to run back into the kitchen and try to see my reflection in the side of the kettle, Sophie appeared, looking anxious. Hissing through her teeth, she ground out, "What the fuck are you doing?"

I opened my mouth to answer, but was interrupted by

the decidedly too close voice of Dave. "Hi again, Jess."

A blush eked its way up my throat, as if it, too, wanted to say hello.

"I think you already know my sister Diana."

Fuck, do I. And as if by magic—just like Mr Ben, the Shopkeeper in the defunct kid's program of the same name, Diana appeared.

"Hi there."

God. That voice. A smile broke out across her face, and I mirrored it. Well, nearly. I mustered a smile, granted, but mine was more the kind of smile that typically denoted the village idiot.

"What a nice surprise."

Surprise?

"When Dave said he wanted me to come to dinner with a work friend, I didn't expect to already know her...well, both of you."

Back to me smelling a rat—a big, bright red one. Scrap that. Two bright red ones. Dave and Sophie were both trying unsuccessfully to hide their glowing faces. What I couldn't understand was why? Why would they be embarrassed about having dinner? Was it because they were uncomfortable about being alone with each other? Why didn't they knock it on the head then and not meet at all?

"Yes. It is a surprise, isn't it?" I gave Sophie a quick glare, and she took that moment to fuck off and sort out the wine glasses.

Dave scampered after her, and if you've ever seen a six foot three man scamper, it is not the easiest, or the most elegant way to move. He almost looked like a newborn fawn chasing its mother.

"A lovely surprise, though." Another smile slipped

effortlessly across Diana's face, making her eyes twinkle and reintroducing those adorable rays of light I had seen from her lips when she had first smiled in class.

When the penny dropped, I'm sure the whole street could hear the clunk of the metal against the tiled floor. I could try to claim that it was the recently discovered skills that made me believe I could work for CSI that were enabling me to see the wood for the trees. But, like Sophie, then I would have been a liar. It was actually the simple phrase Sophie yelled from the kitchen that alerted me, which, I hasten to add, had been preceded by whisperings between her and Dave.

"Why don't you two make yourselves comfortable in the living room and get better acquainted? We'll bring the drinks in."

I should have known Sophie was trying to fix me up. But how on earth did she know that Diana was a lesbian? She couldn't have found out from Dave in the short space of time she had spoken to him in the canteen, and I couldn't imagine Diana introducing herself as the one and only lezza teacher who wanted to get up close and personal with her absent friend. That would be too wacky for even my deluded imagination. So, what gives?

"Shall we?" Diana said, snapping me out of my inner forensics.

She was wearing an expression of confusion. Diana was trying to read my face, and I wished her luck. If I couldn't understand what was going on inside my head, she had no chance.

"Sure," I eventually answered.

I slipped my hand under her elbow to lead her in the direction of Sophie's living room. God. I honestly couldn't tell you what happened when I grasped her arm, but I experienced the weirdest sensation I've ever felt. It seemed as if a jolt of electricity raced from her and into me. Springing away from her, I saw the same expression flash over her beautiful face as I knew I was sporting.

"What the…?" I was so glad I didn't spout the epithet that was trying to slither through my clenched teeth.

"Is it this room?"

Diana recovered more quickly than I did, that was for sure. Her face turned away, and she was crossing the spacious living room at an alarming speed.

I was hovering in the doorway like a prize one tit, wondering why I felt the need to run.

Before I regained my ability to move, preferably rapidly towards the front door, Diana turned around to face me, a smile fixed solidly in place. "So, shall we?"

Shall we what?

"We can't start to get better acquainted if we are in different rooms, can we?" One eyebrow raised itself into the darkness of her hair.

I snorted at the comical expression on her face. Relaxing, I stepped through the doorway and into the room.

"Close the door."

Close the... Huh?

"I think we need to talk."

Shit. Didn't this conversation typically happen when you were actually dating someone and not when you had been invited to someone's house for dinner and realised that you were half of a couple who was being set up? Now that is what I call a long and complex question. However, I didn't say anything to her, just turned, closed the door, and sidled to the sofa nearest the window. At least I could just jump out, if it got too uncomfortable.

"Are you thinking what I'm thinking?"

I doubted it. Unless she, too, was eyeing up the pros and cons of diving headfirst from a ground floor window. "Urg!" Please translate that as, "Although I think I am aware of what you may be thinking, the rational side of me disagrees."

Diana seemed unfazed by my lack of ability to formulate a sentence, and she sat next to me on the sofa. "I think my brother is trying to play matchmaker."

I was going to say urg again, but decided against it. I didn't want to overstimulate her brain with my witty repartee.

"I'm sorry, Jess."

Did she actually remember my name, or had someone reminded her? Dave. He had. Bollocks. Why was I finding it difficult to stay focused? And the reason I thought the last bit was because I know for a fact she had continued to talk, but I wasn't listening.

Blue eyes turned to me, the bluest eyes I had ever seen so up close and personal. How easy it would be to drown in those eyes. A sigh left my lungs, and I know my shoulders hitched with the effort.

Hang on a minute. She apologised? For what? Crap. I felt my eyes widen, giving the impression that I looked surprised by what she had said. Maybe if I knew what it was, I would've been. Should I just go for a grunt again?

"So what do you think? Do you think that's silly?"

Shit. I could've just gone with the "I'll agree with what you think" or the bloke response of "absolutely," but I knew that Diana would see straight through it—whatever "it" was.

"Can..."

Honestly, I was going to ask her to repeat her idea, but the door popped open and two smiling faces walked in carrying wine.

After much subsequent reflection, I believe I missed one of the most important conversations I could've had in my sad little life. Pity I didn't think to ask her to tell me again what she had planned. It might have stopped me making a total fool out of myself.

All through dinner, Diana paid me attention. Everything I said was marvellous, and she found even the crappiest joke to be highly hilarious. It was a bit disconcerting at first, as I had never had that overwhelming feeling of being so popular. However, as time and courses went on, I was beginning to feel something that must have resembled what it felt like to be high. It was intoxicating to hear that musical laugh ring out at my delivery of too many jokes that could have been gleaned from Christmas crackers. I was having a ball. I wish I could have said the same about my interfering hostess. At one point in the evening, I saw Sophie glare at me and gesture sharply with her head for me to follow her into the kitchen. I grinned and ignored her.

After dessert, Sophie verbalised her need for me to go with her on the pretence of getting coffee started. Her tone was clipped, and there was no way she was taking no for an answer.

In the kitchen, I felt the air change from friendly to "Jesus Christ, Jess! What are you playing at?" in mere seconds.

"Jesus Christ, Jess! What are you playing at?"

"What do you mean?"

"What do I mean?"

That's what I said, isn't it?

"You. The way you're acting. Did you slip something into your drink?"

"What do you mean?"

"What do I mean?"

This was getting monotonous.

"All the joke telling—the bad joke telling. What's gotten into you? Is this payback or something?"

I felt the giddiness disappear. Had I make a dick out of myself?

"Okay, I admit it. I invited Dave and Diana over so I could...so Dave and I could fix you two up. Happy?" Turning away from me, she slammed cups onto the saucers before filling the coffeemaker with water. "It was so obvious that Diana was playing along."

Obvious?

"Dave said if she got wind of it, she would pretend to like you to get him off her back."

Pretend to...like me? Pretend. Pre-tend? Wasn't I worthy of being liked without the pretence?

"I'm sorry, Jess" followed by a *"So, what do you think? Or do you think that's silly?"* That must've been what Diana was saying. As soon as she had realised what her brother and Sophie were up to, she had wanted an out. *"Or do you think that's silly?"*

No. I'm silly. Actually, I'm a fucking idiot. I had pushed all that to the back of my head and gone with just feeling good in someone else's company for once.

Without saying a word, I left. Left the kitchen, left the hallway, left the house. Left everything behind without a by-your-leave or a backwards glance. Quite possibly, I cried all the way home too. How sad is that?

Chapter 4

My mobile phone rang somewhere in the depths of the jeans I had thrown on the floor of my bedroom. Five, six, seven times it blasted the naff ring tone before it started on the even naffer text alert.

I pulled my duvet up over my head. I knew it would be Sophie trying to get hold of me. The reason I knew this was because she had tried to call me incessantly as I had marched home in anger, tears, and self-deprecation.

Eventually the phone stopped making the noises that let me know there was a person who desperately wanted me to pick up. She was probably catching forty winks before trying to call again.

There was one thing I hadn't counted on when I had become absorbed into the age of mobile phones and instant communication; that was the old way of communicating. The very old way of making contact with someone you wanted to get in touch with. No. Not a letter. Not even one flown in, tagged ungraciously on the leg of a pigeon. It was in the form of demented banging on my front door followed by shouting. Sophie shouting, to be exact. Her phrasing was predictable. "Open up. Gonna kick your door down" followed by the thudding of someone trying to mimic either Starsky or Hutch, but without success.

My head momentarily poked from under my covers when the knocking started, but now I turned over and faced away from the noise.

Apparently deciding enough was enough, Jeff from two doors down was yelling out of his bedroom window, "Do you know what fucking time it is?"

This was not good. Jeff was a moaning bastard at the best of times, but when he actually had something to moan about, he was in his element. What he didn't know was Sophie was someone you didn't start with, especially when she was pissed off.

"Time you fucked off, asshole! Jess! Come on! Open up!"

"How dare you speak to me like that? I've a good mind to phone the police," Jeff yelled back.

"Look, whoever you are, I'm not in the mood to discuss whether or not you even have a mind. So why don't you shut your mouth, shut your window, and climb back into your sad little life. JESS! FOR GOD'S SAKE!"

Slam. Not my door again, but the sound of Jeff's window closing. That would mean only one thing. He would now be calling the police. And even though I was still fuming at Sophie, I didn't want her getting dragged to the cop shop on account of me ignoring her because she told me the truth.

As I was making my way down the stairs, Sophie must've remembered I had a doorbell, as it started to ring with abandon.

"What?" I think I surprised her, me answering the door I mean. Although I don't understand why, as she had made it apparent she wasn't going anywhere until I had let her in.

She visibly relaxed as her eyes met mine. "Baby." Her voice was soft and motherly, the glint of tears appearing like magic. "Why? Why did you leave?"

Instead of answering her, I turned and walked towards the kitchen. I could hear her behind me, but, like Orpheus, I didn't look back to check if she was there.

Filling up the kettle, I called over my shoulder, "Coffee?" Then I set out mugs without listening to her response. I felt her behind me, felt her waiting for me to give her some attention, but I knew if I turned to face her, I would break down in tears. I had made an idiot of myself in front of everyone, and I was ashamed. Well, not just ashamed, deflated. No...that isn't right. I was totally gutted. Diana was the first woman I had felt an attraction to for so long, and I had cocked it up by being a dick head. And then to top it all off, I had left without a word—not even an "I'll catch you later, got to dash" as I ran screaming silently for the hills to bury my head, preferably up my own arse.

Clink. Clink. The spoon hit the sides of each mug with finality, and I knew that I had to face the music. I lifted the mugs, then turned and offered one to Sophie. Without looking at her face, I said "I don't want to go to art class anymore." Then, like a leading lady in a silent movie, I drifted towards the living room.

I plonked onto the armchair and gathered my legs underneath me, almost as if I was trying to get my body as small as it would go.

Sophie followed me into the room and sat on the edge of the sofa.

The ticking of the mantle clock was louder than I remembered it being. Weirdly enough, I think it was the first time I could remember being in Sophie's company and being able to hear anything other than our conversation.

A bluish light flitted across my front room and made it seem even more surreal than it already was. The bell sounded with one sharp ring. Delicately, I placed my mug on the coffee table and went to the door.

A solitary policeman was on my doorstep, and I smiled pleasantly. "Good evening, Officer. Can I help you?"

"Sorry to disturb you, Ma'am, but we've had a complaint about noise coming from this address."

"This address, Officer? I don't understand." Another smile, a little lean forward to show a glimpse of cleavage, "My friend forgot her key and knocked a while back. Is that what you mean?" As expected, the policeman tit clocked, and I made sure he knew I had seen him by tugging gently at the V of my t-shirt. "You can come in and see if you like, although, as you can tell, I am ready for bed."

Where was this going? What was I doing?

"Well, it would be better if I checked out the complaint completely."

As he made a move to come inside, I said, "If you don't mind me asking, did the call come from 120—a man named Jeff Barnes?" I watched him as he deliberated telling me. "Because, Officer…" I can't believe I leaned towards him again and flashed the curves of the girls. I never flashed for effect, well, not for a man at any rate, "Mr Barnes is not a very nice man. I'm sure you've heard from him before." I looked over my shoulder, as if checking to be sure I couldn't be overheard. "He has a tendency to complain about anything and everything. Actually, he was quite abusive to my friend earlier."

"You cheeky cow. How fucking dare you blame me when you know for a fact your so-called friend was—"

"Calm down please, Sir. There is no need for that kind

of language in front of a lady."

"A lady! A fucking lady! You must be joking. She's a fucking ru—"

He didn't get the chance to finish his rug muncher jibe, as the officer had stepped out and grabbed Jeff by the arm and spun him around.

"Get your fucking hands off me. I pay my taxes to keep the likes of you in a job."

You would think that Jeff would have had the sense he was born with, but no. He apparently felt that it would be okay for him to twat the officer who was trying to restrain him. Not a solid punch by any stretch of the imagination, but a definite swipe all the same.

Five minutes later, Jeff was being taken down to the police station, and I was guiltily closing the front door. I had other things to worry about than the bloke who constantly complained about his neighbours being carted off by the bizzies.

Sophie was still waiting on the edge of the sofa. "Everything okay?"

I gave her a look of nonchalance.

"Come on Jess. What's up? Why did you leave?"

My jaw dropped. How could she even ask me why I had left? Wasn't it blatantly obvious?

"I said I was sorry for trying to fix you up. It won't happen again."

At that point I cracked. Why? Fuck knows. But I did. A sob tore from my chest and hit the air in front of a stunned Sophie. Then another one. And another. Tears were racing down my face, and I wanted to get up and do the dramatic running-from-the-room-whilst-slamming-doors, but I couldn't move. I crumpled up like a tired tissue waiting for the inevitable throwing away into a bin. Warm hands circled me, and my face was pulled against a waiting chest. The comfort that brought me caused even more tears to flow from my depths. Sophie started a rocking motion, and I wanted to be completely absorbed into it. It had been so long since I had let myself cave in, so long since I had let my guard down that now I couldn't stop the emotional meltdown.

Minutes seemed to drag but speed up. I don't know how long Sophie held me, but she never stopped rocking, whispering, stroking my hair and rubbing my back. Even though I had been angry at her for what she had said in the kitchen, there was never a point in my life where I didn't feel more safe in my best friend's presence.

It was quiet. So numbingly quiet that I felt as if I was in another dimension, felt as if I was looking at the situation from above. There I was, looking and feeling so small and insignificant, being held by my guardian.

"You want to tell me about it?" The words seemed too loud, deafening. "It's not just what I did, is it?"

I shook my head.

"Come on, baby. Tell Aunty Soph." She waited. "And if anyone has upset my girl, I'll kick the shit out of them."

A spurt of laughter shot from my mouth, followed by the harrumphing of someone who has cried for too long and too hard. "I like her." My voice was small, and it didn't help that it was muffled by Sophie's chest. Little wonder she asked me to repeat what I'd said. Lifting my head, I looked her in the eyes. "I said I like her. Diana."

Sophie's eyes widened.

I leaned back on the chair, leaving Sophie kneeling at my feet. I turned away, as I felt too exposed to keep staring into her face. "And, as you so delicately pointed out—she isn't, and won't ever be interested in me."

Once again the quiet seeped between us. I could hear the living room mantelpiece clock announcing every second that thrummed by.

"She likes you too, Jess."

I huffed before rubbing my face with my hand to dispel the sticky feeling of drying tears.

"She does. Honest. You should have seen her after you left." Sophie's hand cupped my chin and gently turned me to face her.

Part of me wanted to know how Diana Sullivan had reacted, whilst another part of me was a little fearful. What if she had said "Oh, right. She's gone, has she?" Would that be enough?

"She hoped she hadn't offended you by suggesting the two of you play along with her idea of tricking Dave and me into believing our matchmaking attempt was working."

I wanted to feel some semblance of righteousness at guessing what had happened, but I felt too miserable.

"Even Dave was surprised. He said afterwards that he had not seen Diana look so crestfallen in ages."

In ages? What did he mean by that? And how many people used the word crestfallen in this day and age?

"Listen to me. She likes you." Sophie made sure I was looking straight into her eyes before she continued. "And I'm sorry I made you feel like she didn't."

What could I say to that? "You should be."

Sophie's eyes narrowed, but I laughed and nudged her, a little harder than I intended. The sound of her splatting on the floor, followed by a string of delectable epithets not to be used in front of minors, somehow made me feel even better than the admission of my friend's fault and the possibility of the gorgeous art teacher being interested in Yours Truly.

"You could help me up, maybe even look a little apologetic."

I did neither.

Chapter 5

Wednesday came around too quickly. I did and didn't want to go to class, but the "did" part won out. It wasn't just because I had made a dick out of myself at the weekend that had made me reticent about going to class, either. It was seeing her...seeing *her* and knowing that I liked her. No. Seeing her and finding out that I was, in fact, just another student she had been nice to at a dinner party. However, I did say that I caved and went along, right? The reason? It was seeing her. Just...*seeing* her. And, I have to admit, I had enjoyed the class the previous week.

Sophie was late. Git. I had been hovering outside the building for twenty minutes before she finally texted me to let me know she was stuck in traffic and wouldn't be in class for at least another thirty minutes. I had two choices: stay outside and wait, or go in and grab our seats.

I was nervous. Stupidly nervous. It wasn't the "teenager seeing her crush" kind of nervous; it was more a case of waiting for Diana to comment across the classroom about me fucking off before coffee on Saturday night. I would've been so much happier walking through the door with

Sophie by my side. That way, Diana could've said it, but people wouldn't have been sure who she was addressing.

Funnily enough, Diana never said a word when I went in. She didn't even acknowledge my presence. It seemed as if my legs stuttered in the doorway, almost as if they were deliberating turning me around so I could make my escape. Weirdly enough, I didn't. The little buggers decided that onwards and forwards were the way to go, and before I knew it, I was sitting in the same seat I had been in the previous week.

After I unpacked my stuff, I allowed my eyes to drift around the room. Two things stood out. One—Sophie was still absent. Two—so was Dave. Coincidence? Methinks not. It was just too convenient that they were both late. Definitely. And because of that, I found I couldn't look at Diana. Stupid, I know, but what else was a girl to think? Two absentees and blanked as I entered the room? This woman was as far from interested as a woman could be.

As we began to draw the still life arranged for the class, I decided that I would split when we had a tea break. I had convinced myself that Sophie was not coming, and Dave's absence made my mind conjure up scenarios where brother and sister had almost come to blows because of what had happened over the weekend.

It's amazing what a mind can do, isn't it? I had totally convinced myself that I would be swanning off at half time, but when it came down to it, I didn't. I was too caught up in the activity we were doing to pay any mind to what had happened at Sophie's dinner.

As I was queuing up in the canteen, I remembered that I had been planning to leave, and that was only because I heard the dulcet tones of my best friend from behind me.

"Coffee for me, ta."

I just grunted and kept my eyes on the front of the line. The Babs Hepworth wannabe was hovering to the side, and I was definite she was going to make a jump for it as it neared my turn. Not on my watch, she wasn't.

It was my turn, and the Babster made a move to nip in.

"Two coffees please, love," I called, as I pushed the bespectacled art student almost into the following week. When had I become so aggressive? To be honest, I didn't care. All that concerned me was not allowing someone to push in. That wasn't British.

I think Sophie was expecting me to crack off at her for leaving me in the lurch, but I was busy thinking about the drawing I had created. Every time she spoke, I felt her wait for me to have a go at her, and every time I didn't, she seemed more confused.

"Time to get back." With that, I cleared our cups and headed back to the room, Sophie scurrying behind me.

Upon entering, I spotted Dave talking agitatedly with his sister in the corner of the room. Furtive glances in my and Sophie's direction indicated we were the topic of conversation. Not good. All the feelings of wellbeing and wanting to actually be there to study the topic seemed to fade.

"This yours, Jess?" Sophie was looking at my drawing of trinkets, and I made a noise in the back of my throat. "Wow. You are good."

Opening my mouth to disagree, I was stopped by the familiar sound of Diana Sullivan's voice.

"Excellent work, Jess. You have captured the perspective wonderfully well."

All the moisture in my mouth evaporated, and swallowing became a near impossibility.

"How are you both?"

I chanced a glance at the enigmatic teacher. Those blue eyes were firmly fixed on Sophie, and the smile she flashed was warm and inviting. But only for Sophie. Her voice was like nectar—coating, delicious, intoxicating. Also aimed only at Sophie. It was then I realised something. Diana wasn't interested in me at all. Not judging by the sparkle in her eyes every time Sophie spoke. I was beginning to feel like a gooseberry, a gooseberry fool.

I stood and watched how Diana placed her hand on Sophie's arm when she was speaking, the way she leaned forward as if bringing Sophie into her confidence, the way her body turned more and more away from me, nearly blocking me out of the conversation. Too fucking obvious even for a complete dick head like me to ignore. Diana Sullivan wanted Sophie, not me. She was interested in my best friend, getting to grips with my best friend, making the beast with two backs with my…best…friend. I spent far too long gazing at her hand touching Sophie, fascinated by the circular scar I could see between her thumb and index finger.

Fuck. What was a girl to do? Back down gracefully? Slip away and hide in the corner and hope no one noticed? Make a scene? Demand that Diana Sullivan like me, the lezza, and not Sophie, who had never indicated that she could be persuaded toward Sapphic love. Don't get me wrong. Sophie didn't dislike lesbianism; it just wasn't her bag. She liked her men too much.

But that didn't stop Diana liking her, did it?

The class seemed to drag by. Sophie's drawing was half-hearted at best, and for the most part, she was making faces and mouthing things to Dave across the room. I didn't want to get involved, I just wanted the evening to be over so I could get out of there and get on with my sad little life.

At five to nine, Diana called for the group's attention. I already had my bag packed and was sitting there with my coat on.

Diana started her plenary for the lesson and pointed out our objectives once again. Just as she was finishing up, I began to stand.

"Ah...Jess. I was just about to come to you."

I looked at her with complete disinterest, which made her frown.

"I would love to show the rest of the class your drawing, as I think it sums up everything we were trying to achieve."

Without saying a word, I pulled my art pad out of my bag and tossed it to the centre table. I think every pair of eyes in the room watched its transition from me to the table with avid interest. I heard a whispered "Jess?" from the side of me, but I didn't even look at Sophie.

Diana seemed flummoxed. The confident face she usually wore at the front of class was missing, and her eyes searched mine out. A flicker of hurt darted through the blue, making it seem lighter, if only in my imagination.

"Erm. Well. Thank you, Jess."

I nodded and waited for her to be done with the display so I could leave.

At nine o'clock, I was walking out of the door, Sophie acting like a human sticky bob. She said nothing, not a word, until we got to the car park.

"What the fuck is up with you?"

I ignored her and continued to walk.

She grabbed my arm and I stopped, but kept facing away from her.

"I said, what the fuck is wrong with you?"

Without looking, I muttered, "I'm just tired, that's all."

Sophie dug her fingers in harder. "Bollocks."

I tried to deny it, but she just kept repeating "bollocks" every time I started to speak. "Look Jess, I have known you too long to believe that. Something has crawled up your arse and died. What is it?"

I turned to look at her. She wasn't angry, just confused, nearly as confused as I was. "Honestly, Soph. I've had a crap day. I am absolutely knackered. Actually, I don't feel too good." That bit was true. I didn't feel good. I felt sick to the stomach. "I'm finding coming to class a bit of a strain... you know, mid-week. It wouldn't be so bad if it was on a weekend."

Yes. I was paving the way to stop going to class.

"But, Jess..."

She looked so disappointed, I felt bad. I wanted to not feel the way I did, wanted to not like Diana Sullivan as much as I did. That way I could keep going to the class where I had felt myself coming alive again.

"Can we at least talk about it...this Saturday? Girly day. Shopping, the works."

I nodded and forced a smile. "Come here. Give me a hug."

As Sophie put her arms around me, tears surged up from deep within, but I shoved them back. If I broke down now, I would end up telling her everything. Tell her how I felt jealous that a woman I barely knew but had a huge attraction for was hankering after her instead. Tell her that even though I knew Diana had no chance with Sophie, I couldn't stand to see her not looking at me the way she looked at my best friend.

How sad is that?

By the time I reached home, I was in such a funk. I know. I was in a pretty bad funk by the end of the class, but now I was even lower. All I could see was Diana's expression, the way she absorbed Sophie, laughed with her, touched her arm. I really wanted to hate her, even just dislike her intensely, but it wouldn't come. I had this ache in the pit of my stomach that I couldn't get rid of, and I knew it would be a long time before I could persuade it away. I also knew something else. However much I loved going to class, I wouldn't be going again. Added to that, I knew I would not be telling Sophie. What was the point in telling her? All she would do would be to try and talk me out of it, and that was not going to happen.

Now all I had to do was get through Saturday. That was something I never thought I would say when I was talking about a day out with Soph. Usually our time together was something I really looked forward to, but I knew that I would spend the day dodging questions and trying to forget that I wasn't her.

Chapter 6

Saturday came around; that's what time does. It doesn't fast forward or freeze because you want it to. Despite thoughts to the contrary, it does tick by at the rate it always does, although the perception of speed, velocity, and anticipation does depend a great deal on a person's state of mind. Sophie and I had made arrangement to meet for lunch before going shopping, and, because of time, I was thirty minutes early.

Or I would have been, if Sophie hadn't arrived five minutes after me. That was so unlike her. In all the years I had known her, she had never turned up that early for anything in her life. That was alarm bell number one. Number two came in the form of her hanging up her phone in mid conversation as soon as she spotted me waving wildly at her from the table in the small bistro we had chosen for lunch. Not good. On to number three...that was her voice and expression when she walked over, maybe throwing in a dash of her looking furtively at the door about fifteen times in the twenty feet from where I spotted her to where I was sitting.

"Hey, hon. You're early.'"

Too right. And also beginning to want to leave even before I was supposed to arrive.

"You too." Why did mine come out even more accusatory than hers? Maybe because I was a cynical, untrusting woman. However, it didn't stop the knowledge flooding through me that her voice had actually been a tad accusatory as well. "What's going on?"

Sophie mustered a counterfeit grin and moved in to hug me, which I graciously, albeit stiffly, accepted.

"You are up to something, Harrison. I can sense it."

She didn't answer. Just sat down and grabbed at the drinks menu. "Fancy a cocktail?"

Huh? A cocktail at 12:30 in the afternoon?

"Go on. A little snifter will liven us both up."

Or numb me from the forehead down.

"Just a cranberry juice for me, thanks." I leaned back in my chair and watched her fidget her way through the menu. Her eyes were everywhere except on me. Even when the bum-chick-a-wow-wow sounded from her handbag, she made no move to drag herself from the obviously huge chore of selecting a drink that had more of a kick than a fruit juice.

"You've got a text message."

Nothing. Not any kind of acknowledgement of my stating the fucking obvious. So I told her again.

She grunted, squirmed, and looked shifty.

So, I did what any normal girl would do in that situation—I called her. On her mobile. When she was less than a foot and a half away from me.

"You'd better get that."

Sophie made a gesture to indicate she was too busy to pick up her phone and looked back at the menu, before she did a double take and saw me with my phone next to my ear. Grinning, she plucked her phone out of her bag and tried to go for the sexy response. "Hey there, big boy. What's up?"

I ignored her attempt at humour as I spotted a familiar figure looking in through the glass of the bistro. My heart hit my stomach. I was actually surprised that Sophie didn't hear it. However there was no mistaking that she had seen the blood race from my face, leaving me white and sweating.

"What's up?"

Sophie was still speaking to me through her phone, which I was glad about, to tell the truth, as it gave me the prime opportunity to say and do the next thing.

"When were you going to tell me we were going to have someone else joining us on our girly day?" Click. I wanted to glare at Sophie, just to let her know how very pissed off I actually was, but I couldn't take my eyes off Diana Sullivan as she walked into the bistro.

"Erm."

I wasn't listening. I was too interested in Diana's body language as she began the dramatic walk to our table. An outsider would have assumed she had been ordered to walk the metaphorical plank, but my money was on the fact that she'd had no idea that I would be there. Unlike me, Diana Sullivan was too much of a lady to turn around and walk out. And I would have done it, too, if Sophie hadn't gripped my wrist as I stood and told me to "sit the fuck down and stop acting like a four-year-old." Weirdly enough, if I'd had toys in front of me, I definitely would've thrown them out of my pram.

"Hey." Diana tried to sound upbeat, but there was a tremor in her voice, as if she had announced she was shitting a brick. Then she leaned over to Sophie and kissed her on the cheek.

It was like someone had reached inside my mouth, pushed a fist down my throat, and squeezed my stomach into a clump.

"Hello, Jess. Good to see you again."

Yeah, I bet.

"How're you feeling? More rested?"

Fucking Sophie had been talking to her behind my back. I hated that. "I'm good, thanks." And seething. "A little tired, but I'll live." I tried to give a wan smile, but it came out more like demented. "How're you?" Still lusting after the straight woman?

Diana's smile became a little more natural, and she pulled her chair out and sat down. The waitress finally turned up to take our drinks order, which let me focus on something else for a couple of minutes.

All the way through lunch, Diana fiddled with anything she could lay her hands on—the napkin, the salt and pepper pots, even the other condiment pots. To say the menu was safe would have been lying. It ended up folded into the shape of a flower before it was torn up and piled neatly to the side of her plate. I was fascinated. Not because she was expert at origami, but because I noticed what beautiful hands she had, even with the scar. I'd even forgotten that those beautiful hands would never be making me into something delicate, never guide and mould me into a shape that could be considered creative and engaging. I could definitely relate to the feeling of being torn and discarded.

"Fancy going to the mall?"

The mall? Stockport didn't have a mall. A cheese and egg market, yes, but the closest "mall" was in the city centre. Unless Merseyway was now classed as a mall. And why was I having an internal monologue about whether my hometown had a mall when I should have been answering Sophie?

"I'd love to." Diana answered.

Yeah. I bet you would. More time for you to get to know Sophie. It was time for me to make my excuses and leave the love bird. Yes, singular. Soph wasn't a man-in-the-little-boat licker like me, and the deliriously misguided Ms Sullivan. Fuck. Me and my delectable turn of phrase. I'm still surprised I'm single.

"You coming, Jess?"

I bet you can imagine what shot through my head when I heard the word "coming" in conjunction with my name. And I also bet you followed that with something negative. If so, you are getting to know me pretty well. "I—"

"Yes. Jess would love to come to the city with us. I'll drive." Sophie stood up quickly, as if she was making a point of taking charge. "I'll follow you home so you can drop your car off, and we can all go in mine."

I turned to look at Diana, the question about her car hanging from my lips.

"I walked in."

Yes. Maybe so. But how did Sophie know that? Was it when they were arranging my embarrassment behind my back? And this made me question whether Diana was as innocent to my presence today as I had thought. What I couldn't understand was—if she knew I was going to be here and she wouldn't be alone with Sophie, why did she bother turning up in the first place?

It wasn't long before I was driving back to my house, followed by Sophie and Diana. All the way there, I tried to think of a valid excuse to get out of going to the mall with them, even contemplating a family crisis. Well, it was, wasn't it? I mean, I was in my family, and I was in a sort of social crisis.

As I pulled into my driveway, it hit me. Not the driveway, but a realisation. Why was I acting like a spoilt brat? What if Diana liked Sophie? What if Sophie suddenly had the urge to jump over to my side of the fence and sample the delights of the lesbian world? It was out of my control, and also something I would have to get used to. Who was I to act all mard arsed and teenage? Obviously, I was gutted that I wasn't the reason for Diana turning up today, wasn't the focus of that addictive smile, wasn't the reason her eyes lit up when Sophie spoke. The last bit held the clue. Sophie. And Sophie was my best friend.

Two minutes later, I was buckling up in the back seat of Sophie's car, meeting her tentative smile with a wide one of my own. Relationships come and go, so do crushes, but best friends are for life. There was no way Diana Sullivan would come between us. No way. Never.

Manchester was buzzing. Actually, it was heaving. Funny expressions to explain that Manchester was busy and there were a lot of people knocking about, but who am I to dispute the English language? We spent a while roaming around the Arndale Centre—something that I would never have done by choice, but Sophie wanted to go, so we did.

Manchester is impressive on many levels—scary, yet definitely impressive. Many people who have never been above London tend to think of the city as full of factories and smoking chimneys, but it is far from that. The architecture is magnificent, although it can be intimidating. It is so easy to get lost there, even within the Arndale Centre.

Shop after shop after shop, all screamed: "Bargain!" "Free!" "Closing down!" "SALE SALE SALE!" A girl can only take so much. Unfortunately, that girl wasn't Sophie. She had the ability to work through each shop like a Duracell rabbit—never tiring, never flagging, never giving Diana or me an opportunity to wander off and sit on a bench, wishing for the world to end. We had to do that standing up. The number of times we caught each other's eye and pulled faces was untrue. More than once we set off giggling like schoolgirls. I have to admit, it felt good to not be so angsty. Acceptance was a good thing after all. It gave me the opportunity to pull the stick from up my arse for a while.

It was just turning four by the time we stumbled out of one of the many exits, and the fresh air—if car fumes could be considered the twenty-first century air freshener—was a tonic.

"Damn!" Sophie took a step back, as if she was going to re-enter the shopping centre.

There was no way on this earth that I was going to be following her.

"I have to go to *Next*. I reserved a jacket online, and they will only hold it until closing."

Thankfully I didn't have to say a word; my facial expression indicated my reticence. You know, the one that screams "For fuck's sake!"

"Look. You two can go somewhere else whilst I pop in."

Where? More shops?

"I know. We're right near Mosley Street. Why don't you two go to the art gallery, and I'll meet you there."

That would mean I would be alone with Diana. Or, I

should say, that would mean Diana would be alone with me. I didn't think that would be something she would want, considering the reason she was there was to be with Sophie.

"An excellent idea," Diana said. "Jess?"

Huh?

"Erm." Not much of a response, but at least I tried.

"Or you could come to *Next* with me. Actually, I think I need to nip into *Boots*, too."

How hard could it be to be with Diana whilst Sophie ransacked a few more shops? "Mosley Street it is then."

Sophie tried to look disappointed, but she couldn't hide her sneaking grin. I was beginning to wonder if she wanted to get rid of me, Diana, or the both of us. I also couldn't help my creeping suspicion that she was up to something.

After promising to meet at the front entrance of the gallery in an hour, Diana and I were on our way.

It had been years since I had been in Manchester Art Gallery. I think the last time had been a school trip. If my memory served me right, Sophie had been chucked out for copping off with Alan Henson in a side room where the workers were setting up an exhibition. She never did tell them how she had managed to get in there. Weirdly enough, she had spent the rest of the day in the Arndale, whilst we were all making sketches of famous paintings and writing down loads of shite we could have Googled later. But, being there with Diana Sullivan was something in itself. To be there with someone who loved art, who knew about art—but still wanted to cop a feel of Sophie in the side room—was exhilarating.

Walking into the building gave me the same feeling as walking into a church. The hushed tones of the people milling around, the staff acting as if Jesus was just about to make his second debut added to the ambience, and I felt myself becoming slightly giddy.

Then I felt it, felt her hand slip through my arm and pull me closer to her. Felt the heat of her body rush over me like a delectable rash. Felt her breath on the side of my face as she whispered, "So, Ms Taylor. Where do you want to go?"

At the precise moment she asked me, there was only one place I wanted to go, wanted to be, but that was nowhere near the art gallery.

"If you are thinking what I am thinking..."

I doubt it.

"I know exactly what you want."

I doubt you do—unless you can feel my heart racing through the tips of your fingers.

"You are more into the masters, yes?"

Well, it begins with master...phonetically, of course.

"Hey. You okay? You look kind of flushed."

I was surprised, as I truly believed all the heat in my body was definitely in a spot she couldn't see, not that I didn't want her to. "Just hot."

I stole a sly peak over my shoulder and saw her lips twitch, but she didn't respond.

"How about the Pre-Raphaelites?"

I shuffled, the contact of her still unnerving me.

"Waterhouse? Millais? They have a wonderful collection here." She paused, and I swear I could hear her brain whirling. "Or 18th century—Gainsborough, Constable, Turner..."

"Pre-Raphaelites would be great." Did I actually sound as bored as I thought I sounded? I had wanted to sound enthused, as I really did want to see the pre-Raphs, but I was still having difficulty concentrating on anything but the sensation of her hand on my arm, the presence of her body behind mine, not to mention the smell of her. God, she smelled so good. I couldn't name the perfume she was wearing, but I doubted that it all came from a bottle. Most of the scent I was inhaling was pure Diana. That was the sensation that affected me the most, and the one that brought me the most sadness. Being there with Diana was the closest I would ever be to actually *being* with her.

Diana moved from behind me and stepped into my line of vision. "Shall we?"

Considering I had been blown away the very first time I saw her, the sensation coursing through me as I looked at her perfect face was one of the most powerful I believed I had ever experienced in my life. Her brows were furrowed as she tried to figure out why I was having difficulty answering her; blue eyes were slightly darker than I'd ever seen them; red lips were parted, as if she had stopped in mid word. She was the most beautiful woman I had ever seen, and I doubted the gallery held anything as exquisite.

"Are you sure you are feeling okay, Jess? Would you like to sit down?"

From the depths, I dredged up a beaming smile, God knows how I did it, but I did. On seeing my smile, she nodded and her face moved closer to mine, her smile mirroring my own.

"Come on. We haven't got long. Impress me," I said.

Diana's laugh echoed through the entrance hall, and we were favoured with a few dirty looks. She grabbed my hand and tugged me forward to get us moving. However, her tug was a little overzealous, and I stumbled and ended up falling straight into her.

If I thought the feeling of her being behind me was heaven, God only knows where I thought I was in her arms. Purgatory? No. However much I knew this was a fluke, an accident, an incident that should have made me think I was living in my own personal hell, it was far from it. Have you ever been in someone's arms and known it was the only place you should ever be? Fit perfectly together, like you have finally found the other half of yourself? Known, without a shadow of a doubt, that as soon as the contact was broken you would feel as if part of yourself had been torn away? And had Diana just inhaled me? Had she breathed me in just as I had breathed her inside me? Did *her* eyes flutter as she snapped herself back to the actual moment? I felt as if I was drowning in her, submersing myself in her, losing what little dignity I had left, for her. But I wanted this, wanted her, so much. So fucking much. And at that moment, she wanted me. I could feel it, sense it, almost taste it.

"We are closing in thirty minutes."

Bastard.

And she was gone, torn from me by the announcement, and I was left nursing a wrenching loss in my chest.

"Come. Let's check out the Pre-Raphs, then, before we are hoofed out." Diana barely looked at me, and part of me was thankful for it. Otherwise she would have seen the longing on my face.

Walking up to the Pre-Raphaelite Gallery on the first floor, Diana bombarded me with snippets about the paintings and the movement. Even if I had had the heart to tell her that I already knew about them, I couldn't have conjured the words. At that moment in time, I didn't care about the painters' cause, didn't care they were rebels, didn't care that they had stepped away from the norm and wanted to show modern life—religion, morals, and emigration. All I cared about was that in those few seconds, Diana Sullivan had made me feel more alive than I had ever felt.

This was bad. Very very bad.

Before I knew it, we were in the Pre-Raphaelite Gallery. It is weird the way people act when they step into a gallery that houses such wonderful pieces of art work. The only way I can describe it is solitary. It doesn't matter how many people go with you; it seems as if the experience is very personal. Seeing something so sublime seems to draw you in until you think you are a part of the painting, like you could step inside. The moment is yours—viewing one of the true masters seems to make you expand and absorb, makes you block out everything else around you. What I'm trying to say is, as soon as we entered, Diana went one way and I went another.

Truthfully, this solitary time came to me the moment I stepped in front of Arthur Hughes' *Ophelia*. It was the innocence. I had never thought of Shakespeare's Ophelia as being as young as she was depicted by the artist—maybe because Arthur Hughes was so young when he painted it. She looked like a fairy or a sprite—her face radiating the sadness that accompanies unrequited love, the madness seeming to take a back seat. This is the moment where she gives up, renounces the world and Hamlet, dresses her deathbed with such clarity and knowledge of her fate—a young, rejected woman who was caught in the crossfire of hatred, greed, and revenge. I could empathise, although I couldn't. I wasn't the type to give it all up because I couldn't have the person I wanted. I wasn't even the type to ready myself for any kind of important action in my life, never mind arranging my watery funeral pyre. Could I empathise with the unrequited feeling, the sense of loss of father, lover, mind? Was I humiliated and used, like Ophelia? Would I fade, die offstage and be forgotten, like the tragic lover of the Prince of Denmark?

"Beautiful, isn't it?"

I mumbled a response.

"Have you seen Millais' *Ophelia* at the Tate?"

I shook my head.

"We'll have to go sometime. You would love the Tate."

Snapping my head to look at her expression, I saw her intent gaze on the artwork. Blue eyes studied the small painting, seeming to digest every brush stroke.

"There's rue for you, and here's some for me." Diana shook her head slightly before turning my way and flashing a wonderful smile "Oh, you must wear your rue with a difference."

As I smiled back, I saw something lurking behind her eyes, something sad, something that seemed impenetrable, and then it was gone, and I was left wondering if I had imagined it.

"We are closing in five minutes."

The words uttered by the attendant seemed to bounce off the walls and hit the silence surrounding Diana and me.

I felt as if I should fill the void, but I couldn't drag anything from the depths to help me out. I was nervous, apprehensive, expectant, yet not. The silence seemed to drag and drag, and I was as useful as a chocolate teapot. I wanted to blurt out that I liked her—just so she'd know. No strings. Wanted to tell her that Sophie was straight and she didn't have a chance, but how could I?

"I want to talk to you about something."

Fuck. She wanted to ask my advice on how to get to grips with Sophie.

"The other night, when we were at Sophie's ..."

God. She looked embarrassed. The words she wanted to say kept jamming in her throat, and she was swallowing rapidly.

"Well, actually it's about Sophie that I wanted to talk to you."

See? I told you so. I knew she had the hots for my best friend. All the time I had been telling myself this over and over and then still falling for her smile, her eyes, her fucking scent, even getting a little excited about a trip to the Tate. I always knew I was an idiot.

"I've been...erm...talking to...erm...Sophie since, and..."

Why couldn't she look at me? Why was she actively avoiding my open-mouthed stare? Acting nervous? Fidgeting? All she had to say was she fancied Sophie, and did I think she had a chance? Simple.

Yes. Simple. Something even I could have done, or not, as it happens. I could have told her at that precise moment that I found her attractive, alluring, breathtakingly beautiful. But no. I was standing there waiting for her to say the words I knew were coming, and I did nothing to soften the blow for either of us, did nothing to make myself stop staring at the circular scar on her hand.

"You see...I... erm...wondered if you..."

My head shook from side to side, partly saying that Sophie wouldn't be interested and partly trying to negate the situation. I watched her face fall, watched as the light drained from those hopeful eyes.

"Oh. Never mind. Forget I said anything."

But how could I forget, even if she hadn't *actually* said anything?

And in the words of Ophelia "There's Rosemary. That's for remembrance." The only thing I believe I will remember is the abject disillusionment of knowing that I came second best.

⋅⊱⋆⊰⋅

Sophie was waiting for us outside and, as expected, she was loaded with shopping bags.

Funnily enough, there wasn't one from *Next*.

I thought about asking her where the jacket she had ordered online was, but all I really wanted to do was go home. It was time to pull myself out of the situation, time to move on and away from a one-sided relationship and at least salvage some self-respect.

Thirty minutes later, Sophie was pulling up outside my house, and I believe it was the longest half an hour of my life. Soph had tried to start a conversation, tried to invite us both out for a drink and something to eat, but I just couldn't. Neither could Diana, for that matter. She declined Sophie's offer even before I did.

As I stepped out of the car, Sophie wound her window down. "You going to your parents' tomorrow?"

My eyes flicked to Diana's before landing on my friend's. I nodded sharply.

"Can I come? I haven't had a roast beef dinner for ages."

For some reason, I wanted to say no. "Sure." Where did that come from? I thought I was going to refuse.

"I'll meet you there about one, if that's okay. Let me know if your mum says it isn't, alright?"

"My mum loves you, you know that." And so did everyone else, by the looks of it. The smile I attempted faded, so I tried to cover it up by lurching through the open window and giving Sophie a hug. Closing my eyes, I tried to imagine a time without her in my life, past and future, and I couldn't do it. The thought made me hug her tighter and inhale her.

"Hey. What's up?"

Her voice was soft in my ear, and I wanted to cry.

Pulling away, I noticed Diana looked uncomfortable. Maybe because I had caught her staring at me hugging Sophie, or maybe because she wanted to be the one getting to grips with my best friend. "I'll call you later, okay?" I stepped back from the car, pulling my handbag onto my shoulder like a nineteen forties film star.

"Oi. Sullivan," Sophie said. "This isn't *Driving Miss Daisy*. Get in the front." A smile broke across Diana's face, but it didn't seem genuine to me.

Hark at me and my ability to read people. As if.

Five minutes later, I was standing in my kitchen and wondering what the fuck I was going to do. I didn't want to lose Sophie. God no! I needed to give up going to art class, although getting that past Soph would be a problem. But how could I sit there week after week and watch Diana make the moves on someone that wasn't me? Don't get me wrong, if Sophie liked Diana in that way, I would have stepped back and given her space. Or would I? Of course I would. Wouldn't I? God. I was arguing with myself about my ability to be a bigger person.

Slamming my bag down on the table, I followed the thump with my backside on the chair. Then my head decided to flop onto my arms. And that was the way I stayed for over an hour as my emotions mixed, and churned, and fought amongst themselves.

Finally tearing my head from my arms, I sent Sophie a text to tell her I was exhausted and was calling it a night at not even seven in the evening. It didn't make it better when

I got a text back saying she was still with Diana, followed by a kiss. I thought Diana had refused—quickly—when Sophie's invitation had been put out to the both of us.

I had a sleepless night.

Chapter 7

The next day was different. I felt a little better about the situation. Or that was what I was telling myself. I had to stop being a whinging git and get on with life. I couldn't understand why Diana Sullivan affected me as strongly as she did. No one else had made me feel such intense emotions. Was it because I had never been in the situation of someone liking Sophie when I liked them? Well, that isn't true. My ex, Sam, had fancied Sophie, but she fancied anyone. That was one of the main reasons I had split with her. That, and the fact I actually hadn't liked Samantha James in the first place and had only gone out with her to get her off my back. I know, not the right way to start a relationship.

Twelve o'clock Sunday found me pulling into my parents' driveway. As expected, my mother was over the moon when I told her Sophie was coming, although I hadn't actually spoken to Soph since leaving her outside the previous day.

As usual, Mum was in the midst of steam and gorgeous smells in the kitchen. Dad, I knew, would be talking lovingly to his garden. So, after giving my Mum a kiss and cuddle, I went to find him. Initially I couldn't see him, so I called out.

"Shhh."

Huh? "Dad?"

"Shhhhh."

I still couldn't see him, but gauged he was somewhere near his garden shed. What was he up to? Silently as silently as I could, I moved in the direction I had heard the shushing coming from. I still couldn't...

"BAHHHHHHHHHHHHHHHHHHHHH!!! Git outta it!"

Fuck. As he yelled, he also ran out of hiding and across the lawn. I briefly saw the ginger backside of the neighbourhood cat scrambling over the fence.

"Bugger!"

You can see I didn't share my love of profanity with my parents.

"Bloody cat keeps crapping on my lawn."

My heart was still hammering wildly in my chest, but I still had to stifle a giggle.

"What's so funny?"

Watching a seventy-one year old man chase a cat across the lawn, after he had been crouching near his compost heap for God knows how long—that's what was funny. "Nothing, Dad."

His angry expression was suddenly replaced by a huge grin. "Hello, sweetheart. Come here." The customary hug was given, and I was blessed with a guided tour of his garden. He explained all the preparations he had been making for the up and coming bad weather, and I really did wish I understood what he was talking about. I was too fascinated by the empty pill bottles he had shoved at the tops of his plants.

"Growing your own stash, Dad?" I thought it was funny, although I didn't as much when he explained it was his way of catching earwigs just before lifting one and tapping out a couple of the ugly buggers.

"Pity you couldn't get a pill bottle the size of Mrs Walsh's cat." I could see by his face that he was contemplating it. "It was a joke, Dad."

"I know, I know." But it didn't keep his face from scrunching up in thought.

"Jess!" Saved by the bell, or my Mum's call. "Want a cuppa?" I was surprised at that. Not because my parents never offered me a cuppa when I visited, more like because I had actually got through the kitchen, been part of a covert cat scaring operation, talked drugs and earwigs, and also tried to steer my dad away from catching the ginger cat from next door in a giant empty pack of Paracetamol before the usual asking of did I want a brew. Quite a feat.

"It's a dry old ship, Jess. I never get a brew when you're not here." Dad said it loud enough for Mum to give him the British salute and then turn her attention back to me.

"Ignore him, love. He gets plenty."

"Of earache," was whispered loudly in my ear.

"I heard that." Mum turned away, then turned back. "Well? What are you waiting for? Your cuppa's getting cold."

God I loved my parents. Mad as hatters and still in love after nearly forty years of marriage. I wanted that—wanted the tennis match comments, wanted the closeness and knowing every single thing about the other and loving them all the more for it.

Diana's smile flashed in front of my eyes, and I shook my head to clear the lingering image. I couldn't quite get rid of the ache that appeared in my chest.

"Come on, love. Can't keep the lord and master waiting."

⚜

At ten to one, the doorbell went nuts. There was only one person who would dare to do that at my parents' house, and that was Sophie. My dad answered the door, and I could hear them chatting in the hallway. As they walked in, Sophie was telling my dad that she didn't know where he could get a big jar shaped like a pill bottle.

"Dad! You can't do that to Mrs Walsh's cat!"

Both Sophie and my dad started laughing. "Told you we could get her."

I knew lunch was going to be a meal to remember. And it was. In a good way. There was no angst, no longing, no thinking about Diana Sullivan fancying Sophie, just good food, entertaining conversation and, unfortunately, lots of washing up.

Sophie packed my parents off into the front room, declaring it was up to her and me to clean up. I was just thankful my mother had cooked; if my dad had, we would have still been there at midnight cleaning up.

As we worked, we chatted. It was good to have Sophie all to myself again, just like when we were kids and she had spent nearly every Sunday at my house having lunch. Her mother didn't cook "a mean roast" like my mother did, and for ages I thought it meant that my mum's cooking was something magical. It wasn't until I discovered that Sophie's mum much preferred a liquid lunch at the local rather than cooking for her two children, that I accepted that it wasn't magical, just a cooked dinner. My parents had half adopted my friend, and she became the second daughter they couldn't have. I didn't mind. Actually, I loved it.

"So, what's the deal between you and the gorgeous art teacher?" Sophie asked.

Smash. Thank God it was only a mug. I crouched down and gathered the pieces together as I gathered the words for my response. Sophie crouched next to me, dustpan and brush ready to collect the bits.

"I'm waiting."

"There's nothing to tell."

"Bollocks. You both had a face on you when you came out of the gallery yesterday. It was like sharing a car with a cold front."

"Nothing happened." Apart from Diana trying to get me to help her ask you out.

"I kinda got that. You both came back single and arsey."

Turning away, I got a piece of newspaper and wrapped the broken pieces inside before placing it in the bin. With my back to Sophie, I answered, "I honestly don't understand why you are so interested, Sophie. People might think that you fancy her yourself." Where the fuck had that come from? The little jealous spot nestled somewhere near my cantankerous butt?

Thankfully, Sophie just laughed. "I doubt it, Jess. I'm more into her brother."

That is the problem. Not for me, for Diana.

"Actually, I'm meeting Dave later tonight."

I felt her come behind me, then felt her chin rest on my shoulder.

"I think Diana could be there too if you want me to call her."

I knew she was only trying to help, but it wasn't helping at all. There was her with both brother and sister lusting after her, and I had no one. Instead of a Billy No Mates, I was a Billy Birdless. Resigned, I turned to face her. "No thanks, Soph."

I didn't need to be fixed up with someone who would be looking at someone else and wishing she was with them. Then it hit me. Dave. How did Diana feel about Sophie and Dave getting it on? "How does Diana feel about you seeing her brother?"

"Huh? What do you mean?"

Shit. "Erm...teacher thing. How does she feel about you seeing her brother and she is the teacher?"

She snorted. "It's not as if I'm seeing the teacher, is it?" She paused, as she must have realised what she had said. "And even if I was, it's not as if we are at school, Jess." Her face scrunched up. "Eww...imagine copping off with Mr Dickson, the General Studies teacher from school?"

I looked at her blankly.

"Okay. Mrs Deagan."

My stomach lurched. I could still remember the Design teacher who looked uncannily like a skunk—smelled a little like one, too. This was my moment to tell Sophie that I wouldn't be going back to art class. Again.

"Do you know what is weird?"

I shook my head at her question.

"I'm loving spending time with you in class. I know I'm crap, but it is quality time with you." Okay. Maybe not the right time to tell her I was quitting after all.

It wasn't until I got home that I remembered something Sophie had said. "You both came back single and arsey." It was the word "single" that stood out. Why would Sophie say that? One minute she was trying to fix us up, then telling me I had gone overboard on the finding out and acting like an ass. But now...now it seemed as if she had made sure that Diana and I went off somewhere on our own yesterday. If I remembered rightly, there had not been a shopping bag from *Next*, and no jacket, either. Even I, and my capability at being stupid, couldn't ignore that she had no evidence from *Next* to support her story. What I couldn't understand was why? Why would Sophie try to get me fixed up with a woman who obviously had no interest in me?

Sophie had always been overly protective when it came to my dates. She didn't like Sam, though I didn't know anyone who actually did, but Sophie had always given my girlfriends a hard time over the years. Honestly—I almost expected her to produce a clipboard with questions on it the first time she met someone I was interested in. At least it saved my dad from having to do it.

I wanted to call Sophie and ask her, but she was seeing Dave, or maybe Dave and Diana, and I was at home, considering watching the omnibus *Eastenders* to cheer myself up. And if you have ever considered watching the Walford-based soap opera as a cheering up technique, then you will understand how truly miserable I was feeling. In a way, I felt left out. They were all out and having fun, and I was at home making Dreamtime tea at not quite eight o'clock and considering an hour and a half of gurning, shouting, slapping, and hysterics—courtesy of *Eastenders*, of course, although I felt I could have given them a run for their money in the "pity me" stakes.

Actually, watching the soap made me feel a lot better. At least my life wasn't as hateful as the lives of those characters, and I am damned near certain that I would be able to name the father of my baby, would not break up my friend's relationship because I didn't want to be on my own, am not addicted to booze, fags, and crack—and when I say crack, I mean cocaine, not a part of the anatomy. Thankfully, all the drama in my life had spaced itself over thirty-one years instead of trying to cram itself all into one TV program.

And it was still only half past nine. Bollocks. Furthermore, by ten o'clock I was even antsier. I needed something to relax me, so I picked up a book. An easy read. Yeah. If I was of a mind to sit and wade through pulp fiction when I could have been out making my own stories. Another Dreamtime tea, another half hour of fidgeting and rereading the same sentence over and over again. Why was it so difficult to just chillax on a Sunday evening? I had been doing the same thing for years, and being alone had never before made me so restless.

A sigh slithered through my gritted teeth. Philosophising about my inability to wind down was not getting me anywhere. My eager eyes scanned the room for something to distract me—and then I spotted it. My art pad. The gritted teeth slowly parted to allow a smile to slip onto my face. How could it hurt to have a little doodle for a while instead of going to bed and tossing and turning for God knew how long?

Decision made, I plumped for a cold drink and grabbed my pad and pencils. I don't know why I did it, but I decided to draw just one eye...one eye framed by a shapely eyebrow and the hint of a nose. Instead of giving the impression of eyelashes, I dutifully sketched in each one as if it was the crux of the whole picture.

Before I knew it, the evening had slipped away and I was tiredly folding the cover of my pad closed. Instead of an early night, I was slipping under the covers of my bed at nearly one o'clock in the morning. Amazing how absorbed I had become in drawing just a solitary eye. I hadn't even given it an inspection after I had called it a night.

Chapter 8

Monday and Tuesday sped by. Work was hectic, and I didn't have much time to do anything but eat, shower, and sleep when I got home. I would like to say that my mind didn't drift when I was sat at my desk and that I was totally focused on my job, but if I did, I would be lying. I don't have to tell you where my head skipped off to when it wasn't sorting through the shite at the office. I spoke to Sophie a couple of times, but she didn't mention her evening out with Dave, or even "The Siblings," and I didn't bring it up.

Wednesday came around again, and I was not looking forward to class. I lie. I was looking forward to class. Am I lying now? Ah fuck it. I was apprehensively looking forward to not looking forward to a night at class. That will do.

Work, once again, lived up to its four letters, and I found myself running around like a dick head to get to class on time. Why rush? Why not just stroll in late, like Sophie probably would? Maybe it was because I was too anal to be late for anything, or some similar reason.

When I walked into class and saw Sophie already there—pad out, pencils out, focused—you could have knocked me down with a feather, or something even more cliché. As I got closer, she turned and gave me her signature grin.

"Evening, gorgeous. You're late."

I looked at my watch and noted aloud I was actually five minutes early.

"Yes, I know. But for you, that is late." Sophie patted the chair next to her. "Kept it warm for you."

As I pulled the chair out, I saw a Starbucks coffee cup on the seat.

"Well, your coffee kept it warm for you. Thought you could do with a pick me up."

I smiled at her.

"Why are you smiling like you are chewing wasps?"

"Because you're being nice."

Sophie tried to feign shock, but failed miserably.

"Could you take your seats, please? We are just about to start."

Huh? I didn't recognise the voice.

"Could you please get out your equipment? Pads and pencils to the ready."

Fuck. Who was it? Margaret Thatcher? Turning, I believed I had hit the nail on the head. At the front of the class stood the epitome of a school teacher—a nineteen-fifties, girls' boarding school teacher who would have been more suited to teaching PE.

"What's going on? Where's Diana?"

"Could we have less of the chitter chatter and more focus?"

Crap. I had been transported back twenty-six years and was reliving my first day at school. I quickly moved the coffee cup and settled myself into my seat.

"As you can tell, I am not Ms Sullivan."

A genius! We had a Mensa member teaching us mere mortals.

"My name is Mrs Bright."

See? Mensa. All this accompanied by a childlike song ringing in my head "Mrs Bright had a fright in the middle of the night."

"Ms Sullivan had to be away. She asked me to step in for tonight's session."

Why? To both. Why did Diana have to suddenly go away, and why did she have to leave the nanny from *Count Duckula* in her place?

"Tonight we will be studying the form of vegetables and fruit."

I looked at Sophie. She was intently sharpening an already extremely pointy pencil, fully focused on preparing a weapon that could be used by Vlad the Impaler. I wanted to ask her what was going on with Diana; I knew she would know. Or I could ask Dave. I scanned the room and spotted Dave sharpening his pencil the same as Sophie. Were they making an army of ultra sharp pencils? Resigned, I began to sharpen my pencil.

Break time couldn't come quickly enough. Not that the Stephen Hawkins of the art world was a bad teacher; that wasn't it at all. I wanted to get the skinny on what was up with Diana. Our cups had barely hit the table before I asked, "So, where's Diana?" Subtle.

"She had to go away." Sophie's voice was raised over the first syllable of what Dave was saying, and I knew he had been about to tell me the real reason for Diana's absence.

Fixing him with an engaging look, I asked, "So, *Dave,*

where's Diana?"

His eyes flicked to Sophie and he swallowed nervously, then sat back and gave us both the "I don't believe you" look when he repeated what Sophie had said.

Time trickled by, and I kept on changing my focus—Sophie, Dave, Sophie, Dave. Leaning forward, I prodded, "Why do I think there is more than you are telling me?"

Sophie wasn't put off by my attempt at bad cop. She shrugged, picked up her cup, and scrunched her lips before replying, "Because you're paranoid, Jess."

That was true, but it didn't answer my question.

"Diana had a call from a friend last night."

The word "friend" was given a little extra stress, and it didn't take a rocket scientist to understand that the "friend" in question was an ex. Or maybe it was a current girlfriend. I grimaced.

"She had to go to London."

That was a long way to go for just a "friend," wasn't it?

I watched Sophie trying to open the small packet of biscuits—the way she tugged, pulled, and tried to tear it with her teeth before she held it out to me to open. One movement and the biscuits were free from their plastic confines, and I passed them back and received her trademark grin.

Nah. London from Manchester wasn't far to go for a friend.

"What do you think of Monica?"

Dave's voice broke into my mental meanderings. Who the hell was Monica?

"She knows her stuff, doesn't she?"

Hang on. Who's Monica? Is that who Diana went—

"Granted, she's a little stricter than Diana, but she isn't like that when you get to know her."

Ah...Mrs Bright.

"Actually, the rest of the family think she's a little eccentric. I think she's trying to impress Diana."

Why? I was keenly aware of all the unspoken questions I was thinking.

"You wouldn't think she was our aunt, would you?"

Not on your nelly. Aunt? More like a front man for the Conservative party.

"She's a lovely cook," Sophie added.

What the fuck?

"I couldn't believe how quickly she whipped together the meal on Sunday."

I was definitely out of the loop. I knew I should have gone with Sophie on Sunday when she'd asked me.

"Not saying I wasn't fit to burst when I left *your* mum and dad's, Jess, but man...you should try Monica's Pavlova."

Chance would be a fine thing.

"Hello, there."

Definitely Mrs Bright. Or Monica. Or Aunty.

"May I join you?"

Of course. Come on. Anyone else want to join and make me feel even further pushed out of the loop?

Brown eyes settled on me. "And you must be Jessica."

Huh?

"Oh, sorry...Jess."

A hand reached out in invitation, and I shook it.

A warm smile lit her lips, and her face scrunched in happiness. "I've heard so much about you. My, Diana was right. You are a beauty."

I felt the blood freeze in my veins, and I squeezed her hand more tightly. A sidelong glance told me that Sophie was shaking her head at Dave and he was making the universal two handed gesture that said "I don't know." When my hand was released, it stayed in the air for a few moments more before lowering itself slowly to the table top.

"That's one of the things I love about Diana. She has the eye." Lifting her cup to her lips, Monica blew softly into the coffee and then took a sip.

Nobody said a word; we just waited to see if she would go on.

"That Lauren was a beautiful woman—boy, that she was. I really thought Diana had found the one with that one." Another sip, more shuffling from Dave and Sophie. "Elegant. Poised. Refined." Three things I certainly wasn't. "But so ugly on the inside." A sigh escaped her. "Nearly broke my little Dee Dee's heart. I'm surprised she went to help her out after what she did."

Questions all answered without me saying a word.

"Erm...are you enjoying teaching again, Aunt Mon?"

Nice try, Dave. A little late, but a nice try. Hang on a minute. Why were Dave and Sophie uncomfortable about me knowing about Lauren? What had it to do with me?

"You are a wonderful teacher, Monica. I didn't think there was any way you could top your cooking."

Sophie—you are a lick arse.

"And I'm loving it. I would do it again in a flash." She looked at her watch and made an oohing sound. "Come on, kiddies..."

Yes. She called us kiddies.

"Time to get back to the grindstone."

Then she was gone like a whirlwind. Considering she was touching sixty, she could move like an eight-year-old.

I conjured up a smug smile. "What an interesting woman." Then I left the table, to return to my picture of a half-finished fruit formation.

It wasn't until bedtime that I mulled over the new information I had acquired. Diana had been in love with Lauren. Lauren had been bad news. Diana had her heart broken. Dave and Sophie had tried to fix us up. It would be easier both on the eye and the structure to bullet point at this stage, but I can't be arsed. I believed Diana fancied Sophie; I knew now that she didn't. Apparently it was obvious to everyone but me, until now. Now that it was a little too late. Diana was in London with the woman who had broken her heart, and she also believed I wasn't interested in her. She hadn't been asking for me to help her ask Sophie out; she was going to ask me out, to the Tate. Even though that was an assumption, it was all beginning to make sense. Why else would her aunt say that Diana thought I was a beauty? Why were Dave and Sophie acting like the most inept Secret Service agents the world had ever seen? And why was I such a dick head?

I had blown it. Too bloody right I had. After the way I had behaved, there was no way Diana would believe that I returned her attraction. Even when she had plucked up the courage to nearly ask me out, I had shaken my head and warded her off. To anyone watching, it would have looked like a definite knock back. But Sophie would have told Diana that I liked her, wouldn't she? Yeah, just like an urban myth—a friend of a friend told me they like you. I know it was only a one friend chain, but I was feeling overly dramatic. Could anyone blame me? I blamed me. If I hadn't been so pig headed, I could have been eating dinner, or sharing a movie, or anything with the woman for whom I felt the strongest attraction I'd ever experienced.

I turned onto my side and stared at the shadows dancing on the wall. I was stupid. So bloody stupid. Why couldn't I just be normal and allow my feelings to bear fruit? From the very first time I had heard Diana's voice, I had felt a connection. Then when I saw her, it was as if my soul knew. I should have recognised that ache for what it was, although to recognise it, a person would have had to have experienced it before. Strangely enough, it seemed that I had, but not in this lifetime.

"Christ!"

This was getting me nowhere and fast. There was no point lying in bed thinking of what could have been, how I had acted, how I felt. I had to do something about it; I had to let Diana know how I felt. Upon reflection, I decided that I should probably calm it down a little. It would frighten the life out of her if I started talking about soul mates and reincarnation.

But what if I was too late? What if she got to London and found out Lauren wasn't the evil, conniving bitch she once was? What if they decided to have another crack at what might have been?

I turned over and faced the other wall. All I could do was to try. What harm could come of that?

⚜

The rest of the week went by without much happening. I was more focused on what the weekend would hold than with thinking about work. Sophie and I had made plans for lunch on the Saturday, and I was secretly hoping a certain blue-eyed beauty would turn up too.

Nope. Just Sophie and me, as it happened. Still, I turned

and looked at the door every time it opened.

Eventually, Sophie slammed her knife and fork down and demanded, "What's the matter with you? Hiding from the Feds?"

I shrugged and continued to eat.

After lunch, we decided to put off the shopping for a while —much to my delight—so we could relax over coffee and catch up. I adeptly skirted the topic of Diana , even though she was the main thing I wanted to talk to Sophie about. If anyone knew what Diana was up to, it would be Sophie. Instead of grabbing my metaphorical cojones and asking, I went via a more circuitous route.

"How's it going with you and Dave? Are you seeing each other now?"

A grin broke out on her face, and she nodded shyly. "I really like him, Jess. I know I've said it before, but this time it seems different somehow."

Thoughts of Diana slipped from my mind as I watched my usually gregarious friend blush like a teenager.

"I know that when I first started talking to him, it wasn't because I wanted to date him." She bit her lip and looked at me sheepishly.

The blush was seeping up her throat, so whatever the reason she was with Dave, it couldn't have been about sex and only sex. Don't get me wrong, Sophie was not a slapper. She didn't sleep around, as I've said before. However, Sophie was not shy about telling me about her escapades. I already knew that the only reason she had started talking to Dave was to get the goss on his sister. This was not the time to pump her about that; I really did want to know what she was feeling, how she was becoming more involved with Dave Sullivan.

"Does he feel the same way as you?"

A relieved breath left her, her eyes glistened and her lips curved, totally different from her usual cocksure expression that suddenly seemed like a figment of my imagination. "I hope so. God. I really hope so, Jess. I want him to be the one."

"Don't you *know* that? I mean. When it's the one, you should know it, right?"

She shrugged.

"Well, that's what I think at any rate."

"For me, yes. For him, I don't know. He's attentive, funny, intelligent, gorgeous, and single. Stress on single. But why on earth would he want to be with someone like me?" The smile slipped away and was replaced by a definite sadness. "I'm not exactly catch of the century, am I?"

"Soph..."

"Look at me, Jess. I'm in my thirties, have a crappy job, a family who doesn't give a flying fuck about me. I'm not exactly Marilyn Monroe, am I?"

"No. She's dead."

"Okay. Cheryl Cole, then."

"She's overrated. And you're a better singer."

She snorted, but then the sad look returned. "Honestly, Jess. Why would he want to spend the rest of his life with a 'no hoper' like me?"

This was news. In all the years I had known Sophie, my best friend had never mentioned anyone she would want to spend the rest of her life with.

"Looks like someone is feeling sorry for herself." I grabbed her hand and squeezed. "Dave would be the lucky one, Sophie. Any man would. You are everything a person would want and more besides. You are beautiful, do you know that?"

She was silent for a moment, before a quiet, "You

hitting on me, Jess?"

"Git."

A laugh shot out of her mouth, echoed by one from me, followed by all-out laughing until the waitress hovered near us in a bid to make us be quiet and stop scaring the regulars.

I recognized that I was feeling the same way as Sophie, and realised that it all had to do with perception. When you like someone, really like someone, do you automatically go through the stage of not feeling good enough for them to wipe their boots on your back?

I had seen the way Dave looked at Sophie, and it was the look of someone who was totally smitten. What I needed to do was to make sure that Dave Sullivan told my thick headed friend how special she was to him rather than just gazing at her longingly. But how was I was going to do that? I wasn't Casanova. I had no clue about the romantic side of life. I definitely needed my own crash course on revealing feelings.

"Are you seeing Dave later?"

Sophie shook her head.

"Why not? It's Saturday night."

"He's got to sort out some family matter."

Hmmmm...

"Diana is still not back, and he's worried she has done something stupid."

"Like?" Please don't say she got back with The Bad One.

"Well, Dave is worried that Lauren is trying to get Diana back. Diana was devastated by what happened between them the first time."

"What did happen?"

We have all had times when we want to know the

answer to something, and then when we find out, we wish we never had.

"Lauren was abusive—verbally and physically."

And that meant emotionally and spiritually too, in my book.

"Have you ever noticed Diana's hands?"

What?

"Have you looked at the part where her thumb meets the fleshy bit?"

Confused, I nodded.

"The scar she has? Circular."

No. No. NO! My voice barely a whisper, I asked, "Why?"

"It's a burn. A cigar burn."

I felt sick to the pit of my stomach. I didn't want to know, didn't want to think that someone would do that to another person and still be walking around as if nothing had happened, let alone still be expecting their victim to come when they called for help.

"Lauren did that. She is not a nice person, Jess. She thought it was okay to knock the living daylights out of Diana too. A fit of jealousy from a woman who could have had everything if she hadn't been such an evil cu—" Sophie picked up her cup and drained it. "The burn was the last straw, though."

The waitress had apparently decided we had been sitting there for too long and wanted to get rid of us, as she popped up beside the table. "Everything okay here?"

To be honest, I wanted to leave, wanted to go so I could deal with the anger welling up inside me. I wanted to find Diana and tell her she would never have to go through that again, would never have to be a punching bag for anyone. I would take care of her, love her, wrap her in tissue paper and cherish her for the rest of her life. But I had an awful feeling that I was too late. Too late to take away the pain she must've gone through and the mental agony she undoubtedly still dealt with on a day to day basis. And now she was back with the one who had done that to her, probably believing Lauren's lies of "I've changed," or "I love you—come back to me, please."

I couldn't grasp why would anyone do physical harm to another living, breathing person. A sob tore from my throat, and I covered my mouth. I needed to find Diana. I needed to protect her. I barely knew Diana Sullivan, but I felt I knew her soul. How could I not? It seemed as if it was a part of my own.

Outside, the welling of anger almost choked me. Lunch was clambering up my throat, and I knew it was a matter of seconds before I expelled it all.

A hand landed on my shoulder; a reassuring hand, a familiar hand. Even as a kid, I had responded to Sophie's touch. She could calm me even when I thought there was no way I could be calmed. Today was no exception.

The arm moved around me, circling and pulling me closer to her. I was fully absorbed into safety and familiarity, the scent of her a balm to the rage brewing inside. Instead of exploding in anger, I released it in tears, my body supported by the strength of her. Through my tears, one stuttered word. "Why?"

All the time I cried, Sophie held me, her voice shushing, cajoling, calming. She didn't try to move me from the middle of the sidewalk, wasn't ashamed of her hysterical friend standing outside a restaurant in broad daylight being passed by Saturday shoppers. It wasn't until I had calmed enough to be rational that Sophie led me to her car and got me settled inside. We sat there for ages, me just staring out of the window at nothing, and her staring at the side of my head. What a pair, eh?

"How did you find out?" My voice was barely audible, and I thought that I might have to repeat myself.

"Dave."

"Did you know from the start?" Why that should make any difference to me, I didn't know.

Sophie sat quietly beside me for so long that I turned to look at her. After a few seconds more, she released a sigh.

"No. Not from the very start." She sighed again. "I think I should tell you from the beginning, don't you?"

Yes. Yes I did.

The story that unfolded was nothing like what I would have linked to the beautiful and confident Ms Sullivan. She had been a very successful graphic designer living in London. In my short-sightedness, I had believed she had always been an art teacher at Stockport College in Cheshire. That was her getting back into society again after everything that had happened with Lauren Baker. Sophie didn't drag it out…didn't elaborate on the details, just related the bare bones of it.

"I overheard Dave in the print room talking to a work colleague about how his sister was starting an art class, and it needed it to be successful. The family was hoping Diana could find something to look forward to every day instead of being too damned ashamed to carry on living life as it should be lived." She took a breath and looked at earnestly. "I didn't know the details, I promise you, Jess. I just thought she'd had a bad split."

I nodded. I didn't have the strength left to reproach her.

"So, that same day, I made a point of cornering Dave and asking about the class."

I watched in fascination as Sophie's colouring darkened

as the blush appeared.

"I told him about you, about how special you are. How talented. How beautiful, both inside and out."

I opened my mouth, but Sophie held her hand up.

"You are, Jess. And I also know you would never treat anyone the way Diana had been treated. If anyone could make a woman feel special, it would be you."

I found all that hard to believe, but I continued listening.

"It wasn't until just before you were coming around for dinner that Dave told me the rest of it—how Lauren had led Diana a dance pretty much from the beginning."

Sophie started the engine and turned on the heat. I think she thought I was shaking because I was cold. Far from it. It was the growing rage racing through my veins that was making my body shake.

"Lauren is an actress. West End. After her opening night last season, she received a less than favourable review. Took it out on Diana."

I was grinding my teeth, my jaw was aching.

"It hadn't been the first time Lauren had used her fists, but she always put it down to the stress of work, not being truly recognised, Diana not loving her enough, blah de blah and all that shit. But that night was different."

"How?"

"Lauren did it in front of everyone—most of the cast, their friends, everyone."

Fuck. I didn't know how to react. Part of me was screaming, "At least there were witnesses," and the other part of me was objecting, "It should have never happened in the first place. Public or private." I could feel the shame Diana must've felt when that happened. Knowing that everyone had witnessed you at the lowest point in your life... Hang on a minute. It wasn't the lowest point in

Diana's life; it was the lowest point in Lauren's. Gutter low.

"What happened?"

"Lauren was arrested, and the play was in jeopardy of closing. Lauren was released two days later, but Diana was already back in Manchester. Dave went and got her." She sighed. "She didn't call him. He'd read about it in the paper."

Now that was strange. A woman burning another woman with a cigar and then giving her a good hiding was something that would be in a local paper, so how could Dave have read it in Manchester?

"I know what you're thinking—how did he read it in a national paper? Yes?"

I nodded.

"He knew Lauren was in *Hamlet*, playing at the London Criterion Theatre. When the play's three evening hiatus was announced, the press took hold of the story. Apparently, lesbians fighting over bad reviews is newsworthy."

Sophie's voice continued, but I wasn't listening.

Hamlet. Ophelia. Ophelia's Hamlet. Millais. The Tate. *"Beautiful isn't it?" "Have you seen Millais's* Ophelia *at the Tate?" "We'll have to go sometime. You would love the Tate." "There's rue for you, and here's some for me. Oh, you must wear your rue with a difference."*

All these snippets raced through my memory, but the strongest memory I recalled was the sadness lurking behind her eyes, impenetrable—the sadness I believed I had imagined. I knew the answer to my question before I asked it.

"Did Lauren play Ophelia?"

"How did you know that? And does it matter?"

No and yes. Yes and no. It seemed as if Diana Sullivan

was still yearning after the fucker who tried to ruin her life.

You heard about it all the time—women going back to their abusers because they had no other choice. But Diana did have a choice. That choice was me, or someone like me. Someone who would never hurt her, never take her for granted, never take out their anger on the one they loved best.

Did Diana love Lauren so much that she ignored the abuse, or was it just easier to fall back into something that had become routine?

Nah. I hadn't a fucking clue what I was thinking. I had never been in that situation, never had to pick up the pieces of my life, however much I thought most of the time my life was shite.

"Have you got Diana's number? I need to call her."

Sophie's eyebrows lifted slightly. "Erm…yes. But she's not picking up."

I didn't care. I was going to keep calling until she did.

Three weeks. Yes. Three weeks, and I'd not heard a dickey bird. Don't get me wrong, I did call Diana. Called and called and called, and I didn't even get through to her voicemail, not even once.

Sophie told me that Dave had heard from her, but it was more of an "I'm fine. Don't worry. Ask Aunt Mon to cover for me." Token reassurance. Dave was worried. No. Scrap that. He was beside himself. Lauren didn't live at the same address she had at the time of the incident. Moving wasn't a crime, I know, but it didn't fill any of us with any ounce of calm. None of us had a clue what was going on, and to say our imaginations were running wild would have been an understatement.

It would have been so much easier if I could've just spoken to her, just heard her say that she was happy and things were going great. I wouldn't have jumped for joy, but at least I would have known that she wasn't tied up, battered and bruised, and being kept in someone's cellar.

So, for three weeks I continued with the art class. For three weeks, I looked longingly at the door, wishing for Diana to come in and take over the class. And for three weeks, I sat through art formations, fruit and miscellaneous household junk, in hopes that the tall, raven haired beauty with the stunning blue eyes would become the focus of my life once again.

Who was I kidding? Once again? Pffft.

The weird thing was that the longer Diana was out of my life, the more I knew I wanted her in it. It was beginning to hurt. Physically. I would leave each class with an ache akin to being booted in the stomach each and every time she was a no-show.

So, there we were at the fourth week. Why should I bother to keep going? If Diana was coming back, Dave would have told Sophie, who, in turn, would have called me. And as of six-fifty-five, I hadn't had a call from my best friend.

Sophie hadn't been in class the entire month. I knew she was coming this week, though. She told me so when I had spoken to her for about the fifth time that day.

Monica stood at the front, looking nervous, and I didn't have a clue why. I did notice the absence of the pots and pans and shit from the table. In their stead was a heavy, dark crimson cloth draped over the wood table top. I wanted to be intrigued, but to tell the truth, I couldn't be arsed.

A noise alerted me that someone had entered the room,

and I looked up, expecting it to be Sophie. But, no. Standing in the doorway was an unfamiliar woman. Strangely, she looked as if she had just climbed out of bed, as she seemed to be wearing only a robe. For God's sake, this was nearly November. Why would a woman be standing in a classroom in just a robe? She must be freezing.

Talk about freezing, that's what happened to the question on my lips as Monica beckoned the woman over. Monica had lightened up considerably since her first outing as our teacher, but tonight she seemed a bit cold, almost defensive. "As you can see, class, tonight we are going to be studying life form."

Aw shit. That's the last thing I wanted to do in a class that promised we would get to draw nudes. Please note the sarcasm.

"If you would like to make your way to the table."

If that had been me, if I had been the one who was entering a classroom full of people ready to draw all your bits and bobs, I would have been crapping my pants. The robed woman didn't seem fazed in the slightest. She almost glided over, her smile fake and full, making sure everyone in the room paid her attention.

As she reached the table, she lowered the robe from her body, much to Monica's disdain. "Not yet. We are only drawing your shape tonight."

The woman grinned at her and slipped the robe back up, but not before we had all had a good look at her breasts.

I have to admit that even though I was still hankering for the absent art teacher, I couldn't pull my eyes away from the full, firm breasts that had been on display. Oddly enough, they did nothing for me. They just seemed like breasts. Pity the blokes in the class didn't feel the same way, as I heard the collective intake of breaths when the silky material had slipped off to reveal something I truly believe they had dreamed about for the majority of their lives. Well, certainly since they had hit puberty.

In fact, I took a mini stance by deciding to sharpen my pencil instead of eyeing up the woman, the woman who had suddenly spotted me and seemed a little too interested for it not to become disconcerting. Her smile was cocky, brazen, unfeeling yet full of unspoken promise. I didn't like it. It was fake. It was cold. And it certainly didn't hold the charm of Diana Sullivan's lopsided grin.

Shaking the pencil shavings into my pencil case, I once again wondered where Sophie and Dave were. Must have been the smell of shaved wood that reminded me of them and their army of pointy headed soldiers. Just as the thought flittered into my head, the door opened again and they stepped inside, Sophie mouthing her apologies to me and edging towards her seat like people tend to do when they get up in front of you in the cinema. Dave stayed in the doorway, his eyes fastened on the woman seated on the table.

It was fascinating to witness the smile slipping from his face and replaced by a surge of something almost dangerous. What the fuck? Dangerous? Dave? If the situation hadn't been so fucked up, I would've laughed at that: Dangerous Dave Does Drawing. But...

"What are you doing here?"

Huh? That wasn't me. That was Dave. He wasn't talking to me, either. Thank God.

"Where is she?"

Who? Was this his ex? And why had I thought that?

Sophie was standing next to me, and she looked exactly how I felt—bloody confused. The students were all looking at Dave, and, like me, their head turned to follow his gaze.

The woman on the table leaned back, the shoulders of the robe slipping down to reveal strong, tanned shoulders.

"Hello there, David." Her voice was rich, trained, alluring, in a cat and mouse kind of way. "Miss me?"

He snorted as he strode towards the woman on the table. It appeared as if he had no idea of where he was, or maybe he didn't give a shit. His attention was definitely riveted on the woman lounging in the centre of the room.

"I said, where is she? Where's Diana, Lauren?"

Snap. Even I wouldn't have expected the pencil between my fingers to break so easily.

The class was utterly quiet. I believe if I had still been sharpening my pencil, it would have sounded like a Harrier Jump Jet taking off. But, alas, my poor broken pencil was still being gripped—a piece in each hand.

"I'm here, Dave."

I wanted to turn and look towards the door, wanted to see that, in fact, Diana was there and it wasn't my imagination that had led me to believe that she was standing mere feet away. Instead I looked towards the centre of the room, at the almost panther-like movements of the notorious Lauren Baker.

Her self-satisfied smile was accompanied by the tilt of her head, long auburn hair falling easily over her shoulder as she tossed the locks into photogenic disarray.

I knew what Monica had said the first night I had met her was spot on—Lauren was beautiful, painfully so, but that beauty was only on the surface.

Brown eyes turned and met mine. They should have been as perfect as the rest of her physical appearance, but they lacked depth. No. That was wrong. Could cruelty be classed as depth? I couldn't bear to look at her, couldn't bear the intense nothingness in her eyes, so I caved and looked towards where the siblings were standing.

"Can I just have word?"

Diana had reached Dave and had slipped her hand around his arm. "Outside?"

He didn't answer, just moved towards the door with his sister.

Sophie was shuffling her feet, and I knew if I turned to look at her, she would start analysing everything that had happened. I didn't want to analyse anything; I just wanted to leave. But if I got up now, it would be like announcing that I was uncomfortable with the events. I was uncomfortable with what had happened, but I didn't want everyone else to know it.

If I left, I would leave Lauren there. I knew by the way she had looked at me that I wasn't a random "catch of the eye." She had set out to intimidate me for some reason, and me leaving was what she wanted. She would win.

Pretty fucked up. And no. I don't know what I am talking about either.

Let's try again. If I left, I would meet Diana in the corridor with her brother. That seemed more logical. I would disturb their reunion. It had been nearly a month, and a couple of phone calls wouldn't have been enough to relate what had happened in the interim, would they?

"Pssst!"

"Not now, Soph."

"Spoil sport."

"Let's continue with life form, shall we?" Monica's voice seemed a little shaken, but she did her utmost to keep herself together. "You need A3 paper and charcoal for this...for this...erm...form."

I could've changed the word "form" to so many different words, but I kept my mouth shut and stuffed my broken pencil back into my pencil case.

Monica explained our objective for the evening—living, breathing form. We had to show the shape of the "subject" and try to intimate movement, hence the use of charcoal.

No one said a word. Not one person asked a question. It was almost like the room that was housing twenty-plus people, was, in fact, just me following an art class on the telly.

As soon as we were told to begin, Sophie leaned over. "I wonder what's going on," she whispered.

"Why didn't you tell me she was back? I spoke to you an hour ago."

My whisper was more like gritted teeth with words escaping. I tried not to look at both Sophie and the woman sprawled on the table who was looking directly at me, one eyebrow raised, as if she was issuing a challenge. This was becoming a nightmare. I was drawing the abusive ex of the woman I had the hots for, and all I wanted to do was get up, walk over, and smack her between the eyes.

Hmmm...who is the violent one now, Taylor? a little voice whispered in my ear.

"Oh fuck off."

"I didn't know, Jess. There's no need to—"

"Shush, ladies. Concentrate."

I wanted to tell Sophie I was telling my inner voice to fuck off, not her. The smug smile that crossed Lauren's face made me clam up and put more pressure on my charcoal stick. A dark line scarred the paper, and I eased up on the pressure. Given the rate at which I was destroying my art supplies, I would soon have vandalised all the contents of my pencil case and be left drawing in blood.

Click. The door opened and closed softly, and I heard

Dave's muttered apologies as he resumed his seat. Sophie leaned forward, and I knew that she was gesturing to him. I couldn't resist, so I looked down the line of people and saw him doing the "I don't know" gesture with his hands and a shoulder shrug.

Monica stepped in front of him and leaned over to whisper in his ear.

At that moment, I really wished I was Batfink, with hypersensitive radar ears, but all I could gather were the shush and hiss of whispered words. Turning my focus back to the front table, I was greeted by a wink from the woman I was beginning to loathe. My top lip quivered before twisting into a snarl.

A laugh escaped, but Lauren quickly stopped herself.

I knew at that moment that I was Lauren Baker's next challenge—something that filled me with both dread and a sense of sadistic excitement.

It was the longest hour of my life. Honestly. How could an hour seem like a lifetime? We had drawn Lauren in four different positions, and each time she tried to strip off, only to have Monica remind her that we would not be drawing a full out nude that evening. Was she thick? Or just thick skinned? Maybe she was just trying Monica's patience. By the look on the teacher's face, Lauren was succeeding. Actually, by the looks on Sophie's and Dave's faces, Lauren was winning whatever private little game she was playing.

I couldn't wait until the break. Couldn't wait to get out of there and into my car and into my house and into my bed. As soon as the break was announced, I began to slam my equipment into my bag.

"You're not leaving, Jess? Come on. Don't let saggy tits get to you."

Saggy tits? Had Sophie not seen those breasts? They

were straight from the pages of *Plastic Surgery Triumphs*.

Dave was beside us and trying to wrest my bag from my hands. "You are not leaving." Ah...Dangerous Dave. "I need to speak to you, both of you."

I wanted to say no, I kept on shaking my head and trying to get my bag back, but it wasn't having the effect I wanted. Dave still had it. I didn't.

"Going so soon, Jess?"

Shit. Shit shit shit, and even more shit.

"I was hoping to get to know you a little better." Lauren had come up behind me, her voice too close, her body even closer.

I was rendered mute. It was a good job, too, because the words I was conjuring were a little strong even for me.

"Why don't you just get the fuck away from me, my friends, and my sister?"

"Oooohhh. I see you haven't lost your charm, Davey." One minute Lauren's voice was treacly sweet, and the next... "I don't give a flying fuck what you want, Da–vid. Just keep your interfering face out of my and Diana's life, okay?"

At that moment, Diana reappeared, her blue eyes darting from her brother to her...her...lover? Friend? Ex?

"What's going on? Dave?"

"I hate to break up this little reunion, but I'm freezing, darling." A girlish laugh broke out of that hateful little mouth. "Can you show me where we left our clothes earlier? I mean..." another laugh, "where I left my clothes?"

Looked like lover, then.

A short sharp nod, then Diana guided Lauren towards the door. Just before she left the room, she said something to Lauren and came back over to us. "Please just ignore her. She loves to wind people up. Gets off on it."

I shrugged and looked away from her intense gaze. The other two didn't move a muscle.

"Can I speak to you in the break?"

Dave didn't answer.

"Don't leave, will you?"

Still nothing. Then I felt a poke in my side. Turning, I was surprised to see that Diana was staring at me.

"You won't go, will you, Jess?"

She had been talking to me. Me?

"I need to talk to you. Can you give me five minutes?"

I was so surprised that she wanted to speak to me, I agreed without argument. I could feel Sophie relax next to me. She was used to my stubbornness, and had been expecting a refusal. So had I, for that matter.

So why did I stay? Why did I set myself up for listening to Diana tell me about how great Lauren was, how much they'd missed each other, how fabulous their lives were going to be now they had found each other again?

Probably because, deep down—actually, not all that deep down, I was holding onto a molecule of hope that wished more than anything that Diana and Lauren were not an item. It was the same feeling a person gets when they buy a lottery ticket. Part of them really believes it will be them who becomes a millionaire, but the reality is that the prize goes to someone they believe doesn't deserve it, who will squander and waste it, who won't see what good they could achieve through this stroke of good fortune. When actually, would the loser act that differently if they had been the winner?

I knew that my thoughts were making no sense whatsoever. And that was probably the reason I stayed—because I have no sense.

After telling us that she would meet us in the cafeteria

in less than ten minutes, Diana left with Lauren to get her clothed, and I went to the cafeteria with Dave and Sophie. None of us discussed what had happened until we were secured in the farthest corner of the cafe.

Sophie was the one to break the silence. "We didn't know she was back, Jess. Honestly."

I shrugged and picked up my coffee. The smell of it made my stomach roil.

"The first we knew was when we turned up tonight."

I shrugged again. "It doesn't matter."

After an awkward silence, Dave chimed in. "I'd been trying to get hold of her, you know that. We said we would let you know, and we would have...if we had. Known."

Slamming the cup onto the table, I looked into the blue eyes that were so like his sister's. "Listen, both of you, it doesn't matter. It has nothing at all to do with me what Diana does and who she wants to screw—"

"Really?" Diana's voice broke in. Her voice was trembling, and I knew she was on the verge of tears.

I had meant to say "screw up her life with," but I don't think that was the way it came across.

I felt a little ashamed of my outburst, but, stupidly, I didn't apologise. Actually, why should I? Diana had been the one to flee to London, spend nearly a month there with no word to anyone, and then saunter back, toting the bitch from hell on her arm. And another thing—

Lauren "letting slip" the "our" clothes hadn't been a slip at all. It was as if she had cocked her leg and pissed all over Diana, warning me to back off.

And why should I have been at all affronted? She was my art teacher and the sister of my best friend's boyfriend. I didn't have a claim on her, or any say about anything she decided to do. I felt more shame, followed by heat as the blush raced up my throat and spread along my face. I needed to apologise.

Lifting my gaze to meet Diana's, I could see she was on the verge of breaking down right there in the middle of the cafe. Opening my mouth, I started to say I was sorry, but Diana lifted her hand and waved me off, trying all the while not to cry. God, I felt like a shit. So then I got up and tried to grab her arm. I had to make her understand how sorry I was, but she flinched, as if she thought I might hit her. Why would she do that? I would never, ever...

"Hello again." Lauren was behind Diana, her hands on her waist and moving her to one side so she could take centre stage.

That fucking bitch. The way Diana's body almost folded inside itself as soon as Lauren's hands made contact, it was obvious. It wasn't me she was frightened of, it was the poor excuse for a human being trying to push her way into our lives that had turned the vibrant art teacher into a shell of the woman I knew.

Gripping the cup in my right hand, I had to physically restrain myself with my left, as I had the urge to throw the remainder of my coffee over the smug faced twat of a bitch grinning in front of me.

"Look, Lauren," her name almost spat from my mouth, "don't you ever try to join in any conversation I'm having, you got me?"

The shock that whipped across her face was fleeting, and the smile she had been sporting was dramatically replaced by an expression that could only be described as dangerous. "You little cunt."

Diana attempted to pull Lauren away, but she was having none of it. "Think you're something special, eh? Think you have one over on me because this spineless..."

with the word, Lauren shoved Diana away, "twat fancies you?" Lauren leaned forward.

Sophie move towards me in defence, only to be pulled back by Dave, who had been held back by Diana.

The look on Lauren's face should've frightened me, but in fact it did the opposite. I calmly edged around the table to brace my opponent. And even though I was physically smaller than Lauren, I felt ten feet taller. "As I said before—don't ever, and I mean ever, try to join any conversation I am having." I leaned forward, my face inches from hers. "You like to push people around? Well, I am not the kind of person you can push. Got it?"

Lauren sneered, a half snort leaving her mouth.

"Does it make you feel big and strong to hit another woman?"

I heard Diana gasp, and admonish, "Dave."

I wanted to apologise for mentioning the abuse, but I was too riled up. "If you ever hit Diana again, I will personally knock the living shit out of you."

Lauren's cocky grin disappeared, and I knew I had hit the mark. One thing a bully can't stand is being found out to be a coward.

Diana didn't wait for me to finish. She was gone in a flash, and so was her brother. I wanted to follow her and tell her I was sorry I had broadcast her life to anyone in the cafe who had a mind to listen, but I wanted to stare Lauren out.

"You'd better watch your back," Lauren muttered. With that, she turned to leave.

"That would be your style, wouldn't it."

Her shoulders stiffened.

"You can only get people when their back is turned." I knew she wanted to thump me, could feel her hatred seeping through her skin like poison. "Coward!"

Her fists clenched, but she walked away.

I looked around the cafeteria and was surprised to see that no one had paid a blind bit of notice to the altercation. They were too involved in their own lives to worry about ours. To say I was shocked would have been an understatement. Aren't we the race who love to feed on other people's misery?

Sitting down at the table, I was glad of the support of the chair, as I truly felt as if my legs were going to give way. Fuck. What was I thinking? I wasn't a challenger, a fighter, a defender of the realm, or even someone who would help a damsel in distress. I was just me, Jess Taylor. I had never had a fight in my life, and I really wanted it to stay that way. I wasn't a teenager anymore.

"I'm too old for this shit."

A giggle came from beside me. I'd forgotten Sophie was still there.

"I thought you were magnificent. Told you art class would be good for you—just like being at school."

My hands were shaking as I lifted my coffee again, and the contents sloshed around alarmingly.

A calming hand landed on my own and lowered the cup. "I'm really proud of you, Jess." A sigh left her mouth. "Although announcing to Diana that you know about what happened..." Sophie sucked the air between her teeth before releasing it in a whistle, "Looks like Dave will have some explaining to do."

Shit. I should look for Diana, tell her I didn't mean it to come tumbling out that we knew about her history with Lauren. I needed to explain that I only did what I did because I was protecting her. But was that my only motivation? Was it solely for Diana's benefit that I had turned into Sir Lancelot with a twist, the twist being I was female and not usually one for heroic deeds? Or was it jealousy that had made me react the way I did? Maybe a little, but wasn't it because I was attracted to Diana that I had stood up and threatened Lauren? It was the way Diana had flinched when she thought I was going to be exactly the same as her previous partner that made me flip my lid, wasn't it?

"Don't worry, Jess. Diana will understand. I promise."

Even though I wanted to believe Sophie's assurances, there was an edge to how she said it that made me think she wasn't totally convinced herself.

"Come on. Break's over." Sophie stood. "And if you think you are racing off into the sunset on your white charger, you have another think coming, lady. Up. Class awaits."

Everyone else was already back in the classroom by the time Sophie and I turned up. Monica was in the centre, hastily rearranging the display. The pots and pans were back, and there was no sign of Lauren. Or Diana. Or Dave, for that matter.

Monica called over her shoulder, "Our life class has been put on hold for another week. Please switch back to pencil for the remainder of the evening."

"No. Keep the charcoal out," said a voice from the doorway

Huh?

"You were promised a life class tonight. It is only right you should get one."

It was Diana. I looked towards the door and saw her standing there, her face ashen, her black hair making her skin appear even paler. Red lips captured my attention, and I was surprised to see them moving.

Diana went over to the centre, swept the pots to one side, then clambered onto the table. "Hope you don't mind, Monica."

The substitute teacher's giggle said she didn't mind at all.

"Okay. What you have to remember is not to be overwhelmed by considering the picture as a whole. Choose a section to concentrate on and work on that," Diana instructed.

Babs Hepworth put her hand up.

"Yes?"

"Do you mean to choose a part of you and focus on just drawing that?"

How did that woman get from Point A to Point B without getting killed?

"Yes."

How had Diana said that without sounding sarcastic?

"For example—if you wanted to draw just my hand..." Diana leaned back and grabbed a glass from the array of kitchen items on the table, "you might show the way it grips the glass, but you don't have to draw the glass in full, or the arm, for that matter."

Why was she doing this? Why had she come back? She was putting on a brave face, but I couldn't understand why she was putting herself through this. Monica was leading the class tonight, so it wouldn't have been weird if Diana had just gone home after everything that had happened.

"How long do they get for the basics, Mon?"

"Ten minutes?"

"And your time starts...now."

For the first couple of minutes, I stared at the blankness of paper in front of me, the whiteness of it making my eyes blurry. The only sound in the room was the scratching of charcoal on paper. I lifted my face and was met by a sea of blueness—so fucking blue, so enticing, so addictive I could have drowned in those blue depths, been swept away in them and loved every minute of it.

Slightly, oh so slightly, one eyebrow twitched first, then her lip, almost as if she was trying to suppress a smile.

Why would she be smiling at me after what I had done? Was that a wink? My heart was racing, and I was finding it difficult to breathe. Her eyes were so intense, I was lost in them, lost in her and her perfection. I could see the colour coming back in her face, and it was as if I was watching a rose bloom.

"Okay. Time."

Time! But I...

"Let's have a look at what people have done, shall we?" Monica began moving about the class, and I could hear her praising and critiquing people's work. Head down, looking at my blank page, I was dreading her getting to me.

"Maybe less time studying your subject and more hands on might help next time, Jess." I looked up at Diana, who raised an eyebrow and gave me a lopsided grin.

"Yes, Miss."

"Miss?" Sophie's laugh boomed out before she thought to stop it. "Miss? How old are you? Twelve?"

I grinned shyly and looked at Diana. My heart sped faster. Yep. Twelve, and having the first taste of a real crush. I felt good. Fucking good. Actually, I felt A-plus.

The rest of the class proceeded along the same lines. Each time Monica set us up with a task to draw Diana, I found myself too engrossed in just absorbing her to make much use of the paper and charcoal I had waiting. Even Sophie was getting stuck in, and got on with her work. When Monica was getting the students to share what they had, she mercifully avoided me. I didn't care. I was learning a lot about art by being an observer.

Diana was a masterpiece. She was one of those paintings that have the eyes that not only follow you around a room, but look straight inside you. To be honest, I don't think I could've drawn her if I'd tried. Not just because I couldn't replicate what I saw, but mainly because I doubted I could even guide my charcoal across the paper. My hands were numb in places, tingling in others, and shaking all over, all as a result of the changing expressions on Diana's face.

"I think she wants you. Badly."

"Shut up, Soph. Haven't you got a picture to vandalise?"

"Touchy subject, Miss Taylor?" She sniggered. "I believe someone is going to be a busy little knight in shining armour later."

"Would you like to show the class what you have done, Sophie?"

Monica's voice sounded from behind us, and we both jumped and scraped a charcoal line across the page.

"Aw fuck."

Thankfully, Monica didn't hear the delightful turn of phrase that popped from Sophie's mouth, as she had already moved to the front and was awaiting the picture from hell.

"Erm...well, erm..." Sophie held her picture out at arm's length in front of her and closed one eye, as if viewing it like a critic. "I don't think I truly captured the moment."

"What? Saddam Hussein's first day in hell?" I muttered. She glared at me, and I grinned at Diana. "I think you've caught it beautifully."

To be honest, I wasn't too sure what part of Diana's body Sophie had meant to be drawing. It showed a mishmash of lines, a lot of smudging, and a doodle of a cat with buttons down its front near the corner. I was struck by the lack of laughter when she turned her pad around. My, we were in a room full of polite people.

Monica coughed, then coughed again. "Would anyone like to make an observation?"

Not a peep. Nada. Zilch. Tumbleweed.

"Any strengths?" Again, silence.

"Anything you think Sophie could do to improve in the future?"

Apart from leaving out the buttoned cat? Nope. It was purrfect.

"Well. We can call it a night then."

I had barely picked up my bag before Diana was beside me. I felt her presence. It was like an aura of electricity coating me, making all the hairs on my body stand to attention.

"Would you, erm, can I... Crap."

My eyes met hers, and I grinned. "Do you need to?"

"Huh?"

"Never mind. What did you want to ask me?"

It felt like an age before she actually stopped moving her lips around and allowed the words to come out. "Would you like to do something on Friday night? Erm...with me, I mean."

Amazing to think how calm I felt. It was usually me that was struggling for words and blundering my way through a conversation in hopes that I actually was conveying what I wanted to say. Diana was waiting for my response. I was pretty sure she was holding her breath.

"I would love to. Call me. Yes?"

She nodded, and those thick dark locks dancing over her shoulders and the broadening smile made me feel way too much about what was, in fact, just the prelude to our first date.

God. If she made me feel this way with the promise of a date, how on earth would I cope when we were actually on one? That concern didn't stop my insides from dancing, and my brain began to wish away the next two days.

Chapter 9

Thursday was a bitch. No. I take that back. It would have been a bitch if Diana hadn't called me when I got home from work to arrange our date. I liked writing that—"our date." Where was I? Thursday being a pseudo bitch. The reason why I initially said the day wasn't my favourite kind of day was because of work. I know most people would say the same, but I believe my day was even worse because of anticipation, the anticipation of making arrangements for our date.

Diana called on Thursday to arrange for us to meet up the following day. Man. That sounds cold. Fuck it.

Friday night came around slowly, slowly, quickly, slowly, almost like a fox trot, and I was nervous as hell. I know I've rattled on—in detail—about how much I liked Diana, but the knowledge that it would just be her and me for the whole evening was killing me. At times I felt I couldn't breathe because of excitement, and then I processed into the "I'm not worthy" train of thought. I'd never experienced that in my life—that wanting, I mean. Diana Sullivan was out of my league, and there was nothing

I could do or say that would change that. At least that's what I was thinking when I was in my 'I'm not worthy' stage. Thankfully, my mood swung like a pendulum, and before I knew it, I was on a forward stroke and getting all excited again. Talk about rapid cycling.

As the big hand on the mantelpiece clock approached ten to and the little hand hovered at not quite seven, I caved. "Sophie. Can you come over?"

"Fuck off."

"But I'm having a crisis."

"You will have, if you call me again." Click. Brrrrrrr.

Why had I called Sophie? Maybe because deep down, or maybe just beneath the first epidermal layer of the skin, I was a coward. I wanted to go out with Diana. Wanted to sit and be entertaining, delightfully engaging, deliciously sexy. But how could I, when I was just me?

Ding dong!

I hate doorbells. They make you want to wee. Not all the time, just on first dates that matter, and maybe Halloween when I was a kid.

Ding dong!

Insistent doorbells were the worst.

Inhaling a deep breath, I made my way to the door, glancing at myself in the mirror one last time. The outfit I had chosen was smart yet casual. We were going to grab something to eat, and then go and see a film. All in all, a traditional first date. Dark green cargo pants topped with a white, short sleeved shirt said, "Yes, I'm going out casually, but can be accepted at places like—"

Ding dong! Which translated to "Who gives a fuck where you're going to eat? Just answer the door before I blow my batteries!"

My hand was shaking when I lifted it to turn the

latch on the door. The metal clunked against the ring on my index finger. Turning the knob was a feat in itself, as if I was a ninety year old woman answering the door to carpetbaggers. I took another deep breath before I yanked the door open.

Standing half on half off my doorstep was Diana. Obviously. But she wasn't the assured woman I had seen on Wednesday night. Don't get me wrong. She was breathtakingly beautiful, had those amazing blue eyes, that gorgeous body, that everything, but she was almost white. Her lips stood out against the paleness of her face, and for a moment I thought she was going to be sick. I could see her mouth moving, and for a split second I thought she was about to lose her lunch all over my doorstep. Then it hit me—she was as nervous as I was. I know that shouldn't have made me happy, considering she looked so terrified, but it did cheer me up to find out it wasn't just me who wanted this date to work so goddamned much.

"Hey...you okay?"

She swallowed hard before quickly nodding her head twice.

"You want to step inside? I'm not quite ready yet."

I was, I had been since a quarter to six, but it would give her time to adjust—if that was the right word—and me too, for that matter.

Diana stepped into the hallway, and I was again aware of how tall she was. I never had to be reminded of her beauty, however unwell she looked.

"Here. These are for you."

Flowers. Tulips. A dozen of them in blazing glory. Initially I thought they were roses, and had a fleeting urge to go and check out the meanings. Talk about insecure.

"You seem like a tulips kind of girl."

A slight smile, a lifting of those perfect lips, lips that I was suddenly fascinated with. Just the sheer movement of them, the way they seemed so soft and kissable, so alluring and enticing. Before I could think it through, I found my own lips pressing against hers. In that brief moment, as lips held lips, all my anxiety seemed to evaporate. It felt so right to be kissing her. Although it was a mere brushing, a sampling, the connection was so unbelievably strong, I found it difficult to drag myself away.

Just before I moved away, my eyes sprang open and I saw her startled look change into something more primitive. Blue eyes darkened as her pupils dilated and almost covered all the colour. And you know something? That perfect moment when I saw her reaction was utterly wonderful.

"Erm...thank you." The smile I sported was huge, and my heartbeat quickened as she smiled in response. Even I wasn't sure whether I was thanking her for the tulips or the kiss, but it didn't really matter, did it?

"No, thank *you*." I could see some colour flush her face just before she shyly looked away and then back at me. "Shall we go inside?"

Memories of the first time Diana has said those two words at Sophie's came flooding back. "Sure." But why was I finding it so difficult to get moving? It seemed that all I wanted to do was stand and stare at the vision before me.

"Is it this room you want me in?" Diana asked, indicating the living room.

Her voice drew me out of my idling and ogling and reminded me of my manners. "Yes." As I turned, I was anticipating it. Not just her hand on my arm, but the feeling of electricity sizzling through me, that feeling I had once classified as weird but now was coming to expect every time we touched. Not that it wasn't still thrilling; it was. My reaction paid testament to that. I couldn't help jumping at contact.

Diana was looking just as confused as I was. Unlike the first time, she voiced the question. "Did you feel it too? That...erm...jolt. When we...when I touched you."

Words eluded me, so I nodded. What I couldn't understand was why there hadn't been that electricity when we had kissed. No. I didn't mean it to sound like that. There is something desperately wrong if there are no sparks when you kiss. God, I'm rambling. Even I don't understand what I'm trying to say.

She chuckled, and slowly shook her head from side to side. "Never mind. You need to get sorted. The table is booked for seven-thirty." A grin split her face and she looked more in control, at least more than she had when she'd first arrived. "In here?" She repeated, pointing towards the lounge, and I tipped my head in confirmation and fled the scene.

In the bathroom, I stood in front of the mirror. I looked the same. The same green eyes, the same blonde hair, the same everything. So why did I feel so radically different? Happier. Lighter. Why was I grinning stupidly? Considering I had a huge knot forming in my stomach, I was feeling pretty good. I tentatively lifted my fingers and trailed them along my lips. I had kissed Diana Sullivan with these innocent pilgrims. God, that kiss, that connection. That look she gave me just before I pulled away… Jesus. If that's how she could make me feel with a brush of lips, an expression of want, what on earth would I be like if she actually made a move on me?

Grinning at myself, I ran my fingers through my hair

and turned for the door. There was only one way to find out.

⚜

Being with the Diana was beyond even what I had imagined. I knew I liked her, had known it from the very first time I had heard her voice in the classroom. But being with her, being alone in her company and being the focus of her full attention, that was more than I could have ever believed possible. Initially, I had just been attracted, forcefully attracted, granted, but just attracted after all. However, the more I got to know her, the more I got to really *see* her. I knew it wouldn't take much for me to fall hard for the gorgeous art teacher.

There's the rub. I had never been a person to fall for anyone. All my ex-girlfriends were exes for a reason. I liked them, sure, but loved them? Think I could ever have fallen for them? No way. They were just girlfriends. I know that doesn't seem fair, but I don't think I've explained it the way it was. I didn't set out to have just a girlfriend I just liked. I wanted to fall, wanted to love, wanted the white picket fence and everything that came along with it. But it never happened. After the blast of sexual attraction had fizzled, I was left feeling a little deflated, wondering whether there was something wrong with me. Not now, though. Not after sitting in Diana's company at dinner. Not after seeing those blue eyes digest me along with each course.

In a nutshell, I can guarantee I have never wanted anyone more than I wanted Diana. It wasn't because she was intelligent, charming, beautiful, and sexy. God, was she sexy. It was everything about her. It was the way she threw her head back when she laughed, the way her eyes sparkled when she looked at me, the way she smiled her half crooked smile. It was the feeling of excitement when she touched me as she was explaining something, the racing charge of expectation alongside the current rushing between us. And I still don't think I have clarified why I knew, beyond the shadow of a doubt, that I could so easily fall for her. To be honest, the thought didn't just scare me, it terrified me.

You know what is coming now—doubt, insecurity, unworthiness. Just because I felt all of that wonderful stuff about her, didn't mean she would feel the same about me, did it? Not to mention that I was only halfway through my first date with Diana, and I could see myself spending the rest of my life with her. That was freaky enough, but to suddenly get hit by the jitters over her intentions… Where was my dad when I needed his input on her plans for my future? Better still, where was Sophie?

"Are you okay, Jess?"

Diana's melodic voice broke through my mental meanderings, and I focused on her concerned face leaning over the table and dangerously close to the candle.

I brought a grin out and nodded. "Never been better, Ms Sullivan."

Her nose wrinkled adorably, and she returned my smile.

Butterflies danced merrily in my belly. At that precise moment I didn't care about the future, because at that precise moment, she was with me. Smiling at me. What more could a girl ask for?

"Excuse me. I have to make a trip to the ladies room. Won't be a tick."

Erm. Not really what I had in mind at that precise moment, but it was a start. A woman had to relieve herself at some point in the evening.

Alone at the table, I took the opportunity to look around the restaurant she had chosen. Couples were huddled all around, and if my vision served me, they were all female. I sighed, then gasped. Seated at the far side of the room was Samantha James. Yes, *the* Samantha James. My ex, Samantha James. She wasn't alone. The woman was all over her, and Samantha was loving it. I wanted to look away, but I couldn't. Samantha James was looking straight at me. Fuck. I hadn't seen her in months, not that I was complaining. The more time that passed without me seeing her, the better.

Out of the corner of my eye, I could see Diana talking to a member of staff. That's all I needed—Diana meeting Samantha. More to the point, Samantha getting her claws into Diana. Anger welled up inside me and balled my fingers into fists, ready for battle. I wasn't usually the type to fight for what I wanted, so the action surprised me, but it didn't make the anger go away. Or unclench my fists.

Samantha grinned over at me as she extricated herself from the woman she was with.

Fuck again. She was coming over. I looked past her to where I had seen Diana, but she wasn't there.

"Hello, stranger. Long time, no see."

Man, that woman could move when the mood struck her.

Samantha leaned over the table, blocking my view of the exit where I had last seen my date standing. This was all Diana needed after all what had transpired with Lauren on Wednesday—me getting all arsey and knocking Samantha on her backside in the middle of a restaurant. That would fill Diana with absolute joy, wouldn't it? Going from one woman who was happy to use her fists, to another who was just as ready.

"What do you want, Samantha? It can't be me, surely?" Good. My voice was steady; I sounded in control. Big tick to me.

"Just thought I'd say hello."

A grin that was almost predatory appeared on her face, and it made me think of the Cheshire Cat from Alice in Wonderland but without any of the cute qualities—just a freaky grin that seemed as if it would be there even when she had left.

"Who's the date?"

Ding. That was the sound of that old proverbial penny dropping into place. It wasn't me she was interested in, but Diana. Samantha James was all about conquests.

"New girlfriend?"

"Why don't you just fuck off, Samantha? I'm not interested." I leaned closer, my face mere inches from hers. "And I never was. Got me?"

A sharp laugh shot out of her mouth. "You weren't saying that when I was fucking you, were you? If I recall, you seemed to want me around then." She squinted one grey eye and looked me up and down. "Must admit, you were pretty good in the sack. Well, when you lost that stick up your backside."

Reading her face, I knew she meant it as a compliment, as if being told you were a good lay when you loosened up was something to write in your diary as a "My achievement of the day today was…"

"If I was so good, why did you sleep with all the others? Hmmm? Was it the stick getting in the way?"

Why wasn't I ignoring her, or telling her to sling her hook? I tried to look past her to see if Diana was there, but the human slinky moved with me.

"So, as I was asking, new girlfriend? Or is it open

season?"

I frowned.

She tutted and leaned towards me. "I mean, is she available?"

God help me if I didn't lift my fist a little. I wanted to smack that self-satisfied, shit-eating grin off her face. How dare she come over to my table and try to pump me for information about my date, when her own sat glowering on the other side of the restaurant.

"No, she isn't."

Fuck. Could that response have been any colder? And the best thing was, it hadn't come from me; it came from behind Samantha. I have to admit, the look on my ex's face was pure quality. Talk about how to confuse an idiot. Her upper lip lifted, and her head tipped to one side as if to say, "How did you do that?"

"So, if you don't mind, I would like to sit down at my table with MY girlfriend." Diana's voice was cold.

Part of me wanted to jump up and down and shout hurrah, then race around the restaurant telling each and every person individually that Diana said I was her girlfriend, but the older, less teenaged part of me decided to sit with a smug grin on my face.

"I was just—"

"I know what you were 'just' doing. Now move, or I'll move you."

Samantha straightened up, apparently believing she could intimidate Diana with her height.

At that point I really wanted to laugh, as Samantha was at least three inches shorter than my gorgeous defender.

Diana stood with her hands on her hips, one eyebrow raised in challenge, her lip slightly curled.

God, she looked sexy. It wasn't the most perfect time to

feel a rush of arousal, but come on. I would have had to be dead not to feel even more desire for Diana at that perfect moment of Samantha getting her just desserts.

"Well? Do I have to physically move you, or will you move your own dumb ass?"

"Who the fuck do you think you are?"

A sardonic laugh shot out of Diana's mouth, and she leaned towards my ex.

It was a good feeling—watching Samantha step back as if she fully believed Diana was going to crack her one.

"I am the woman who will never treat another woman the way you do." Samantha tried to get a word in, but Diana lifted her hand and silenced her. "Do you think I don't know about you? Don't know that you haven't a clue when you've got it made?" She laughed as she slowly shook her head. "You are one sad fucker."

Samantha's body language spoke volumes. She was livid, absolutely livid. I was loving it. Or maybe I was still loving the "MY girlfriend." I didn't know for sure.

"You are going to end up one very lonely woman."

Samantha pushed Diana out of the way to get past her, but Diana caught her by the arm and pulled her in close. A growl came through her teeth as she spat out, "Don't you ever fucking do that again, understand? Or I will knock you into the other side of next week."

I didn't get it. I'm sorry if I sound dumb, but I didn't get it. This wasn't the same woman who had suffered physical abuse from her ex-girlfriend, the ex who was smaller than Samantha. So what was up? And how did Diana know about my past relationship?

Samantha didn't say a word. She tried to shrug off Diana's hand, but it stayed put. Grey eyes met blue, and I could see some level of unspoken understanding pass from one woman to the other. Diana removed her hand and Samantha moved away, more slowly than she had approached.

Diana watched every step before she turned to me and gave me a stunning smile. "All done. You fit?"

It was if nothing had happened.

"The film will be starting in twenty minutes."

I just sat there, staring.

"What's up?"

I shrugged. What could I say? Should I mention the transformation from hunted to hunter? I had to. I loved seeing Samantha James put in her place, but my head couldn't compute the events. I'm not saying that I felt threatened by Diana's actions, far from it. I felt a sense of the damsel saved from distress, and it felt good. Very good. Exceptionally good, actually.

"What about the bill?" I asked. "We need to pay."

"All done." A huge grin lit her face. "You fit?"

So, that's what she had been chatting about to the member of staff. I moistened my lips to begin a tirade about how I wanted to pay my way, but she surprised me beyond what she had already done.

"Hey." Her voice was so soft, so delectably enticing. She looked over her shoulder at Samantha James, who was arguing with her date, then turned back and captured me in her blue gaze. "If I'm going around telling everyone you're my girl, can't I at least pay for your meal?"

A small smile glimmered across that perfect mouth, but I knew underneath her cool appearance, she was as nervous as I was.

I could feel the electrical charge dancing between us. I could almost see it. "In that case... I would hate for you to lose face. Thank you."

I dropped my eyes, as I couldn't hold her intent gaze any longer. When my eyes reacquired her, she had dialled back some of her dynamic sexuality, and I was able to continue breathing at a steady rate.

"Come. We're going to be late."

Diana held out her arm, and it seemed the most natural thing in the world to link mine with hers.

It may have been my imagination, but I could swear that I felt, and heard, a click—just like two pieces of a jigsaw puzzle snapping together. Oddly enough, I didn't react. Apparently I was becoming used to sensations pulsating around me when I was with Diana.

❦

Case 39. That's the film we went to see, although I honestly don't know why. The evil spawn looked like the kid from the Cadbury's advert, and I felt that her eyebrows should have won an Oscar. It was supposed to be a horror film, but to be honest, I have been more scared when opening my gas bill. Still, I made the most of the situation. What sane girl wouldn't?

To tell the truth, I did jump a little for real and knocked Diana's Coke out of her hand and over the man sitting next to her when the "thing" came out of the closet. I could make a joke about coming out of the closet, but that would be a little too obvious and I doubt anyone would really want to hear it. Neither did the bloke next to Diana. Talk about overreacting to a little spilt Diet Coke. The way he acted, you would think I had peed on his kids as they were opening their Christmas presents. Thankfully, Diana handled the situation, giving him money to get his shite shirt and Primark jeans dry cleaned, whilst I just sat silently praying for my seat to swallow me up.

As soon as the first credit came up, we were out of there. Neither of us wanted to hang around and have Diet Coke shoved in the unmentionable places that the sticky, stained man had threatened.

The drive home was made in silence. It didn't feel uncomfortable, just a little deflated. The evening had been perfect and I didn't want it to end, especially since I didn't know when I was going to see her again. I know she had said "MY girlfriend," but as the evening wore on, I hadn't seen any more evidence from Diana that indicated that what she said hadn't just been to piss Samantha off. There had been no attempt to sneak her arm around me in the darkened theatre, no leaning against each other as people do when snuggled down in their seats, watching a film. The only action I had seen was the movement of the badly dressed and spattered man who was unfortunate enough to catch the remainder of a soft drink.

"Here we go."

I hadn't even noticed we had arrived in my street; I had been too busy feeling sorry for myself. Considering I had enjoyed every single moment of being with Diana, I couldn't understand why I should be feeling any sadness about the evening. Maybe it was because I wanted it to happen again, and was worrying myself stupid about it not happening. That's me in a nutshell—busy thinking about stuff, but not much action.

"Yes." Last of the big orators, that's me.

"Thank you, Jess. I had a lovely time."

"Yes." Oh God, say something! "So did I." Bravo. Can I rival Henry V and his historical speech? Methinks not.

"We'll have to do it again soon, yes?"

"Yes!" That came out a little loud. "I'd love that." A

lot better, more normal; the volume didn't hurt anyone's eardrums.

We were both fidgeting with seatbelts and bags, twisting rings around, flicking glances at the other but too shy to actually make eye contact.

"Erm…"

"Yes?" Did I sound eager? You bet.

"Are you free tomorrow?"

I could feel the grin leave my stomach, travel up my throat, and appear on my mouth like magic. "Yes." One word answers; I was doing well.

"Shall I call around about eleven?"

"Yes." Come on, Taylor. You can do better than that. "I'd love to see you again. Actually…" I hesitated, wondering whether I should say what was on the tip of my tongue. "Would you like to come in for coffee? We can make plans."

She sighed, the only sign that she had been holding her breath. Then she smiled, that perfect crooked one I liked so much. "I thought you'd never ask."

We both started laughing and went into my house.

God, having her in my house seemed the most exciting thing in the world. Why was that? She was just a woman in my home. Well, that isn't it at all, is it? She wasn't just any woman,

she was Diana Sullivan, the woman I had been lusting after, and I didn't want to screw it up. But if anything could be screwed up, I would be the one doing the screwing.

I made coffee and delivered it into the lounge, where I found the Diana leaning back on my undeserving sofa. I know I keep saying how beautiful she is, but at that moment, the moment I saw her reclined—her legs stretched out, her head against the back of the sofa, her eyes closed—I thought I was being visited by a messenger from God. It was either the light from the lamp or she actually did have a halo around her head, or I was losing my mind big time and hallucinating. To be honest, I didn't care if I was. I stood there taking her in, unobserved. I didn't care about the heat of the coffee burning my fingers, didn't care that I must've looked gormless, I was mesmerised.

"You okay?"

Fuck. Caught in the act. My hands shook, and the coffee splashed over my hands and along my wrists. "Fuck." More splashing as I tried to put the cups on the table and missed completely, spilling the full contents on my trousers. "Fuckity fuck fuck fuck."

Dancing around with hot coffee seeping through my trousers was not the best way to impress the woman who was trying to help me. I doubt me stripping off the trousers was any more of a heart grabber, either. But thankfully, it stopped my Morris dancing.

"Jesus, that was hot."

Diana didn't say anything. She was half on, half off the sofa, copious amounts of tissue in hand, attempting to soak up the brown liquid pooling on my carpet. But her eyes were not on her task; they were on me—the woman who was now standing in front of her with no trousers on.

It should have been sexy, shouldn't it? Me stripping off for the object of my desire. However, standing there with brown speckled legs and shoes was about as far from sexy as I could get. Told you I could screw things up, even without planning it.

"Hot." Diana's mouth moved around the word, and her eyes were riveted on my naked legs.

"Erm…yes. Very." I'm a dumbass. Especially because I was finding it difficult to do anything but watch her reaction. There was no laughter, no sound, no rushing for a clean pair of trousers to cover my stupidity. I stood there like a first prize dick head.

"You should…erm…you should…"

Dress? Get a brain? Dig a huge hole and bury myself in it?

Diana leaned towards me, her tissue filled hands outstretched in an attempt to blot the dripping drink from my legs.

Thing is, I let her—let her wipe even more coffee down my legs. I was fascinated with her facial expression. She was so engaged in her task, I don't think she realised she was making matters worse.

Grabbing her wrist eventually, I put a stop to her cleaning effort, and for a few seconds she just stared at my knees, totally ignoring the way the drink seemed to bob on the top of my socks. "I think I should…"

"Yes."

"Before it…"

"Yes."

Leaving the room sharpish, I had to take a last look at Diana. She was still in exactly the same position, her gaze on me. Her expression showed some element of confusion, like she was just realising she was on her knees on the floor of my lounge and I was running for the door half naked. Not quite what she envisioned on our first date, I imagined.

In the bathroom, I continued a running commentary on my stupidity. At that moment, I should have been sipping Colombian coffee, making chit chat, even—fingers crossed and God willing—getting a little bit of a grip of my date. Instead, I was washing off the stain on my legs and cussing like a sailor. Why was I an inveterate dickhead? Why couldn't I just breeze into the room, slip the cups effortlessly on the table, and then sidle up to the delightful woman downstairs? I wanted to call Sophie and ask her how I should dig my way out of this one, but that's not really what one did, was it? After all, I was a grown woman.

"Soph, Listen."

Yes. I had snuck into my bedroom and snapped up the phone before slinking back into the bathroom again to make a surreptitious call to my best friend. It was lookingmore as if I was, in fact, fourteen after all.

"I know, I know, Look. I fucked up." I furtively glanced at the door, fully expecting Diana to barge in and accuse me of having no common sense whatsoever before marching off to live her own life. "I poured coffee all over myself."

Sophie's laugh filled me with dread. It was the same laugh I'd heard when I fell off the stage doing the Nativity in Primary School.

"What's the big deal? Everyone spills coffee all over themselves at some stage." She paused, then asked, "What did you do?" The stern mother voice came out. "Jess? Tell me you just cleaned it up." The woman knew me too well.

"Erm… I…erm…well, I…"

"Jess?"

"Itookmytrousersoffandstoodtherewithjustmy shoesandshirton." When you say it more quickly, isn't it supposed to sound better? If that was the case, I mustn't have said it quickly enough.

That laugh again. God, I hated that laugh. That laugh indicated I had been a total melon.

"And the problem about you being half naked in front of the woman you are lusting after is?"

I bit my lip. Then bit it again.

"My advice is—make the most of the situation."

She waited. When I didn't respond, she sighed. "You ran off, didn't you? You chicken shit."

"I…"

"Jess, go. We'll talk tomorrow, okay?"

I tried to get a word in, but she wasn't listening to my plea for guidance.

"Slip into something more comfortable, and dry, and get back in there. Laters, lady."

Panic snaked up my throat at the sound of the disconnected tone. Then I thought, "Why am I panicking? What is the worst thing that could possibly happen?" A laugh slipped out of my mouth, and I hastily covered it with my hand.

After donning sweatpants, I made my way downstairs. The lounge showed no sign of the mess, and Diana was seated on the sofa, acting as if nothing had happened.

"Hey, you." My voice sounded brilliant. No wavering, no stuttering, nothing but normalcy. I grinned inwardly.

"Hey, you too." Diana leaned forward, and she looked a little uncomfortable. "Look, I'd better get off." She stood. "We'll have to do coffee again sometime." The smile she gave me was tentative at best.

So, what's the worst that could happen? Diana leaving after my display of ineptitude, that's what.

"I've had a lovely time."

I nodded. I knew if I opened my mouth, I would probably start crying. Weren't we supposed to be meeting tomorrow?

She reached down and picked up her handbag.

It seemed as if everything was moving in slow motion. I wanted to remind her about our sketchy arrangements for the following day, but I thought I would give her the easy opt out by not mentioning it. Maybe after my display of being the new but not improved village idiot had made her rethink her invitation.

Diana was standing in front of me now, and I had to tilt my head up to meet those blue eyes.

"So," her voice was husky, thick and so enticing, "are you still free tomorrow?"

Amazing to think that one moment I was feeling almost suicidal and the next, ridiculously exultant. A grin spread like lightning across my face, and I grabbed her face and pulled her to me, my lips claiming hers again as they had at the beginning of the evening. This time it wasn't a brushing, wasn't a sampling. This time it was total ownership. And it felt so good, so damned good. This time she didn't hesitate, didn't give the appearance of being startled; she reciprocated my yearning with full abandon. Deep, sensual, open, wet, hot, pagan. My fingers effortlessly slipped into her hair and tried to pull her closer, tried to absorb her, claim her, possess her, my tongue flicking over her lips until her mouth opened and allowed me access.

Her strong arms circled my waist and lifted me, until my feet had to rely on my toe tips for support. My whole body pushed against her until I knew for definite that the sofa was behind her legs, then I lowered her onto the soft cushions and climbed on top of her. My body pressed against hers, my knee separating her legs, allowing me between them. Cool fingers slipped down the waistband of my sweats, and her hands cupped my backside and pulled me closer, pulled me in, allowed my pubic bone to hit the apex of her thighs in perfect rhythm. She met each thrust; each grind of my hips made her gasp into my mouth. Heat and wetness originated from between my legs, and I was sure I could feel a trickling sensation at the tops of my thighs.

"God, Jess, yes, please." Her hands were scrabbling with my shirt, trying to lift it off; kisses peppered my face and throat. "I want you…want *you*…please."

My hand removed itself from her hair and slithered its way between us. Our lips never breaking contact, I fumbled with the button of her trousers. The anticipation of finding the same wetness between her legs blinded me to what we were about to do. Plink. Open. The zip put up no resistance, and then my hand was inside her panties. Slick, wet, wanton, mine. I pushed down, separating the folds to find treasure, to find the quivering mass of want waiting for my touch. I wanted to take it, love it.

Leaning back, I pushed her shirt up to expose her bra and the curves of her delicious breasts. Lips met skin, suckling, nipping, licking the tender flesh. I could hear bells ringing. Was I in heaven?

"Jess, God, please…ignore it."

Ignore it? Ignore what? My hand was forcing her trousers down, the panties giving me more room. Long, hard strokes, followed by flicking and circling.

The bells again, followed by a thudding.

My teeth moved the bra aside, and I could see her nipple straining to meet my mouth. I was so close, so damned close. My fingers were in position to enter her, to feel the closeness of her as I made love to her.

"Jess!

Why did her voice seem so deep?

"Open up!"

I'm trying, honestly, I am trying.

"Diana!"

Huh? Why was she…

Bells and thudding and a man's voice at my front door eventually made me sit back on my haunches and look at

Diana's expectant face. My hands froze—one inside her pants and the other on her breast. Our chests were heaving, flushed with arousal.

"It's Dave," we both said at the same time. Then "It's Dave? *Dave?*"

I scrambled off her, and we both hurriedly tried to sort out our clothes before answering the door.

Dave stood on the doorstep, his face filled with panic. "Thank God for that. I thought I might be too late."

Had he planned on stopping us from getting to know each other?

"I thought you might have gone to bed."

Well...

"And Diana gone home. I...I..." Dave was having difficulty speaking. It was obvious he was upset and out of breath. "It's Monica."

"Monica?" Diana pushed passed me and pulled Dave inside. "What about her?"

"She was attacked. Someone broke in and attacked her."

The colour disappeared from Diana's flushed face, and the contrast was disturbing. "But she...she was at my house tonight, using the studio."

Dave gave a half-hearted shrug, his face showing his confusion. "I don't know the specifics. I got the call on the way home tonight. I knew you were here, so I came instead of calling."

Diana staggered, and I caught her around the waist.

"We need to go to the hospital, Di."

"The hosp-i-tal?" Another stagger.

"Diana, come sit for a minute."

She tried to argue, tried to pull away, but I wouldn't let go.

"Just one minute. You won't do Monica any good if you go to see her in this state."

Dave nodded and helped me take Diana into the lounge. Cushions were scattered on the floor, and the sofa indicated two people had very recently been disturbed. It was embarrassingly obvious that we had been making out. It felt wrong somehow that we had been doing that whilst Monica was in the hospital with God knew what injuries.

After sitting Diana down, I turned to Dave. "Do you know what happened?"

He shook his head. "Mrs Greenall from Number 32 called me. She heard a disturbance and went around. Aunt Mon was already down for the count."

A sob broke from Diana.

"The ambulance took her away, but Mrs Greenall said the ambulance guys told her that Aunt Mon will be okay." He leaned forward and grabbed Diana's hand, then squeezed her fingers. "The police want to talk to you."

"I want to see Monica. I can talk to the police after."

Understandable.

Dave patted her hand. "Come on. We'll go in my car."

Typically, at that point I would have bowed out, would have let them sort out what they had to do without any involvement from me. But this wasn't a "typical" relationship. I'd had only had one date with Diana, but I knew deep down that I needed to be with her.

"Just let me get my shoes on."

Two sets of blue eyes turned to me, and both seemed thankful.

"Shall I call Sophie?"

Dave released a sigh of relief. "That would be wonderful."

I turned to go make the call.

"Jess?"

I turned back to Dave.

"Thank you."

I gave him a small smile, fishing around in my bag for my mobile before realising it was under the towels in the bathroom.

Sophie picked up on the third ring. Her greeting consisted of, "What the fuck have you gone and done now?"

In less than a minute, she was on her way out her door.

See? That's what friends do, isn't it? Be there. Just be there for whatever unexpected event should crop up. I hadn't even told her Dave would be there, just said I needed her. And for some friends, that's all it takes.

Sophie was already at the hospital when we arrived. Checking with Reception, we found out Monica was still being tended to. Sitting on the plastic chairs in the waiting area was the worst part. That didn't come out right. I meant waiting for news was the worst part; the comfort of the chairs was immaterial.

Two hours. That's how long we had to wait for news—two fucking hours. Eventually a tired looking doctor came out and asked for relatives of Monica Bright. Considering we were the only ones there, it was more like a rhetorical question. A glimmer of guilt flitted through me as I remembered meeting Mrs Bright for the first time. All the internal piss taking—Mensa member, the nanny from *Count Duckula*, not to mention calling her Margaret Thatcher in my head. All I can put that down to is disappointment at Diana's absence, because later, when

I wasn't being a mean bitch, I found out that Monica was one of the nicest, gentlest women I had ever met.

Monica had sustained a nasty blow to the back of her head, the suturing of which required twenty-four stitches. Unfortunately, the blow had caused her to fall and smash her face on something sharp, which resulted in twelve stiches across her eyebrow, a black eye, and a broken nose.

Diana started crying again, as she had been doing off and on ever since we had climbed into Dave's car. "Can we see her?"

The doctor thought about it before nodding. "You can see her, but she's under sedation at the moment."

"So she won't be able to come home tonight?"

"With head injuries, the patient has a greater chance of concussion, so she has to stay in hospital for a minimum of twenty-four hours for observation."

After thanking him, the four of us made our way to Monica's room. Inside, we all inhaled at the same time. Gone was the feisty woman who had led the art class in Diana's absence, and what was left was an old lady with a face the colour of clay on one side and a rainbow on the other. I thought I was going to be sick. Not because of the stitches or dried blood, but because of what had happened. How could anyone harm this gentle woman? In fact, how could anyone do this to another human being?

As the question flitted through my mind, I immediately thought of one person I knew who could, who would. Lauren. She had proven time and time again that she was free with her fists and wouldn't think twice about hitting someone. Nah. Even she wouldn't stoop so low, would she? I mean, she hit Diana. Although I still couldn't give credence to her reasons, she had done so because Diana was her partner. No excuse, but the only one I could conjure. But to hit an old woman on the back of the head and then leave her bleeding? That was even beneath her level of fuckster.

Monica had been in Diana's house. Maybe Lauren had thought Diana was there. Maybe she had a key to Diana's place and let herself in to confront her ex-lover, and found Monica there instead. Bam! Wrong woman, but message put across.

I had to stop my suppositions. I was not the lead DI in *Prime Suspect*. All I had was an intuitive hatred for the actress. What I needed was evidence, a chat with the police. It could even have been a botched burglary.

"You need to talk to the police, Diana."

That wasn't me. That was Sophie the organiser. It was amazing how she always seemed to know what I was thinking.

"See if anything was taken."

See? Sophie was definitely on my wavelength. I wondered if she, too, thought it could have been the Bitch from Broadway, the Wanker from the West End.

Diana and Dave went over to the bed, whilst Sophie and I hovered in the doorway. Both of us knew this was family time, not the time to all overcrowd Monica's bed.

After a few minutes, Soph indicated with a tilt of her head that we should leave them alone for a while. I nodded and silently followed her back to the waiting area. No sooner had we arrived before Sophie started.

"It was Lauren. It had to be."

Considering I had thought the same thing, I surprised myself by shaking my head at my friend's statement.

"Look, Jess, who else could it have been?" Soph glanced around the empty corridor as if she was fully expecting Lauren to come tumbling from one of the side rooms in a prison outfit and toting a swag bag. "The facts speak for themselves. One..." she lifted a finger, ticking it off with her other hand, "Lauren has a history of violence. Two, she is still in Manchester."

I frowned. To be honest, I hadn't really thought about where Lauren had gone after the night class. Truth be told, I hadn't really given a shit.

"Three, she would know where Diana lived."

"But how did she get in?"

Sophie snorted. "That's easy. Monica let her in."

Huh? Why would Monica let her in? Why would Lauren hit Monica if she knew Diana wasn't there? Whatever had transpired between Diana and Lauren had nothing to do with Monica. Man, this was getting confusing. It was almost like the opening to the old TV series, *Soap*.

A sigh hit the air and drew my attention back to Sophie, who was leaning back in her chair, her fingers steepled, a look of absorption plastered on her face. Minutes ticked by, and neither of us said a word. More minutes. So quiet, too quiet.

"Or, she had a key."

I had already thought of that, but why would Lauren have a key to Diana's house? They'd broken up before Diana had gotten the place, hadn't they? A person who has escaped from an abuser doesn't then give them a key to her home, does she?

And usually, the person doesn't go running back to her ex when she calls, do they? But Diana did. Quite quickly, if my memory served me right.

A feeling of nausea hit me, a swirling vortex of nausea. People who did such a thing usually still loved the person, didn't they? That's one of the main reasons why a victim would go back—love, the "I can't live without them" gene.

What else was there? Diana didn't need Lauren financially, didn't have dependents, but perhaps she had loved her—or still loved her.

I gagged. Couldn't help it. It was the thought of what I had been doing with Diana just before Dave had come to my door that made my stomach roil. Diana wanted Lauren and not me—not the one who would never hurt her, but the selfless bitch who beat the shit out of her on a regular basis. Talk about the perfect example of lusting after the Bad Girl.

"You okay, Jess?" Sophie was leaning forward again, her eyes trying to meet mine.

I nodded, but gagged again.

"You gonna hurl on me?" I started to shake my head, but the contents of my stomach made a bolt for it, so I followed suit—made a bolt for the nearest toilet and lost everything I had consumed that evening.

Warm hands slipped over my shoulders and held me in place before one slid down my back and began slow, circular movements over the sensitive skin. "Come on, love, get it all up."

Again and again I retched, eventually stopping when there was nothing left to bring up.

I slumped on the floor, brought my knees up and wrapped my arms around them. It was the only way I felt as if I could protect myself. From what, God knew. Tears slipped down my face, something that wasn't unusual. I always cried when I felt ill.

Sophie sat next to me, the cold tile giving no comfort to either of us. A strong arm wrapped around me and pulled me close.

I always felt so safe in Sophie's arms, always. Even when we argued, I never felt threatened, never felt ill-at-ease. Part of me wished that everything was different, that Sophie was my girl and we were just sitting there being happy and complete in each other's presence. How much simpler life would be if we were a couple, if Sophie and I were in love, were together. If we could move past friendship and make a life with each other. Then I wouldn't be sitting on the floor of the toilets feeling my heart breaking into a thousand pieces. I would have it all, wouldn't I?

"Bad pint?" Her voice was gentle, but she was trying to make me laugh, trying to get me to open up.

I shrugged and shook my head.

"What is it, honey? You coming down with something?"

I could barely shake my head.

"You lovesick? Huh?" Sophie must've felt my body stiffen, because she leaned in closer. "I know you, Taylor. You think Diana's still in love with Lauren, don't you?"

How did she know?

"I know you well, lady." Her hand cupped my chin and lifted it so I was looking directly into soft, concerned eyes. "For the record, I know for a fact...for a FACT...that Ms Sullivan is absolutely smitten with you."

"But—"

"No buts. She told me."

"She told…"

A grin changed the serious expression into the woman I knew. "She told me ages ago. Why do you think I have been doing everything I can to get you two together?" A laugh shot out. "Do you know she was shitting a brick the day we all met in the bistro? It took all my persuasive powers to get her to join us. After the way you acted in class on the Wednesday before, she thought you'd tell her to sling her hook."

Come to think of it, she had looked like someone

walking the plank.

Another laugh from Sophie. "The art gallery was my idea, though, a good one, I thought. Then you both come back without the balls to do anything about your obvious lusting."

"That long?"

"Yes, Taylor. Long before she mogged off to London to see the twattette. Satisfied?"

No wonder Sophie had said something about coming back from the art museum single and arsey.

"She really likes me?"

"Yes, you muppet. She really likes you." At that point, Sophie tried to move back, but her knees and butt had other plans for her. "Fuck me. Fuck."

I laughed, must've been from relief.

"Oi, git. Don't laugh at my aged bones. I've fucking seized up."

I made a move to help her and realised I was in the same boat. We looked like two eighty year old women attempting to breakdance—if eighty year old women punctuated every movement with a euphemism for pain and surprise.

After I rinsed my mouth, Sophie and I hobbled back to the waiting area, where we sat in the chairs and waited. This time, I couldn't seem to keep the grin off my face. Not really the expression a woman should be wearing when waiting in a hospital after a friend has had the crap beaten out of her. Thankfully I changed expressions when Diana and Dave came out. Just.

Deciding to get the interview over with, Diana called the station and arranged to meet the police at her house as soon as she could get there. There was no point leaving it until the morning; evidence might be gone by then. Without discussion, we all went to her house. All for one, and one for all, is what I say. Lauren didn't know what was going to hit her— Erm...if it was Lauren, that was. My money was on her as Public Enemy Number One, even if it turned out she was innocent.

Chapter 10

To my surprise, the police were at Diana's place before we were. I was afraid that they might not pay much notice to something they could have put down as an aborted burglary. As it turned out, they were very interested in what had happened to Monica, especially as there didn't seem to be any evidence of a break in. The doors and windows hadn't been tampered with, so that left one of two scenarios—either Monica let the person in, or the intruder had a key. As it worked out, the only other people to have a key to Diana's place were Monica and Dave.

"What about Lauren? Did she have a key?" Dave asked Diana.

The two policemen sat forward—pens lifted, ready to take notes. "Lauren?"

"Erm...not that I'm aware of."

Huh? Should be cut and dried—either a yes or a no answer.

"I keep a spare key in the glove compartment of my car."

The Bobbies stared at her expectantly.

"But my car isn't here."

It was outside my house. We had all piled into Dave's car to go to the hospital.

"Erm."

The policemen were still staring. To be honest, they were giving me the creeps.

"Do you want me to go and check?" Diana asked.

The older of the two policemen gave a sigh that could only be interpreted as boredom before shaking his head. "Just let us know if it turns up missing."

What a stupid fucking statement. How can anything turn up missing?

I think he realised what he had said, because he paused before standing up as if to dismiss us all. "This is a serious incident, Ms…" he glanced at his notes, "…Sullivan. We need your full co-operation. Please check around and see if anything is missing."

I couldn't help myself. "And what are you going to do about it?" They had spoken to Diana as if she had robbed her own house and whacked Monica on the head for effect. "Where is CSI? A Community Officer? Is this all you are going to give us?"

The bored sigh again. "I'm sorry to disappoint you, *madam*, but this isn't a television show."

I hate being spoken to like I'm an idiot. "Well, I'm sorry to disappoint you, *Officer*, but this isn't police service. A woman is in hospital with head injuries, and you are behaving as if it is a waste of your time to look into who might have done it and whether they might try something else."

The look he gave me could have given Medusa cause to worry about her lock on the position of Gorgon. "We can only go on evidence." He shot a glare at Diana. "And we have no evidence—no break in, nothing. For all we know, the old dear fell over."

I was thoroughly pissed off now. "So, let me get this straight. You say this was a serious incident, but also say there is no evidence and the old dear could've fallen over."

"There is no need to be aggressive, madam."

Aggressive? If he wanted aggression, I would give him aggression.

"I am just stating the facts."

"Badly."

He stiffened, then half closed one eye and looked me up and down. "And you are?"

I was on the verge of snapping "Does that matter?" when he continued. "Where were you between the hours of 9 pm and 10?"

WTF?

A small smile flickered over his face as he brought out his pad and pen again.

It was my turn to heave a bored sigh.

Thirty minutes later, after I had been interviewed within an inch of my life, and Sophie too, as she couldn't keep her gob shut, Dave came back with Diana. Whilst the coppers were tearing into me and my best friend, they had decided to go check for the spare key. To no one's surprise, it was missing from Diana's glove compartment. It didn't take a rocket scientist to figure out that there had only been two people in Diana's car in the time since she had last seen it—me and the lovely Lauren Baker. I didn't have it, so that left the absent actress as the magpie.

At that news, the officers seemed to get their act together. They said that it was something they could work on, but I was still under the impression that a woman with the shit knocked out of her from behind was kind of the thing they should have been focusing on, not who had stolen a house key. Maybe I was just losing faith in the legal system. Diana gave them the name of the hotel Lauren had checked into after she had stormed out of class the previous Wednesday, and the policemen left, hopefully to arrest Lauren Baker.

Obviously Diana couldn't stay at her house whilst her key was on the loose, and it was too late, and expensive, to get the locksmith out at such an hour. The next day would be fine for changing the locks, considering that her insurance company wouldn't cover the cost if a key was used and there was no break in. Stupid, I know.

I wanted her to stay at my house, but I couldn't seem to voice the invitation. Would she think I was offering so we could continue what we had started before Dave appeared? That would have been callous, understandable, but callous. Dave suggested that Diana stay at his house, Sophie kept nudging me, trying to get me to say something. She punched me in the arm at one point, but I even muffled the "ouch."

Dave was oblivious to our interplay as he grabbed a holdall and helped his sister stuff her clothes and toiletries inside the bag. "You can stay as long as you like, sis, you know that."

Another punch on my arm. I turned and glared at Sophie, who tried to look innocent.

"You can have my room," Dave offered gallantly.

Punch. A visual "Fuck off."

"Or…" Sophie tried to interrupt Dave's rambling, but he wasn't listening.

However, Diana looked hopefully in our direction.

"She could stay with either of us."

Blue eyes flicked to mine, and they seemed to sparkle a little as a smile lit her face. Was that relief?

"I know this is a crappy thing to have happened, but I

love having you stay over, Di," said Dave.

Fuck.

"We can spend the night going over everything in detail."

Her shoulders slumped as resignation set in. It was now gone four in the morning and everyone, apart from Dave, seemed to realise when enough was enough.

"Yeah. That would be fantastic, Dave."

He grinned at her and lifted the bag to signal he was ready to get going, so we all got up and made our way outside.

Sophie was going to give me a lift home, and I knew she would end up spending the night. Before we parted, she gave Dave a kiss and a hug, and they whispered for a moment. I'm definite I heard Dave say, "Well, I didn't know, did I?"

That left Diana and me.

"Hey. Sorry about tonight—erm…last night."

What on earth did she have to be sorry about?

"Not the best way to end our first date," she continued.

A laugh drifted between us, so soft and delicate it was as if I could catch it in my hands and treasure it like a prized butterfly. Then there was a slight frown as she looked down at me.

"Are we still on for tomorrow? Maybe a little later than eleven?"

Instead of answering her straight away, I leaned in to capture those perfect lips again. I have never, ever before been so lost in anyone's kisses. All I could feel, all I could taste was her. Nothing else mattered. Breaking the contact was agony, but it was either that or standing outside in the cold until we both froze to death.

Like a lovesick teen, I watched Diana climb into Dave's

car, staring after her until the interior light dimmed after mere seconds. But, if I looked hard enough, I could still see her looking at me as the car pulled away, and believe me, I looked hard.

"Come on, Romeo. Home." A firm hand gripped my elbow and pulled me over to the car. "And I hope you don't think I'm Diana tonight. I'd hate to punch you in your sleep if you get fresh."

Aw shit. Now that idea was in my head.

I barely got any sleep. Thoughts of what had happened to Monica kept drifting in, thoughts of Lauren, too, the smug fucker. But truth be known, the two main thoughts that kept me awake were nothing to do with the incident at Diana's house. One—what if I did feel Sophie up in my sleep? I would die a thousand deaths, both literally and metaphorically. Two—Diana. How could I not think about Diana? I had come to grips with her in the most intimate of ways, tasted that mouth, touched her hot skin, seen those gorgeous eyes up close and personal. God. And then back to worrying about reason one again—dreaming I was still doing all of the above and being rudely awakened by my best friend strangling me.

But she liked me. Really liked me. Fancied me, in fact. Not Sophie, Diana. A grunt came from next to me; the air of my friend's breath hit my face. Wistfully, I wondered why I couldn't just become comatose like her. She had no problem sleeping, and definitely no problem nicking my Tina Turner t-shirt and sprawling like Leonardo da Vinci's *Vitruvian Man* across my bed, leaving me with a handful of duvet and only enough mattress to balance one cheek of my arse on. I couldn't even lie on my back, or facing away from her—I had to face the grinning, somnolent, snoring woman who had pegged "left hand side" as she had raced for my bedroom.

My teeth were beginning to grind together. I wanted more of this bed…more duvet…actually, some of the pillow would be nice, too. Nudging Soph, I whispered, "Move up, mate." Nothing. So I repeated the nudge once, twice, three times, until I half stumbled out of the bed and shoved her hard. "For fuck's sake, Harrison! Shift your fucking arse over!"

Soph muttered groggily, "Oh, Diana, Diana… Kiss me again."

My hand hovered over her left shoulder with an impending punch. What had she said?

"Your lips are like velvet, baby."

Lips like velvet?

"Mmmm…yes."

When I heard a laugh, the churning in my gut was suddenly replaced by the urge to throttle Sophie.

"Got ya, Taylor."

"You fuckster!" Thump. My punch landed on her shoulder. "Now shift. My bed, my duvet…your arse, move!"

Sophie was still laughing as she slid over, rubbing her arm whilst I muttered how she had better sleep with one eye open for a while.

Back to back. That's how we started to sleep again. However, the next morning I was sprawled over her chest, the spit dribbling over Tina Turner's grinning mouth. That'll teach her. No, not Tina—she was innocent, unlike the person inside the shirt. Funnily enough, I couldn't help grinning as I snuggled in deeper.

Chapter 11

Diana arrived at two-thirty. I'd expected her to be earlier, and part of me had believed that she had slept on it and decided that she couldn't be arsed seeing me on the Saturday, after all. Call it low self-esteem if you want, but I imagine many people go through that "I'm not worthy" stage within a relationship. Sophie had left as soon as she cleared out my fridge, promising to call me later. So, I had been left to my own mental meanderings for almost two and a half hours. A lot can go through a girl's mind in that length of time, most of it fruitless, pointless, and random. I also had the cleanest window sill and phone in the world, considering how many times my hands went over them with the duster as I toyed with either calling her or looking out of the window in hopes of her turning up.

When she did, I was at the window, and I hoped against hope that she hadn't seen me craning my neck, trying to see further up the road, almost falling off the ledge in the process. I even waited a respectable time before answering the door with a look of shock firmly in place.

"I didn't expect to see you so soon."

Her face showed confusion, and her hand gestured weakly at the living room window before she shook her head.

Shit. She had seen me. So, my attempt to be reserved and chillaxed in front of her was pointless.

"What are you waiting for? Come in." I wasn't going to admit my faux pas. I wasn't an idiot. "I was just cleaning the windows." Shut up. Just shut up now. "They can be a bugger, can't they?" Why won't you listen to me? I was sounding not only desperate, but like a clean freak to boot. "Enough about me." Please. "Any news on Monica?"

We had made our way into the living room that was spotless by now, and Diana slumped on the sofa, kicking her shoes off in the process. "I've been to see her this morning. She has no idea who hit her." She sighed as she patted the cushion beside her.

Obligingly, I sat next to her, and was pulled into her arms, landing my head on her chest.

"She was working on a project when she thought she heard me come home."

Long, dextrous fingers started stroking my hair, and I was trying my hardest to concentrate. This was important after all.

"She had just got into the hallway when she felt something hit her at the back of the head. That's it."

I lifted my face to look at her. A frown was burrowing onto her face and making her eyebrows almost meet. I began stroking the lines, trying to ease the worry I could see there. Warm breath hit my wrist, and tingles spread like butter over my skin; the hairs on my arm raised and danced stupidly.

"So, what happens now?" I whispered.

A slight shrug of her shoulders meant my body moved

with hers.

"Change the locks. Go through my stuff to see if anything is missing."

It had to be Lauren. It had to be. Nothing obvious was taken, so the purpose for being in Diana's house was not robbery.

"I called the locksmith this morning, but he can't make it until after seven tonight."

Jesus. She mustn't have had hardly any sleep. She must've got to bed at the same time as me, but she had called the locksmith and visited her aunt in hospital already today. All I had done was fart about pseudo-dusting and keeping to my guard tower, also known as the living room window ledge. There were faint dark circles underneath Diana's eyes, tiredness mixed with worry. I knew if the circumstances were right, it wouldn't take long for her to nod off.

"Why don't you grab a cat nap? You must be beat."

Blue eyes opened wider in an attempt to show she was fine, but it was obvious she wasn't. "I'll be fine after a good strong coffee. Honestly." A smile appeared. "And anyway—why would I want to sleep when I can be here with you?"

Bam. My heart thudded against my ribcage, and I was sure she could feel it against her breast. Thoughts of what we were doing on the same sofa the night before darted into my head. But she was knackered and should get some rest. It wasn't as if we would never get the opportunity to relive the moment if we didn't do it right now, was it?

An idea came to me. "But you would still be here with me, wouldn't you?" I stroked around her eyes, making lazy circles with my fingertips, smiling when I saw the lids fluttering. "We could both have a nap. Here. Together. On the sofa." More caressing, more fluttering, more thumping inside my chest.

Her hand had begun a light rubbing motion on my back, and I was in no hurry to leave the comfort of her arms.

The quiet was marred only by our breathing. Nothing else actually mattered. I could feel her chest rising and falling beneath mine, and it was as if I was on board a small boat bobbing gently on a lake. It was hypnotising, relaxing, perfect.

"Okay. Five minutes. Then we should get on with our date."

I couldn't help the smile on my face, but I buried it against the softness of her sweater, nestling in deeper and inhaling the scent that was pure Diana Sullivan.

If I had to choose between the erotically charged encounter we had shared the previous evening and the one I was now experiencing curled up on the chest of the woman I was falling for, I would have been hard pushed. Cuddling was delicious, intoxicating, but in the most ethereal way imaginable. I believed I had waited all my life to experience that feeling. I was home. This being together was home. She was home. My home.

It was almost three hours later when I woke up against the warmth of her. Her arms were wrapped tightly around me, keeping me firmly in place. My face was against her throat, and my hand was tangled in her hair. Legs intertwined, and bodies pressed together. All in all, it was the perfect way to wake up, one I wanted to experience again and again and again. Diana's breathing was regular, the breathing of someone who was sound asleep. A need to see her in such a peaceful pose made me gently lift my head to look at the woman I was using as a human pillow.

Blue eyes met mine, and I was startled.

"Hey, you. Sleep well?" Her voice was husky with sleep, and it sounded so sexy.

Without preamble, the southern part of my anatomy sat up and screamed, "I'm awake!"

Diana didn't wait for an answer, as she leaned forward and brushed her lips over mine.

I wanted to continue, but knew if we did, there would be no way either of us would be going anywhere for the rest of the day. It wasn't just the thought of Monica, the thought of the locksmith, the thought of everything we had to do that stopped me. It was because I didn't want to rush this, rush us. Last night, although wonderful, had been too soon. Although I wished the circumstances had been different, I was happy that we hadn't fallen into bed with each other on our very first date.

"What's the matter? You okay?"

"Perfect."

"I know that, but are you okay?"

God, this woman was smooth. I leaned in for another brief touching of lips before whispering in her ear, "You, Ms Sullivan, are a charmer. A silver tongued charmer."

Her laugh glittered in the stillness of the room. "Me? A charmer?" More laughter.

I just stared at her and nodded my head solemnly.

"I am as far from charming as they get."

I rose up so my legs were straddling her waist, and I stared down at her, my head canted in question.

Diana cleared her throat and tried to look repentant. "Ms Taylor, I can assure you, I only ever speak the truth as I see it. You are perfect." She cupped my chin; her thumb stroked the side of my face. "So utterly perfect." Gone was the laughter, and what replaced it was a look of concentration, like she was deliberating her next move. "I know it is early in our relationship, Jess, but..."

All the moisture in my mouth dried up.

"But I think I'm..." She swallowed nervously. "Never mind. It'll keep."

"No!" Crap. Too loud. Try again, Taylor. "No." That's better. "Tell me." I grabbed the hand that was caressing my face and brought her fingers to my mouth, kissing the knuckles as my eyes never left hers.

There was a slash of panic flitting through the blue, and the colour changed like moving water. A tongue tip appeared and nervously moistened already moist lips. Then it disappeared to make way for her bottom lip to be sucked inside whilst she chewed on it in contemplation.

"Just tell me, Diana." I turned her hand over and kissed her wrist. "What's the worst that could happen?" Tempting Fate again, maybe, but I had to know what she was going to say.

"I think...I'm..."

Come on. Say it.

"I'm falling for you." Blue eyes closed, and she shook her head before cracking one eye open and peering at me. "I know, one date, and I'm scaring you away already. I'm sorry."

"I think I'm falling for you, too." Liar, Taylor. You know you are.

"If you want to take things slowly, I totally understand. You don't have to say... What did you just say?"

"I said..." I brought my face to hers, making sure she was looking as deeply into my eyes as I was into hers, "I think I'm falling for you, too."

The kiss she gave me was hard, soft, deep, light—everything a kiss should ever be, and more. Her hands held my head in place as she showed me just how my admission had made her feel, and I felt became lost in the taste of her all over again.

I was definitely falling, falling hard. I even had a certain four letter word popping in and out of my head. But, like the lady said—it had only been one date. If I'd voiced my actual thoughts, I believed I would be the one doing the scaring. Talk about being the punchline of every lesbian joke I had ever heard: second date, U-Haul truck; third date, turkey baster.

Reluctantly, I pulled away, the separation making my body ache for the feel of her. "We need to talk." Christ! I was going for fourth date now—the "let's talk seriously" one.

"About?"

Sighing, I pushed myself back even further and shifted myself off her. I sat nearer the end of the sofa, and it wasn't long before Diana did the same. How do you start a conversation about cooling things off before you have even let them heat up? I didn't want to cool things off with her. Shit. I was no good at this. What I wanted to say was that I didn't want to rush into making love with her, not that I didn't want to make love with her. GOD! How inept was I? All I wanted was for us to take our time, get to know each first, make our first time perfect and special. I wanted so much more than some quickie on the sofa for us.

I looked at Diana tentatively. Her body had folded into itself, and it took me a couple of minutes to realise that it was me and my staring at the living room rug that had done it.

I released a colossal sigh. "I just don't want to rush us,

that's it. I want to get to know you, and I want you to get to know me before...before we..."

Realisation dawned on her face and her eyes opened wide, followed by a knowing grin. A solitary nod and a half smile told me she knew exactly what I meant. "I would like to get to know you, Jess. And not just physically." Her hand slipped across the sofa, and she twined our fingers together. "When the time is right, we'll know."

My body was trying to tell me that the time was right now, but I wanted everything to be perfect. Maybe I was being old fashioned, maybe I was expecting to feel what I had read in novels, but the one thing I knew for certain was that I would enjoy the waiting, the learning, the journey with the intriguing woman who was right next to me.

"Hungry?" No point in dragging it out, was there?

Diana gave me a saucy grin before nodding.

I knew that it was going to be very interesting discovering Diana Sullivan, and I also knew I was going to find out a lot of things about myself in the process. And that was a scary, yet definitely exciting thought.

Whilst the locksmith fitted new locks on both her front and back doors, Diana went through her personal belongings. Whoever had been there had taken one very specific thing—a necklace with a pendant on it. It was the only thing Diana still had that Lauren had bought her. Evidence to suggest the actress had something to do with the events of the previous evening, perhaps?

Nope. The police reported that they had interviewed Ms Baker, and she had an alibi for the whole of the Friday evening. I knew it was the same officer I had pissed off the night before, as he refused to go into detail about the alibi, just vaguely mentioned another party being involved. Considering Monica hadn't seen who had hit her, the police had no other choice but to do fuck all. No evidence, no witnesses—no crime. It didn't matter about Lauren being the last to be in the car when the key was taken, didn't matter about the pendant and necklace, didn't matter that a woman had stitches for being in the wrong place at the wrong time. Seemed like Ms Baker had once again gotten away with being violent.

Sophie and Dave met us at the hospital and, thankfully, Monica seemed more like her usual self—if being beaten black and blue and having a total of thirty-six stitches could be considered normal. The doctors informed Diana that her aunt could go home the next day.   Not   surprisingly, Monica didn't fancy staying over at Diana's again, even though the locks had been changed. She didn't want to go home and be by herself, either.

Before I'd even thought it through, I said, "You are more than welcome to stay with me, Mon." I know she could've stayed with Dave, but as much as we all liked him, we also knew he would have difficulty letting the matter of the attack drop. To say he was livid about his aunt being attacked and the police not doing anything productive, in his mind anyway, was an understatement.

I was embarrassed when I saw Monica's eyes fill with tears, and I shuffled in place for a few moments.

Diana slipped her arm around me and pulled me to her, whispering in my ear, "You're an angel, do you know that?"

That made me shuffle a little bit more. Looking over to Sophie, I saw her mouth, "Lick arse," but I chose to ignore her.

We stayed until we were asked to either keep the noise down or go home. It was fun being in the hospital, not that I would have ever thought I would write that. Being in hospital is never fun—especially if you are the one sprawled out in the bed.

Monica looked tired, so we decided that the best way we could keep the noise down was if we buggered off somewhere else.

"Anyone fancy a curry?" Dave asked as we all stepped outside.

My stomach churned at the mere thought of being stuck in an Indian restaurant inhaling the smell of Hell itself.

"Sorry. Forgot you hate the stuff."

I looked at him gratefully, but realised he was talking to Diana.

"You don't like curry?"

She looked embarrassed, but pretended to stick a finger down her throat and made a gagging sound. "I know, I'm weird. Everyone likes curry except me."

"Not me. I even hate the smell of it."

She tilted her head and gave me one of those gorgeous half-cocked grins of hers, the dark hair slipping over her chin in the process.

"Awwww... A match made in heaven. Look, Dave, two curry haters find love."

I ignored Sophie. It seemed as if that was the best course of action to follow with her that night.

"No breaking of naan bread for these two whippersnappers. No googly eyes over the pilau."

"Shut the fuck up, Soph." Sorry. Trying to ignore Sophie was like trying to ignore a mosquito. Turning more to Diana, I asked. "Do you like fish?"

A snigger from Sophie was less than polite.

I thought I'd specify. "Fish and chips?"

"In the paper?"

I nodded.

"You're on." Diana turned to the other couple. (I liked writing that—other couple, meaning we were a couple—and I'm getting on my own mushy tits now) "You two up for it?"

Five minutes later, we were on our way to the chippy. Twenty minutes after that, we were standing outside, tucking into fish and chips in the paper. It reminded me so much of when I was a teen hanging about on a Saturday night with my mates, eating chips just to keep our hands warm. Looking at the members of our foursome, I felt a sense of nostalgia. Sophie was still in the group, and I wouldn't have wanted it any other way. But instead of a gangling, acned youth trying to cop a feel of my best friend, she had a good looking, caring man beside her. It was at that moment that I truly absorbed the way he looked at her. For all Sophie's worrying about him not liking her, I was more than certain this man would tell her the same thing his stunning sister had told me earlier in the day, if he ever got the chance to get a word in.

To say it was a wonderful feeling would be an understatement. To know that Sophie was in line to get her heart's desire was just what my own heart yearned for. Well, one of the things my heart yearned for. The other was standing right next to me, offering her fattest chip in my direction.

After eating, we decided to walk through the park and enjoy the cold autumn air. Arms linked, Diana and I walked behind Dave and Sophie, our feet kicking the leaves to the side of the path.

"Tell me something about you?"

Her expression looked questioning, as if to ask me to be more specific.

"Anything. Your job. You do more than teach at the college one night a week. So..." I drifted off, inviting her to continue.

Diana looked at the darkened sky as if she was trying to formulate a response. "I'm a graphic designer."

Something I already knew, but I didn't say anything.

"I used to work in an office in London, but in my line of work, it is just as easy working from home."

But that wasn't the real reason why she worked from home, nor was it the reason why she decided to teach a night class. I didn't want to push, didn't want her to feel uncomfortable by making her feel she had to open up to me, but...as I said, I wanted to get to know her. How could we start our journey if we never moved past the introductory stage? "Here. Let's sit on the bench."

Minutes passed, and still we sat there, our only contact, holding hands. Dave and Sophie had stopped at the next bench, about ten or so metres from us.

"I think I need to explain what happened. I know Dave told you some of it, or he told Sophie and she told you."

Blue eyes flicked to mine, and I nodded reluctantly, muttering, "Sophie only told me a little."

"Thought so."

Diana's voice was sombre, and I knew what she was about to tell me was something that was going to be hard for her to say. I didn't have any idea how hard it was going to be for me to hear until I heard the full story. There is no point in me recounting, word for word, the events in London. But, like me, you need to understand what had happened to know what made me hate Lauren Baker even more than I had when we sat down on the bench.

Like love's young and naive dream, the relationship had started well. It had to have done. Lauren could never have had so much of a hold over Diana if she had been a cunt from the outset. Sorry. Bad word. Shouldn't really resort to the "c" word, but in my mind, that was all she would ever be from then on.

They had met when Diana's firm was hired to do all the graphics for the theatre company Lauren was working for at the time. You know—posters, programmes, fliers, even the billboards. Lauren was the main draw of the show, and it was Diana's job to promote the actress in every way possible. Lauren had suggested that they spend more time together, something that I could tell Diana regretted.

Of course, Lauren had been charm personified, making sure Diana was well and truly under her spell. No. That's not quite right. Let me rephrase that. Diana was not out at work, and Lauren made it progressively more difficult for her to stay in the proverbial closet. It wasn't a case of Diana living a lie; she stressed that she just didn't want people at work to know her private life. Lauren had her. Little innuendos at meetings made Diana easier and easier to manipulate. Rather than causing a scene, it had seemed easier to go along with Lauren's wishes.

"I'm not proud of who I was back then. I should have just called her bluff. She had as much to lose as I did. Even more, maybe." Diana's eyes fixated on our clasped hands. "I mean, who would go to see a woman in a romantic role with a man if they knew she batted for the other team when she was offstage."

True. But I doubted Diana was the kind of woman who would ruin someone's career for revenge—unlike her ex.

"By the time we moved in together, I already knew it was over. I tried to get out of it. Lauren wouldn't take no for an answer. Then the guilt... God, the guilt."

Diana shook her head. "I wasn't even attracted to her anymore, and that made me feel even more guilty. I couldn't give Lauren what she said she wanted—love, commitment—all of which she professed to have for me. And she knew it. That's when it started. Just a push now and again, apologies, the ever useful 'It's because I love you so much' or 'Look what you make me do.'

"As in all destructive relationships, the abuse didn't stop at words or pushes, it escalated to slaps, thumps, and good old fashioned 'putting the Mrs in her place' beatings, which were always followed by her begging for forgiveness. She would promise, 'I won't do it again. I just love you so much' until the next time the fists came into play. Every time, guilt. 'You make me do this. You make me hate myself.'

"My work suffered, how could it not? I never said a word. How could I tell my bosses why some days I would just sat staring at the computer screen for hours, why sometimes I couldn't even stand up straight because my back was a mass of bruises.

"Then opening night... Actually, it was closing night for us. Lauren was playing Ophelia. Ever since I had started on the publicity campaign, she had bragged endlessly about what a fantastic opportunity it was for her. When the review painted her in a less than favourable light, it seemed to serve as the catalyst that made her show her true colours to everyone. Even though the article hinted about Lauren's sexual preference, that wasn't the reason she..." Diana fumbled with her composure, then rushed out, "... stubbed out her cigar on my hand."

When Diana was telling me that part, I couldn't help rubbing my thumb over the circular scar between her thumb and index finger. I wanted to wrap my arms around her and hold her close, while I told her she was safe now. I would promise her that Lauren would never, ever get the chance to hurt her again.

"I'm not sure if it was because it happened in front of everyone, or, in my fucked up logic, I didn't feel I deserved to get a beating because of a bad review."

"You didn't deserve a beating, full stop."

The snort that left her formed a mist in the cold, dark night. "By that time, I thought I did." Diana pulled her hand from mine and pretended to straighten the collar of her coat.

Instead of backing off, I grabbed her hand again and brought it to my lips. Her fingers were cold, so I blew warm air on them before gently kissing each and every finger. I could feel her eyes watching my movements, and I knew I had to very careful what I said and did at that moment.

Considering how angry I was, I surprised myself with my gentleness. Slowly, I pulled her against me, guiding her head to my chest and wrapping my arm around her shoulders. I could feel her body shaking, and I knew she was crying. I didn't want her to cry, but I knew she needed to release the pent up emotions before she burst like a pressure cooker. If that happened, there would be little chance of putting her back together again.

I realised I was stroking her hair, long, rhythmic strokes that seemed to calm her. Nestling my face against the back of her neck, I whispered, "I've got you. Come on, love... get it all out. I've got you."

And I did. I would have her back, protect her, for as long as she let me.

174

Chapter 12

It had been two weeks since the night on the park bench when Diana had told me about her history with Lauren. I wanted to talk about it, wanted to know how she was feeling, but Diana hadn't mentioned it again, and I didn't dare bring it up in case I put my foot in it. She seemed fine, happy, in fact, so why rock the boat? I knew that excuse was a cop out. She knew that I would always be there to listen, didn't she? What was the point in her brooding over the worst time in her life, when the future could be so much brighter? At least I hoped that was what she was thinking— that I could make her future brighter.

We picked Monica up from the hospital on the Sunday, and she stayed with me for nearly a week. Diana came around to see her every day, usually flanked by Dave, and, on occasion, Sophie. Although I loved having them all drop by, they never stayed long enough, always with the excuse of being a bother. Considering that two months earlier it had been a struggle to get me out of the house rather than being in bed by nine-thirty, I realised my attitude toward life had changed considerably. I no longer wanted to curl up in bed with a book, preferring now to spend my evenings doing things that made me feel as if I was actually part of the human race.

I have to admit it was nice coming home from work and having someone there to talk to. But, man, Monica could talk. After about an hour and a half each evening, I changed from fully interested and responsive, to nodding and grinning inanely.

It was fun having her staying with me, but I would be lying if I said I didn't jump for joy when she announced that she missed being in her own home and was ready to return there.

Art class was in its ninth week. We only had three more sessions before it would be over and Wednesdays would go back to being just Wednesdays—even if it was still curry day at work. At least when I went to class, I knew I would be seeing Diana.

I feel as if I should explain that last comment, shouldn't I?

I wanted to see more of her. Who could blame me? Not knowing when I would see her again was driving me nuts, and although I loved Sophie dearly and thought the world of Monica and Dave, I wanted alone time with Diana. Was I being selfish? Yes. Did I care that I was being selfish? Y… No. Well, yes and no.

It wasn't anyone's fault—except maybe Lauren's, even if we couldn't pin it on her—that Monica had moved her stuff back to her own home the previous Sunday, and then insisted we all stay for Sunday lunch, then tea. Diana had to go to the offices in London for project discussions on Monday and Tuesday, so that left Wednesday at class for me to see her.

How could I nurture a budding lesbian relationship

when a man was sitting on a bench in the middle of the room wearing nothing but a smile? Not easy. But at least I saw her, got to chat with her, could gaze into those amazing blue eyes all I wanted. All the while being teased mercilessly by Sophie, though to give her credit, she did shut up when the bloke stripped off, much to Dave's dismay.

I was once again rubbing out the model's private parts to draw them over—he seemed to like Sophie—when I heard Diana's dulcet tones in my ear.

"Maybe you should leave that bit until last." She chuckled. "Unless you like rubbing a man's—"

"Ms Sullivan!"

Fucking Babs Hepworth. It was a conspiracy.

"I can't seem to get the angle right."

I wondered what part she was drawing.

"The curve won't curve right, and the hair is getting in the way."

God, I wanted to laugh. Would you admit that out loud in front of everyone?

"And the fleshy—"

"Okay, Sylvia."

So that was her name—not The Babster.

"I'm coming." Leaning down next to me, she whispered, "Wait for me at break, okay?"

A stupid grin spread over my face, and I felt rather smug.

"Look at my dick. It is huge!"

Sophie, not the man, although I totally believed he thought the same. Sophie thrust her pad in front of me, and I was face to face with every lesbian's nightmare.

"You are supposed to draw the whole figure, Soph, not just..." I lowered my voice "...the bits that interest you."

Dave's head snapped up, and he looked at the both of

us before shaking his head and giving Sophie a feigned glare.

"Life should be full of interesting bits. I can draw his face any time." She held her pad out in front of her. Using it to mask her mouth, she whispered, "Do you think Dave's jealous yet?"

Rolling my eyes, I tutted and continued rubbing out.

"Suit yourself."

From the other side of the room, I heard Diana explaining that the man's moustache should accentuate the lightness of the nose and enhance the curve. Given the chuckles in the room, I knew I wasn't the only one with a filthy mind.

*

I waited for Diana. Of course I did. And as soon as the last person left the room, she was over to me, dragging me into the storeroom and closing the door behind us. I was pressed against the wall by her firm body. I didn't care that it was dark in there, although I wished I could see her eyes.

Her arms wrapped around me and pulled me closer and closer. A hot, wet mouth found my throat, her lips opening to taste my skin. God, It felt so good to feel her breath travelling over my neck and up to my ear.

"I've wanted to do this all day." Diana's voice was deliciously husky and enticing. A slight nip on my ear, and her mouth was moving again, and so were her hands. One slipped up the side of me, as the other pressed lower and grabbed my ass cheek. Another tug, and I was straddling her thigh, pressing against muscle.

I pushed harder, moaning into her hair. When I heard her moan echo mine, the heated moisture bubbled between my legs. Jesus. She hadn't even kissed me yet and I was pooling, melting, pressing against her to intensify the contact.

Her lips found mine. The kiss was not gentle, not soft, not a brushing. It was almost possessive, a claiming. It was the kind of kiss that could drive a person mad with want; it was everything, but not enough. My hand pushed through her hair and she groaned into my mouth, making me wetter, making me want to swap places so I could press my body against hers like she was doing to me. I was rocking against her, building a rhythm.

Diana was meeting each thrust, the kiss deepening, the sounds of our pleasure punctuating the connection, making it more intense, more sensual, more primitive. She tore her lips away, emitting a soft groan before she took my mouth again. But still it wasn't enough.

I slipped my other hand inside her blouse and traced the edge of her bra, taunting her. Instead of dipping inside, I cupped her breast through the cloth, her nipple hard against my palm. I couldn't resist. I had to feel the flesh, had to feel that pert bud on my skin, in my mouth, against my breast.

It was my turn to break the kiss, but her moan of disappointment turned into pleasure as I burrowed my face between her breasts, inhaling her. God, she smelled so fucking good…edible, delectable, divine. A swift push to the side and her bra was gone, and my lips hovered over her puckering areola. I wished I could see it, too, but the darkness of the storeroom precluded that. Any thoughts of taking things slowly deserted my brain.

My panting breaths hit her skin. With each puff, she gasped and pushed forward, but I moved my mouth before she could make contact.

"Jess, please."

That's all it took. Two simple words, and my mouth enveloped her and sucked. She tipped her head back, and her chest pushed against my face.

"God, yes!"

A flick. A dragging of teeth. Wetness coated the hard stub as my tongue loved her. I couldn't help bringing my hand up to massage the rest of her breast. Her hands were in my hair and gripping, pulling before pressing me into her even harder. My other hand was on her hip, moving with the rhythm of her thrusts, wanting to join in, to take her. Wanting this to be somewhere other than in a darkened room with the knowledge that twenty-odd people would be piling back into the classroom in a matter of minutes.

"Jess! Are you coming?"

God. Nearly. If she would just slip her hand, or use her thigh, her mouth— Yes, her mouth...

"You've had nothing to drink yet."

Oh, I have, but I wanted so much more. Nothing could quench this thirst. Nothing but her.

"For fuck's sake!"

Light. Blinding light. Light that made me squint and draw away from the ample breast.

"Oops. Sorry, mate."

Diana quickly moved so my face was covered. Considering it was by her chest, I didn't protest.

The door closed slightly, leaving a slit of light to peek through. I heard a giggle before Sophie collected herself enough to splutter, "Meet you downstairs." More giggling. "If you want."

Her footsteps scurried away, and I knew Dave would know all about the tryst in the storeroom in less than three minutes.

Diana's chest was heaving. So was mine, actually. It

wasn't from embarrassment; it was arousal. Obviously. No one could have such a close encounter with Diana Sullivan and not be aroused, or out of breath, for that matter. The heat of her was still on my face, my one hand was still cupping her delicious breast, whilst the other was digging into her backside. Glancing at her, I saw that crooked smile that only Diana can pull off, her blue eyes dancing with laughter.

"Looks like we've been busted, lady." Diana's voice was husky.

I grinned, then briefly kissed the curve of her breast before moving away from her. I gently slid her bra back into position, and made a point of patting her shirt into place and buttoning it up. "There you go. Good as new." Another pat. Another grin. Then, on my tip toes, I raised up and placed a chaste kiss on her gorgeous mouth. "Come. We have people to entertain." I grabbed her hand and led her from the storeroom.

Just as we expected, Dave and Sophie were grinning stupidly when we arrived, my best friend giving me a knowing wink and a nod.

"Y'alright?" She lifted an eyebrow, leaned back in her seat, and eyed us both up. A frown appeared on her face, and she leaned towards me, her hand reaching out for my neck. "Someone has a hickey."

"Fuck..." I tried to look down, but was stopped by Sophie's finger flick.

"Gotcha."

Instead of calling her a myriad of names, I gave her a serene expression, which unnerved her more than a curse would have.

Dave just grinned that charming grin of his and absently stroked his goatee. Although I didn't know him well, I had the feeling he was worrying about something, as the few times I had seen him play with his chin whiskers was when he was deep in thought.

I wondered what might be making him worry. Me? Diana? Diana and me? God, I was so self-absorbed. Was it him and Sophie? Were they okay? Back to me again—was Dave okay with Diana and me? Of course he was…he set me up with her. So what was the matter?

"Did you know there is an exhibition of Gauguin at the Tate?" he asked.

Huh? Why did he look worried about that?

"I know." Diana picked up the coffee that Dave or Sophie had gotten her and shrugged as she took a sip. "Started end of September. Can't get tickets for love nor money."

"Really?" More goatee fiddling, then a grin. "You loved Gauguin when you were a student, didn't you?"

"Still do." Diana nodded. "Love his work. A true master." She glanced at her watch, and then knocked back the rest of her coffee.

"It's your birthday in December."

My ears pricked up. Someone was having a birthday and wasn't going to tell me.

A blush spread over Diana's face, and she gave me a quick glance before standing.

"When—"

"Come on. I'm the teacher, and I say it's class time."

Dave laughed and dug into his back pocket. Slap. A white envelope hit the table, and we all stared at it as if it would either explode or get up and start doing a song and dance routine.

Diana tentatively snaked her hand out and drew it toward her.

"Happy birthday, sis."

Shaking fingers peeled back the flap and lifted out several pieces of paper.

"Thought you might want to get away for a breather."

Sophie snickered, and then realised she was almost thirty-two and arranged her face into a smile.

Train tickets. Two nights at the Plaza. And, to top it all, two passes for the Gauguin exhibition.

"Fuck me, Dave. This must've set you back."

One might have expected the expletive to have come from Sophie, or me, as we were both known for our ability to say what we really thought and felt—to a degree, usually with profanity, but it came from Diana.

"I can't accept—"

"Yes you can."

Silence as the siblings stared at each other. Looking from one to the other, it was a dead heat as to whose eyes started to fill up first.

"Thank you."

Despite being quietly spoken, Diana's simple words accentuated the moment, as her tears conveyed how very touched she was by Dave's thoughtfulness. Then Diana grinned and launched herself over the table to hug her brother, coffee cups rattling off in all directions.

Dave made the usual grunting noises of happy embarrassment, and Sophie and I made faces at each other—something we had been doing for most of our lives.

Eventually Diana released him and tried to reorder her clothes, and my mind immediately darted to watching her perform almost the same actions as we left the storeroom not very long before. Once again, heat hit me, and I don't mean in the face. The woman who was staring at the tickets was aglow, and she looked even more striking than usual.

That was no mean feat. I hadn't realised she could be anymore enchanting. The breath I didn't realise I'd been holding hit the air in a soft whoosh, drawing the attention of three sets of interested eyes.

Sophie looked concerned. "You okay, Jess?"

"Just hot." Even that didn't get me a snicker. I wondered whether Sophie was feeling okay.

"Ms Sullivan?" The Babster, I mean Sylvia, was leaning over the table. "Isn't it way past time for the lesson to resume?"

Diana smiled her teacher smile. "Oops. Sorry. Yes." Turning to us, she pulled a face, which made the muscles in her neck stand out. "Better go and earn a living." With that, she was gone, Dave following closely on her heels.

I leaned down to get my bag and was surprised to see Sophie staring at me. "What?"

She didn't answer, just half closed one eye and gave me a searching look.

"What?"

She leaned towards me. "What's up? I thought you would be dancing all over the place after what I witnessed."

Huh?

"But you look as if you lost a pound and found a penny."

I started to answer, but she cut me off.

"Is it because Diana didn't ask you to go to the exhibition with her?"

Shit. I hadn't even thought of that.

Sophie patted my hand like an old aunt might. "Don't worry, Jess. Judging by what I witnessed, she will definitely ask you." After another pat and a saucy wink, she stood to go back to class.

"Erm…"

"Enough with the long speeches, lady. We're officially

late for class. Willy Man is waiting for us."

And that was that. Well, that wasn't exactly that. I couldn't help thinking about what Sophie had said. Shouldn't it be obvious that Diana expected me to go with her? I was her girlfriend after all. Wasn't I? She had said as much to Samantha James on our first date, hadn't she?

Wait a minute. She had said it then...but not since. Was I or was I not Diana Sullivan's girlfriend?

I tried to dismiss the thought. Of course I was. People didn't do what we had done in the storeroom, or on my sofa for that matter, without being girlfriend and girlfriend, did they? I snorted as I realised that of course people fucking did. I wasn't living in the nineteen-twenties. It wasn't required, or even expected, that undying love be declared to the world before a little snogging session could occur.

Sophie was back to shading in her penis. Excuse the phrasing, but I was having a mental and nervous breakdown. I wanted to ask Soph was Diana my girlfriend. But seeing her intense scrutiny of her artistic attempt at pubic hair, I decided to suck it in and stop racing ahead without a definite finishing line. I knew I was flirtarded. I also knew I could make mountains out of molehills, but I was a skilful bluffer who could usually talk my way through most situations. Sometimes. With the help of the guru herself, Sophie Harrison. The same Sophie Harrison who was drawing flying lice around the scrotum in her drawing.

I was so absorbed in my own drama, I didn't even react to the feeling of my hairs lifting at the back of my head and the sensation of something slipping down my drawing board and hitting my hand. I saw a folded piece of paper with a smiley face on the front. A quick turn of my head revealed Diana's retreating figure. I unfolded the paper and found a very brief message written in her flowing script:

What are you doing on December 17/18/19? Fancy seeing Ophelia *at the* Tate?

I have to admit, the grin shooting across my face was gloriously painful, the muscles being stretched to the limit. Lifting my head, I was met by blue eyes looking at me intently from across the room. It might have been my imagination, but I thought she looked a little nervous. In what universe could she honestly think I would turn her down? And why did the sparkle begin to fade? Fuck. My brain seemed to kick start and I nodded enthusiastically, heaving a sigh of relief when I saw the light reappear in her eyes, followed by a grin that could have rivalled my own on the stupidity scale.

"Okay?" she mouthed. "You want to come?"

I nodded again and held up the paper, wanting nothing more than to run up her and give her a kiss of confirmation.

"Good."

Her wink made my heart pitter patter even faster.

"My pubic lice are wrong." Sophie mumbled from next to me. "They look like wasps."

Ignored her, I returned Diana's wink, holding eye contact until someone called for Diana's attention.

"Jess? I said my lice look like wasps."

I knew she was staring at the side of my head with an expression of faux sadness, but I didn't look at her. Picking up my pencil, I tipped my head towards her pad before uttering, "Maybe you shouldn't put the stripes in. Colour in the bodies instead."

A few seconds passed before I heard her, "Oh yeah, cheers."

God, I loved Sophie. A quick look over at Diana, who at that moment lifted her head from a student's work and graced me with one of her wonderful smiles, made another thought flash through my mind. Heaven help me, I was beginning to think the L word was creeping not too softly into describing the feelings I had for Diana Sullivan. The worrying thing was, I didn't even know if I was still her girlfriend or not.

Back to the drawing board. Literally and metaphorically.

Chapter 13

You would think that Diana and I would have gone back to her place or my place to continue what we had started in the storeroom, wouldn't you. We didn't. It wasn't as if I didn't want to, or she didn't want to, but we had agreed to take things slowly. Kissing *could* be just kissing. We didn't have to have full blown sex just because we got a little overheated. Did we?

I lie. I lie I lie I lie I lie.

I wanted nothing more than to have hot, passionate, earth-shattering sex with Diana, but it had been my idea to take things slowly. I knew I couldn't kiss Diana and not want to go further. Call me weak willed, spineless, chicken shit, anything you want to, but I freely admit it. When it came to Diana Sullivan, I had no self-restraint. We could just hop into bed and do the deed, make the beast with two backs, plump the hairy pears, but somewhere in the vacuous self-sacrificing neurotic brain of mine, I had a wish for something more. I wanted our first time to be special, wanted this relationship to be something more than sex.

After class, I told Diana I had to get home and do some

work that had to be finished. Stupid, I know. I just wanted to go home and take stock of what was happening with me, with us. Sit and ponder the miracle of the universe and everything that was the dark haired, blue eyed woman who I hoped beyond hope thought of me as her girlfriend. I knew she was disappointed, knew she wondered why I was blowing hot and cold, but I did have some serious thinking to do. To be honest, I wasn't too sure what the serious thinking would entail, but I had decided that I would at least have a crack at it.

Sprawling out on the sofa, the room lit only by a lamp, I stared at the ceiling for far too long. Images of Diana came easily, mainly because my head was so full of her, so full of her smile, those lips, the strong jaw, the high cheekbones, the way she tilted her head when she laughed, the smell of her... God, the smell of her. And the feel of her skin under my unworthy fingertips, the softness of her breasts. The way my mouth seemed to come alive when it closed upon a taut nipple. I tried to conjure the darkness of the skin surrounding the nipple—the picture making my mouth water to taste it again. A sigh, long and hard and definitely rising from exasperation. Why was it that I had decided to take things slow and steady? Given the sensation whirling around in me, the lower half of my body was not at all happy about my decision, and was demanding why it had not been asked its opinion before I had gone all virginal. It wasn't as if I hadn't ever slept with a woman on a first date. So, why not now? What made me turn holier than thou and believe I could re-experience the first time another person touched me intimately?

But this wasn't like the other times. This wasn't just another person. This was someone I held feelings for, feelings that I was a little bit worried about airing to anyone, especially myself. If I did, and then she didn't feel the same way, where would that leave me? Devastated, most probably.

And then it struck me: If I was too afraid to admit my feelings, wouldn't I feel just as devastated by not knowing she didn't care for me as by not knowing at all?

"Ohhh—ohhhh—your text is on fi-re!!!!" Trust my phone to interrupt my serious thinking.

I honestly believed I had reached an important part... or maybe an impasse. I plucked my mobile off the table. I don't know why I was surprised to see the message was from Diana.

"U ok? U smd quiet 2nite. Wnt 2 tlk?"

After working out the bloody message, I pondered for at least five seconds before clicking the call button. One ring later, I heard Diana breathing out a hello.

"Hey."

Now that it came down to it, what did I want to talk about? I doubted that my insecurities would be a good topic of conversation, especially not those feelings that were building up inside me. "Of course I want to talk to you. I always want to talk to you."

I heard her sigh and could imagine her expression, could imagine the tilt of her head as she cupped the phone next to her ear.

"Sorry about the message. I erm...well..." A delightful laugh of embarrassment left her mouth. "I just wanted to make sure you were okay after...erm...what we did in the...storeroom."

I pulled the phone away from my ear and stared at the block of technology in amazement. I hadn't thought of that. "No! I mean yes! You know what I mean!"

Diana laughed again.

"I loved what we did in the storeroom, you know that. I just..." had to come home and have a ponder about my virginity "...had to finalise some reports for work tomorrow."

"Good."

"Good?"

"Yes. Good. I like it when my woman works hard and brings home the bacon."

My woman? Insert huge fuck-off grin about now. Is "woman" one level above girlfriend?

"Oh, you do, do you?" For once my attempt to sound sultry actually succeeded, but not as well as when she replied with a simple yes. It is amazing how all the moisture in your mouth can suddenly emigrate to other, needier regions with one uttered word. Not that I minded. Not that I minded in the slightest.

"So, what do you want to talk about?" You? Me? Us? Our future? How I can't seem to get through one day without thinking about you? How, since meeting you, I have devolved into a love struck, teenage boy?

"How about our trip?"

And we did. We talked and talked and talked about art, about the Tate, about our plans for the future. It was over an hour later that I made the usual noises of someone who is about to end a conversation.

"Before you go, Jess, I just want to say something."

The blood stopped in my veins, figuratively, as of course I know that only happens when one is dead—if it does even then. Once again, my mind was digressing. And stressing over the apparent hesitation in her voice, if the pain in my chest was any indication.

"I know we've only known each other for a few weeks, and we said we'd take things slowly."

I grunted. Couldn't do anything else, really.

"Well, I..."

I sat up for this part. Had to.

"Really like you."

"And I really like you." Really really like you, to be painfully honest.

"But... How can I say this?"

I was standing now. Wouldn't you be, if you were just about to be told that the woman you were falling for wasn't falling for you as hard as you wanted her to? Yes, Diana had hinted that she might fall for me, but she hadn't said for definite. What if she was going to say this wasn't the be-all and end-all for her? Why I thought that last bit, I didn't know.

"My relationship with Lauren was difficult."

She wasn't ready to date again, that had to be it. She was trying to let me down gently. I couldn't stand still; I began to pace.

"And, to be honest, I was hurt pretty badly by what she did."

At that moment I hated Lauren even more. "I know, honey."

"But I didn't love her."

Huh? Why would she say that?

"The only hurting she did was physical and to my pride."

I understood that Lauren was a bitch and that Diana might be in the stage of licking her wounds, but I didn't really comprehend what she was trying to tell me. I even stopped pacing in hopes my brain would harness the excess energy.

"You understand?"

"Erm, I think so." Why couldn't I just say no, say I was completely confused and needed clarification?

"Good."

"Okay."

Diana paused before asking, "You want to add anything?"

Something like, I don't understand what you are saying? Am I officially your girlfriend? Or even the best one...could you ever love me? There. The L word in the open. Therefore, when my response wasn't as good as it could've been, it should be blamed on the mental duress of thinking about the ultimate four letter word.

"Nope. I think we've covered it all for now." I have to admit, I did hear an element of disappointment in her voice when she muttered a weak "okay."

It wasn't until I was climbing into bed that something struck me. Was Diana telling me she felt more for me than she had for Lauren? It was reviewing the way she had said, "You understand?" that set off bells in my head. It was just a pity the bells were retarded and had not sounded the alarm an hour earlier.

"Shit!" I climbed out of bed and searched for my phone. "Shit, bollocks, fuck, and wank."

Should I call Diana and tell her I hadn't understood at all, and could she please explain what she had been trying to tell me? Or should I grow a spine and make the first move?

Click. New message.

I wud lke 2 add tht I thnk u r de mst btfl wmn n de wrld x

Send. Then a flash of foresight. How could I send her

that without using real words?

Click. New Message.

I would like to add that I think you are the most beautiful woman in the world x You deserve this message to be written in full and not in text speak x

Send.

A smile slipped onto my face, and I hoped beyond hope she was telling me what I wanted her to be saying—that she felt the same as I did. That the "liking" part was more than like, that the reason she had said she had never loved Lauren was because she might be falling for me as hard as I was falling for her.

"Ohhh—ohhhh—your text is on fi-re!!!!"

My hand was shaking as I clicked to open the message. Dancing about on my screen was an emoticon doing a jig and grinning widely. Then the sound of another message came through.

"No. You are the most beautiful woman in the world. No take backs. And I will always give you everything I have in full. I promise. Good night, my Jess. X"

My Jess. Those two words seemed to sneak behind me and take my knees out from under me, and my body sank onto the bed before I even realised it. *My* Jess. Hers. I was hers, and she was *so* mine. Mine. She was mine.

I wasn't aware of the lone tear tracking down my face until it plopped onto my thigh. Why do people cry when they are really happy? Simple. If they didn't, they would explode or implode—either way it would be messy. I wanted to reply to her text, but I couldn't see the buttons.

I don't think I could've typed the response anyway; my hands were shaking too hard. I had never felt so deeply about anyone in my whole life, never wanted someone so much, never needed to hear she felt the same way I did. It was scary, gloriously scary, to feel so much so soon, but I knew I'd never find this feeling with anyone else, ever. She had to be the one. My one. My woman. My Diana.

I also knew, beyond a shadow of a doubt, that I was in love with her, totally and utterly and completely in love with Diana Sullivan. Was that what falling for someone actually is—falling in love? Up until that moment, I had thought that love just meant a strong attraction, a crush. Amazing how I had lived for thirty-one years and didn't even know the rubric of love.

I flumped back onto the bed and looked at the dancing emoticon. The way I was grinning stupidly, it could've almost been my reflection there on the screen. Although I didn't know for positive how Diana felt, this was not the time to worry about that. Tonight I wanted to go to sleep with the idea that she felt the same way I did, and we had the rest of our lives to tell each other so.

It wasn't every day that someone fell in love. Especially me. I'd never been in love in my life. I'd felt an intense attraction to the odd woman before, but to be in love? Nope. Never.

Fuck. I was in love. I. Was. In. Love.

The abrupt move from prostrate to standing shot pains down my back and legs, but that wasn't why I shouted "Shit Shit Shit!" into the air. I was in love. With Diana. With someone who had not even officially said I was her girlfriend. This was not good, not good at all.

My phone was still in my hand, and I clicked on the second message. "My Jess." But not "I love you, Jess." Not

"I want to be with you for the rest of my life, Jess." I threw the phone onto the bed, covered my eyes, and pressed my face against my palms. They felt cold on my overheated skin, and also wet. The single tear that had appeared when I first read the message had been joined by an army of its friends.

Was this still happiness? And where did the "I wanted to go to sleep with the idea that she felt the same way as I did" go to? No one had ever told me that falling in love would make me paranoid, scared, apprehensive, and a myriad of other adjectives that seemed to point out that falling in love was a fucking disaster.

At least Diana liked me.

The first sob fell into my hands, followed by another and another and another. Yeah. At least she liked me.

Chapter 14

Thursday came around slowly, maybe because I had spent most of the night trying to force images of Diana out of my head. Whether the thoughts are good or bad, something like that will annihilate any chance of a good night's sleep. However, when I say images of Diana, they weren't the glorious ones where we were up close and personal, or with her admitting her undying love for me. They were more of the type where I spilled my guts, and she either laughed or gave a sad shake of her head and told me she didn't feel that way about me.

Come to think of it, why on earth would Diana love me? I was insecure, clumsy, spineless, and I couldn't seem to say what I wanted to say. She was absolutely gorgeous, talented, funny, witty, intelligent, and had a body to die for. I was just me—boring, thirty-one, and single. Living my life day to day in a rut of routine, and the first time I had moved totally out of my comfort zone was when I found Diana. Diana Sullivan. The most beautiful woman in the world.

Did I mention insecure?

It had just gone one o'clock when my office door opened and a very familiar head poked through.

"You had lunch yet, git face?"

I don't know who was the most surprised—Sophie or me—when I shot off the chair, raced over to her, flung my arms around her neck and began sobbing.

Initially, she froze, then she wrapped her arms around me and covered me in a safety blanket. Minutes passed, and she didn't push me to tell her what had happened; she just allowed me to gather myself up and regain some measure of composure before leading me back to my desk and sitting me down.

Kneeling in front of me, Sophie grabbed my hands and pulled them to her chest, held them there a moment before moving them up to her mouth. Her lips brushed over my knuckles. Still, she didn't say a word.

I was calming down, and along with the composure came the hiccoughing that comes with crying hard. I wanted to tell Sophie what had happened, or what I believed would happen if my stupid heart got a chance to spill itself over into the real world. But the hiccoughing actually kept me from speaking.

Twenty past one. Twenty minutes had passed by with Soph on the floor and me harrumphing on the chair. Eventually I swallowed, tested my lips to see if they were numb, and gave the words life.

"I'm in love with Diana."

Sophie's grin spread like a bush fire, the heat palpable, before she realised I wasn't smiling.

"She doesn't love me."

Brown eyes widened in shock before slitting into anger. Her hands gripped mine harder, and I actually saw the wheels begin to turn inside Sophie's head.

"It's not her, it's me."

"Fuck that, Jess."

Standing sharply, Sophie turned her back to me. The stiffness of her shoulders told me she was livid. There was a quick flash of those brown eyes back in my direction, before she lifted her head higher and straightened her back. The last time I had seen her do that was when she had found out about Samantha James' infidelities, and it had taken a lot of fast talking on my part to stop her from knocking my ex's teeth down her throat.

"I hate liars."

Liars?

She turned sharply and crouched on the floor again. "Did she tell you this? Tell you she didn't love you?"

I was still shocked by her anger and could only shake my head slowly, erratically.

"Have you told her that you love her?" Her voice was softer now.

Once again, I shook my head.

"Jess? When did you know you love her?"

"Last night."

Sophie laughed. She laughed! Head back, hearty booms of laughter. Had she gone mad? More to the point, had I?

Eventually, after much chest heaving and aborted attempts to speak, she blurted, "You realised last night and are a fucking wreck because you're in love with a woman who hasn't said either way whether or not she loves you back? Correct?"

Put that way, I began to understand why Sophie laughed, not that I felt like laughing myself. I was too caught up in my very own pity party.

"You are a nugget."

"But—"

"Nugget."

Tightening my lips, I tried to give her a look, the one Diana could pull off so easily. "I don't even know if she's my girlfriend or not."

More laughter, punctuated by a thigh slap, and then Sophie was standing in front of me, her hand outstretched in invitation. "Come, nugget. Lunch. You're buying." As I grabbed her hand, she looked me squarely in the face. "I fancy chicken nuggets today. What about you?"

I had to laugh, shakily, but a laugh all the same.

Over lunch, Sophie put me in the picture about a few things, specifically the fact that Diana and I were girlfriend and girlfriend. In her words, it wasn't just what she had witnessed in the storeroom, but every touch, gesture, and look Diana and I shared screamed "couple."

I was appeased, somewhat, but I also decided to ask Diana if I was more than a fling, more than someone to help her get over Lauren Baker. And that would be a start— me actually voicing my thoughts to the person I *should* be sharing them with. Definitely a novelty.

After about thirty minutes of Sophie stroking my ego, things went a little quiet. Then it hit me. Why had Sophie just "popped" into my office on the chance I would be up for lunch? Great mate I am. I should put "self-absorbed" on my list of qualities. "How're you?"

Brown eyes lifted and met mine. The twinkle, that was almost her trademark was brighter than ever.

"How's Dave?"

God. I was sure I saw a flash as the light sparked from her eyes.

"He's in love."

My mouth moved to form the words "with whom?" but noting her expression, I didn't have to. Oddly enough,

I never knew I could squeal in as high a pitch as I did then. Squeal, lunge, and hug, actually. Sophie's body jerked against me, and I knew that when I eventually let her go I would see a huge grin and maybe a few tears. The happy kind.

I was right.

"Are you?" Almost rhetorical, but I had to ask.

"What do you think?"

My face hurt with the smile I gave her. If there was one person in this world I wanted to find true love, it was Sophie. She deserved the best, to be treated like a queen, to be loved and loved and loved by someone she loved in return. Dave was the one. He may have taken his time about it, but he did well in the end.

"Can I be your bridesmaid?"

The sip of tea she had taken shot out her nostrils. "Fuck sake, Jess, give us a chance." Using wadded napkins, we both made the job of cleaning up her mess. "And no, you can't be my bridesmaid."

I paused, wet paper in hand.

Sophie looked fleetingly serious before allowing the smile to surface. "Maid of Honour.

I squealed again, lunged, missed, and head butted her in the face.

"Jesus, Jess!" But she grabbed me into a hug and pulled me to her.

Thoughts of my own insecurities went to the wind as I embraced the moment. I had waited far too long for Sophie to get her heart's desire to dampen the mood with my own worries.

"Awww," I heard a woman's voice say from behind us. "Look, Helen. Isn't that adorable?"

"Love's young dream, eh?" answered the person who

must've been Helen.

Sophie and I froze before slowly pulling apart.

It wasn't that Sophie didn't want to be classified as a lezza, or that I was embarrassed by people thinking we were a couple, but come on. Someone thinking me and Sophie were at it? That was too fucking weird even for me.

Chapter 15

Friday night saw me pulling up outside Diana's house to pick her up. I had spoken to her on the phone the previous day, and she'd dropped the bombshell about me meeting her parents. Thankfully, I wouldn't be the only one under scrutiny. We had arranged to meet Sophie, Dave, and Monica at the restaurant, which, I was later to find out, equated to seeking safety in numbers. Initially I had been surprised by the plan to meet Diana's parents, and I wondered why they'd never been mentioned before, considering Monica was such an influence in Dave's and Diana's lives. Weird that in all the time we had known each other, neither brother nor sister had indicated whether their parents were still alive, serial killers doing a stretch, or even more boringly, lived in the area. As it turned out, the latter was the reason I hadn't met them before. They didn't live in the area. They lived near Chester and rarely came to visit. It wasn't until I actually met them that I realised that even if they had lived next door to either one of their children, it would still have been a while before I would have been introduced.

Diana was quiet on the way to the restaurant, and it wasn't until we pulled up outside that she turned to me, her blue eyes looking unusually dark. "I will apologise beforehand for what you are about to endure."

I cocked my head in question.

"My parents are not really the nurturing or friendly type."

A little late for me to do a runner. In truth, I didn't really care if they were Fred and Rose West; at least I was going to spend the night in Diana's company—girlfriend or not.

I should drop that topic. I'm getting on my own tits now.

The first thing I noticed about Mr and Mrs Sullivan was that they were snobs. The second...they ignored my outstretched hand. The third...they ignored Sophie's hand. Soph and I did the raised eyebrow thing and she mouthed, "Hark at me and my working class roots."

Another notable thing was the relationship between parents and children. If I said cold and loveless, I would be buffing it up from what it actually was. A nothing. No familial greeting other than a "My dear, you look drawn," followed by an air kiss. What amazed me even more was how different Diana and Dave were from their parents. It was as if they had tagged onto Mr and Mrs Sullivan as we entered the restaurant, and the folks thought we were wait staff. It didn't take long to work out that the only reason they had come to Manchester was because they had tickets for a performance at the Opera House. Having dinner with their children was just a side order they could shove around with a disinterested fork.

I was seated at the very end of the table, and that gave me the opportunity to watch the interaction between parents and children. Now, I don't think of my relationship with my parents as anything different from other children's relationships—apart from my dad's addiction to catching the cat from next door—but I would classify mine as being normal. This was as far removed from normal as abnormal could get. Conversation was stunted. It revolved around social climbing and business—both things none of the younger Sullivans had the slightest bit of interest in. Except for a striking resemblance between the family members, no one would have ever thought they were related.

Over the course of the evening, another thing became apparent. Monica was the "mother" in this "family." She was the one who made Sophie and me comfortable, the one who asked Dave and Diana how their days had gone, the one who told Dave to eat all his veggies. Mummy and Daddy were more interested in the wine menu and pontificating shite. I would be lying if I didn't say I was a little put out at first, but after about five minutes, I was more than happy they were ignoring me. They didn't even ask Monica if she was fully recovered from her attack. It was as if it had never happened. Not that I was privy to their conversations to date, but I definitely got the impression that they didn't give a shit.

Throughout dinner Diana's hand frequently rested on my leg, giving it a pat or a stroke. I know she did it to reassure me, but the feelings jangling through my body had nothing at all to do with being reassured, more like being expectant. Very expectant. Every time she touched me, I turned to look at her; and every time I looked at her, she gave me one of those dazzling smiles I was beginning to think she saved just for me.

It was when dessert was being served that things changed. Derek Sullivan apparently made a conscious decision that he should direct his discourse to something other than how much money he earned a year, what changes were happening in his club, and his take on the world at large.

"Diana, you seem to have forgotten to introduce us to your little friend."

Was I being transported back through time to Primary School? I shot a quick look at Sophie. Nope. She had all her teeth, and was definitely a lot taller than twenty-five years ago.

"Is she a colleague?"

Diana's body stiffened. "You know full well, Father, that Jess is not a colleague."

"Jess?"

Just the way he said my name made the hairs on my neck stand to attention, like they do in all horror stories.

"Jess? I thought this was Lauren."

More prickling of hairs, more wishing I was in a horror story so I could chop off the evil monster's head with an axe and glory in the gushing of its blood.

"So why did you ask if she was a colleague, then?" Diana's eyes locked onto her father's daring him to continue. He didn't get the hint.

"I was hoping that you had grown out of that deplorable behaviour by now."

What deplorable behaviour? Contradiction?

"It is about time you stopped all this...this..." he waved his hand in my general direction, "*abnormal* behaviour and settled down."

I heard Diana's teeth click together and a definite grinding began. "I am not abnormal. I am a lesbian."

I was amazed that she could get the words through her clenched teeth.

Mother Dearest put in her tuppence worth. "Diana!

How dare you say that disgusting word in public! Have respect for your father."

Sophie had had enough. "Respect? You two talk about respect?" She snorted her disbelief. "You two have no idea how lucky you are to have such wonderful—"

"And who are you?" Judith Sullivan's eyes dragged themselves over Sophie as if it was beneath her to mix with the lower classes.

Sophie stood, holding her wineglass as if she was going to lob the contents over someone. "Look, lady, don't cut me off when I'm talking. Got it?"

Aw fuck. Sophie was well and truly pissed off.

"Soph, sit, love. I'll handle this."

"Dave, keep out of this. It's between me and the white witch."

Aw shit again. Monica started laughing and a part of me wanted to join her, but my laughter would have been because I was becoming hysterical.

"No. I will do this." Dave stood and placed his arm protectively around Sophie, and stared, first at his mother, then his father. "No more. No more telling me, or Diana, who we can and cannot see."

Derek threw his napkin onto the table and shifted as if to stand.

"I'm in love with Sophie, and she loves me back." He turned and gave her a smile, a nod, and a quick lift of his eyebrows. "We're going to get married."

Monica stopped laughing, Diana stopped clenching her teeth, and I stopped the hysterics dead in their tracks. Big Daddy and Mummy Bear froze...but more to the point, Sophie sat down. Sat down with her mouth open and stared at the table top. Even I—and as everyone knows, I'm an idiot—could tell this was the first Sophie had heard about marriage.

Completely unaware that he had blown Sophie away with his declaration, Dave continued, "As for Diana, she's gay. Get over it."

Derek leaned forward, his face hard. "No daughter of mine is gay. This…" he waved his hand over me as if he could make me disappear, "…is a phase."

"Jess is my girlfriend."

I would like to say that at that point my facial expression became smug, but honesty makes me go with relieved.

"And I can guarantee she is definitely *not* a phase."

I felt an ache in my chest so sharp, I had to suck in a breath.

"Will you keep your voice down? People will hear."

Judith Sullivan was not only a homophobe like her husband, but she was more concerned with social acceptance than the love and happiness of her daughter.

"Really?"

God. Diana sounded so fucking sexy when she used that tone of voice. I know it wasn't the ideal time and place for that observation, but God…

"Jess, baby."

I just about swooned.

"We're leaving." Diana stood and held out her hand and I took it willingly, smiling up at her.

"You have brought shame on our family, Diana. What you are doing is disgusting."

It was as if there was not another sound in the restaurant, as if all the other diners had stopped eating and talking. To be honest, I would have, too, if I had been at another table. However, I was holding hands with the woman I loved in front of her mother and father, and not expecting to get their blessing any time soon.

"Judith." Monica's voice sliced through the silence. Blue eyes, so like and unlike Diana's, flicked to her sister with a look of utter contempt. "I think you mean what *you* are doing is disgusting."

"This has nothing to do with you, Monica. Diana is my daughter, not yours."

"You certainly don't act like her mother." Throwing her napkin on the table, as most of the people at our table had done at least once in the short span of time we had been there, Monica stood. "Come on, kiddies. I've got a Pavlova at home with our names on it."

The five of us stood.

I knew it was hard for Dave and Diana to move away from their parents after what had transpired, as no one wants to leave a situation still bubbling, even if their relationship was not the best to start with.

"How dare you leave your mother!" Derek was on his feet, trying to block our way. "I demand you apologise at once!"

"Oh, shut up, Derek, or you'll ruin your reputation as a cold hearted bastard. You've never stuck up for your wife before."

To hear those words come from Monica's mouth was what Sophie and I would call "absolute class." In other words, something we would consider a perfect put down.

"As for you, Judith, you're the one who has brought shame on our family." She leaned over to her sister. "You seem to forget, I remember you when you didn't have two ha'pennies to rub together and didn't walk around with a stick up your backside." Judith opened her mouth to speak, but Monica held her hand up. "And I remember Carol."

Judith blanched at the mere mention of the name.

"I am proud to be related to Dave and Diana. Gay,

straight, whatever—I love them as if they were my own."

I couldn't swear she did it on purpose, but when Monica turned to leave, her backside hit the table. And hitting the table made the glass of scarlet wine wobble dangerously. And I did know for definite that the second bump was done on purpose, knocking the glass onto its side and spilling the contents over Judith's previously immaculate tailored dress.

Monica's voice rose above the scream emitting from injured party at the end of the table. "I think it's time to go, don't you?"

Outside the restaurant, the laughter started. I think it was mainly a release of nervous tension, but it felt good. With tears running down her face, Diana spluttered, "Well, I think that went better than expected." More laughter. When she could speak again, Diana turned to Monica. "Who's Carol?"

Monica slipped her arm through her niece's and pulled her along. "My secret weapon."

Intrigued? Nah. Even I understood that Carol was someone that Judith wanted to forget, and to bring up her name when we were talking about her daughter's sexuality... It didn't take a rocket scientist to work it out.

"Jess? Come here." Monica slipped her free arm through mine, and we walked to the car park arm in arm.

It wasn't until I got to my car that I remembered what Dave had said about him and Sophie. Was his declaration of marriage a spur of the moment something to piss off his parents? God, I hoped not. Not with the way I knew Sophie felt about him.

The car park was dark, but I could make them out. Their foreheads were touching, and the silhouette showed two people obviously in love. If their body language was any indication, I wouldn't have to wait very long to be Maid of Honour.

And to make the night even more perfect, Diana Sullivan was my girlfriend. She said so. In front of everyone, too.

Now that was an evening to write home about. Decidedly a better-the-longer-it-went-on kind of evening. The best bit was—it was still early. It made me wonder what else the night would hold. It wasn't what I thought it would be.

Diana didn't say a word all the way home. Even though I knew she was fuming, she was still gentle as she absently stroked my thigh. Pulling up outside her house, I left the engine running. Something about the way she was staring out of the side window gave me the impression that she didn't feel up to continuing the evening after all. We had already turned down Monica's Pavlova, and I was beginning to think that was not the only sweet thing that would be off the menu that evening.

A few minutes ticked by without her even realising the car had stopped. The air was thick with unspoken words, but oddly enough I didn't feel uncomfortable.

"Do you think it is wrong?" Diana's voice was hushed, as if the words were sacred, painful, or sinful.

Eyebrows scrunched, I gave the side of her face a confused look.

When she turned and looked straight into my eyes, she seemed lost, and I had the urge to pull her close and comfort her, even though I didn't know what she was talking about.

Diana seemed to read my confusion. "This. Us. Being abnormal."

Fuck. There was one thing I thought I knew beyond the shadow of a doubt about Diana, and that was her comfort with her sexuality. Never before had she mentioned that she thought being a lesbian was wrong, but then again, I had never seen her after her parents had Rottweilered her. I'd been so lucky in my life—my parents loved me, gay or not.

I gently cupped her cheek, my thumb touching cool skin. "There is nothing... NOTHING...wrong with being you. Being us. Please don't ever think we are wrong. Some people don't understand that lo...erm..." Shit "Relationships come in all shapes and sizes. Just because it isn't as common as a man being with a woman, it doesn't mean it is abnormal." My thumb brushed her lips slowly, softly, in hopes that would comfort her, as I was more than definite my shite speech hadn't come anywhere close.

A sigh left her mouth and trickled over my fingers. "Sorry, Jess." She grabbed my hand and kissed it, shooting sparks up my arm and through my body. "Sometimes I get a little self-conscious. It doesn't help when my parents believe I'm the spawn of Satan."

I wanted to say that if the way her parents had behaved was any indication, in theory she *was* the spawn of Satan, but I was too busy relishing the feel of her fingers stroking my hand. She sighed again, then smiled, the first smile I had seen since leaving the car park.

"You're so right, Jess."

Huh? Me? Actually right?

Diana leaned forward and captured my mouth with hers, giving me a searing kiss, her lips opening and sucking in my bottom lip. God. My spine lost its ability to keep me upright. However, as quickly as it began, the kiss stopped and Diana pulled back, a grin firmly in place. Her voice was husky as she whispered, "There is nothing common about being with you, Jess Taylor." Another kiss, this time more chaste. "So, are you up for a nightcap?"

Amazing how quickly her mood had changed from forlorn and dejected to sounding quite upbeat.

"Sure. Sounds like a plan."

A short while later, we were flopped on her sofa nursing a coffee. Although I wanted to continue the kissing we had started in the car, the greater, nobler, and nosy part of me wanted to delve into her thoughts about being gay. Her parents had given her a hard time, but she had shut them down, stuck up for us, called me her girlfriend, and made sure they knew that being gay wasn't a phase. However, judging by her solemn mood in the car, her even voicing the shite that people come up with about being gay being wrong, had me concerned.

"You okay?"

"Y-es. Erm... Sure, why?"

"You seemed a little out of it just then." Diana placed her cup on the table, grabbed mine and set it there too. "I think I know what is bothering you." I started to respond, but she shushed me. "You think I'm ashamed of being gay, don't you?"

I didn't answer.

"Thought so." She sucked in a breath and then allowed it to seep slowly from her mouth. "I think I need to explain."

If she was going to say she was ashamed of being a lesbian, being like me, then I would rather she keep it to herself. Instead of sharing that bit of information, I nodded. What was the point of delaying the inevitable?

"My parents, as you're now aware, don't agree with my lifestyle, don't agree with who and what I am. I have been subjected to their views for nearly fifteen years." She reached out and took my hand. "When you're constantly told your way of life is the wrong way, an aberration, it kind of knocks you off kilter now and again."

I didn't know how I should feel. Was she ashamed, even if only on occasion? And if she was, how would I deal with being hidden?

"I'm proud of who I am, Jess. I just thought, well, maybe you might not be."

What the fuck? "What the... No way!"

My outburst made her giggle before blue eyes met mine once again, the serious look back in place. "I just, well, you didn't comment or confirm when I told my parents you were my girlfriend. I wondered if you hadn't thought we were, or..."

Oh. My. God. In all my stupid churning over events and scenarios, I'd never given a thought to whether Diana doubted that I wanted her to be my girlfriend. Told you I was self-absorbed.

Pulling her to me, her face inches away from mine, I whispered, "I've been waiting for you to claim me for so long, Diana." I kissed the tip of her nose. "I know I shouldn't have waited for you to make the first move, but I didn't want to freak you out." That, and I was a chicken shit.

Instead of her grinning and understanding, she just looked confused. "But I did."

"I know you did. I was there. Parents, arguing, exclamation."

Diana pulled back slightly so she could scrutinise my face. "Not then. The text message. I know it wasn't the best way to express it, but I thought it would give you an out if you didn't feel the same way."

Text message? She hadn't asked me to be her girlfriend in a text... "My Jess." Fuck. And I hadn't replied, either, because I was doing a happy dance before realising I was in love with the woman who was staring at me with a look of utter confusion. Fleeting images of me crying myself into a fitful sleep crept in. What a waste. If only I had called her and said something back. Sophie always told me off for not being able to share my thoughts and feelings with those that mattered. Considering I worked alongside countless people, managing complaints and orders, I was completely shit at communication. "Shit."

"Not really what I was going for, but at least you've stopped staring at my forehead as if it is growing horns," Diana said.

"I'm so sorry, honey." The endearment elicited a brief smile, and I felt a little embarrassed. I wasn't the kind of woman to call another my other half, sweetheart, love, darling, or the classic, baby. But this felt different. Maybe because it was. "So, am I your Jess?"

Without pause, she answered. "Do you want to be?"

Instead of answering, I launched myself at her, my arms grabbing hold and pulling her hard against me. My lips found hers and tried to show her how I was feeling. Lips pressed lips, teeth clashed, tongues claimed. I was above her, her body stretched beneath mine. The feeling of her hard, yet deliciously soft body, met my own. I separated her thighs with my knee and slipped one leg between hers.

Pushing against the vee of her thighs, I actually felt her groan seep into my mouth. It was addictive, utterly addictive. I wanted to hear it again. I pushed. God. The way that sound felt as it travelled through my mouth, down my throat, and into my body... I was lightheaded, but I felt alive, felt that I needed more. My hand was at the base of her shirt, my fingers playing with the hem. Her hips came up to meet mine and it was my turn to gasp, her thigh hitting the need that was flooding throughout me.

Without further deliberation, my fingers slipped beneath her top and touched hot, smooth skin. They trailed up the side of her waist, luxuriating in the curve of her before slipping behind her and pulling her closer still. Her hands were gripping my backside, fingertips digging, pushing forward to press me against her even harder. A rhythm was building between us, me thrusting against her, my thigh chafing, her thigh hard against me. Sensations were rippling, climbing, and I was lost in her.

Her mouth left mine to kiss my cheeks, my eyes, my nose, then down to my throat. The heat of her mouth pulsated on the join of my shoulder and my neck, and I bucked against her even harder. I leaned back to give her better access, my hand leaving her back to slip around the front, and I spread my fingers over her skin as if I was assessing her like a fine piece of art, except instead of feeling cold, hard marble beneath my fingertips, the skin was hot and silken. Her teeth nipped, and then her tongue licked my throat.

I didn't remember her hands moving inside my top; didn't remember lifting my arms to allow her to remove it—all I remembered was the sensation of cool air swirling around me before the heat of her hands on my skin. I was straddling her now, my bra the only barrier between her hands and my breasts. She cupped them, my aching nipples hard against the palms of her hands. A thumb flicked over the sensitive peak, making it move sideways before appearing erect through the silk of my bra. Long arms snaked around my back. A quick flick, and I felt the confines of the material loosen. Diana's expression was sultry, sexy, primitive. Wetness pooled between my legs in anticipation.

Slip. Slip. Gone. The bra was tossed to the floor, and I waited for her next move. Her eyes glistened in the lamp light as her fingers traced the curve of my breasts. I felt revered and desired at the same time. Her eyes followed the movement of the soft fingertips. Her mouth opened, and she moistened those glorious lips. It was as if she had read my mind as to what I wanted her to do, because she raised up, her breath hitting my skin, making my nipples pucker and tighten, before she enveloped the nub in that hot, wet mouth.

"God!" My eyes drifted closed, almost as if I couldn't keep them open and still fully experience the sensations surging throughout my body. I jerked against her, seeking more contact. Slow, deliberate suckles, licks, flicks, her teeth grazing along the tip of my nipple. Her free hand left its perch on my hip and trailed along the underside of the other breast. Sparks sizzled through me.

"Look at me, Jess."

That voice. It trembled within me. Diana's voice had been the first thing that attracted me to her, and now that same voice was talking directly to me.

My eyelids fluttered open, a simple act that was more difficult than I would ever have thought. However, once I saw the vision underneath me, my eyes effortlessly opened wide. Diana's dark hair was swept back over her shoulders, framing a delectable throat. Her face was flushed with arousal, blue eyes almost violet with desire, pupils dilated to almost fill the colour. Moist lips, the lips that had recently been loving my breast. We were undulating against each other, so close, but not close enough. I longed to feel her skin next to mine, her breasts against me, the length of her underneath me—naked, hot, wanting.

I traced the buttons to her blouse, up and down, down and up, until the temptation to pop them open became too strong to resist. One, two—a glimpse of the curve of her breasts. Three, four her bra was fully exposed, and so was my longing. I wanted to taste her, bury my face between those perfect breasts and drown in the feel and scent of her. Sliding the straps from her shoulders, I dipped my head and brushed my lips over her skin. I felt her trembling; the shiver of it exciting me beyond what I had ever experienced before. This was the skin that I loved. The smell that I loved. The woman that I loved.

But I couldn't tell her that. Couldn't whisper it into her ear and let it trickle through her body. Couldn't divulge my inner longing to be loved by her in return. It was too soon, too soon for both of us, although I knew as surely as I knew anything in my whole life, I was in love with Diana.

Warm hands cupped my face and tilted it up to hers. Unspoken words lay in her eyes. Her lips moving slightly, but it seemed she was having difficulty voicing her thoughts. We had gone too far this time to stop. This would not be a fumble on a sofa, a session in the storeroom. If I couldn't tell her I loved her, I could show her.

Licking my lips, I saw that she was fascinated with the movement of my tongue. "I want to…" make love with you "…move this upstairs."

Her thumb began to caress the side of my face, and her touch radiated through all of me. Without waiting for her to answer, I drew back and stood up by the side of the sofa, immediately missing the contact with her. I offered her my hand, smiling when she clasped it and allowed me to pull her to her feet and up against me. I had to tilt my head to look into her face, such a beautiful face. Our bodies were slick against one another, the top half allowing more contact, but not nearly enough. I wanted her closer. All of her closer.

Diana rested her forehead against mine, a sigh escaping before she tipped her face to meet my intent gaze. "I'd love to. Come."

Her hand holding mine, she led me to the stairs. It seemed like time had stopped and we were the only people moving in the whole world. It was deliciously surreal. Although the anticipation was growing inside me, I was having thoughts of not being good enough, not being able to satisfy the woman who was taking me to her bed, the place I had wanted to be for so long. Even though I was terrified, I was also exultant. This was me and her. Us. Her and me taking the next step in a relationship I wanted so much.

Click. A lamp gave the room a sensuous glow, and I saw Diana's bedroom for the first time, not that I was interested in interior design at that moment. My focus was definitely riveted on the woman standing beside the bed. She looked magnificent, the light behind her accentuating her curves, allowing the true beauty of the woman to stand out as she waited for me to move from the doorway and take what I was being offered.

I wanted to take it all in, etch it all into memory as the most perfect moment in my life. And with each step I took toward her, I fell deeper in love with Diana. Part of me was bloody scared of feeling the way I did. I was digging myself ever deeper into a situation which I knew could end so badly. I knew that even if our relationship stopped now, my heart would be forever lost to her. When at last I was standing in front of Diana, I trailed my fingers up her belly, up the curve of her muscle, watching in fascination as it rippled under my touch. I moved along the underside of her breasts, along the silk of the bra, across the bump of a very interested nipple. I wanted to taste it, as I had done two days before.

I slipped my arms around her, found the clasp of her bra and undid it. A second later, I pulled her into my arms, and the feel of her breasts against mine for the first time was almost my undoing. There is something so sexual about a woman's breasts, something so delicious. The way they mould against a hand, the way they pillow and excite. I lifted my face and received a kiss so deep... I wanted to stay like that forever. It was as if my whole soul was coming alive in that instant.

I pressed her backwards until I felt the backs of her legs touch the bed. We lowered ourselves to the bed, and I spread myself over her like a blanket. The kiss was hot, all-consuming, but I wanted more. Her hands were holding me close, gripping my shoulder blades as if to keep me from leaving her. I had to have more. I wanted to unwrap her like a present, wanted to feel her skin slip against my skin, wanted to luxuriate in the scent of her, deliberate over which part I should touch, kiss, honour.

Diana seemed to recognise what I needed; maybe she felt the same way I did. God, I hoped she did. Hoped beyond hope that Diana Sullivan wanted me as much as I wanted her.

"Here." She pushed me back slightly, and her fingers slipped to the waist of my trousers.

I felt every movement as she popped the button, drew my zipper down and eased the cotton over my hip and down my thighs, leaving me in only my panties. Then they were gone. Instead of feeling exposed, I felt cherished.

Hungry eyes feasted on my body, and I could feel tingles appear wherever she gazed, almost as if she was touching me with her eyes.

I shifted closer to her and slid her trousers down muscled legs, her panties getting caught up in the movement. Moments later, we were both sitting on the bed, completely naked in front of each other for the first time. My eyes were ravenous. Only by absorbing the whole of her could I satiate their hunger.

Now that we were naked, her eyes moved over my body, making me feel revered. When she lifted a shaking hand, almost as if she was too scared to touch me, I grabbed it and placed it on my breast. Blue eyes disappeared briefly behind closing eyelids as a moan escaped her mouth. Want surged inside me, and I knew if she put a hand between my legs, she would know how much I wanted her.

Diana leaned forward, her lips seeking mine. Slow, deliberate kisses—gentle, yet forceful, then they moved, and she sucked the pulse point on my neck. Leaning back, I gave her more access. Her hand slipped around my waist and pulled me closer. My fingers slid into her hair and tangled in the silky strands. Her mouth moved lower and kissed along my collarbone. I could feel my hips moving, trying to find something to press my need against. I was so turned on, so ready, so focused on making love to this woman. With every kiss, I had to bite back the urge to tell Diana I loved her. It was agony holding back the words. The only time in my life I had ever wanted to say them, had ever been on the precipice of uttering them, and I couldn't.

I pressed Diana away from me, then stopped her from retreating by moving over her, my body lying flat against hers for a coveted moment of connection. We merged together, each moaning into the air. It seemed as if we clicked, like a puzzle missing its other half for centuries being reunited in this room, on this evening, in this lifetime.

Breaths were ragged, erratic. Noises of pleasure danced from mouths onto skin, inside my heart, my soul. I moved down Diana's body, my lips worshipping each and every part of her. Her skin was soft, taut, delicious, silken, and my tongue danced across it in adoration. I wanted to show her how much I needed her, longed for her; but more than that, I wanted to love her. It was consuming me, the emotion blurring my vision, something I didn't want to happen. I wanted to commit every facet of this night to memory, every taste, touch, smell and image, so I could play it over and over in my head every time I was not with her.

Her fingers were insistent—dragging, trailing, touching, reading my body as if it was imprinted in Braille. Each movement seemed as if it had been choreographed eons ago, and now it was time for the performance.

Her breasts felt divine, the pert nubs rising up to greet my greedy mouth. I loved them. Made love to them. Caressed them with my tongue, my lips, my breath, my eager fingers and palms, but it didn't diminish the hunger churning inside me. I needed more. She needed more. And who was I to refuse the woman I loved?

Moving lower, my lips and tongue traced a path along her stomach, down her thighs, then back up. Then down and up. Her fingers were now in my hair, her hands guiding me to the place I so urgently wanted to go. Diana shifted, her legs opening wider and giving me access. The glistening of her folds invited me to sample the nectar I knew could satisfy my wanting. I couldn't resist.

Sliding my hands up the insides of her thighs, I pressed them apart to open her more fully. She was a magnificent sight. Diana Sullivan was offering herself to me, offering something so personal, so vulnerable.

I leaned forward and released a soft breath over her wetness. A jolt shot through me when she groaned, "Please, Jess." She was trying to rush me, trying to make me dive inside her with my tongue, my fingers, my all, but I wanted to take her slowly, take her my way, take her in the way I would cherish forever in the memories I was making. I had to taste her, touch her, find every hiding place and make it mine.

My tongue didn't listen to my reasoning. It wanted to sample the delights of her, and so it became a defector. A flick. A swipe. Diana crushed her hips towards me, to increase the contact. Then a sweeping stroke along slick folds… God. The taste of her…the essence of her. Her scent was addictive, and I was totally absorbed in everything that was her. More strokes, more tasting, more and more and more. But not enough. Never enough.

Gripping her thighs, I dipped my head and covered her clit completely with my mouth, then drew it in. Her hips shot off the bed, increasing the contact between my mouth and her clit, but I carried on, as my own need danced in my core. A flick, a grazing of teeth, more bucking. Being at the centre of her was deliciously intoxicating; I was drunk on her. I didn't see how anything could ever surpass what I was feeling at that moment. How could one go beyond perfection? Diana was grinding her centre into my face, slick juices covering my chin and mouth. I knew she was close; I could taste it, feel the thickness of it.

We were rocking, the rhythm rising perfectly, as if we had been together a million times before, yet this was new, this was our first. Moving my lips, I mouthed 'I love you' inside her before slipping my tongue beyond the folds and deep within her. Then out. Then all the way in. I was loving her, showing her how I needed her. Faster, faster, deeper, deeper, the tempo increased, the wanting intensified, my fingers gripping her thighs, slowing her hips to allow the moment to gloriously drag on.

"Jess! God! Jess! Yes!"

Sweat was slipping along the side of my face, her essence dripping from my hungry lips. I kept thrusting, pumping, dancing inside her.

Long fingers in my hair orchestrated my movements— gripping, pulling, pushing me. I could barely breathe, but I didn't care. I was making love with Diana Sullivan, loving her fully with more than my mouth. Diana was frantically twisting her hips, her orgasm imminent. She was riding my face, my tongue, peaking, cresting, clenching, stilling…

"GOD! Jeeeeeessssss!"

Hearing my name on her lips was nearly my undoing. I almost tipped over into the sweet light alongside with her.

"I… I… God!" Her groan was guttural.

I didn't slow. I knew she had more to give me, just as I had so much more to give her. I pulled my tongue free from her spasming muscle and pressed it against her clit.

"Fuck! Jess! I… God!"

Her growl was pure animal, but the feeling of her cumming for the second time into my mouth was all woman. All my woman.

Shaky hands tried to lift me, but couldn't, so I moved up her body like a panther, leaving small kisses in my wake. Her skin tasted wonderful—salty, musky, perfectly Diana. Her eyes were hooded, her lips slightly parted with the fragments of her cries. I stopped to adore her breasts, mouthing silent epithets of love against the soft flesh.

As I reached her face, her mouth claimed mine

accompanied by a crushing hug, her fingers digging into my back. Diana's hips lifted, and I slipped between her legs; her wetness coated my skin. It was a mix of her and me, a blend of our connection—my love, and what I hoped was her love too.

Slam. I was on my back, her hands caressing my breasts, her mouth on my throat. I could feel her trying to control her actions, trying to slow it down so she could take me as slowly as I had taken her. But I didn't want that. I wanted more, much much more. I wanted her to spread my legs, climb between, and press two fingers inside me. I wanted her to thrust inside, push and plunge and lunge and take. I wanted to see her eyes mist over as she drove into me deeper, dipped into me harder. I was so wet, so ready, so hers. My reactions encouraged her to own me, but she didn't budge from loving my breasts.

Lifting my hips, I urged her on. Pressing down against the apex of her pubic bone, I found some relief, but not nearly enough. "Di-a-na." The word staggered, stammered, stunted. My ability to form a sentence failed me; I was lost all over again.

One hand made its way down my side, along the curve of my waist and down the back of my thigh. Her lips were intent on consuming my breasts, and I was engulfed in the sensations of her fingers and her mouth. Then those delicious fingers dipped down and grazed the wetness pooling at the very core of me, and I knew where my focus lay. With her. Instead of lifting to press into her body, I pressed down and tried to make those digits claim what was theirs. But she moved them away, taunting me, making me inch backwards in hopes of capturing her hand.

"Please. God. Please." I felt her smile against my skin, and I knew it was the crooked one I loved best. That only fuelled my need for her.

"Patience."

The word echoed over my skin, rumbled inside me. Blue eyes lifted and caught my gaze; my breath caught. Diana Sullivan was the most beautiful woman in the world, and she was with me—and she was moving slowly down my body, her eyes dark and erotic, her tongue and lips trailing their way to between my thighs.

Knowing where her journey would end made my heart beat harder than I would have thought possible without passing out. Even though I wanted her there—God knew I wanted her there, I basked in the knowledge that she would get there. Eventually. Weird, I know. One minute I couldn't wait; the next, I was happy to.

Hot breath met wetness, and my groan was primal. Diana parted my legs and released another breath up and down the length of me, and I surged forward in an attempt to press against her mouth. I wanted to beg her, plead with her to just take me, but, for a split moment, words were lost to me. Then a flick, followed immediately by another and another and... God...the ripples sizzled through me like lightning, and I had to force myself to stop the words "I love you" from escaping and exposing me.

"Fuck!" It was the only word I could allow to slip from my lips, as telling her I loved her at that precise moment terrified me. I would not have been able to continue making love if she didn't say it back or, even worse, if she told me she didn't love me. And I needed her. God, I needed her.

Her mouth captured my clit, dragging and holding, pulling and sucking. Soft moans bubbled from my throat and my hips bucked against her to increase the pressure, but she was too quick for me. She drew back, and the cold air hit the heat that was aching for her return. Diana slipped her hands down my quivering thighs, and I wanted to grab her and pull her back where I needed her at that instant.

Just as I thought she was going to move away, her hand slipped back towards my clit. Diana leaned forward, her face coming towards mine, her dark hair brushing my skin. Breath hit my face in short, sharp puffs.

"Jess, I... I need to...' Diana closed her eyes.

"Yes." I didn't know what I was agreeing to, but I had to tell her she could do anything.

Without preamble, fingers were at my entrance, blue eyes locked on mine. I watched in fascination as her lips moved as if she were speaking, but there were no words, just breath.

Two fingers slipped inside, filling me. Deeply. And then they stopped. She drew them out with agonising slowness, her eyes gauging my expression. Back in. So deep, so full, so fucking good. The inside of me was trying to hold her there, pull her in and keep her prisoner in the depths of me. Out. And back in. Out and in. My hips were thrusting towards her, encouraging her to increase the tempo. Her hair was still brushing my skin, blue eyes still held my gaze. Our skin was slick with sweat, and our bodies moved delectably against each other as our breaths mingled between us.

The feeling of her taking me was exquisite, but it wasn't enough. I wanted her to take me harder, faster, deeper. I wanted to release the words I was so scared of saying, professing my undying love for her. But most of all, I wanted to hear those three cliché words slip from her lips with the promise of our future.

I think it was this realisation that made me want to break eye contact. I didn't want her to see the tears that suddenly filled my eyes. I eliminated the space between us and claimed her mouth. The kiss was all-consuming, allowing me to hide my vulnerability beneath it. I cupped the back of her head and pulled her harder against me.

Her fingers dipped deeper, the penetration acknowledging the neediness of my kiss. Her fingers were plunging inside me faster, my hips reaching and plummeting with each thrust. My essence was dripping from me, the slickness on her fingers mingling with my wetness and making the motion fluid.

A third finger thrust inside, the tightness yielding almost immediately. One of my hands was in her hair, the other on the curve of her ass. Feeling her work so hard as she made love to me made it so much better, as I knew she wanted to please me as much as I wanted to please her. Frenetic, wild, decadent, primeval—each stroke brought me closer. I had never experienced what it would be like to be completely and utterly taken by someone I loved before. Loved. Loved.

When my orgasm hit, I thought I would die. The light. The sensation of floating. The stepping out of my body and seeing myself being loved by someone as wonderful as Diana Sullivan. My cumming was a cleansing, a connection, an epiphany of what I wanted for the rest of my life. Spasms raced through me, hitting every nerve ending with precision.

And as the lights curled and danced, I uttered her name before I began to cry.

Strong arms slipped around me, and Diana cradled me against her body. Soft kisses brushed my hair, and I could just barely hear the shushing sounds she was making. Having her so close to me didn't stop the tears; it only made me more aware of how much I loved her, and that she didn't feel the same way as I did.

"Jess? What's the matter, honey?" Her voice held a hint of fear, and I realised Diana had no clue why I was blubbering like a baby after we had finally made love. Her fingers shook as they stroked my cheek, wiping away my tears.

I opened my eyes and looked at her.

Blue eyes held more than concern, more than questioning. My breakdown had caused a glimmer of hurt in those beautiful eyes, making me feel even worse. It wasn't Diana's fault that I had let my unrequited love for her mar what should have been one of the happiest times of my life. It wasn't every day a person fell in love for the first time.

"Jess?" Her voice broke, and so did my heart.

"Nothing, baby. I'm...I'm just so happy."

By the way her hand stilled and her eyes widened slightly, I could tell she wanted to believe me. But then I saw her deflate, felt her draw away.

Shit. I didn't want her to move away from me, physically or emotionally.

"Honestly, I am." I cupped her chin and rubbed my thumb against her cheek. With each stroke, I could feel her relax a little more. The loudest sounds in the room seemed to be our breathing.

Touching her was a balm to my soul. I really needed to connect with her again, not just to ease her concerns, but to stop the incessant doubts I couldn't seem to shake.

In one fluid movement, I pulled her to me and claimed her mouth in a searing kiss, as if I was attempting to kiss away her doubts. For a split second I thought I had succeeded.

Diana pulled away, her hands moving to cup my face and hold it still. Dark blue searched my green, and I knew there was no way I was going to get away with crying and not explaining.

"Tell me, Jess."

I opened my mouth to lie again, but she saw it coming.

"Is it because you wanted to wait?"

Wait?

"I know you said we should take our time and…" her eyes fluttered closed, a sigh slipped through her parted lips, "and I couldn't wait for you any longer."

The air was still around us.

"But it just felt so right, now felt so right."

It was. But was it right to tell Diana I was in love with her? Was it right to make those beautiful blue eyes widen, and then cringe as she made up some excuse as a way to escape an embarrassing situation?

"It was perfect, Diana." I leaned forward and placed a gentle kiss on her adorable lips. "You are perfect." I smiled and tipped my head to look up at her. "Ignore me. I was just overly emotional." A frown tried to appear on her face, but I kissed her again. "Believe me. You were spot on. This was the right time, and I feel wonderful."

I was grateful that she didn't push the issue. Although it was the perfect time to make love, oddly enough, somehow it wasn't the right time to proclaim it. I think I would call that a paradox.

Throughout the night, we awoke to continue discovering one another. Hands, fingers, breasts, stomachs, lips, tongues, and everything else that we could press against were sampled, tasted, stroked, loved. And each time, I wanted to pour those three little words over her skin, into her mouth, inside her most intimate places. I also wanted to hear those words from her, wanted her to tell me she loved me just as much as I loved her.

Seven twenty-three Saturday morning, I was staring at the sleeping profile of the most beautiful woman I had ever seen. It was as if I wanted to record her each and every nuance to memory, just in case she woke to realise she had made one of the biggest mistakes of her life. Though why she would feel that way was beyond me. It wasn't as if we had been under the influence of anything but each other.

I wasn't used to having negative feelings about sleeping with someone, and to be perfectly honest, I was beginning to freak myself out. I hoped I wasn't going to become one of those needy, insecure types who text, call, stalk, and terrorise their partner twenty-four hours a day.

"Good morning, gorgeous." Her voice was husky and deliciously addictive, as always. "Don't tell me you're ready to get up."

A smile formed in my stomach and raced to my face. Not a bad greeting to start the day. No sign of "Fuck me! Was I pissed?" I decided I could put my stalker suit in the closet for a wee while longer.

Snuggled against her, I could feel her chest lifting and falling in an easy rhythm. I moistened my lips and asked, "Did you sleep okay?"

"Sleep?" Her laughter rattled around her chest, and my head bobbed with the motion. "What's that?" Another laugh. "I think that was the last thing on both our minds last night, don't you?"

Actually my insecure, fucked up thinking was probably one of the leaders in the running for the thought most on my mind the night before.

"Not that I minded." Her lips brushed the top of my

head, and then she sighed.

I don't think I had ever felt so contented in my life.

"Hungry?"

I was just about to say I was fine, when my stomach gurgled.

"Looks as if I have my answer." Her laugh rumbled through me, and the hairs on my arms stood to attention, just knowing I was close enough to feel it. "Come on. Let's get that monster fed."

I hoped Diana would join me in the shower, but she didn't. She cooked breakfast whilst I got ready.

Breakfast was wonderful; like I expected it to be anything less. Everything Diana did, she did with excellence. Thoughts of her the previous night flitted through my mind, making parts of me glow with the memory. I watched in fascination as she tucked into scrambled eggs and bacon. How anyone could make eating eggs and bacon sexy, I will never know, but she did.

I wasn't sure how long I'd been staring, don't know how long she had been holding the fork halfway to her mouth, but I eventually tore my eyes away from the fork and up to her parted lips. I licked my lips reflexively.

"You okay, Jess?"

"A-huh."

"You want this?"

Her mouth? Those lips? Of course I did. I felt my head nodding.

"Here you go."

Why wasn't she moving closer?

"Jess?"

Was she waiting for—

"Jess!"

Snap. Back to reality. Back to a forkful of scrambled

eggs right in front of me. What the...

"You seemed to drift off a little there, my woman."

I liked the way she said that—my woman.

"Are you not interested in my eggs? No?" She chuckled. "Maybe you were thinking of something more tempting?" Blue eyes twinkled, and she placed the fork on her plate and then leaned over the table. Her face was so close to mine, our breaths mingled. "Well, what would you like?"

Diana's throaty voice trickled over my skin, and my eyelids fluttered.

I wanted to say "I want you, you and only you," but that would be exposing my inner longings, the ones I had wanted to spill all over her last night.

Diana came closer, her lips almost touching mine. "Hmmmm...let me see."

Being so close to her beautiful face was both blindingly wonderful and absolutely terrifying. I was so aware of how I felt about her, that fear had snaked its way into what should have been a glorious experience, both last night and at this moment.

"Well?"

I brushed my bottom lip against her mouth. The blueness of her eyes turned darker.

I could hear the crockery on the table rattling as she pushed closer to me. I leaned back, but she kept coming, the sound of breaking plates not stopping her advance. A strong hand cupped the back of my head and drew me closer to her; our lips met in a kiss that was deep and fulfilling. My chair was tilting backwards, but I couldn't pull away from her. The kiss was too perfect to worry about insignificant things like landing on my back on the tiled kitchen floor. As long as she was on top of me when I fell, I didn't care.

I needn't have worried about that. Diana slipped

effortlessly over the wooden table and straddled my legs. I could feel her heat through my trousers. My hands slid over her muscled back, and it didn't take me long to realise she wasn't wearing anything other than her thin t-shirt. Fuck. I wanted her. Wanted to tip her backwards, lay her over the table, and take her—make mad passionate love to her all over again.

My hand made the decision for me. It tucked itself between her open and ready thighs. God, so wet. So hot and wet and ready for my fingers. She groaned against my mouth, and I pushed deeper, her intimate walls clutching my fingers. Diana rotated her hips and groaned again. Breaking away from her mouth, I looked into her face. Red lips parted, breath ragged, while her body moved against my fingers in perfect rhythm. A vision.

Dipping my head, I growled as I tugged her t-shirt with my teeth. Diana's grin told me she understood my message, and she pulled the obstructing material off her body. Seeing her naked and straddling me was sublime.

I placed a gentle kiss on her collarbone, inhaling the scent of her. Venturing lower, my tongue teased the curve of her breast as I pulled my fingers free.

"Please, Jess."

My tongue dipped lower, finding a path between the cleft of her breasts, my fingers stroking the length of her making her buck against me.

Everything about my mouth's journey seemed right, perfect, seemed as if I had travelled this path all of my life. It didn't make the experience any less intense. In fact, the feeling of familiarity made it even more wonderful. Diana's lips found the curve of my shoulder, and their heat caressed the skin, almost as if she was inside of me.

Inside again, inside the heat of her. Inside the core of

her. Inside the woman I loved. One finger, two, three. Deep, thrusting, wet. Her legs opened wider, thighs lifting to wrap around me and the chair, trying to absorb me. Hips rising and falling. Thrust, thrust—fingers seeking her touchstone. The rhythm was irregular, wild. Her fingers were digging into my flesh, pulling me closer, giving me a gift.

I could feel it building—the maelstrom of climax swirling through her, the slickness of her juices gathering and charging for release. I knew I had it in the palm of my hand. At that precise moment, I knew, too, that I had her in the palm of my hand and the tips of my fingers. There would never be anyone else for me.

As the first spasm hit, I captured her nipple with my mouth and sucked. Diana clamped down and around me, her arms engulfing me and shutting out the world. The sound of her cumming made me ache with love for her. I slipped my fingers free and embraced her, the wetness coating them sliding along her skin.

We sat like that for God knows how long, rocking against one another, neither of us wanting to end the moment. It seemed as if we were two parts of a puzzle that had somehow re-united its individual pieces after an eternity of separation. I'd felt it before—on our first date, and again the first time we'd made love, but the sensation of reconnection was so much stronger now. Part of me urged me to tell Diana I was in love with her, but the more rational part of my mind still thought it was too soon.

Diana's mouth was moving against my neck, but it wasn't kisses. It seemed as if words were being impressed on my skin, but I couldn't make them out.

Lifting my head back, I saw her face half turned to me, her lips parted, dark hair splayed over her shoulders and mine, but I could not hear her speaking.

"You okay, Diana?"

A lazy smile slipped across her face, followed by a nod. "Perfect."

Yes you are. And beautiful—don't forget that.

My hands moved over her back, and I could feel the morning chill on her skin. She was naked and sitting on my lap in the middle of her kitchen at the end of November.

"Come on, lady. You need to get some clothes on. You're cold." I slapped a loud kiss on her mouth, then was surprised to see her brow furrow.

"I'm hot."

"Yes you are."

She snorted, and leaned back to look me fully in the face. "Git."

I patted her butt. "Grab a shower and warm up. We have the whole day ahead of us."

She kissed me, and then made an attempt to slip my top off.

I laughed at the face Diana made when I pulled her hands from me. "We have all the time in the world to carry this on...*later*."

Diana's eyebrow lifted, and her eyes flashed. "Promise?"

My fingers made the appropriate X gesture across my chest, as I said, "Cross my heart and hope to die."

Diana tilted her head as if to ponder what I'd said, and then the grin was back. "That'll do." Then she was gone, half running, half skipping out of the room, the picture of naked perfection.

I immediately missed her heat, but when I looked at the wetness on my leg, I couldn't help the stupid smile that plastered my face. I still had the essence of the woman with me after all.

Whilst Diana showered, I tidied away the broken crockery and poured another cup of tea. The newspaper had come, and I idled away some time flicking through the events in the world outside of Diana's house. I was so immersed in a story about a kidnapped dog that when her mail came, I jumped and knocked over the cooling cup of tea in front of me.

"Shit!"

Diana's voice drifted down the stairs. "What did you say?"

I hastily tried to clean up the mess whilst replying, "Nothing, honey."

After I had cleaned up, again, I collected her mail and placed it on the kitchen table. I didn't even flick through to have a snout at whom the mail was from. Weird, considering I would class myself as a woman, and being a snoop was part of the job description. I turned back to the paper. Back to violence, hatred, war, and death. Cheerful stuff.

Ten minutes later, I felt Diana behind me, her mouth close to my ear. "Anything interesting?"

Without looking up, I answered, "Mail."

I felt her tense slightly before asking, "Male?"

"Over there. Table."

"Ah...*mail*."

I stifled a grin and peeped up from my reading to watch her flick through the letters.

Her face crumpled a little before she ripped open an envelope. Blue eyes flicked through quickly, an eyebrow raised in contemplation.

Interest piqued, I folded the newspaper and observed the storm of emotions sweeping across her chiselled features.

"Strange."

I didn't comment, just waited for her to elaborate.

"Why on earth…" She turned the letter over to see if there was anything written on the back before meeting my quizzical look. "Would you believe it?" Diana held the letter out to me, and I hesitated before taking it.

Unlike Diana, my eyes went to the address, London, and then to the signing off, Lauren Baker, before I read the note. What the fuck. It was as if I had been punched in the gut. Talk about timing. I tried to read through the letter, but I couldn't seem to absorb the words. All I could focus on was the "Love ya loads, baby, Lauren x."

"As if I want to know she's moved." Diana's voice seemed miles away. "I can't believe she actually thinks I give a damn."

I looked up at her and noticed two things. One, she was pale. Two, she looked like she had been punched too. I doubted it was for the same reason as me. What I couldn't understand was why she had told me, why she had let me read it. Why on earth had she not ripped up the letter and thrown it in the bin with all the broken crockery?

"Jess?"

Time for the acting. "Weird, isn't it? I'm surprised she would draw attention to herself after what happened to Monica." Not to mention Lauren must have put two and two together and realised Diana had come back to me that night.

I folded the letter, placed it on the table, and slid it over to where Diana stood rooted to the spot. It seemed as if time stopped—no, everything around us stopped and we kept moving. Slowly. It seemed as if I was moving backwards and she was moving even more slowly towards me, thus creating a distance that I could not have envisioned half an hour earlier.

Her slender hand reached out to touch me, but I must've given her some signal that said this wasn't the time, and she placed it over the letter and scrunched it in her hand.

Turning away from me, Diana spoke. "Yeah. She could never understand when she was not a welcome intrusion." Her voice sounded thick. "I still don't understand why the police believed her denials."

That made two of us.

Diana sighed and determinedly straightened her shoulders before walking over to the bin and slamming the letter into the trash. "She always had a way of making people see things from her perspective. Must be part of the training to become an actress."

What was I doing? I was allowing a letter from Lauren to ruin what should have been the happiest morning of my life. And for what reason? Jealousy, that's what. The green-eyed twat of a monster herself. Given the way Diana reacted, she hadn't asked Lauren to keep in touch. Just because I thought she should rip the fucking letter up, didn't mean she would do what I would have done. For that matter, why should she? So Lauren had signed it "Love ya loads, baby." Was I acting this way because I couldn't seem to say those words to Diana? I had entirely too many questions. I needed to act, instead of sitting on my arse being all rhetorical.

Before I could pose any more asinine questions to my moral self, I stood and moved over to Diana. I slipped my arms through hers and pulled her back against me. Initially she was rigid, but she soon relaxed. When Diana turned around, I had to look up to see her eyes. It seemed as if there was a storm brewing in the blueness, as the hue shifted and changed in intensity like clouds collecting above water.

"I…" I wanted to tell her I loved her, wanted her to know that she was the only one for me. I wanted her eyes to settle and stay focused on us, not think I was a jealous bastard who was one step away from clouting her because she hadn't reacted the way I thought she should. So, what I said was, "I'm sorry, love."

Her brow furrowed, but the ghost of a smile edged its way around her mouth.

"It was a bit of a shock."

She snorted. "Tell me about it."

Standing on my tiptoes, I leaned in and placed a kiss on her mouth, a quick one, one that was intended to test the waters. I was thankful that my lips met no resistance. So I kissed her again, just as briefly.

Diana feigned a growl, grabbed my butt and dragged me to her. Her mouth claimed mine in a searing kiss, and my knees buckled. I felt as if I was drowning in her, and at that moment, I knew I could die a happy woman. But not today. Today was our day. Today was a day that was full of wonderment and unlimited possibilities.

Tearing my lips from hers, I grinned. "Let's go out. What about Buxton?"

Diana laughed. "Buxton? Why on earth do you want to go to Buxton?"

"Just because."

"Just because what?"

"Just because."

She laughed again, a musical sound that I knew I would never tire of hearing, and one that I promised myself I would try to elicit every chance I got, for as long as she would let me.

"Okay. Let me get my boots on." After another kiss, she released me and went in search of her footwear.

Energy rushed through me, and I felt like a six-year-old at a funfair. "I need to go and get changed first."

A muffled "okay" came from under the stairs, and I grinned stupidly. I lifted my hand to sweep my fingers through my hair, but stopped abruptly and lowered my fingers. I inhaled the perfume clinging to them. Not mine, not Diana's.

Amazing to think how the realisation of having your girlfriend's ex's perfume on your hands could make them feel like they were on fire, isn't it? Why would Lauren douse her letter with perfume? And why hadn't I noticed it when I was holding the letter? Maybe because I was too fucking busy being jealous.

I splashed hot water over my hands, followed by lashings of liquid soap. Although I scrubbed the skin until it was nearly raw, it didn't seem to take away the stench of the woman who had once had what I wanted.

"Ready?"

My teeth were gritted together, but I mobilised my jaw enough to answer.

I needed to call Sophie. Someone who had their head screwed on tight had to give me a verbal bollocking and tell me to stop trying to fuck up my life with stupid thoughts and even stupider actions.

Lauren Baker was not in the picture anymore. I was with Diana. Diana was with me, not with Lauren. She was in London, not here in Stockport. She wasn't the one Diana had climbed over the table to this morning; she wasn't the one who had spent the night loving Diana; she certainly wasn't the one who was going to be spending the day with Diana. And she definitely wasn't the one who would be trying with every fibre of her being to get Diana to fall as much in love with her as she was with Diana.

No. That, without a shadow of a doubt, was me.

Chapter 16

We spent the whole of Saturday in Buxton. It was wonderful being with Diana; I even willingly succumbed to Christmas shopping. The only downside to the day was that thoughts of Lauren Baker kept creeping into my mind. I couldn't seem to stop them, couldn't erase the image of her smug face the last time I had seen her. My stomach roiled every time I envisioned Lauren, and I mentally pushed her out, time and time again.

What was the matter with me? I knew Diana wanted to be with me. She didn't want Lauren. She couldn't… not after what we had shared the previous night and over breakfast. At the slightest opportunity, she stole a kiss, even held my hand as we walked through the town—that told me that she wasn't afraid of letting everyone know we were together.

But still, why had Lauren written to Diana? No. Diana had thrown the letter away. That should've been enough. Shouldn't it?

What the fuck was happening to me? I'd never been

one to be jealous over someone's ex. But then, I'd never been in love before. Before I met Diana, I'd never felt so gloriously wonderful and so fucking insecure in my whole life. If I didn't curb my irrational thinking, I was going to cock things up for good and all.

I should have been happy that Diana was with me, ecstatic that our relationship was taking off. Granted, I had fallen in love with her a tad too soon; and although it wasn't a case of love at first sight, it was damned near it. All through my life, I had scoffed at the tired romance stories of people seeing "the one" and swooning. In *my* life book, there had been no such thing as the elusive love at first sight. Lust, yes, but love took time, didn't it? Two people had to get to know each other and not be responding only to physical attraction for it to be classified as love— that much I was sure of. Or was I?

God! I needed to call Sophie. I know I said that earlier, but I'd been with Diana all day, and it wouldn't have looked good—me phoning Sophie to ask for relationship advice. Imagine: "Excuse me a mo, Diana. Soph? It's me. What do you do if you are being eaten up with jealousy and think your girlfriend may run back to her ex?" Nope. Not the best course of action, even I could see that. Just.

So, when Diana asked if it was okay if she stayed over at my house Saturday night, I was a little torn. Who am I kidding? I desperately wanted her to stay over. It would mean another night with the woman I wanted to spend every night of my life with. Sophie could wait.

We stopped at Diana's to collect an overnight bag, and then went back to my house. Within half an hour, we were soaking in a bath of hot water, easing aching muscles and chasing away the chill of a cold November day. Candles lit the room, and their scent added to the sensual atmosphere of heat and steam. Diana's hands stroked my stomach. The movement of her fingers seemed choreographed, as they danced over my skin in a dance of semi seduction. Luxuriating in the feel of her body behind me, I leaned back.

"Did you have a good day?" Her mouth was right next to my ear, the vibration of it resonating through my body.

I nodded, a grin splitting my face.

"Good."

Her breath trickled over my skin, and goose bumps sprouted up all over my body and made me squirm back against her. I heard a gasp from behind me and realised I had made contact with her most sensitive spot. My fingertip trailed down the thigh that was fortuitously positioned alongside me. I could feel the trembling of her muscles as my lone digit made its way up and down. Another shift back, another gasp from Diana.

"What about you?" I couldn't make out the mumble that came from behind me. "Did you have a good time?"

Lips massaged the sensitive skin of my neck; teeth nibbled gently before her mouth sucked gently. Of course I was wet already, but certain areas became even wetter.

"I loved it." A hand slithered up my belly and cupped the underside of my breast, the nipple straining for contact. "And this." Her other hand snaked downwards and through the apex of my thighs. A single stroke of her palm jangled every nerve ending. "And…this." Teeth nibbled my earlobe, one hand slipped higher and covered the expectant breast whilst inquisitive fingers parted my folds and dipped into heat.

"God!" I could feel her pushing against me, and I wanted to turn around and capture her mouth—her body, her soul, her heart, but the sensations racing through me placed me on a one track course: I wanted her to make love to me.

Her fingers became more insistent, pushing down, dragging up; her palm began a kneading motion, while her tongue stroked my throat. Her scent was intoxicating, mingling with the candles and steam.

I was thrumming with sensations, all of them battling for pre-eminence, but I couldn't focus on any one of them. Together they made up the whole, they all made me *feel* whole. Seeing her hands, her thighs, the peculiar shapes dancing on the walls…hearing her mutterings so close to my ear, the splash of water…the feel of her body underneath mine, her lips, her fingers, her breasts, the heat of the water, the heat of her… I knew my cumming was close. More stroking, more heat, more mutterings, more more more…and I needed her *so* much more. I wanted her deep inside of me, wanted her to climb inside me and stay, needed to know that she would always be with me, body and soul.

I tried to turn, tried to cover her body front to front, her breasts pressing against mine, guide her fingers inside me as I slipped inside her, but she held me fast, her fingers delving deeper, her palm cupping my breast.

Instead of resisting, I succumbed. Surrendered to her inquisitive fingers…yielded to her kisses…gasped as a lone finger entered me and held me in place. It circled, pushing against nerve endings that were throbbing for attention. And she gave it to them. Another finger, more circling, circling that turned to pushing and pulling, pushing and pulling that transformed into taking. My hips pushed downwards, trying to increase the penetration of Diana's fingers, increase the pressure. A beautiful ache sparked inside, an ache so all-encompassing that I could feel the seed of it blossom and sprout, as if its mission was to completely cover every molecule of my body. I turned my head and was met by hooded violet eyes. Diana's deep concentration didn't mask her expression of desire. Her breasts pressed so close I could feel her taut nipples on my skin, our bodies moved in rhythm. Red lips were parted, breathing ragged. A slight twist, and I covered them with my own. That little bit of additional contact released me, and my orgasm erupted in a tidal wave of euphoria.

White. Everything blindingly white and deliriously wonderful. I felt the safest I've ever felt in my life with her one arm around me, the other drawing her fingers from inside and trailing them up my side. Now that I could turn fully, I covered her body and kissed her properly.

I was just in position when she pulled her mouth away from mine.

"Jess."

I didn't want to stop. I wanted to love her as she had loved me.

"Jess, let's go to bed."

That was worth stopping for, as long as we were stopping to start all over again.

I gave her a quick kiss and then lifted off her, sloshing water over the rim of the tub. Holding my hand out, I gripped hers and pulled her up.

Dry towels swaddling us, I led her to my bedroom. I wanted to remember every single detail of this night—the way she held my hand as we walked, the look on her face, the way her eyes glistened, the soft smile she gave me as I closed the door behind us.

Not once in all the times we made love to each other throughout the night did Lauren Baker invade my thoughts and try to ruin what Diana and I were sharing. It was a pity that I couldn't stop it sneaking in as I lay in Diana's arms in the early hours of the morning. It was beginning to freak me out. Why couldn't I just let it go? Call me insecure, but I prefer the term "twat."

The next morning we were woken by my dad calling to ask if I was coming for lunch. That was a first. Dad called me to give me updates about world news—how he hated the Prime Minister, Mrs Walsh's cat and its pooing habits—but never to invite me to lunch. That was a given. The only time I didn't go for lunch was when I called to say I wasn't going.

I could hear my mum's voice in the background asking how many were coming, and then it hit me. They knew I wasn't alone. And the reason they knew? Only one possibility, and that came in the guise of one Sophie Harrison, AKA, the Gob of the North.

"Erm…your mum wants to know if…erm…anyone else is coming," Dad mumbled.

I grinned over my shoulder at Diana sprawled naked on the bed. "Just a minute, Dad." Holding the phone away but with the mouthpiece uncovered, I asked, "You up for a spot of lunch with the in-laws?" As soon as I realised what I had said, I could feel the blush surging up my throat and into my face.

Diana grinned and nodded, mouthing, "I'm starving."

I hoped that she hadn't noticed my verbal faux pas, but I quickly turned away from her so that she couldn't see the redness covering my face like spray paint.

"Yep. Make it two for lunch."

I heard him whisper something to my mum before he

said nonchalantly, "Not our Sophie, is it?"

A laugh shot from my mouth. "As you well know, Dad, no…it's not Sophie. Happy?"

"Too bloody right I am. Got to dig out my clipboard."

I opened my mouth to tell him he'd better keep his bloody Inquisition to himself, but he fired a "see you both later" and hung up.

Fuck. I knew my parents. Better still, my parents knew me. As soon as they clocked me with Diana, they would know I was smitten, and they would make damned sure Diana was good enough for their little girl. This was not good. This was like Sophie times two on crack.

"I'm looking forward to meeting your parents, Jess." Diana's voice drifted from behind me and I pulled a "fuck me" face before plastering on a casual smile and turning to face her. "I've heard such wonderful things about them." Her hands slipped around my waist and pulled me to her. "And…anyone who can make something as magnificent as you must be pretty special."

A small kiss turned into something a little more promising, but we didn't have the time to finish what would inevitably start if we continued. I didn't want us turning up at my parents' smelling of sex, although at least it would likely shut them up for a little while.

As soon as we arrived, the Inquisition began. Don't get me wrong, my parents were all smiles and courtesy, but the questions they asked were not the kind of questions you would ask someone unless you had an agenda. "What do you do?" Granted, that might show interest in the person's life. "How much do you earn a year?" was a stand-in for

"What are your intentions towards our little girl?"

Initially, Diana looked a little startled, but, after a grin in my direction, she answered "More than enough."

That didn't quite answer the underlying question of "What are your intentions." To be honest, I wouldn't have minded hearing the answer to that one myself.

The look on my dad's face spoke volumes, and for a split second I believed he was going to ask, "More than enough to take care of my daughter?" Mercifully, the phone rang and he scuttled off to answer it, muttering his apologies whilst leaving my mum grinning and nodding.

"It is wonderful to finally meet you, Diana. We've heard so much about you."

Not from me, they hadn't.

"You're a Graphic Designer, yes?"

Not again. Why did they always have to re-enact the Spanish Inquisition?

"Come into the lounge, and let's chat."

Diana made a move to go with my mum, whilst I was stopped by my dad yelling for me. Shit. Divide and conquer—that's what they were up to. Get both of us on our own and play good cop and…erm…good cop, until they had all the information they needed to make a full and valid assessment.

"Jess! Sophie's on the phone!"

Now I was torn. I wanted to save Diana from a fate worse than a day with the lead interrogators from the MOD, but this also was a prime opportunity to talk to Soph.

"About time. You deaf?" He leaned closer, his grin devilish, "Or in love?"

Before I could turn my disapproving look into a sarcastic comment, he was gone.

"Jess?" Sophie's voice calmed me, but only slightly.

"See you've taken your bird for the interrogation. How's it going?"

"Thank God you called. I need to talk to you."

A moment's silence echoed from the other end. "What's happened?" The jokiness of her previous tone had vanished, and I knew she would be sitting upright, the look of the Defender on her face.

"Lauren Baker, that's what."

"WHAT? She been bothering you? Little fuck—"

"She wrote a letter to Diana and—"

"Hang on a minute. She wrote a letter?" Sophie paused, and I knew she was thinking it through. "You going all paranoid, Jess?"

"Well, it came yesterday. I know I'm being stupid…"

"Yes. You're being stupid. Look, Jess, do you really want to fuck everything up?"

Of course not.

"Get over it. How would you like Diana to go all moody arsed every time she thought about your exes?"

Obviously, I wouldn't.

"Lauren is very much in the past, and if you don't want your relationship with Diana to go the same way, then get over yourself."

I didn't want to jeopardise my relationship with Diana, but that didn't stop the jealousy from rising.

"So, give us the goss. Did you shag?"

"Sophie!"

"Looks like a yes. Any good? Earth moving, the works?"

"Sophie! Pack it in."

"Looks like a yes again. Nice one." Her chuckles came down the line crystal clear. "I have to dash. Meeting Dave in a few. Good to know it's all going well." She paused.

"And Jess? Don't fuck it up, okay? Leave Baker in the past and move on. Diana is the one, and you don't want to fuck it up, do you?"

No. Obviously.

"Speak later. Love you." And she was gone, like the proverbial whirlwind.

Back in the lounge, my parents were listening in rapt attention as Diana said, "Well, that's how I would do it if I had that problem."

"What problem?" I asked.

"Oranges," Diana supplied.

Oranges?

My dad turned his grinning face my way. "My. You've got yourself a cracker here, love. Oranges."

What the fuck with the oranges already?

"Fancy coming into the garden, Diana? You can tell me where I need to put them."

I looked at Diana, who gave me a wink before saying, "I'd love to."

Left alone with my mum, I had to ask. "What's all this about the oranges?"

"Not a clue, love. I was busy watching her body language." She got up from the chair and came over to me. "She's beautiful, Jess. And funny." Loving arms wrapped around me and pulled me close. "She's in love with you, you know."

"Pffft!" Still, I felt my heart stop for a moment and then begin banging against my ribcage.

"No pfffts. Mums know. It's written all over her." She kissed my cheek, and then pulled away. "You want a brew?"

Of course I did. But I also wanted to know more about what the oracle had seen. Diana was in love with me?

Diana. In love. With me? Why couldn't I see it? Why was I holding back on telling her that I loved her? Should I just go for it, say, "Look, I'm not expecting anything in return, but thought I would just get it out there." But I was expecting something in return. If Diana nodded, thanked me, and then carried on with her life, I would be devastated.

"Well, are you coming or not, Dolly Dreamer?"

By the time we got to the kitchen, there was evidence of ravaged oranges all over the counter tops. Mum just picked up a cloth and started wiping the counters, her attention otherwise engaged. Looking out the window, I could see Diana and my dad talking animatedly at the end of the garden, his arms waving about like a human windmill. Before I knew it, I was standing next to them, thoughts of having a cuppa long gone.

"Let's see if that ginger moggy likes this, shall we?"

Glancing at the ground, I saw orange peel and segments scattered along the borders of Dad's garden.

"That should stop the cat. If not, back to the giant pill bottles." Diana turned and flashed me a smile, and my stomach flipped.

"You've got a belter here, love. She's a keeper."

I know, Dad, I know.

"Tea's up!"

Dad scuttled back to the house, leaving me alone with Diana for the first time in what seemed like ages. I opened my mouth to apologise for the Twenty Questions, but Diana spoke first.

"I really like your parents, Jess. They're so different from mine."

Too right. They actually gave a shit—and that's why they give the third degree to anyone they think I like.

"I was surprised your dad hasn't used oranges to keep

the cats off his garden before." She snorted. "A lot better than me designing a huge pill bottle to catch them in."

Fuck. He never asked her that.

"Are you two coming?"

Time for Round Two.

<hr/>

It was a wonderful lunch. Mum and Dad left off grilling my girlfriend for the remainder of the day, indicating she had passed the Taylor Test. Which was good. By the time we left, the day was nearly over. The time was quickly approaching when I would be leaving Diana's company.

Diana drove me home, and we sat in the car, each waiting for the other to say something. I wasn't ready to say goodnight, but I knew we both had to work the next day. I wanted to invite her in for a while, just to extend our time; however, I knew where we would end up if I did. Not that I would mind, but I knew Diana had to work on a project that was due by the end of the week.

"So." Diana's voice broke the quiet of the car. "Here we are."

"Yes."

More silence, a little fidgeting, a lot of expectation.

"So. Erm… I'll say goodnight."

Do you have to? Can't you say you want to come inside? Stuff work; let me make love to you again. I met her intent gaze. Those eyes got me every time.

"Do I get a kiss?"

A grin spread over my face. "Do you want one?"

Diana didn't even answer. Her avid lips found mine, and I was lost in her. Hands fumbled inside jackets, underneath tops as they searched for skin. Diana pushed me backwards until I was pressed against the door, her body trying to climb on top of mine. The interior of her car was too small to accommodate her body trying to shift over the handbrake, and I could hear her frustration as a growl emanated from the depths of her. I laughed, and felt her stiffen before she relaxed against me.

"It's not going to happen, is it?" Her voice was joking and slightly muffled.

"Not here, it isn't."

Her head shot up, and I was questioned by blue eyes and a raised eyebrow.

"And you have to work, honey."

She slumped. "I hate work," she muttered against my neck. She sounded like a teenager denouncing school. "I want to play with you."

I laughed again.

Her face assumed a serious expression. "You laughing at my misery, Taylor?"

I nodded.

Diana emitted a long sigh and leaned against me.

Minutes passed as we half sat, half lay like that, neither of us wanting to end the day. But, like all good things, an end had to come.

I stood in my doorway and watched the tail lights of her car disappearing into the distance. Turning, I was just about to enter when I heard someone say, "Fucking dykes."

"Night, Jeff."

Grinning, I made my way into the house and closed the door. It was time for a little loud music to liven up the neighbours before bedtime. At least whilst I was pissing off Jeff Barnes, I would not be pondering the meaning of life, love, Diana Sullivan, and my incessant desire to throttle the life out of Lauren Baker.

Chapter 17

I didn't get to see Diana until class on the Wednesday, three whole days later. We'd spoken on the phone, but it'd been rushed. Diana's boss wanted the proofs of the project asap, and she had to get them to him before Friday—meaning Thursday. Considering she was teaching on the Wednesday evening, that didn't leave her with much time to get on with it. Part of me was smugly pleased that I had made her go home on the Sunday so she had more time to work, whereas the other, needier part was still wishing I had ignored the responsibilities of her life and had taken Diana inside.

Diana looked perfect, as usual, but she seemed unfocused. It was as if her mind was elsewhere all evening, although she did make her way over to my desk more than once to whisper in my ear. Sophie was in her element with her piss taking. She hummed *Hot For Teacher* throughout the first session, even though I glared at her repeatedly. Eventually she decided that losing her teeth down her throat was a good incentive to pack it in.

Break time came and went without Diana joining us,

but Dave and Sophie seemed unfazed. As for me, you can gather what was going through my head. Rushed phone calls, no real contact, unfocused... I knew she was busy with work, knew that she was drawing the classes to their planned conclusion in the next two weeks, but the rational side of me worried that there was too much evidence that argued that she just didn't want to see me.

Had the weekend been too much too soon, like I thought? I mean, sleeping with each other and meeting each other's parents all in the space of a few days—a lot. And the letter from Lauren. I wanted to stop that memory from eking inside, but it was a prime exhibit in the court case taking place inside my head. Was Diana thinking about Lauren? Even if it was to do with how the bitch had treated her in the past? Did she need to talk about it?

I decided to go and seek out the missing Ms Sullivan and ask if she needed my help. That's what girlfriends do. They help to sort out problems. I stood suddenly.

"You going for a pee?"

I wondered why Sophie felt the need to ask about my bladder.

"Hurry up. Class starts in a few," she said, as if I didn't know.

Making my way to the classroom, I salved my neediness with the excuse that I was being a good girlfriend. I was mentally berating myself for forgetting to grab her a coffee and bring it back with me, when I was stopped dead by Diana's voice.

"I can't just drop everything here right this second. I have commitments."

I couldn't see her, but I knew she was somewhere ahead of me.

"I'll try to get to there tomorrow, okay?"

Where?

"I know you need me, but…"

Who? Who needs her?

I heard her sigh of resignation. "Okay. I'll be there about 11. I'll catch the commuter. You happy?"

I wasn't. And her voice was getting closer. I didn't want to appear to be ear wigging, although that was exactly what I was doing. I furtively looked around the hallway for an escape hatch. Doors surrounded me, but I knew they would be locked.

"See you then."

Fuck. I ran a little down the opposite way of her voice, turned around, and started strolling back. Diana appeared around the corner, her mobile in her hand.

"Hey, baby. I was just coming to meet you."

I forced a grin. "Same here." With knobs on.

"You okay? You look a little pale."

I nodded and squeaked a "Fine" before launching myself at her.

"Hey, what's all this about? Not that I mind." The warmth of her seeped into the fear of me, and I held her tighter. "Has something happened?" She pulled back far enough that she could look into my face, as if trying to read me.

"Nope. Just missed you." I saw that she was gauging my response, so I grinned up at her. "Can't a girl miss her woman once in a while?"

The crooked grin came out, the one, as you know, I really loved best. "Too right." A soft kiss brushed my forehead, and she pulled me to her and held me tightly. It was like we were saying goodbye at a train station, never to see the other again. "I've missed this…us."

Tears welled up in my eyes, and I can't really explain

why. Too much had happened in the last five minutes for me to compute. All I knew was that Diana was going away tomorrow, and she was holding me like it would be the last time.

"Jess? About after class…"

I knew it was coming before she said it.

"I've got to get straight back. I'm leaving for London tomorrow."

London. Lauren Baker. Love ya loads, baby.

"Work needs the project as soon as. I have to walk them through it."

I squeezed her to me harder before releasing her. "I understand, love. Work is work, after all."

To be honest, I think I did pretty well when I spoke. My voice was perfectly pitched, light, understanding, pleasant. Although if anyone who really knew me was standing near, they would have added "empty" to the list.

"I might be away for the rest of the week…maybe into next. Is that okay?"

What did she expect me to say? No. I want you to quit your job and stay with a woman you have only known for ten weeks?

"God, baby." I laughed for effect. "I'm sure I can entertain myself for a few days." Either my imagination was playing up or I saw a fleeting look of disappointment cross her face. "You need to get a drink. Class should be starting now, *Teach*." And dismissed.

"Erm…okay." Diana stood there as if she was waiting for me to continue metaphorically brushing her off. "I'll… I won't be a minute."

And then she was gone, and I was left mentally kicking myself up the arse whilst standing alone in the corridor.

The second half of class seemed strained. I mean, a naked woman sat in front of us all, flashing her bits and pieces, and none of us could muster even a giggle. Not even Sophie. She, for once, was concentrating on something less private than when the man was in the same position last week. There were no epithets like the "Look at my dick!" or even wasp-like pubic lice. Granted, she was drawing the woman's breasts, but she did have the choice of drawing intimate places as the woman had decided to sit facing the pair of us with her legs raised up. Not the most flattering position.

"I'm sure her flower keeps winking at me."

I ignored Sophie and focused on getting the peak of a mischievous nipple to seem almost chiselled.

At nine, Diana was pleasantly chatting with Dave as Sophie as I packed our things away. A little part of me wanted to slink away into my car, go home, and bury myself under my duvet. However, I was getting on my own tits. I had to stop all the insecure bollocks and carry on, get a grip of what I was stupidly doing. What Sophie had told me when I spoke to her from my parents' was going to come true. At this rate I was going to fuck up the only good relationship I'd ever had. I knew that Soph would tell me to talk to Diana about things, get them out in the open, but how could I? It would be like admitting I was a fucking insecure idiot who was becoming obsessed with Lauren Baker—the same Lauren Baker who Diana had told to sling her hook because she was an obsessive, violent, insecure wankette who didn't know what side her bread was buttered. A bit like me as it happens. So, if I didn't want to be kicked to the kerb, I needed to behave like a normal human being for once.

"Hey, you." Diana tore her eyes from Dave and grinned at me. "Fancy a little you and me time before you go?" I suggested.

God. That smile.

"Night, Dave," Diana moved away from her brother, who was looking a little confused. He began to speak, but Diana repeated, "Night, Dave," and moved closer to me. "You need a lift?"

"Nope." I moved closer. "Just a kiss to keep me going."

Strong arms wrapped around me and pulled me into her.

Sophie shouted her goodnight from the doorway, giggled, and then told Dave to move it. That left just Diana and me in the room.

"I think I can manage a kiss." Her voice was sultry, husky, alluring, and so close to my ear that ripples raced through me.

Tilting my head, I gazed up into a sea of blueness. So open, so trusting, so goddamn beautiful and enthralling.

She dipped her face to mine and delivered the most tender, yet powerful kiss I'd ever had in my life. Pressure deepened, and I felt myself becoming absorbed, almost as if I was morphing inside of her. Nothing else mattered but that moment. Nothing else existed but Diana and me. Nothing could change the way I felt about this woman. That was a lot of nothings, but this was everything—*she* was everything.

We parted in the car park, and in my rear view mirror I observed her watching my departure from where she stood beside her own car. I wanted to slam on the brakes, get out of the car, and run to her; hold her, gather her up and slip her inside my coat, and run. But that was just idiotic. I had to start acting like a thirty-one year old woman who had just realised love actually existed, and stop being a teenage Facebook addict updating their status to "confused," "lovesick," "angsty," and all the other adjectives dredged up by hormones and insecurity.

Diana said she would call. That was enough. Diana was my girlfriend. My girlfriend. And I was happy with that.

Just under an hour later, I was at home making Dreamtime tea.

Chapter 18

Thursday saw me checking my mobile every few minutes. It was as if I was awaiting the results of a test and couldn't concentrate on anything else until an "All Clear" beeped through. She called at seven thirty-one p.m., just as I was climbing into the bath. I nearly broke my neck getting to the phone, which, with fortuitous foresight, was right next to me. I could hear voices behind Diana, like she was in a public place, and although I spoke as loudly as I thought appropriate, she had difficulty hearing what I was saying. I heard a woman shout her name, but it didn't sound like Lauren Baker's voice. The speaker sounded older, or so I convinced myself.

"Baby, I have to go. We're sitting down to eat before going back to the office. I'll call tomorrow, okay?"

"Sure. You get going." What else could I say?

"And Jess… I miss you."

I absorbed the words. She missed me.

"Got to go, honey. Until tomorrow?"

"Yes…okay. And I—" But she was gone, and I was left holding the phone to my chest and wishing it was her.

That was pretty much the pattern of the next six days. I knew she was busy, knew the project was important, but I was also missing her. Diana was popping home for Wednesday's class and going back to London the following morning. I hoped I would get a little private time with her during her brief return.

As soon as I walked in the classroom, Diana grabbed my hand and pulled me into the storage cupboard and slammed the door behind us. I was extremely happy I had made it to class thirty minutes early, which gave me more time for Diana's kisses. It wasn't long before we were both panting, the deprivation of separation apparent to us both.

A soft knocking sound came from outside the door followed by, "Are you two at it again?"

We giggled like school kids caught behind the bike sheds by the teacher on duty, but I didn't mind.

Diana straightened my blouse and took my hands. "Are you free after class?"

I grinned and nodded.

"Can I come over? You can say no if you want."

Standing on my tiptoes, I kissed her gently. "I would love you to come over. I've missed you."

"Have you? Really? You're not just saying that to make me feel better, are you?"

I wasn't sure whether or not she was joking, but the look on her face told me she meant every word. That made me feel so fucking good.

Class dragged by. Don't get me wrong, I loved being there with Diana, loved taking part in the drawing exercises, but I wanted time alone with her. You can't blame me, can you? I hadn't seen her in a week and had only spoken to her at intervals.

By nine-twenty, we were in the hallway at my house. By nine-twenty-three we were naked and on my bed. Our lovemaking was fierce, passionate, demanding. Every touch, stroke, taste was filled with a hunger for more, as if we could never be satisfied. It was gone one o'clock in the morning by the time we both fell asleep, her half sprawled over me, both completely satiated. It didn't seem as if even five minutes had passed before she was gently shaking me awake and murmuring that she had to leave.

My eyes flicked to the clock on the side table. Five-forty-five. Sitting up, I watched her dress. Her movements were fluid, sensual. Clothes slipped over the glorious expanse of her body and hid the tantalising skin.

"You're up early."

"Hey, baby." Diana's smile brightened the room. "I know, but I've got to get home and get my work stuff. My train leaves at eight-ten."

She leaned over, and her face was mere inches from mine. I could see the tiredness around her eyes, and her normal vibrancy was slightly dulled.

"I…thank you for last night. I needed that."

Funny thing for her to say— "needed that" not "needed you," like I would have said but didn't.

"My pleasure, love."

Was I easy? No. I didn't want to go down that path. Didn't want to start thinking she only wanted me for a quick release.

"When will you be home?" Did I sound eager, or just interested?

Diana sighed, her shoulders slumping. When she looked back at me, I could see sadness lurking just below the surface. "To tell you the truth, Jess, I don't want to go back to London."

I grabbed her hand and squeezed.

"I want to stay here with you. I missed you so much last week."

I felt the ache in my chest crack and the balm slipped out and coated the inside of me.

"Can I ask you something?"

Anything. I nodded.

"Do you wish I didn't have to go too?"

Why would she ask that? Wasn't it obvious?

Diana shook her head. "Never mind. I've got to get going."

She stepped away from me, but I drew her close. "I wish more than anything that you didn't have to go back. I've missed you so bloody much." I wanted to add that I loved her, but didn't.

"I just can't wait until you're back for good."

A hot kiss brushed my cheek. "I can't either." When she leaned away, her eyes were sparkling and full of life, the fatigue banished. "You mean so much to me, Jess. I just want you to remember that when I'm not here."

Cupping her face, I made sure she was looking straight into my eyes before I said, "You mean a lot to me, too, Diana. I just want you to remember *that* when all the women in London are hitting on you."

I grinned to let her know I was joking, although a bit of me wasn't. This woman in my arms was gorgeous. Any fool with two eyes could see that. I was still surprised that she had decided to be my girl instead of getting someone who was worthy of her. "You need to carry a big stick around with you to beat 'em off."

God, I loved her laugh.

"Yeah, right. Can I borrow yours if you're not going out?"

"In the vernacular of today's teenagers … LOL!"

"LOL?" Her puzzlement showed on her face in the most adorable way.

"Never mind. Go on. You're going to be late."

Ten minutes later, I was waving her off. There was no point in going back to bed. There was no way I would be able to go back to sleep. There was only one thing for it—a cup of tea and morning TV. Now that was living.

⊷⊶⊷⊶

Why was it getting harder the longer Diana was away? Shouldn't I be getting used to it? I mean, she had been gone again for five days and a bit, only popping back for class again. At least she had taken the time away from her busy life in London to call me more often, though not often enough to assuage my insecurities.

I spent Saturday with Sophie, who told me in no uncertain terms that I was well on my way to a strait jacket and a one way pass to the Obsession Ward. My parents were no better on the Sunday, and they thought making goo goo faces at me when I was talking on the phone with Diana was perfectly acceptable. As soon as the call was over, they tried to dig me out of my self-induced funk, but I couldn't snap out of it. Even I knew that was not good, but I couldn't seem to nail the reason I was acting like such a twat. It wasn't because I loved Diana, that much was obvious. People in love didn't do that. Jealousy wasn't about love—it was about possession, and instead of the other person falling madly in love back, it would only scare them away.

I didn't want to scare Diana away. I had to do something about my out of control anxieties before I lost the only woman in my life I would ever love.

Chapter 19

The Tuesday before the last drawing class, and therefore Diana's return, I was in bed at nine-thirty. I couldn't bear to sit downstairs and watch TV or do anything else as mind numbing. So, I lay in bed staring at the ceiling and thinking about me and Diana. I should say I was thinking about how I was going to get past acting in a manner that would drive her away. Every time I pictured her face, I got a clawing feeling in my gut. A little bit of that was fear, but the majority of it was the anticipation of seeing her the following evening.

I had just nodded off when my mobile sounded. Through blurry eyes, I saw Diana's name flash up. My grin was instant, even though I was still half asleep.

"Hey, did I wake you?"

Why is it that when people ask you if they've just woken you, we always insist we were awake, as I did now?

"Oh? That's strange."

"What is?"

"I thought you'd be asleep, considering all your lights are out."

L.T. SMITH

Eyes that were half open shot to full visual as what she said sank in. If she knew all my lights were out, that could mean only one thing. I shot out of bed, tripped over my rug, and launched head first into the closed bedroom door. I didn't let it affect me, just shook my head and yanked the door open, and then raced down the stairs. It wasn't until I was standing in front of my door that I remembered Diana was still on the other end of the line.

Lifting it to my ear, I could hear Diana repeating my name. Butterflies skipped around in my stomach, and I was definite my legs were finding it hard to keep me standing. I was surprised to see that my hand was shaking as it unlatched the safety chain and made its way to the catch at a snail's pace.

"Are you *ever* going to let me in?"

Her tone was teasing, and a grin split my face.

She laughed. "There you are. Finally." Diana was still talking into the phone, but lowered it to hold her arms out in invitation.

I didn't have to be asked twice. I grabbed hold of her and pulled her close, pressing my face against the nape of her neck. Her scent was like coming home after being away for far too long. It calmed me. It held everything I needed to feel complete. I don't know how long we stood there, but I snapped back from my oasis when I heard her whisper, "Let's go inside. You're shivering."

She thought I was shivering because I was cold. I didn't correct her.

It wouldn't take a rocket scientist to figure out that Diana didn't go home that night. We spent hours knowing each other again, hours of moulding ourselves to one another's willing bodies.

The sun sifted through the partially drawn curtains

and slithered up the covers to illuminate the contours of Diana's face. She looked so young, so innocent. I felt a giggle bubble up as I remembered all we had done the previous night, many of which was as far from innocent as things could get. A contented sigh slipped through her lips as she turned towards me, her body seeking mine in her sleep. That slight movement made my heart glow, and I wondered if she had even known she was doing it. I hoped she did.

My fingers traced the air around her face without actually touching her, etching her chiselled features, her firm jaw, her straight nose. Then my fingers fluttered over the softness of her lips, lips I had kissed only a couple of hours before and was aching to kiss again. I lowered my hand and shifted closer to her, until my breath mingled with hers.

Softly, so softly, I freed the words I longed to say to her. "I love you."

It was amazing how saying those three words made my heart soar. But seeing Diana's eyelids flutter and hearing "Jess?" seemed to do the complete opposite.

Snapping my eyes closed, I feigned sleep.

I felt Diana move, felt her lean over me as if she was checking to see if I was awake, then she said my name again.

I played possum, although I was definite if she had the mind to listen, she would hear my heart banging like a drumstick against my ribcage.

I stayed like that for as long as I believed she was leaning over me. It felt like hours. As soon as I felt her shift, felt her breath move from my face, I smacked my lips together and readied myself for my fake waking up performance.

My eyes fluttered open to a sea of blue. Diana was staring at me intently, her head resting on her hand, her elbow buried in the pillow. I stretched leisurely, or as leisurely as I could considering I was metaphorically crapping myself as I expected her to demand I repeat what I had said.

I batted my eyelids as if to focus them and innocently asked, "You okay?"

Diana seemed to think about it before answering with a smile, "Couldn't be better."

I think the sensation of relief is one of the finest emotions a person can have. Think about it. All the times you have felt really good in your life, weren't they mainly associated with relief? I know the relief I was experiencing was selfish, but at that precise moment I was happily wallowing in it. However, there was a little part of me that felt a sense of disappointment that she hadn't heard me say those three little, yet very powerful words.

"You want something to drink? I'm getting one."

Unable to trust what might come out of my mouth, I nodded.

"Coffee? Water? Tea? What?"

I nodded again.

Diana's face crumpled in question.

"Tea! Erm…yeah…tea."

A laugh shot out of her mouth. "Looks like tea, then." She swiftly leaned forward and planted a kiss on my lips, almost possessive in its intensity. Then she was up and off the bed, grabbing her shirt as she left the room, leaving me breathlessly waiting for her return.

We sipped at our drinks, then snuggled down for another hour before the alarm sounded and told me it was time to get up for work. Diana had a million and one things to get sorted at home before class that evening, so she left my house at the same time I did. I hated parting from her.

All day at work, I was distracted. Had she heard me tell her I loved her? If she had, why hadn't she said anything? Even a "WTF!" would have been a response. It seemed strange that she had woken up when I had whispered to her. God! I was driving myself insane with all the fucking mindreading and possible outcomes that could occur if I had the bloody spine to say something to her. I should've just bit the bullet when I saw her eyelids twitching and her forehead furrow and waited for her to be fully awake before I told her again.

Who was I kidding? That would take balls, backbone, gumption—three things I obviously lacked. I wanted to call my pseudo therapist, AKA Sophie, but I knew she would only take the piss before telling me to get a grip.

The evening came around slowly, because I was looking forward to class. If I had learned anything from the course, it would not just be how to consider perspective. I had learned so much about my life, myself, and my inability to "seize the day." Don't get me wrong, it wasn't all negative. I had also found Diana Sullivan, although I don't think she was actually lost in the first place.

Hoping to grab a few minutes alone with Diana before class started, I got there early. I hadn't expected everybody else to have the same idea. It was the last class after all—something I had acknowledged but not actually acknowledged, if you know what I mean.

She was in the process of thanking a middle-aged woman for a gift when she suddenly stopped mid-sentence and looked in my direction. Her blue gaze transfixed me as she bestowed a breath taking grin on me. She finished her thanks and made her excuses, her eyes darting back and forth to mine all the while.

"Hey, you." Diana leaned forward slightly and, for a moment, I thought she was going to kiss me in front of all the class. Instead, she tilted her head and whispered, "You look amazing." I heard her inhale deeply. "And smell divine."

A blush raced over my face, even heating the tips of my ears. A giggle came up from nowhere, and I was on the verge of shuffling my feet and saying, "Aw shucks." But I was saved.

"Oi! Taylor! You sucking up to the teacher again?" Sophie was standing right behind me, and I hadn't even heard her approach. Strange, as Sophie was a lot of things, but Ninja wasn't one of them.

Diana looked over my shoulder and grinned. "Ah…the sister-in-law. You bring any equipment tonight?"

"Just my razor sharp wit and good looks."

I turned to face her.

"And— Fuck me, Jess! What's with the beetroot face?"

Did I say she had saved me? Maybe I meant to say she embarrassed me to the point that I felt the blush turn into something more like a third degree burn.

"You got a temperature?"

I meant to give her a playful push, but even the people who were on the other side of the room turned to look when they heard the thwack of my hand on her shoulder and the "Ouch! Y'git!" from my best friend and tormenter.

"It's the cold. Erm…the heat."

She was rubbing her shoulder and glaring at me. "Which one? Cold or heat?"

"Both. Come on, let's get settled." I winked at Diana. "See you in a bit," I said. Completely stupid, as I would be seeing her all night—she was the one teaching the class. However, my stupidity was forgivable—I was having a crisis at the time.

Our final project was a still life. A female subject, much to Sophie's disdain. This would be the one that would decide if we would pass or fail the course. By the looks of my friend's drawing, and her inability to focus on what she was doing, I gathered Sophie didn't really care if she flunked. Images of her cat with buttons down its front popped into my head at one point as I was looking at her work—something that shouldn't have been conjured when she was supposed to be drawing a naked woman. At least the pubic lice were absent.

Dave came in about 7:45, nodding to his sister and mouthing his apologies. Diana grinned at him and motioned for him to get stuck in.

When break time came, Dave scooted over to us and told us he needed to speak to Diana before meeting us in the café. I smiled at him, but part of me was a little disappointed that I wouldn't be able to snatch a few moments alone with her.

Why did I have a need to be near her all of the time? Why was it when someone else held her attention, or if she was not right next to me, within touching distance, I felt empty? Was I turning into a sticky bob? We had been together just twelve hours earlier, so why was I feeling as if a lead weight had been dropped onto me when I was queuing for coffee?

Sophie didn't say anything until we were seated, and then it took her the time to stir her coffee slowly whilst glaring at me suspiciously before I got antsy.

"What?"

She continued to stir, and then tapped her spoon on the side of her cup three times.

"Why are you staring at me like I've grown two heads?"

She puckered her lips and closed her eyes momentarily.

"What? Again."

A sigh hissed from between her teeth, and her shoulders slumped. There was a look of resignation on her face. "You're cocking up again, aren't you?"

I pulled the "What the fuck are you talking about" face and snorted.

"Thought so."

"Look, I—"

"So you should be."

"What?"

"Exactly. What the fuck are you playing at?"

A frustrated breath left my lips, and I squirmed uncomfortably on the plastic chair. Grabbing a pen from my bag, I snatched a napkin and wrote, "I've no clue what you're talking about. I'm not even going to try to answer you if you insist on finishing my sentences."

Sophie half looked at me scribbling before giving me a look of disinterest as I pushed the note over to her.

"You know exactly what I mean. You're being all retarded."

Huh?

"No need to look all innocent. I've known you too long for you to give it the angelic one." Sophie leaned over the table. "Jess, just tell the girl how you feel. What's the worst that could happen?"

I didn't answer.

"You're terrified she will leave you. I saw your face when Dave asked Diana for a word. Anyone would think you would never see her again."

"But I didn't do or say anything."

"You didn't need to. All I'm saying is—"

"There you are." Diana slipped in beside me, and I felt the click of connection again. "Dave's getting coffee." She looked from me to Sophie. "What's up?"

"Noth—"

"Just reminding Jess about something she has to do." Sophie smiled showing her perfect, white teeth. "Tell me Diana…"

My stomach clenched. She wouldn't, would she?

"I wanted to know something."

I tried to kick her under the table, but kicked the table leg instead.

"How do you feel about…"

Aw fuck.

"…teaching?" The smile again, this time aimed at me with a raised eyebrow added.

Diana was oblivious to my discomfort, both physically and emotionally, and started to jabber about the pros and cons of teaching a night class. I didn't hear a word of it. I was too busy plotting my revenge on my grinning friend.

I passed; Sophie didn't. I was over the moon, as I had fully believed I would fail. Sophie was really surprised that her drawing hadn't cut the mustard with her "in-law," but she took the rejection as well as she could, with grumbles, piss taking—mostly to do with I was sleeping with the teacher—and loads of face pulling.

However, my excitement at passing the course paled in comparison to what I felt when I found out Diana would not be leaving the following day as I expected. The project was running smoothly, and she didn't have to go back to London until the New Year. It was if a weight had been lifted off my chest. I would be a liar if I said the heaviness of heart I had experienced the last couple of weeks was solely because I missed Diana. It was more a result of my fretting: about how I felt about Diana, about her being around much more interesting people than me, and, mainly—if I was being truthful—about her being in the same city as Lauren Baker. I know, I know, Diana had told me she had never loved Lauren. But she had also told me Lauren had held something over her to keep her with her. That was the crux of the matter.

But that was in the past. I had Diana all to myself, and I was going to be certain sure that I made the most of it.

Chapter 20

With Diana home, I couldn't believe how quickly time flew by. Her birthday came and went, with much celebration and a necklace from me. I had spent ages looking at rings, but decided that it was a little too soon to be frightening the shit out of her with an engagement ring. "I love you" definitely comes before "Will you marry me?" doesn't it?

Before I knew it, I was waiting for Diana to pick me up for our weekend in London. It would be the first time we were away together, but it wasn't as if we didn't know each other intimately by that stage. Good job, too, because I would have been shitting a brick.

The Plaza was everything I could have wanted and more. It wasn't until we pulled up outside, that I realised we were staying at the Park Plaza on Westminster Bridge Road and not the dump I had seen online. Our studio room had a fantastic view of Big Ben framed by floor to ceiling windows. No wonder it was so expensive. God bless Dave.

As soon as the porter scuttled out and the door closed behind him, Diana slipped her arms around my waist and we stood for ages gazing out the window. An illuminated

Big Ben stood guard over the city, and the Houses of Parliament tagged on at the side. It was perfect.

"Fancy a soak before dinner?" Diana's voice tickled my ear, and every nerve ending in my body responded. "Get your bags sorted, I'll run us a bath." A quick kiss on my throat, and she was gone.

I liked the thought of her running "us" a bath. That sounded wonderful.

Five minutes later, I went into the bathroom, where the scent of the bubbling water tantalised my nose. Fluffy bathrobes and slippers were waiting next to the bath, and lighted candles ringed the edges of the room.

Smiling, Diana waited to see my response before she said, "I won't be a minute" and shot out of the room.

I quickly disrobed and slipped into the tub. I sighed as my body relaxed into the gentle massaging of the water. My eyes closed, and I sank even lower.

A voice close to my ear whispered, "Careful you don't drown in there."

A lazy smile slid onto my lips, and I slowly opened my eyes and saw a half-naked Diana, standing with her back to me. Muscles shifted and shaped as she removed her clothes, and I once again wondered how anyone could be so perfectly beautiful. As she bent to pick up her trousers, I was entranced by the mouth-watering image of Diana's backside. God. I felt a surge of arousal, one that had been pretty much on a constant simmer since the night I first heard her voice in the Art room.

It felt natural to scoot forward and let her slip in behind me. So natural to feel her legs slip around my hips. So utterly natural to lean back and feel her breasts on my back, and her breath on the side of my face. We chatted lazily about the exhibition the following day until we realised we didn't have to talk at all. Just being with each other was more than enough.

We bathed each other, every caress of the sponge on my skin provoking the yearning I had for Diana. I could hear her breathing becoming more ragged as she rubbed her hands over the base of my neck. Soft kisses lighted on my flesh and conjured goose bumps along my arms and chest. Even though the room was pleasantly warm, my nipples were as hard as if I was in sub-zero temperatures.

Incited by her soft touches, I shifted around to kiss her. Rather than getting in our way, the water enhanced the pressure of our lips. Her hands went to my butt and pulled me closer, and the lapping water titillated the sensitised area between my legs. The rhythm of her against me was fluid. My mouth left her lips and trailed down her throat, over her collar bone, and eventually to her breasts. The water on her skin mixing with the taste of her made a heady combination. Fortuitously, the bath was wide enough for me to part her legs to make room for my fingers. Thicker wetness than that of the water helped me slip effortlessly inside her. A gasp came from her lips, her eyes half open and expectant. Out. In. The tempo was slow, and she tried to press herself onto my hand. I could tell by the noises she was making that she wanted me to take her quickly, but this wasn't the time for speed. This was the time for a slow, loving reconnection.

Hips pushed higher, fingers dipped deeper as my mouth sucked her breast. I could feel her most intimate walls contracting, pulsating, readying themselves for the onslaught of sensation that was imminent. What I didn't expect was to climax with her as she came; just watching her beautiful face as she tipped over the edge was enough to take me over with her. At that precise moment, I knew that this weekend I would tell Diana I loved her. Leaving the words unsaid would drive me crazy.

❦

Over an hour later, we emerged from the bath, faces flushed, bodies fully alive yet relaxed. I was drying my hair when I heard the door knock and Diana speaking to someone.

"Hungry?"

Turning, I saw a trolley laden with food and my stomach growled my answer.

It was the most wonderful evening of my life. Everything was absolutely perfect—the setting, the company, the food—everything.

Our passion flared throughout the night. I couldn't get enough of Diana, which both thrilled and depressed me. Even in sleep I couldn't escape the fear that Diana would reject my proclamation of love. And even though it was a great comfort to feel her naked body spooning up against my back, part of me was still in limbo. I just wanted to get a grip on myself, maybe even give myself a good shake. But as that was impossible, I fell into a fitful sleep.

The exhibition at Tate Modern opened at 10 am, and Diana wanted to get there before the rush. Breakfast was hurried, and soon we were making our way on foot, as the gallery wasn't even a mile and a half from where we were staying. Half past nine saw us queuing outside the imposing edifice, a gargoyle of a building whose exterior definitely hid the fact it was full of beautiful artwork.

By the time we got inside, we were perished. The wind had whipped around us, making our teeth chatter and forcing us to hang on to each other for heat. That was what

I told myself, at any rate.

It was so worth it. It took my breath away to see all those beautiful pieces in one place. Half naked women surrounded us; the exhibit could have been described a lesbian's dream. I was fascinated with Gauguin's philosophy—the escapism from everything that was "artificial and conventional."

Considering I was as conventional as conventional could get, I was a little surprised at my mental meanderings. It was the freedom of it all, the "fuck it all" mindset. I coveted the ability to throw caution to the wind and follow my dream, although mine didn't include travelling to Tahiti or Hiva Oa. Mine was just about six feet tall, and staring at a wonderful painting titled *The Moon and the Earth*, her fingers outstretched as if she desperately wanted to touch it, just as mine were aching to touch her.

Time sped by so quickly that I was surprised when Diana said we should get lunch and sit for a while. We had been in the museum for over four hours, and it felt as if I had just stepped through the door.

"Right after we eat, we need to get going. Tate Britain closes at six." Diana was perusing the menu and only flicked her eyes to mine.

I didn't answer. Tate Britain?

"If you want to see *Ophelia*, we have to go to Tate Britain."

She shot me a tentative glance, almost as if she was embarrassed about mentioning it. Why would she feel embarrassed about going to see a painting that we had both said we wanted to see? And why was I suddenly going all fucking Secret Squirrel again?

"Sure. I'd love to."

I remembered the first time she mentioned seeing

Ophelia at the Tate. "Oh, you must wear your rue with a difference." I also recalled the impenetrable sadness lurking behind her eyes. Was it still there? Or had I only imagined it the first time? But the sadness didn't linger long. Diana was intently focused on the fare in front of her.

We were quiet over lunch. Conversation seemed unusually strained. Was it my imagination, or did Diana seem uncomfortable? I couldn't work out why she would feel like that. It was just a painting, the same painting she had offered to show me the first time she had tried to ask me out on a date. But, Ophelia also reminded us both of Lauren Baker. I realized I was providing her side of the conversation as well as my own, but it was so damned obvious.

Outside in the cold wind, I spoke without looking at her directly. "We don't have to go to the Tate, if you'd prefer."

For a few moments, Diana didn't answer me, and I thought the wind had whipped my words away.

"I would like to show it to you, if you wouldn't mind."

From the corner of my eye, I saw that Diana was fidgeting, her hands nervously slipping inside her pockets. Considering I was the one who was feeling nervous about making my declaration of undying love, I put her concern on the back burner for the moment. A sudden anger flowed through me, probably stemming from stupid jealousy about a relationship Diana had told me she hadn't even wanted. Simple, when you put it like that. But try telling that to someone as pig headed and idiotic as me, and you would realise it only incited my jealousy.

The walk to Tate Britain was a little further than the earlier mile and a half. We walked past the hotel and over Westminster Bridge, seeing Big Ben, the House of Lords, and Parliament up close and personal. The view should have encouraged cameras to come careering from bags for pictures of stupid poses for entertainment later, but we did neither. Diana seemed lost in her own world, though I could feel her surreptitiously glancing my way when she thought I wasn't looking.

We arrived at Tate Britain just after four-fifteen and made our way directly to the Pre- Raphaelite gallery. Just as we were about to enter, Diana's phone sounded.

"Shit." She fumbled around in her bag and brought out her mobile.

I grinned, as I had dutifully turned mine off before entering the Modern.

"I…*erm*…got to get this. Won't be a tick."

The grin I was sporting slipped into a weak smile and I nodded, indicating I would go on ahead.

Diana mouthed "wait" and indicated she would move out into the hallway.

She was talking to someone, but the words came in spits and spots. She kept furtively looking my way, as if she was checking either that I was still there or that I couldn't hear what she was saying.

My brain went with the latter. The green eyed monster started churning inside me, and I felt a rush of anger and nausea. What was going on with me? When had it ever been a crime to take a phone call?

"Not yet. I haven't had the chance to speak to her."

Speak to me about what? Assuming I was the "her." Many scenarios vied for my attention, some of which were actually pleasant, intimate and perfect. Alas, they were losing, and losing quickly.

"What if it all goes wrong? What if she…"

"Are you lost, madam?" An elderly male voice came from beside me, and I looked into concerned grey eyes.

Lost? Yes. But not in the way he was thinking.

"Can I be of assistance?"

Diana looked over to us and mouthed, "Are you okay?"

What was it with everyone wondering whether or not I was okay? I nodded. I couldn't think of what else to do.

Shapely eyebrows lifted before they furrowed again. "What?" Her attention was back on the person at the other end of the line.

"Are you feeling okay, madam?"

Fuck off. Please. Before I tell you to fuck off and feel even worse than I do already. I had to think of a way to avoid the scene I would otherwise probably start making in the non-too distant future. "Loos. Erm. The ladies room. Can you tell me where to find it?"

The gentleman smiled and pointed in the opposite direction, indicating the foyer of the Clore Gallery.

I thanked him and turned to look at Diana. She was fully engaged in her conversation, her free hand once again fidgeting in her coat pocket. I waited for her to look, and pointed to the end of the corridor before mouthing, "Loo."

She smiled at me, and I felt my heart break with the knowledge of what I was about to do.

Scuttling away, I found myself standing outside on Millbank, the gallery doors behind me. I don't know why I thought running away would solve anything, but that's what I did. As usual. I didn't have the guts to stay and listen to whatever Diana seemed so nervous about telling me, so I left. I would go back to the hotel, get my things, and leave London to go back to the safety of being a loner who had fuck-all in her life.

That didn't happen. I found myself going in the completely opposite direction.

After walking a while, I caught a cab and rattled off an

address I had total recall of, even though I had only seen it the once. Who would have thought I would end up there, on today of all days.

Her self-satisfied smile faded as I looked into Lauren Baker's brown eyes. Her long auburn hair was pulled back into a pony tail, stray locks escaping the confines of the elastic band. I was definite she must've been working out before I rang her bell, as she was kitted out in sweat pants and a vee neck t-shirt.

Her hand went to her throat to finger the necklace there in a nervous gesture. "Well, well, well. The little student." Her lip curled into a sneer and she reasserted her pose of destroyer, leaving me wondering whether she had been nervous at all. "What have I done to deserve the honour of a home visit from my replacement?"

Now I was there, I didn't have a fucking clue what I wanted to say. One thing I did know was that by going to see Lauren, by not trusting in Diana, I had truly fucked up anything Diana and I could have had between us. Sophie had been right. I had totally and utterly mapped out my own downfall. I had let jealousy and insecurity get in the way of something that could've been truly magical. I had been so scared of losing Diana, I had pushed her away. What I couldn't understand was why? Why had I done that to me? To us?

"Cat got your tongue?" Her smirk was back, and then her eyes widened. "Don't tell me Diana's done a runner?" Her laugh was shrill, loud. "You think…" more laughter "you think she is *here*?"

My teeth clenched, and I took a step forward. With sick satisfaction, I saw her step backwards, as if she expected me to clock her. "You are nothing but a bully."

She snorted. "A bully? Are we on the playground?"

I knew she was taunting me, and like a fool, I took the bait. "Hitting a woman, burning someone you profess to love... Yes. A bully." My fists were clenching, and so was my jaw. "No. A coward. You couldn't have Diana, so you made sure she felt as if she didn't have any other choice but to be with you."

"Diana loved me. Ask her."

It was my turn to laugh, but it wasn't because of merriment. "I didn't have to. She told me all about you."

Pain flashed through Lauren's eyes, and then she leaned forward and ground out, "And she told me all about you." A look of disdain crossed her ugly beautiful features as she looked me up and down. "And you ain't all that."

I have never hit anyone in my life, but I now believed it would be a satisfying experience if the circumstances were right. You see it in the movies, and it's easy. Thwack. The other person's head will fly to the side, and they wipe their lip and look at the spot of blood before giving you a look or a smack in return. That was not the case. Agony was shooting through my hand, and I was definite I caught her tooth with my middle knuckle. There was no wiping and snarling, no thump back. All I got was a bloody hand, an aching wrist, and a woman who seemed even more self-satisfied than before.

Her tongue came out and licked her lips, as if enjoying the taste of blood. Lauren cocked her head to one side and looked deeply into my eyes. "And we are so very different, how?"

I think that was the lowest point of my life up to that moment. Turning, I stumbled, my handbag falling on the street and dumping all the contents.

Lauren watched me as I fumbled around, collecting things. She didn't say a word. Eventually I gave it up and left most of my belongings on the floor. As long as I had my purse, I could get home.

But I had to see Diana before I went. I had to explain that in fact the old saying "It isn't you, it's me" held more truth than I'd ever thought.

◦⊰⊱◦

By the time I arrived at the hotel, I felt sick. I had totally fucked up. Totally Fucked Up. By allowing my insecurities to take charge of my actions, I made damn sure that I lost the only woman I had ever loved, and I hadn't even told her how I felt. All I had managed to do was show her that she should run as fast as she could in any direction that led her away from me. I was worse than Lauren Baker and Samantha James rolled into one.

Reaching the door to our hotel room, I realised I didn't have the card key and turned to go back to reception to get another one. I didn't get very far, as the room door flew open and Diana appeared. Her face showed both anger and relief, but instead of biting my head off or saying anything caustic, she disintegrated in a flood of tears and wrapped her arms around me.

She kept trying to speak, but her sobs got in the way. Six foot of shaking, sobbing woman. Six foot of quivering mass, a quivering mass I had created.

I wanted to stop her tears, wanted to lie and say I had left the museum for some reason other than that I was a twat. The lie wouldn't come. I had, as my mother always said, "Made my bed" and now I must lie in it, or not lie, as the case turned out to be.

It didn't matter. I knew that whatever I said would not be enough as soon as I heard the voice behind me.

"How sweet. Love's young dream."

Why had Lauren followed me? How did she know where I'd be?

"You left these."

I felt Diana stiffen, pull back, and I saw her expression turn from concern to something darker, something cold.

"Thought I'd be the concerned citizen, although I really should've called the police."

And then Diana turned to me, blue eyes wide with confusion. "Jess?"

I opened my mouth, moved it as if I was actually speaking, but nothing came out.

"I think it's best if we went inside, don't you? I doubt you want everybody hearing what a fucking bunny boiler you've got yourself involved with." Lauren didn't wait for a response, she just pushed past us into the hotel room.

"Jess? What…why is she here?"

There was such sadness in her voice that I knew she already had worked out what had happened, but was afraid to believe it.

"Nice room. You've splashed out, Diana."

"Jess?"

I pulled away from her, almost peeling her fingers from my arms. It was time to face what I had done, even though I knew it would hurt her even more than she was hurting already.

I scanned the room, noting the disarray—the phone thrown on the table, her coat and bag tossed onto the floor, a small box next to her gloves on the coffee table. I took note of every minute detail, anything to delay acknowledging that my relationship was in smithereens.

"What's going on?" Diana's voice had lost its insecurity. It was sharp, authoritative. There was no evidence of the sultry, seductive lover I had been with less than twelve hours earlier. No lightness, no humour, nothing of the woman I had accompanied to the Tate.

Lauren touched the bruise that had formed on the side of her swollen lip. "I think you should ask her, don't you?"

My principal thought was that I should have hit Lauren harder, then maybe she would either still be unconscious or be finding it too painful to speak.

"Stop fucking me about, Lauren. Why are you here?"

"Diana, I—"

She held up her hand to silence me. A cold glance flicked my way before she focused her attention back on Lauren.

Lauren inflated with happiness at seeing Diana shut me up.

"I said, why have you come here? I told you I never wanted to see your face again. Ever."

Some of Lauren's inflation oozed out of her, as if she had a slow puncture. Unfortunately the deflation turned to resentment, resentment aimed in my direction. After all, I was responsible for this scene.

"I don't know why you are being such a bitch to me. She's..." Lauren's finger jabbed in my direction, "....the one you should be mad at." Silence. "She came around to my place looking for you, and she punched me in the face."

"I didn't—"

"You fucking liar. You punched me in the face because I told you Diana wasn't with me."

You would think I would have learned my lesson, wouldn't you? Unfortunately, I hadn't. I made a grab at the lying, conniving twattette, my hands grasping the scarf around her neck.

Strong hands grabbed me and pulled me off, almost

flinging me aside.

"See? She's a nut job." Lauren's hands flitted up to her throat and played nervously with the necklace, as I had seen her do at her apartment.

Diana froze. Her eyes narrowed and then widened before she ground out, "That's my locket. You've got my locket."

"And? I bought it."

Shit. This was one of those times when a person is nervous, angry, and a little surprised. Although I was in a situation where I wish I had done everything completely differently, I was still a little thankful that I wasn't Lauren Baker at that moment.

"It was you, after all. You hit Mon."

A nervous laugh shot out of Lauren's mouth. "I have no clue what you are talking about. Hit Mon? Who, or what, is Mon?"

"You know damn well who Mon is. She is the woman you nearly killed when you broke into my house." Diana reached for her phone. "Let's see what the police say about this, shall we?"

The room was so quiet that I honestly believed I could hear the three numbers being dialled.

Panic vibrated off Lauren. She had to know there was no way she could convince the authorities she was not guilty. The evidence was hanging around her throat, after all. She turned pleading eyes in my direction, as if she expected me to intercede for her.

I gave her a smug smile, even though I knew it wouldn't be long before I was the focus of Diana's disdain and disappointment myself.

Diana was speaking to Emergency Services, and all the while, her emotionless eyes flicked from me to Lauren and back.

I actually saw the light come on above Lauren's head and then travel to her eyes and illuminate her face.

"Actually, I would like to speak to them too. I've been the victim of an attack, after all."

Shit, again. That had never entered my head. Why had I not realised there would be repercussions other than me losing Diana? GBH or ABH? That was the only decision left to make. Then on to court—prison, or bound over to keep the peace. A record—life over. Aw fuck it. It already was.

Diana had stopped talking. The phone was closing and so was her expression. "You get out now and never contact either of us again, never mention this again, and that's it. Over."

"No. Diana, Monica deserves better than that." I turned to Lauren. "I don't give a rat's ass about what you say I did. You're going down too."

"Just shut up, Jess. It's over." Diana turned away from both of us. "Everything is over."

The excruciating reality struck home as I understood what she had said. "Everything" meant "us," because to me she was everything.

Lauren fled and left us to our silence. The room darkened, and the small lamp struggled to make an impact on the gloom. We sat in silence for over an hour, neither of us wanting to admit what we had to admit, although it was a foregone conclusion: we were over, done with, at the end of the chapter. We'd had our closure with Lauren's arrival, with me admitting what I had done, but we both knew there was one more act to play. I didn't want to be the lead in the final scene of our relationship, and, judging by the agonising quiet, neither did Diana.

My legs going numb from inactivity I shifted in the chair.

Sad blue eyes caught mine, and Diana breathed out a resigned sigh. "Why, Jess? Why did you have to go and see her? Why did you have to hit her?"

Such pain. Not just mine, hers. It seeped from every pore of her and filled the air. I shrugged my shoulders in defeat.

Another sigh, a slight hitch, almost as if the sigh had wanted to be a sob but had been restrained.

"I love you, Diana."

Too late. Way too late. Her face stretched and crumbled all in one fluid motion. A solitary tear slipped from her eye and trickled down her cheek.

"And I loved you, Jess."

Loved.

Standing abruptly, she walked over to the coffee table and scooped something off it. "Do you know why I wanted to see *Ophelia* today?"

I shook my head, but realised she couldn't see me. "No."

Slowly, she faced me, her hands cupping something. "I wanted to…wanted to…" She sobbed, followed by a flood of tears. "Never mind. It doesn't matter now." Her hands fell to her sides, along with whatever she held in them. "I think I should go."

Those words galvanized me into action, and I was next to her, gripping her arm, her body tense, as if I might hit her. "Please, Diana, don't. Let's talk." I could feel the rigidity of her body in just my fingertips, and I knew even before she spoke that I didn't have a cat in hell's chance of changing her mind.

Diana couldn't even look at me as she said, "I can't, Jess. Not now."

"When?" I was becoming frantic.

Her shrug loosened my fingers, and I allowed her to slip away.

Chapter 21

After Diana left the hotel room, I stood staring dumbly at the closed door, numb. I don't know how long I stood, then sat, then lay, before the numbness turned into grief. In the course of that one evening, I went through the five stages. I tried to deny our relationship was over, tried to convince myself there was something I could do to make things right. Then I moved on to anger. God, was there anger. I ranted and raved about everything and everyone, but I never forgot who I should be angriest with. You might think I would blame Lauren Baker, but I knew for a fact it was all my own doing.

And then came the bargaining. That was easy. I promised myself I would be a better person, would seek help, would do anything to get Diana back and show her how much I loved her.

The fourth stage—depression. Full on depression. Tears, tears, more tears. I don't think I can adequately explain the pain that tore me apart. I felt as if I was being thumped in the stomach over and over and over again, and I found myself curling into a ball to deflect it. It didn't help.

The next morning, the sun streamed through the window and I watched it approach the foot of the bed. It was a new day, a day for accepting what had happened and trying to move on. I accepted what I had done, accepted I had totally fucked up the best thing I had in my life with my own insecurities, accepted many things, except for two. One was that Lauren Baker had gotten away with hurting Monica because of my unexplainable actions. The second was that I would never be with Diana again.

I knew that the last stage was to be where everything began to heal through acceptance, but how could I? Diana wasn't dead. She was very much alive, and somewhere in my world. So no, I couldn't accept it.

And I never would.

I had been home for about half an hour when my front doorbell went crackers. I didn't want to answer it in case it was someone who wanted to be sociable, but there was a tiny part of me that was hopeful it might be Diana.

As soon as I got close to the door, I knew it was Sophie outside, mainly because of her shouting and threatening me through the letterbox. Some things never changed.

I opened the door and turned away without saying a word, just made my way to the living room for my roasting over the coals. My actions affected more than just Diana and me; they affected Sophie and Dave too. How could I still be her best friend when she was marrying the brother of the woman I had hurt so badly? And how could I see Sophie, see her and Dave, and act as if my heart wasn't breaking every time?

"What the fuck are you playing at?"

I knew she'd be angry.

"What on earth were you thinking? Lauren Baker?" Her voice got louder as she followed me.

"I told you to leave it, I told you!" Sophie grabbed my arm. "Jess? Fucking answer me!"

In all the years I had known Sophie, she had never spoken to me in that tone of voice. My anger poured from inside and belched out into the air. "Don't you think I know I fucked up?"

Sophie snorted.

"Don't you know I wish it had all turned out differently?"

"It's a pity you didn't think about that before you cocked things up, isn't it?" She stomped to the sofa and threw herself on it.

I could see she was trying to control her anger. Her chest puffed out as she released a slow breath.

"And why is your phone off?"

Oddly enough, I hadn't thought about my phone. I had turned it off as Diana and I had entered the Tate, and had been too busy screwing up my life to think about turning it back on.

"Do you know how many times I've tried to contact you?"

I glanced towards the landline before looking back at Sophie.

"You know I don't have your landline number on my phone."

I shrugged as I went back to the armchair I had been curled up in since my return.

"Come sit next to me, Jess. Tell me why."

How could I tell her why? I didn't know myself. I had acted completely out of character. I couldn't even blame it on falling in love for the first time. Millions of people fall in love and don't act the way I did.

She patted the sofa, and I sat on the far end. "Diana's devastated. Obviously."

Just the mention of Diana's name sent a searing pain through me. Sophie must've seen her, as I knew Dave would have been in contact, if only to see how everything went. It had been his birthday present to her, after all.

"I don't think I've ever seen anyone cry so much."

I vaguely wondered whether Sophie was torturing me on purpose.

"I mean, Jess, not only did Diana leave Lauren because she didn't love her, she left her because she was violent. And what did you do? Used your fists."

Aw shit. No wonder Diana was devastated. I had shown the same characteristics she had suffered through with Lauren—insecurity and violence. Shame filled me, and so it should. I had never thought violence was the answer to anything, so why had I hit Lauren? No one, not even Lauren Baker, deserved to be hit. I was the lowest of the low. No wonder she had tensed when I had gripped her arm.

The tears that flowed weren't just tears of self-pity, they were tears for the hurt I had caused Diana, Sophie, Dave, and Monica. Sophie's arms slipped around me and pulled me to her. Being in her arms had always been a comfort, but not at that moment. I couldn't allow myself to be comforted. I didn't deserve it.

Sophie held me. She didn't say a word. Even when the tears stopped flowing, she just held me tighter.

Why hadn't I listened to her? She had told me to leave it, told me to just tell Diana how I felt, but I had known better, hadn't I. And look where that got me—curled into a ball, half on and half off Sophie's knee, shivering in emotional exhaustion.

My lips were swollen and dry, my tongue seemed too big for my mouth, but I had to ask. "How is Diana?"

Sophie snorted. "How do you think? She's crushed."

I lifted my head to look into Sophie's brown eyes and saw concern there. .

"She loves you, Jess. Can't you see it?"

"Loved."

"Huh?"

"She said she loved me. Past tense. I fucked up for good and all."

As I pulled away, Sophie's hands slipped down my arms and released me. "You want a cuppa?" Without waiting for a reply, I went into the kitchen. I set the kettle on to boil, and I heard Sophie shift into the room behind me.

"What do you mean, 'past tense?'"

I couldn't turn and face her. "As I said, I fucked up. How on earth could she still love me after what I did?" Silence filled the space between us, and I continued to make coffee. "You still off the sugar?" An irritated sigh sounded from behind me.

"What the fuck are you doing, Jess? You've just split with the woman you profess to love, and you are carrying on as if nothing has happened."

I stopped stirring the drinks.

"True, you could've done things differently, but you didn't. What are you going to do about it now?"

Anger flashed through me, and I spun around. "Do about it? DO about it? This isn't some fucking admin error. I, as I keep on fucking telling you, have fucked it all up. I couldn't let it go. Couldn't let go of the…the…jealousy… the feeling that if someone better came along, she would pick them over me."

Instead of looking surprised by my outburst, Sophie smiled. That pissed me off. "Go on. Tell me 'I told you so.' You've never had that problem, Sophie." I moved towards her, brandishing a teaspoon as my weapon. "Everyone always loves Sophie, don't they? Everyone *always* wants to be with you." My laugh was angry, bitter, like the ones that you hear in films when the psychotic killer is unveiling his or her plan of world destruction.

Sophie didn't look threatened by my cutlery weapon. What was I going to do? Stir her to death?

"As for me," that laugh again, "I get fucked over, get shit on. I find out from everyone else that the woman I was seeing was fucking anyone with a fucking pulse." I was close to Sophie now, and her eyes were flicking from me to the utensil in my hand.

"Give me the spoon, Jess."

It should've been funny, should've had us both in stitches, but it didn't. The spoon was my asserter, my right giver, my administrator of justice.

"Give Me The Spoon, Jess."

"No! It is my spoon." Yes. I had lost the plot big time. "Mine, not yours. You have your own spoons." What the fuck was I saying? "You always have everything, and I get fucked over."

"She wasn't worth it, Jess."

"YES, SHE WAS!" The yell emanated from within me, and it alleviated some of the pressure, diminished some of the old anger. "Diana is worth ten of me. I was never good enough to be loved by her."

Sophie lunged and grabbed my hand in an attempt to wrest the teaspoon from my grasp. I wasn't having any of it. She couldn't take the teaspoon away; it was all I had left. And then it was gone, and I was in Sophie's arms, crying again.

"She wasn't worth it, Jess. Samantha wasn't worth it."

Samantha?

"I know… I know… Come, let's sit down."

Sophie led me to the living room and sat me on the sofa again. One minute later, she brought drinks in. I could smell the brandy.

She gave me a tentative smile and offered me a cup. "Helps."

Snivelling, I took the offered drink and sipped. The heat of the coffee and the alcohol flowed through me. We sat there for what seemed like an age, but in reality was only about ten minutes.

Sophie placed her empty cup on the table, then took mine from my hand and placed it next to hers. "We need to talk, Jess. You need to get all this shit out in the open."

I shrugged.

She patted my thigh gently. "You need to accept this and move forward." I opened my mouth to speak, but she stopped me. "Not Diana, Samantha James."

"This is not about Samantha James."

"That's where you're wrong, love. It's always been about Samantha James."

As Sophie told me, in detail, why it was all about Samantha James, I realised something. Just because I had never fallen head over heels for my ex, it didn't mean what she did to me, did to us, wouldn't have consequences. I'd admitted it without even realising, when I had lost my temper in the kitchen. Saying things like "feeling that if someone better came along, she would pick them over me." No wonder Sophie had smiled.

That had been the main problem, hadn't it? Me thinking that Diana would do to me what Samantha had done, and becoming another case of finding "out from everyone else that the woman I was seeing was fucking anyone with a fucking pulse."

"That's one of the reasons I wanted you to meet Diana in the first place. I thought you two could heal each other."

That made me feel even worse.

"Maybe it was a little soon, eh?" Sophie hugged me to her. "I just couldn't bear to see you going more and more into yourself."

I pulled back and looked at her in confusion.

"You were never the one to stay in all the time, Jess. I never had to force you to come out and do stuff. But after Samantha…" She pulled a face, "it was like you wanted to protect yourself from the world by staying alone in your own little space."

Had I? Was that the reason why I'd sat home night after night, going to bed at 9:30 to have a read like a pensioner would do? Was I really trying to avoid getting hurt all over again? Could I even remember what I'd been like before I found out about Samantha's infidelities?

"You were always the life of the party, Jess."

"But—"

"No. You were. I was usually the person that tagged along to whatever you were going to."

"But—"

"Yes, you were, and no I wasn't." She gave me a stern look that was softened by the gentleness in her eyes. "You said everyone loves me, wants to be with me. That isn't exactly true, is it?"

"But—"

"You got interrupting goat disease, Taylor?"

I laughed, my first real laugh since the Tate.

"We have always been a team, always gotten into trouble

together. Remember the school trip to the art gallery? Who dared me to cop off with that munter Alan Henson in the work room?"

Me?

"And remember when you shoved a sharpened pencil into my arse cheek in the middle of a Science exam?"

I laughed again.

"I got two weeks detention for that."

"I tried to get you off."

This time, Sophie laughed. "Telling them I fell onto your pencil didn't cut it, hon. That's what gave me the two weeks."

She regaled me with some other stories from school, from college, and from our twenties, and it seemed as if I was stepping out from under a cloud of amnesia. It appeared as if I'd remembered only what I wanted to support my fucked up reality of my life to date.

"So, you see…you are a wonderful woman, Jess Taylor. You're my best friend, and you always will be. Even if sometimes you act like a total dick."

I rubbed my sore eyes and then the rest of my face. "What am I going to do, Soph?"

She shrugged. "I've no idea, Jess." She took my hand and squeezed my fingers. "It's all down to you now, honey. You have to do this on your own." She waited a tick, and added, "But you're not on your own, if you know what I mean."

Yes, I did. Sophie would always be there for me, but what I had to do to make things right with Diana had to come from me.

We talked and talked and talked—no change there. But this time we talked about the future, how we were in charge of it, how the past could shape it but didn't have to lead it.

I waited until the tail lights of her car disappeared before I did what I'd wanted to do for hours. Searching through my handbag, I found my phone. As soon as it had kicked to life, the tone sounded to tell me I had seventeen text messages and twenty-one voicemails.

Hearing Diana's voice on the voice mails was painful. Hearing her becoming progressively more frantic was like a kick in the stomach. No. Scratch that. It was like being repeatedly kicked in the stomach. She had initially called when she couldn't find me at the Tate. Her voice sounded a little concerned, as she had checked the restroom and found it empty. By the fourth message, she had checked every restroom and café and shop in the whole museum. Then she called to tell me she was going back to hotel.

"Whatever I have done, I'm sorry. So sorry, Jess."

I could hear the emotion in her voice; she was holding back tears. But when I heard her call from our hotel room, her sobbed, "Where are you?" the dam burst.

I'd been so intent on confronting Lauren Baker, I hadn't even considered what Diana would be going through when I went missing. Maybe I thought she would just be pleased she hadn't had to tell me what I believed she was going to tell me. Yes. I had considered that she was waiting for an opportunity to dump me. But had I really believed that? We had spent the previous evening making love. That wasn't consistent with someone who couldn't wait to dump someone else, was it?

I checked my memory to see if I could actually make sense of what happened. I couldn't.

I remembered the look on Diana's face when Lauren

Baker turned up at the hotel room holding a handful of my belongings and the key card to my room. Diana's pained expression had etched its way into my brain and refused to vanish. Then afterwards? After Lauren went? After we had sat for too long in silence? What did she pick up from the coffee table and nearly offer me? It was small, whatever it was. It could hide inside her hands. She'd said, "I wanted to…wanted to…'"

Wanted to what?

It hit me, hit me hard. I should have seen it coming; all the evidence had been there if I hadn't been too self-pitying to see it. Her nervousness, the fidgeting, the phone call with the "I haven't had the chance to speak to her" bit. The "What if it all goes wrong? What if she…" The small box, the wanting to, but not doing…even the "I loved you too." It all made sense now.

Diana was going to tell me she loved me. Maybe the box held a ring. It seemed presumptuous, but what else could it have been?

I dialled the phone, barely giving Sophie the chance to say hello before I blurted, "Was Diana going to give me a ring at the Tate?"

No answer.

"Please, Sophie, was she?"

"It's not my place to—"

"Please."

I heard her sigh, mutter something to the air, and then come back on the phone. "Diana was going to propose to you."

Have you ever had someone reach inside your chest and rip your heart out whilst you looked limply on, completely defenceless and unable to stop it? I choked out a "thank you" and "speak soon" before clicking off.

I had single-handedly ruined my chance at happiness without even giving it serious thought. Diana had been plucking up the courage to propose, and I had taken her nervousness for reticence and tried to counteract that with a pre-emptive negative action of my own.

I made my way up the stairs to my bedroom. I had to lie flat before I literally fell on my face. I'd already done that metaphorically in the last twenty-four hours.

Fully dressed, I slipped under the duvet and stared at the ceiling, waiting for the latest shock to subside so I could start the grieving process all over again.

It was the longest night of my life.

Chapter 22

Thankfully, Sophie was a constant. I wouldn't have blamed her for walking away, since my actions had compromised her relationship with Dave. I tried not to burden her with everything that was going on inside my head, but sometimes it just couldn't help spilling out.

It was as if I had to keep going over and over everything, to try and make some sense of what I had done. It didn't help. I couldn't work out why I had acted the way I had. Diana was not Samantha James, had never shown any indication of being like her, but I had treated her as if she would do me like my ex had. That was definitely not what Diana deserved, or what I had wanted. If I could have turned the clock back, I would have done it in a heartbeat.

I tried to contact Diana, but it was futile. My first attempt had been on the Monday, believing that after a couple of days away from me she might give me a chance to explain. She didn't answer her phone. I also went to her house after work. Again, no answer. Actually, there was no sign of life whatsoever any time I had tried to contact her. I called Sophie and found out that Diana had decided to work away for a while and would not be back in Manchester until the New Year.

It seemed strange that she would leave everyone behind. Dave and Monica were here, and with Christmas coming, Sophie's information about Diana being out of town just didn't sit right. But I didn't argue. What could I do?

Yes. What could I do? Finding out where she was staying would be a start. So, I tried. Sophie was my obvious source of information, but that pot turned out to be a dry pan when it came to Diana. All Sophie would say was that it wasn't up to her to pass on information; I should ask Dave. I couldn't face him, couldn't bear to see the hurt in his eyes knowing that his sister had gone away because of me.

Finally, I cracked. There was one other person who could help me. Monica. Once again, I was in a quandary. Seeing Monica would bring it all back. I had not only let Diana down that day, I had also let Monica down. If I hadn't thumped Lauren, Monica would have gotten justice for her attacker.

And so it was that two days before Christmas, I was ringing Monica's doorbell. I had to apologise to her for what I had done. Instead of receiving the cold shoulder, Monica was happy to see me, which made me feel even worse than I had. It was the "My goodness, Jessie, you look terrible" that made me start to cry on her doorstep. Comforting arms wrapped around me and pulled me inside.

Initially, I thought she didn't know what I had done. How could she know and still act as if I was a lifelong friend she hadn't seen in ages? Maybe because she was a better person than I was.

It turned out that she did know that Diana had sold her out in order to bail me out of a potential assault charge.

Her being Monica, she didn't care about that. She was just miffed that I hadn't hit Lauren harder. I had to laugh at that, laughter that turned into tears.

Monica comforted me until the waterworks stopped. I kept saying I was sorry, so sorry for everything.

I spent nearly three hours with Monica, but at the end of the three hours, I was none the wiser about Diana's whereabouts. I left Monica with the promise that I would come and see her soon.

Christmas and New Years were like a wet rag. I stayed with my parents over the holidays, when all I wanted was to be on my own. I think Sophie had forewarned them, as the topic of Diana was not broached. I resisted all of Sophie's attempts to get me to go out and get "ratted." I didn't feel like going out on the tiles when I felt as low as I did. I knew if I had one drink, I probably wouldn't stop.

By March, I felt like an empty shell. Work was my saviour, whilst all aspects of a social life were on hold. If Sophie thought I had walled myself up when Samantha James had done the dirty on me, she soon realised that it was nothing compared to what I was doing to myself at this moment. It had been months since I'd visited Monica. What was the point? It was clear that Diana didn't want me to contact her, and seeing her aunt would only make me remember how stupid I had been.

The absolute kicker came one evening as I was staring at the TV on mute. I was experiencing the strangest sensation. I was completely devoid of any get-up-and-go, reticent about doing anything but while away the time before I could go to bed, when I was struck with a need to do something else. So, there I was without any motivation, yet full of motivation. Totally fucked up. It was like I had ants crawling inside my veins, and I had to think of something to do to get rid of them without me actually doing anything.

Eventually I got up from the armchair and went into the cupboard under the stairs and pulled out a folder. Inside this folder was my art pad. One might think I would steer away from anything to do with art at that point in my life, but no. I wanted to do something, anything to get the crawly feeling to go away.

Flicking through the pages, I tried to ignore the drawings I had done in class, as each and every one would be painful to see. The speed with which I whizzed through them didn't help, as I could sense each drawing, each evening spent with Diana as our relationship was blossoming.

Then I stopped. Stopped and stared, and held my breath to keep from crying out. In front of me was a drawing I had not done in class, a drawing I had not looked at since the night I had done it. A pencil drawing, done from memory, of just one eye…one eye framed by a shapely eyebrow and the hint of a nose. All in all, it was a drawing of Diana, done when I had started to feel something for her but had been too chicken shit to admit it to myself.

I cried myself to sleep. The ants in my veins decided to fuck off after all, and left me with dreams of loving and losing Diana Sullivan.

It seemed months could fly past when a person didn't give a fuck about time. It might seem that after all the detail I put in to describe the events of just three months, it is odd to skip over five months in the matter of a few lines, but what was there to say? I was upset. Broken. No need for me to reiterate it all over again. I felt like Bella Swan in

New Moon—too focused on my own emotional breakdown to go into detail about the nothingness of my life.

April passed, and May followed. May—spring, rebirth, and fuck all else. Sophie's wedding was the following month, and I was dreading it. Well, both dreading and longing for it, to be perfectly honest. I was to be the Maid of Honour, so there would be no hiding in the crowd. And the reason I wanted to hide in the crowd? In the five months I had been separated from Diana, I hadn't seen Dave, either. There would be no way I could avoid talking to him, considering he would be the groom.

And the reason why I was longing for the wedding? Obviously, I would see Diana again. I doubted she would let a little thing like hating my guts get in the way of attending her brother's wedding.

God. I was shitting my pants. I didn't want to make a scene at the wedding, didn't want to see Diana look at me with revulsion, or even indifference. Indifference would actually be harder to bear. Knowing that Diana didn't care whether I was there or not would be so much more hurtful than her reacting to my presence, even in a negative way.

This was the day I was to meet with Sophie to get fitted for my dress. I had seen pictures of it, countless photos, to be honest, and I was just glad it wouldn't make me look like a meringue. Whatever happened on this day, I would make sure that Sophie enjoyed herself. It was time to leave my misery on the shelf I had been perching on for nearly half a year and go and be with my best friend to celebrate what was going to be the happiest time in her life.

Walking into the cafe at precisely one o'clock, I was surprised to see Sophie was already there. I gasped as I remembered the last time we had met in that particular place, and, once again, Sophie had been early. This time, she didn't look furtive or guilty.

A grin spread over her face, and she stood to greet me with a peck on the cheek. "Hey there, face ache. Ready to have your booty pimped?"

"As long as you don't go for pink, pimp away."

Lifting the menu, she asked, "Fancy a cocktail before we get started?"

Shaking my head, I continued to browse the menu. I think her enthusiasm was beginning to be contagious, as I felt a buzz of electricity flash through me. "What about you? You up for a cocktail?" When I lifted my head for her answer, the grin froze on my face.

Sophie was looking past me, in the region just beyond my left shoulder.

"I think I'll stick to a soft drink."

I knew that voice. I felt my heart trying to force itself up my throat and out of my suddenly dry mouth.

"Hello, Jess."

I had to lick my lips to get them to work. "Hello, Diana."

I turned to see her standing behind me, as beautiful as ever. Her hair was a little shorter than I remembered, but it still brushed her shoulders. The blue eyes seemed to spark as our eyes met, and in that one look I felt my love for her rush back tenfold.

"You're looking well," I said.

I didn't actually think she was, but that wasn't what you said to someone. Telling them they looked tired, maybe a little gaunt, they seemed to have lost a little weight... No. So, the "looking well" thing was the best option.

"So do you. You look great."

Seems like Diana went to the same school of etiquette as I had, because I definitely knew I looked like shite.

"What's all this? The 'let's compliment the arse of each

other' club?"'"

I turned and saw Sophie grinning at me. I couldn't believe she hadn't told me that Diana was going to be joining us, although I knew she was going to a bridesmaid.

"I'm starving, ladies. And then we have to get you dressed up like those toilet roll lady dolls." She waved the menu in the air as she stood and hugged Diana to her. "Good to see you, love. It's been too long."

Yes. It had. But that didn't change the fact that Diana was there, at that very moment, and I wasn't prepared. I had only had five months to work out what I would say to her if I ever got the chance to see her again. I had gone through a hundred different scenarios, but none of them had included us meeting again on the day I was going to get fitted for my bridesmaid dress. Truthfully, none of the scenarios turned out the way I wanted them to. They always ended up with Diana leaving again, saying what I had done was totally unforgivable. Which it was, apparently.

However, Sophie wasn't the kind of person to let a little thing like me fucking up my relationship with Diana get in her way. She carried on chatting, leaving spaces for us to give monosyllabic answers throughout the course of the meal. When she eventually realised that we were not answering her in as much detail as she wanted, she turned her Gestapo tactics on Diana.

"How's work? You still working in London?"

I pushed my lasagne around the plate, holding my breath all the while.

"Erm…well, yes…for the moment."

For the moment? Did that mean she—

"Are you moving back to Manchester?"

Thank you, Sophie.

"Well, that, erm, depends on…on…things."

Things?

"Things? What kind of things?"

Once again, thank you, Sophie.

"Just—"

Everything went quiet. Even the background sounds of the bistro seemed to fade into nothingness. I furtively lifted my face to Diana's and was surprised to see her looking at me intently. Her expression was open, and I believed I could see the old Diana there for a fleeting moment before a screen slipped into place.

"Enough about me." Her eyes held me fast, and then she broke the connection and looked at Sophie. "You excited about getting hitched?"

Sophie had been watching us both intently and seemed surprised to be included back into the conversation. A grin split over her face, and she leaned forward and slapped my arm. "Nearly as much as dressing my best friend up like a fairy."

I tried to laugh, but it came out as a squeak.

Soon after, we were seated in the dressing room of the bridal shop, waiting for our turn to be transformed. Conversation came mainly from Sophie, as the tension between Diana and me was almost palpable. Don't get me wrong, we did speak, but in a more reserved manner than I ever would have thought could be between us. Truthfully, what did I expect?

Fifteen minutes later, we were shown through to the back and into the dressing rooms. Inside mine, I found a rich blue dress hanging from the hook on the wall. This was it. Time to get into my role as chief of the bridesmaids. I sniggered. Chief? Bridesmaids? There were only the two of us, and I doubted Diana would follow any instructions I might give.

"Excuse me, Madam. Glass of champagne?" A young woman was standing in the doorway, the curtain drawn back to reveal a tray with three glasses on it.

I was just about to decline, when I heard Sophie shout, "You'd better have one, Taylor. It cost me a fortune."

Grinning with embarrassment, I nodded my head in the direction of Sophie's voice and mouthed, "God help the groom."

The woman's face split into a wide smile, and she held up the tray.

What the hell? What was the worst that could happen?

I selected a glass, took a sip, and placed the glass on the floor near the doorway. I began to undress, anally folding each piece of clothing before placing it on the floor next to the glass. Lifting my head, I noticed that I could see into the dressing room across from mine, as the curtain of that dressing room had not been pulled fully closed. The next thing I noticed was the mirror, the same style full length mirror I had in my room. Unlike the mirror in my cubicle, this one reflected the most beautiful sight I had seen in months.

Diana's back was to the mirror. The reflection of her smooth, strong back teased me. I could see the muscles moving with the rhythm of her arms as she undressed. I knew I should close the curtain and stop being a voyeur, but I was transfixed. A movement, a turn, I held my breath. Breasts, full and proud, were revealed to my hungry eyes, and my mouth went dry. Diana stretched; the silkiness of her stomach beckoned, and I took a step towards her. Seeing the band of her panties, I remembered a time when I had slipped my hand inside and found a wetness that always seemed to be there just for me. There was a flash of blue, and my heart stopped. For a split second, I thought it was her eyes, that she had caught me spying on her, but it was her dress as it slipped over her body like a caress.

I tried to tear my eyes away, but I couldn't. Watching Diana turn and swish the skirt out was mesmerising. The swoosh of a curtain being draw back belatedly sank into my subconscious, and suddenly I was face to face with a fully dressed Diana. Her gaze moved down my half naked body, her eyes darkening. I felt as if I was being memorised, and heat sparked within me. I wanted to reach out for her, tell her how sorry I was, beg her forgiveness and pledge my love to her. But no. I saw her expression change, saw the coldness come over her features, and I knew that my love for her was definitely one sided.

"You need to hurry up and put the dress on. Sophie wants us to meet in the main room."

And she was gone, leaving me bereft.

Time seemed interminable. After the confrontation in the dressing room, I wanted to leave, but this was Sophie's day, not mine.

Getting dressed in my everyday clothes, I longed for the chance to talk to Diana. We had to be together on Sophie and Dave's wedding day, and it wouldn't be right to have a dismal atmosphere between us. That's the last thing I wanted. I had to explain to her why I had acted the way I had, though I still hadn't fully worked it out myself.

I was just tying the laces to my trainers when Sophie's head popped around the curtain. "Hey, you. I gotta dash. Could you do me a favour?" She stepped into the small space. "I…erm…kind of promised I would give Diana a lift back to her place, but I have to meet Dave at the tailor."

What the fuck? No! Then the more rational side of my brain kicked in. If I gave Diana a lift, then I could explain—captive audience, and all that.

"Sure."

Sophie looked a little surprised that I had agreed so easily. "Erm…right. " She stepped closer. "Sorry I didn't tell you she was coming, Jess. Thought it would freak you out." After a quick kiss on the cheek, she was gone and I was left trying to calm the butterflies that wanted to flutter me to death.

I was waiting outside the shop when Diana came out and looked around for Sophie.

"She had to meet Dave. I hope it's okay if I drive you home." My voice sounded like it actually belonged to me for a change, and, for a fleeting moment, I felt in control.

"No thanks. I'll get a taxi."

She said no? What?

"Why? I can take you." Was I sounding whiney?

Cold blue eyes looked at me, and the blood froze in my veins . Diana moved closer to me, her body seeming powerful and almost threatening. "I said no. I don't want a lift."

"But…"

"But what, Jess?"

I'd never heard her say my name so bitterly.

"Is it because it might be easier for you to talk to me if I was in the car with you?"

"What do you mean by that?" Anger swelled inside me. "Easier?" A harsh laugh crashed from my mouth. "Easier? More like a chance to actually speak to you without you running away to God knows where."

"After what you did to us," she waved her hand from herself to me, "you dare blame me? I told you I didn't love

Lauren. Hell, I didn't even like her, never mind love her. But no. You ruined everything we had because you just wouldn't let it go." She snorted in disgust. "You had to go and make a scene, had to go and hit her because you couldn't handle being in love with someone who would have done anything in the world for you."

True. It was my fault. All of it. I had not believed in myself enough to think I was worthy of Diana's love. They always say if you can't love yourself, you can't love anyone. In that case, I didn't have a cat in hell's chance, because there was no way I could even like me at the moment.

"I wanted to explain, but you wouldn't let me. You just up and went."

Diana started to walk away from me.

"Seems like you always run when things get tough." Then I said something I will regret for the rest of my life. "You ran from Lauren, too, didn't you? You can never stand up to anyone, you just run away and hide."

Fuck. Fuck. And Fuck.

Dark hair whipped around so fast, I thought I was imagining. Diana towered over me, blue ice chips bored into my eyes, and her breath hit my skin like a slap. "Run and hide?"

Her hand was on my shoulder, her power seeping into my body.

"I didn't run and fucking hide."

A slight push made me stagger backwards. People were stopping to watch the floorshow, but neither of us gave a damn.

"If you'd taken your head from up your own backside, you could have found me, but it seems you didn't even try." Her voice hitched, and she plucked her hand from my shoulder, looking at it as if she didn't recognise it. "That's what hurt the most, Jess. You didn't even try to find me."

"I did! I—"

She stopped me with a look.

With that look, I realised something. I hadn't tried to find her, had I? Asking Sophie, going to Monica's, knocking on Diana's door, that wasn't looking for her, was it? That was going through the motions, expecting that everything would turn out as I hoped it would. What had I done in the last four and half months to find her? Nothing. Just wallowed ever more deeply in my own misery, believing I had lost the best thing that would ever happen to me, totally believing that what happened was because that was my lot in life.

"Goodbye, Jess."

And then she was striding down the street in all her perfection whilst I stood frozen to the spot, drowning in my epiphany and wishing more than anything that I could get amnesia.

Chapter 23

Two weeks. That's how long it had been since I'd spoken with Diana in the High Street. It was also two weeks until Sophie's wedding day. And I was doing something I should've done a long time ago—sorting my fucking life out. So Samantha James shagged anything in a skirt, and probably trousers, too, but that was no reflection on me. That was something that I had to accept and move forward from.

Not everyone was like Samantha. Sophie and Dave, my parents—they had relationships without constant drama and strife. They trusted and loved unconditionally. They allowed their hearts and souls to be intertwined with the life of another, believed that this person would always be there for them. And why? Simply because they were in love, and that's what love was all about—being together, loving and trusting each other, things that I'd come to believe were beyond my reach. I didn't want my life to be stagnant, to be just a still life. I wanted be more than a static subject in a painting; I wanted to live.

It was time to take brush in hand and create a different

setting, a different life for me. But for me to be happy, that picture would have to include Diana. And that meant that I had to make amends, had to prove that I would never betray the love she had for me, never again purposely harm our relationship. I had to show her that I had left behind the insecure, selfish woman I had been.

Why had I taken two weeks to come to this point? It had taken me that long to get my act and my plan together.

The first step was to go see Dave and apologise to him. Without his help, I was sunk before I began.

The shock on his face might have been comical if the situation hadn't been so serious. I knew I was putting him on the spot, and a part of me felt guilty about that, but I had to find Diana.

"Please, Dave. I have to tell her how sorry I am."

"I don't know, Jess. She's pretty cut up about it all."

The same day she'd left me standing in the High Street, I had gone around to her house and her neighbour had told me Diana had gone back to London. I had to follow her and do my best to win her back.

"Please. Just give me her address in London. I promise I won't tell her you told me."

If I sounded like I was begging, it was because I was. I had a vague idea where Diana worked, but I wanted to know for sure, wanted to find out which hotel she stayed in when she was there.

Dave nervously shuffled his feet.

I had to convince him I wouldn't hurt Diana again.

"Please, Dave. I love Diana so much, I can't lose her."

"She… I don't know. She's my sister, Jess. I have to look out for her."

He was apologetic, but there was a firmness in his voice. I was gripped with fear. If I couldn't get the information from Dave, I was screwed. If he didn't help me find Diana so I could talk to her, all the promises of never again betraying her or our love would be moot.

At the thought of not having the chance to win Diana back, tears welled. "Please, Dave. I won't hurt her again. I won't hurt her …a-gain."

My voice gave out. I tried to repress the emotions, tried to be strong, but I couldn't. Everything was falling apart. I was falling apart.

Dave clumsily put his hands on my shoulders and patted me as if I was a small child. "Hey, hey, hey. Come on. Don't cry."

I lurched forward and pulled him against me as my sobs became louder. Strong hands slipped around my shoulders and held me.

"I want to tell her I love her. I'm ready to do whatever she wants me to do to prove that to her."

Dave continued to comfort me, his words tumbling over my shoulder. "I know you love her, Jess. But is love always enough?"

Is love enough? Enough? Of course it was enough? Wasn't it?

I tilted my head back and looked up into his face. My vision was blurred, but I blinked away my tears.

"It has to be, Dave. It just has to be."

Our eyes locked, and an understanding passed between us: If I messed this up, I would have him to deal with.

I shook my head. "I won't cock it up." My voice quavered. "If Diana will let me, I will spend the rest of my life loving her. I give you my word."

He sighed, then gave a small laugh. "You've convinced me."

A squeal of delight shot from my mouth, and I leapt

forward and kissed his cheek.

He laughed again, pulling me into a quick hug. "Let me write the address down for you."

As he got pen and paper, I knew for certain that I had been very lucky. Dave loved his sister and would protect her with his life. If he thought for one minute that I could not be the one Diana needed, I am definite I would never have gotten the address from him. His confidence in me made me even more determined to not fuck things up.

As I was leaving, Dave caught my arm and turned me around. "Jess? One thing."

I waited apprehensively for what would undoubtedly be an admonition.

"Love her, okay? Just love her."

I threw my arms around him and hugged him close. "That is all I ever want to do for the rest of my life, I promise." And I would, if Diana would only listen to me.

❧⟡❧

The next thing I had to do was get the people at the Tate to close the one of the galleries so I could put my plan into action. I was put through to a woman called Sally. As anticipated, she said it couldn't be done.

"Please, Sally." My voice was pleading, just as it had been with Dave.

"I'm sorry, Miss Taylor…"

"Call me Jess."

"As I was saying, Jess, closing one of the galleries is not an easy thing to accomplish. Do you know how many visitors we get in there in one day?"

Her tone was sympathetic but firm, and I knew Sally would not be a pushover. I didn't really care about how many visitors would miss a chance to go into the gallery when my life hung in the balance, so I replied with as much charm as I could muster. I was not either charming or persuasive by nature, but I had to try harder than I ever had in the past to summon those qualities.

"I know that, Sally. I know. And it is because of you and your fantastic work with the exhibits that it is so successful."

Even I thought I'd gone over the top with that line, but I heard her mumble a "thank you." I couldn't see through the phone line, but I really hoped she was blushing furiously, because if she was, I was halfway to charming her into helping me.

"This is a matter of life and death—mine, actually." I thought about crying, but it seemed pointless, as Sally wouldn't get the full benefit of my snot-spattered expression and my tear-filled doe eyes. "This could literally change the lives of two people, two people who are very unhappy at the moment."

Sally didn't respond, and I thought I'd lost her interest. I quickly said, "Art means the world to both of us. If I could just see her, talk to her alone in that gallery, I know that we could have a chance." Sadness washed through me, and I actually began to cry without meaning to. "Or I would know for sure that I'd blown the only thing good that has ever happened in my life."

Silence buzzed down the phone line, and for a moment I thought she'd hung up and left me blubbering like a baby on the end of the line.

"I can't close it for very long," she cautioned. "Ten minutes, tops."

I cried even harder, but for a completely different reason. The first part of my plan was in place. There was hope.

Now all I had to do was to get Diana's boss onside, even if he wouldn't be aware he was helping me.

I stepped off the train at Euston, and then caught a taxi to Tate Britain. I was deliberately early, as I had to make a phone call that would display the number from the gallery and not a number from a mobile or a Manchester area code.

With Sally's permission, I called Diana's company on a Tate phone and purported to be the Chief Curator of Tate Britain, which was very interested in promoting a new exhibition entitled The Romantics. The show was to start in early August and run until June 2012, and fliers, brochures, and posters were needed for the promotion of the event. When I told James Turner, Chief of Sales, that we were very interested in hiring his firm for all of the art work, I could practically hear him salivating into the phone. I mean, come on! A graphics company in charge of promoting one of the world's biggest art galleries would have made anyone salivate.

The style of the promotional material designed for The Criterion Theatre's production of *Hamlet*, was exactly what the Tate was looking for. As one condition of considering his company for the job, I wanted to meet in person with the artist who had designed that campaign. Of course, he agreed immediately. And Diana Sullivan, one of their Chief Designers, was scheduled to meet with Sally Rogers outside the Pre-Raphaelite Gallery at four-thirty.

It was four-twenty-six, and I was standing inside the gallery. The plan was for Sally to meet Diana in the foyer, lead her to the gallery, and then say, "I won't be a moment," before slipping away and giving me ten minutes to salvage my entire life.

Keenly attuned to every sound, I heard the distinct timbre of Diana's voice as she and Sally stood chatting in the doorway. Per plan, Sally made her excuses and departed. All of this I heard through the demented beating of my heart. At any other time, I would have been proud of myself for managing to not run toward the sound of her voice, but I had to keep it together for the next few moments.

She was wearing heels. The tip tap of them resounded on the tiled floor, and I knew she was approaching the spot where I was standing with my back to her.

"Hello, there. I thought I was the only…" She stopped walking and stopped talking.

I didn't turn around, just started to speak. "You see Ophelia? See her blank stare, the flowers scattered all around her?"

Nothing. Although I could feel her just behind me.

"See that sadness, that loss?"

I turned and looked into Diana's eyes. I couldn't read them; they seemed closed to me.

"I think I'm starting to understand how Ophelia felt when she lost the one person she loved more than anything."

Still no reaction.

"Before I met you, I used to think that, unlike Ophelia, I wouldn't give up on everything because I couldn't have the person that I wanted. I had everything that I wanted, and needed, and I was the one who ruined it all."

I stepped closer to her.

"It wasn't a case of not wanting to participate in the most important scene in my life, it was a case of being too scared to take centre stage, lest I find out I wasn't worthy of being the leading lady after all."

I reached out and gently grasped Diana's hand. It sat indifferently in mine, so still that it might have been inanimate.

She stared down at our hands as if this was all a nightmare.

"I don't want to renounce the world, Diana. I've spent far too long hiding from it, being too bloody frightened of being hurt to appreciate the wonder of life and living."

A small squeeze of my fingers told me she was, in fact, still with me and not drifting away into another world to escape being here, with me.

"Samantha James humiliated me, Diana. She made me feel as if I was a nothing...a nobody."

"You are not, and have never been, a nothing or a nobody." Blue eyes flicked at last to mine. "Not to me. Never to me."

Warmth seeped from her hand into mine, and I felt a small tug as she drew me closer to her. Being so close, inhaling her scent, losing myself in her mesmerising eyes... I believe I actually felt my heart kick start again. Tears welled in my eyes, and I tried to blink them away. They weren't having any of it, and slipped from under my lids and trickled down my face.

Diana lifted her hand and gently brushed the tears away.

"I'm...I'm so sorry, Diana. I... God." The tears wouldn't stop.

She cupped my head and brought it to her chest, and I could hear the hammering of her heart. Pulling her hand free from mine, she wrapped her arms around me and held me as I cried, stroking my back and murmuring words of comfort. She pressed a kiss to the top of my head, and I cried harder. There I was trying to explain why I'd done what I had, and I ended up blubbering like a baby.

Diana murmured softly, "It's okay, baby. Everything will be okay." Then she just let me cry, as she held me safe in her arms. Eventually, she patted my shoulder, and said, "Look."

I sniffled and lifted my head.

Diana was gazing past me. "Isn't it beautiful?"

I realised she was regarding Millais' painting. Unlike my usual solitary experience when viewing beautiful art, this time I felt a part of something much bigger than I'd ever known.

"But," hands cupped my face and turned me to her, "not as beautiful as you, Jess. Nothing is as beautiful as you."

When her lips touched mine I felt my world right itself. Her lips were so soft, so deliciously perfect, I forgot we were standing in Tate Britain, forgot everything apart from how much I loved her. Pulling away from her was difficult, but I had to tell her, had to say the words I had kept myself from saying for so long.

Diana sighed as she rested her forehead against mine. "I've missed you so much, Jess." Her eyes glistened with tears. "I love you."

My face crumpled, and a sob escaped me. She had spoken in the present tense. And this time, I wasn't going to mess it all up.

"You will never know how much I love you, Diana."

Her eyes closed, then opened, and they greedily drank me in.

"But I swear, I will spend the rest of my life showing you."

Our kiss was not gentle, not restrained, not timid or fearful. This kiss was a kiss of commitment, and of our future. And I felt complete,

A cough sounded from the doorway, and we sprang apart.

Sally stood just outside the gallery doorway looking a bit rueful. "Sorry. But…erm…we need to reopen this room again."

A giggle bubbled up inside me until it overflowed and echoed off the walls of the gallery. I felt as if something I had always dreamed about had magically become reality. I had awakened from a self-imposed sleep, and my life was raring to be explored.

I thanked Sally and received a wink in return, and together Diana and I left the sacred walls of Tate Britain and went out into the fresh air of May.

The door to her hotel room clicked closed, and I embraced Diana and pulled her to me. After slipping my hands underneath her coat, I slid it from her shoulders. Her mouth met mine, and the passion she always roused in me flooded through me. I needed more. My hands fumbled with the buttons on her blouse; I couldn't seem to stop them shaking long enough to unfasten them.

With a ripping sound, Diana tore her shirt to release the buttons from their holes, and my eyes fastened on her breasts, barely restrained by their bra.

Ripping again. This time it was my blouse that got the Diana Sullivan treatment, not that I minded, as it allowed my torso access to her bare skin.

More kisses, more connection, more and more and more. I felt my legs hit the side of the bed, and I lay down on it. Frantic hands searched my trousers until they found the button, then the zip, then the band…and then they lowered. All the time, Diana was kissing me. All the time, I was kissing her.

Naked. Both of us. The sleek movement of her skin over mine was an affirmation of everything good and right. Her knee parted my thighs, and she slipped between my legs. The wetness I had pooling there increased as soon as her pubic bone ground against me, and I lifted my hips to greet her thrust.

"God, Jess." Her mouth was on my throat, and her words seeped through my skin and down into every part of me. "I love you so much…love you…love…you so much."

I felt like crying again, this time with sheer happiness.

Fingers dipped between us, and I gasped as they gathered my juice and brushed it over my swollen clit. I needed more, needed her to cherish and love all of me. My hips bucked against her. My hands glided over her skin, committing each and every muscle to memory, and pulling her closer. Another stroke of her fingertips, another gathering and brushing. My hips were moving to the rhythm she was setting and it was blindingly wonderful, but I needed even more from her.

"Please, Diana. Please."

Her talented fingers were toying, circling, teasing, and I wanted to force myself onto them. I didn't have to. The feeling as she filled me was sublime. "Jesus!" The depth of it, her slow, purposeful taking of me, was elegantly flawless.

Sensations were building to a point where I thought she might drive me mad with need and desire, and I welcomed it. Each touch sealed our future, made me more utterly hers.

I could feel I was close to cumming, ready to tip and fall and explode all over her, before I completely melted into her.

"Go-d! Di…ana! I… I…love you…love you."

There was a flash of light. Bright. Distinctively celestial. A waterfall of emotions crested and broke through me at that instant, but none so clear as my love for Diana Sullivan. My Diana. My woman. My life.

⋯⋯

Throughout the night, we reaffirmed our love, our connection. Each time was like the first, as we tasted, stroked, and joined. Emotions were raw, exposed, and neither of us could seem to stop the flow of tears that came with our lovemaking. Every aspect of every action seemed heightened, making each the most memorable we had yet experienced.

Morning found us wrapped around each other, neither of us apparently willing to relinquish our hold, lest it turn out to be just a dream after all. When I opened my eyes, I saw her gazing down at me, one hand propping up her head, a look of absolute peace radiating from the exquisite blueness of her eyes.

"Morning, baby. Sleep well?"

I stretched my body and made a growling sound. "Sleep? What's that?" Leaning forward, I kissed her tenderly. Even though we had spent much of the night making love, desire flared at even that slight contact.

"Hungry?"

I grinned at her saucily and raised an eyebrow.

"Tsk. I mean for breakfast."

Snuggling up to her, I mumbled against her chest, "You on toast?" God. What was wrong with me? Had I been hit by the mushy stick when I was asleep?

I felt the laugh rumble inside her chest before a kiss

landed on top of my head.

"I like you like this," Diana said.

Peering up from my divine place near her breasts, I looked at her quizzically. "How? Hungry?"

With one fluid motion, she had me flat on my back and was pinning my hands down with hers. "No." Her face came closer, and she scrutinized mine. "I like you relaxed and…" she kissed my nose, "happy and…" another kiss landed on my eyelid, "romantic and…" the other eye received the same treatment, "all mine." Her mouth pressed against mine and sent sparks racing throughout my tired body, and I immediately missed her when she pulled away. "I'll order us breakfast, okay?"

I felt the loss of her as soon as she moved her body away from mine, and sighed as she went into the living area to call room service. Looking around the room, I noted that she had two suitcases stacked on the side, and her portfolio resting against the wall with a laptop bag leaning against it. It looked exactly like the room of someone who was living away from home. I felt a longing for those cases not to be there, for time to go backwards to the moment when we had arrived at the Plaza, five months previous. I also wished for me to know then what I knew now. I would have acted so differently. Or maybe not. Maybe I had needed to go through hell to realise what I had almost lost.

Yawning, I stretched again. I needed to shower, and definitely to brush my teeth. I hadn't noticed if Diana had morning breath or not, but I doubted she could say the same about me. Smacking my lips together, I held my palm to my mouth and tentatively breathed onto it. Yep. Definitely time to freshen up.

After a quick shower and a thorough brushing of teeth, I appeared in the bedroom dressed in her robe.

She was sitting on the bed, a pile of clothes next to her. "I didn't know if you had anything to change into, so I got out some sweats and a t-shirt for you."

I didn't mention that I had brought some clothes with me, just in case my plan actually worked. My overnight bag was still stored in Sally's office. I just had to remember to collect it before leaving London, as I didn't want Sally to wonder why I hadn't. Worse still, Sally might forget I'd left it and bring in the bomb squad to disarm my smalls.

"Knickers?" I asked.

"And to you."

Have I mentioned lately how much I love her smile?

"Will you be needing any?" She lifted an eyebrow and gave me a look that suggested I wouldn't.

I tried to copy her expression, "That depends."

"On?"

Moving close to her, I whispered in her ear, "You."

Her hands on my hips, she pulled me to her, her mouth finding my stomach. The heat was addictive, and I felt I needed to feel it in other places.

"Shower time!" And she was gone, leaving me gasping, half naked next to our bed. Shaking my head, I laughed. She was such a tease, and I loved it.

I'd just finished dressing when there was a knock on the door, undoubtedly announcing the arrival of our breakfast. The shower had stopped a few minutes before, so I knew Diana wouldn't be long and I poured the tea.

A few more minutes went by, and she still hadn't come through. I could hear her fussing with her luggage, mumbling what I surmised were swear words under her breath. Chuckling, I decided I would start eating without her. My stomach was definite that it was time to feed the beast, and who was I to deny it?

I was halfway through my second piece of toast and honey by the time she appeared in the doorway. Her face was flushed, and she seemed to be a little distracted. A grin split her face as she ambled over to the table. Frowning, I asked, "What took you so long? And why are you grinning like that?"

"No reason."

I gave her the "I don't believe you" look, but didn't push. That insecure part of me was laid to rest—I had gone through too much to let her fidgeting and flushing get me all anxious again. It was amazing to think that after all we'd gone through, I would feel so much peace inside.

Breakfast was eaten in comfortable silence; the only words exchanged were relative to passing butter or pouring tea.

"Right. Time to get cracking." I stood. "Fancy exploring London?"

Her hand shot out and grabbed mine. The blue eyes that looked at me held pleading, and I was confused. I could tell she wanted to say something, but it was as if the words were jamming in her throat. I couldn't think of anything that we couldn't say to each other now. Previously, I would have been panicking, would have been thinking that for some inexplicable reason, she didn't want me to be there, didn't want me. But not now. I'd recognised that Diana and I were meant to be together, that nothing and no one could separate us, unless it was me and my stupidity. Thankfully, I had put that folly away and was determined that it wouldn't return any time soon.

My newly confident self knelt in front of her and

cradled the hand she had placed on my arm. Gently, I drew her closer to me. "What's up, love?"

"Jess, I…' Her Adam's apple was bobbing crazily. "I… love you."

I smiled up at her like a mother with an overly anxious child. "And I love you, Diana." My tone included some bit of comfort, but also conveyed that she should continue if there was more she wanted to share.

"When we came in December, I… God, that turned out so badly."

I took a deep breath. She was right. We should discuss it, discuss what had made me act the way I had and put it in our past once and for all. But I wasn't going to come out of it looking good at all.

She sighed. "I think I went about things the wrong way."

Huh? No. It was me and my insecurities that fucked everything up.

"I wanted to tell you how much I loved you, but I was so scared you would run a mile. Turned out you ran anyway."

"No, Diana. It was me. I wanted so badly to tell you I loved you that it was driving me mad, making me do things I would never have normally done." A cracking noise came from my knee and, instead of standing, I swapped over to the other one, still holding her hand. "I was consumed with jealousy over Lauren, because I couldn't believe you loved me and not her. I also blamed Samantha James and how she had treated me, but, in fact, I brought it all on myself."

Diana was looking at me intently, absorbing every word. She gave a quick shake of her head and attempted to stand, but I was too close to her. Her foot moved back and deliberately kicked her chair over. Then in one fluid movement, she was kneeling on the floor in front of me, our hands still joined.

Our heads were not quite level, so she leaned forward and down a touch, until her face was close to mine. "I don't want to go over the past, what happened or what could've been, Jess." The words were calming me, as her breath blended with mine. "I... I..." Leaning away, she released one of my hands and put her hand behind her. I thought she was balancing herself, but instead she brought her hand forward and lifted it to my face.

A small box. An open, small red box, displaying something that glistened in the morning light. The sun's rays filtered through and created a prism around it, and I was momentarily lost in the brilliance of the colours.

"Jess Taylor, will you marry me?"

Would I marry her? Marry? Would I? Me? Jess Taylor marry Diana Sullivan? Do you take this woman to be your lawfully wedded wife? To have and to hold? Marry?

"Wha-a-t?"

My voice demonstrated my inherent stupidity, but by the smile she was giving me, Diana knew I wasn't refusing her. Apparently Diana finally had me and my inability to comprehend perfect moments in my life in the bag.

"Marry me, Jess."

It wasn't a question. This time it was almost as if it was a dare, almost as if she knew I was powerless to refuse her. She was right.

The kiss I gave her tipped her backwards and flat onto the floor, so I straddled her and continued to tell her without words that I accepted her proposal. My display ended with us both breaking into laughter, and I slipped off her to lie on the floor.

Through her laughter, I heard her ask, 'So, is that a yes?' before she climbed on top of me and pinned me with the blueness I loved so much. There was happiness and expectation in her eyes, and a raised eyebrow, but it was the "Well?" that prompted me to speak.

"Yes. Yes! YES!"

And that was the last rational thought I had for the rest of the morning. Not that I'm complaining. Insert a huge grin here.

Chapter 24

The following day, I forced myself to leave Diana in London and spent my entire train journey back to Manchester staring at the solitaire diamond on my left hand. I imagine that most of the people on the train must've have thought I was high or drunk, as I kept grinning and sighing, and constantly jiggling on my seat. If I couldn't stay with Diana, the next best thing was to get back to Manchester and tell Sophie what had happened. I didn't want to tell her over the phone; I really wanted to see her expression when I broke the news. Diana was going to call Dave later, after giving me time to tell my best friend.

"iv nooz 4 u. mt @ mine @ 9?"

It took Sophie less than a minute to respond.

"m already here."

What the fuck? "WTF? + ?"

"u av cable. C u sn"

I grinned at the phone and stared at my finger. Then I did what any woman in her right mind would do—I took a picture of my engagement ring and sent it with the message "I love you," obviously to Diana, not to the woman who was sprawled on my sofa watching TV. I was feeling mighty smug and well loved.

It wasn't until I got my keys out that it dawned on me, Sophie didn't have a key to my place. I knew damned well she had fed my parents a line and got their key from them, probably after she'd scarfed a full Sunday roast and charmed them to bits.

Entering my house, I spotted her exactly as I knew she would be. Sneaking behind the sofa, I knelt down and thrust my hand in front of her, shouting, "TADA!"

"Fuck!" The drink she was holding flew into the air, splattering her in the process. "Shit!"

It was one of those scenes that play out really slowly, but instead of feeling helpless to step in and do something, it just gave me more time to enjoy the show. Watching Sophie try and catch the glass before it hit the floor was a peach. The number of times it scuttled around and flipped from her grasp was amazing, and I couldn't help laughing.

Smash, and scatter.

The only sound in the room was the theme tune from *The Simpsons*. My laughter had died as soon as Sophie turned her aggrieved attention to me.

"This had better be good, Taylor." Brown eyes flickered to my hand, back to my face, then back to my hand again. "What's that?"

"That, my dear, dear friend, is a ring."

"Duh. I know it's a ring, but what is it?"

"My dear, dear—"

"Will you cut out the dear?"

"Sophie, this…" I held my hand aloft, "is an engagement ring."

"A what?"

I pulled a face and grabbed her hand. "See this on your hand?" I put mine next to it. "This is the same."

"No, it isn't." Her lip curled slightly, as if she was talking to an idiot. "I have something to go with this. It is called a fiancé."

I smiled at her.

"You haven't even got a girlfriend. How can… No way! You're not back with that slapper, are you?"

Scrambling to my feet, I lifted my hand and blew on my solitaire. "I doubt your future sister-in-law would appreciate being called a slapper."

I had gotten nearly all the way to the kitchen before Sophie rocketed off the couch. A firm hand caught my arm and swung me around.

"What? Diana… You… Ring?"

"That's what I've always loved about you, Soph, your ability to articulate."

"Just a minute. Where've you been?"

"To London to see the Queen."

"Are you drunk?"

"Only on love, only…on…love."

"You are freaking me out now. I think I preferred you miserable." Sophie leaned her face close to mine. "Now answer me. Properly. Got it?"

I nodded and grinned, and she ground her teeth.

"Are you telling me you went to London to see Diana and have got engaged to her?"

I nodded.

"For real? You're not just hallucinating and buying rings you can't afford to pretend your life fits with your screwed up imagination?"

This time I shook my head.

"Fuck me."

"Sorry, Soph. I'm taken."

She tilted her head to the side as if assessing my truthfulness, or my sanity. "WAHOOOOOOOOOOOOOOOOOOOOO! You're getting hitched!" Her shout was loud, and I fully expected Barnesy from next door to come around complaining again. "You did it, baby. You sorted it all on your own."

"Well not exactly on—"

"I don't give a fuck about anyone else." Sophie grabbed me and clutched me to her before lifting and twirling me around, all the while screaming in happiness.

Fortunately, I had known Sophie for the majority of both our lives, and I knew that it would be a matter of moments before she tripped and we both ended up on the floor.

I was not disappointed.

⁂

My mum and dad were ecstatic. I think they believed they were one step closer to grandkids, and I didn't have the heart to tell them that neither Diana nor I had the tackle to accomplish it.

As I was leaving, my dad pulled me to one side and whispered, "I am so happy, love. She's a keeper."

I wrapped my arms around him and kissed his stubbled cheek.

"Tell her one thing from me will you?"

I nodded against his shoulder.

"The oranges worked."

Leaning back, I looked into his eyes.

"Didn't like to mention it before."

Bless him and his moggy fixation.

So, there we were on Sophie and Dave's wedding day. The bride was radiant, as I knew she would be. Preceding her down the aisle was one of the proudest moments of my life. I could waffle on about how everything panned out, tell you about Dave kneeling at the altar with the price sticker on his shoes, could tell you about Sophie tipping Dave backwards and kissing him hard when they announced, "You may kiss the bride." I could tell you all that and more, but to you it would seem like just another wedding.

To me, it was so much more. It was the day my best friend married the person she loved the most in the world; the day I knew that she would be happy for the rest of her life; the day I'd hoped for so many years that Sophie would have. It was also the day I stood behind her, both physically and metaphorically, like she had stood behind me for twenty-five years.

It was also the first time I had seen Diana since she had popped the question. I know it seems like a long time for us to have been apart, but she had things to do—relocate, for one. We'd spoken to each other every night on the phone, and, unlike the last time she had worked away from home, this time I didn't go half-crazy with jealousy, this time I was content with it. I'm not saying I didn't miss her, that would make me a liar, but I also knew she was returning to me—something that a month ago I would never had believed possible.

I started this tale by indicating that the events recounted within took me by surprise. Doesn't love always do that? Then why do we always act so stunned? It took me a long time to realise that everything that I believed to be part and parcel of my makeup—being alone, being happy alone, working too hard and not enjoying being alive—was not the most brilliant and satisfying time of my life.

Yes. I cocked up. More than once. I gave up, too, something we should never allow ourselves to do. I honestly believe that we are in charge of our own happiness, but sometimes it takes the presence of the people we love around us to make us want to grab those happy reins and steer ourselves in the direction that we have always dreamed we would go.

Yes, Samantha James dented my self-esteem, but it was up to me to push out those dents and smooth the body work once again. It was her shortcomings, not mine, that led to infidelity and disregard of another person's feelings. True, I might not have given her everything she wanted in a relationship and should have ended it long before it turned ugly, but, come to think of it, so should she. Whatever the relationship, it takes two to make it and two to break it.

As for Lauren Baker—what can I say? I was jealous of someone who was so unhappy with her life, she had to resort to making everyone as miserable as she was. Diana had the courage to walk away. It had taken her a while to do it, but do it, she did. No one should ever have to suffer from the wrath and low self-esteem of another. Okay. I cracked Lauren one. But between you and me, I think she had that coming. Pity I didn't hit her harder when I had the chance of a pop. Joking. Not. Yeah… I'm (not) joking. However, she got her just desserts in the end. The week before Sophie's wedding, she was in the Nationals again for hitting a stagehand. This time she got a hefty fine and was bound over to keep the peace. I'm not smirking, honestly, just grinning a little bit.

Before I love you and leave you, I have a couple more things to share. I know, I know, I should just get to it already.

My life before Diana was a mess. Actually, after Diana, it was also a mess. I existed, but I didn't live, and that was such a waste. Work, early nights, and making excuses to do nothing seemed to be part and parcel of my shrunken world. I had slipped effortlessly into apathy and didn't even realise it. Yep. Groundhog Day—that's what my life had become, although I was just living the same shit over and over and not learning from my mistakes.

Apparently all it takes to pull someone out of a funk is an email, a bit of contact, and your best friend in the world understanding what you need. Sophie was my saviour in more ways than one. She didn't allow me to get swallowed up by past mistakes, didn't relent in her love for me and our friendship, and never let me nosedive into OAP behaviour before it was my time.

And here is my two pennies worth for you to take or leave, as you please. Friendship. Proper friendship, not the "I have 547 friends on Facebook" kind, but the ones where you know their eyes close up, can recognise their laugh in a crowded room, know their scent, their troubles... Friends are the gems in our lives that sometimes we take for granted, something I know I am guilty of. A true friendship is priceless and irreplaceable, and my true friend is Sophie Harrison, serial bluffer and shoulder to cry on.

As for love? I thought I was already talking about that. Love comes in many guises, shapes, and sizes, and each and every one of these is a blessing. Be it your family, your friends, your pets, or your partner, love is present and usually ignored or skimmed over in the face of the demands of modern life and her difficulties. Don't do this, okay? Take time. Take their hands and tell them, "I love you." Don't flinch away from those three words as if they will burn. How can they? They are the words that have kept this race of ours going for thousands of year, mainly through the actions of a person rather than just their words. To have the chance to love and to be loved in return, isn't that why we are here? To connect, to belong, to live a life that isn't bland and static, but full, fecund, and joyful.

Diana and I won't make the mistake of not living our lives to the fullest, although it doesn't mean we won't make any mistakes. We are human, after all. But I will try, and hopefully succeed, to make sure she knows how I feel about her every day of our lives together. I want to have a full, fecund and joyful life with Diana, the very woman who is gesturing for me to get off my butt and make a speech to the drunken crowd at Sophie's reception. Like this story, I will try and make it brief. I think you've heard that before.

Okay. I will let you go now. I have speeches to make and a woman to love for the rest of my life.

One last thing, in case you were wondering. I love Diana Sullivan. Maybe you worked that one out for yourself.

About L.T. Smith

L.T. is a late bloomer when it comes to writing and didn't begin until 2005 with her first novel *Hearts and Flowers Border* (first published in 2006).

She soon caught the bug and has written numerous tales, usually with a comical slant to reflect, as she calls it, "My warped view of the dramatic."

Although she loves to write, L.T. loves to read, too—being an English teacher seems to demand it. Most of her free time is spent with her furry little men—two fluffy balls of trouble who keep her active and her apologies flowing.

E-mail her at fingersmith@hotmail.co.uk
Blog: http://ltsmithfiction.wordpress.com

Other Books from Ylva Publishing

http://www.ylva-publishing.com

Conflict of Interest

(revised edition)
Jae

ISBN: 978-3-95533-109-2
Length: 466 pages (approx. 135,000 words)

Workaholic Detective Aiden Carlisle isn't looking for love—and certainly not at the law enforcement seminar she reluctantly agreed to attend. But the first lecturer is not at all what she expected.

Psychologist Dawn Kinsley has just found her place in life. After a failed relationship with a police officer, she has sworn never to get involved with another cop again, but she feels a connection to Aiden from the very first moment.

Can Aiden keep from crossing the line when a brutal crime threatens to keep them apart before they've even gotten together?

Heart's Surrender

Emma Weimann

ISBN: 978-3-95533-183-2
Length: 305 pages (approx. 63,000 words)

Neither Samantha Freedman nor Gillian Jennings are looking for a relationship when they begin a no-strings-attached affair. But soon simple attraction turns into something more.

What happens when the worlds of a handywoman and a pampered housewife collide? Can nights of hot, erotic fun lead to love, or will these two very different women go their separate ways?

Coming Home

(revised edition)

Lois Cloarec Hart

ISBN: 978-3-95533-064-4
Length: 371 pages (approx. 104,000 words)

A triangle with a twist, *Coming Home* is the story of three good people caught up in an impossible situation.

Rob, a charismatic ex-fighter pilot severely disabled with MS, has been steadfastly cared for by his wife, Jan, for many years. Quite by accident one day, Terry, a young writer/postal carrier, enters their lives and turns it upside down.

Injecting joy and turbulence into their quiet existence, Terry draws Rob and Jan into her lively circle of family and friends until the growing attachment between the two women begins to strain the bonds of love and loyalty, to Rob and each other.

In a Heartbeat

RJ Nolan

ISBN: 978-3-95533-159-7
Length: 370 pages (approx. 97,000 words)

Veteran police officer Sam McKenna has no trouble facing down criminals on a daily basis but breaks out in a sweat at the mere mention of commitment. A recent failed relationship strengthens her resolve to stick with her trademark no-strings-attached affairs.

Dr. Riley Connolly, a successful trauma surgeon, has spent her whole life trying to measure up to her family's expectations. And that includes hiding her sexuality from them.

When a routine call sends Sam to the hospital where Riley works, the two women are hurtled into a life-and-death situation. The incident binds them together. But can there be any future for a commitment-phobic cop and a closeted, workaholic doctor?

Coming from Ylva Publishing in Fall 2014

http://www.ylva-publishing.com

Barring Complications

Blythe Rippon

It's an open secret that the newest justice on the Supreme Court is a lesbian. So when the Court decides to hear a case about gay marriage, Justice Victoria Willoughby must navigate the press, sway at least one of her conservative colleagues, and confront her own fraught feelings about coming out.

Just when she decides she's up to the challenge, she learns that the very brilliant, very out Genevieve Fornier will be lead counsel on the case.

Genevieve isn't sure which is causing her more sleepless nights: the prospect of losing the case, or the thought of who will be sitting on the bench when she argues it.

The Return

Ana Matics

Near Haven is like any other small, dying fishing village dotting the Maine coastline—a crusty remnant of an industry long gone, a place that is mired in sadness and longing for what was and can never be again. People move away, yet they always seem to come back. It's a vicious cycle of small-town America.

Liza Hawke thought that she'd gotten out, escaped across the country on a basketball scholarship. A series of bad decisions, however, has her returning home after nearly a decade. She struggles to accept her place in the fabric of this small coastal town, making amends to the people she's wronged and trying to rebuild her life in the process.

Her return marks the beginning of a shift within the town as the residents that she's hurt so badly start to heal once more.

Bitter Fruit

Lois Cloarec Hart

Fuelled by booze and boredom, Jac Lanier accepts an unusual wager from her best friend. Victoria, for reasons of her own, impulsively challenges Jac to seduce Lauren, her co-worker and a young woman Jac's never met.

Under the terms of their bet, Jac has exactly one month to get Lauren into bed or she has to pay up. Though Lauren is straight and engaged, Jac begins her campaign confident that she'll win the bet. But Jac's forgotten that if you sow an onion seed, you won't harvest a peach.

When her plan goes awry, will she reap the bitter fruit of her deception? Or will Lauren turn the tables on the thoughtless gamblers?

Under a Falling Star

Jae

Falling stars are supposed to be a lucky sign, but not for Austen. Her new job as a secretary in an international games company isn't off to a good start. Her first assignment—decorating the Christmas tree in the lobby—results in a trip to the ER after Dee, the company's second-in-command, gets hit by the star-shaped tree topper.

Dee blames her instant attraction to Austen on her head wound, not the magic of the falling star. She's determined not to act on it, especially since Austen has no idea that Dee is practically her boss.

Still Life
© by L.T. Smith

ISBN: 978-3-95533-257-0

Also available as e-book.

Published by Ylva Publishing, legal entity of Ylva Verlag, e.Kfr.

Ylva Verlag, e.Kfr.
Owner: Astrid Ohletz
Am Kirschgarten 2
65830 Kriftel
Germany

http://www.ylva-publishing.com

First edition: September 2014

Credits
Edited by Day Petersen
Cover Design by Amanda Chron

www.ingramcontent.com/pod-product-compliance
Lightning Source LLC
Chambersburg PA
CBHW020258030726
47499CB00001B/245